The Last Skipjack

The Last Skipjack

by

Mary Hastings Fox

Golden Antelope Press
715 E. McPherson
Kirksville, Missouri 63501
2019

ISBN: 978-1-936135-76-9 (1-936135-76-0)

Library of Congress Control Number: 2019945972

Published by:
Golden Antelope Press
715 E. McPherson
Kirksville, Missouri 63501

Available at:
Golden Antelope Press
715 E. McPherson
Kirksville, Missouri, 63501
Phone: (660) 665-0273
http://www.goldenantelope.com
Email: ndelmoni@gmail.com

Dedication

To Larry Pinkett
A worthy model for all the best qualities of my fictional
characters
A real-life hero who shows courage
When everyone else seeks safety

Acknowledgements

Many thanks to Amy Paloski, a goddess among muses, a friend who made me believe that writers can write what and when they want.

To my children Lisa, Cristy and Dave for continuing the family story-telling legacy.

Special thanks to: Lisa Arbareri for taking my words seriously;

My Sister, who still thinks I'm funny.

To my husband Moe, just because.

Foreword

Invictus

By William Ernest Henley

Out of the night that covers me,
    Black as the pit from pole to pole,
I thank whatever gods may be
    For my unconquerable soul.

In the fell clutch of circumstance
    I have not winced nor cried aloud.
Under the bludgeonings of chance
    My head is bloody, but unbowed.

Beyond this place of wrath and tears
    Looms but the Horror of the shade,
And yet the menace of the years
    Finds and shall find me unafraid.

It matters not how strait the gate,
    How charged with punishments the scroll,
I am the master of my fate,
    I am the captain of my soul.

Contents

Chapter One

Before the Depression, the land near the Chesapeake Bay was a major producer of "stoop crops," melons, tomatoes, cucumbers and beans, crops that had to be hand-picked. Between 1930 and 1960, these truck crops were largely replaced with the "new" industry of chickens raised for meat production, and of grain needed for poultry feed – crops that could be machine harvested. (Levy, Civil)[1]

1955

The first time Celie Mowbray saw Isaac, she was only ten years old. It was a typical day in the Tidal Basin — steaming, stinking hot and airless, one of those days when the humidity is so high your body sticks to everything, including itself. Celie had been doing the worst possible chore for a day like this — cleaning the chicken yard. She'd spent most of the morning navigating what her brother Frank called The Chicken Shit Trail, a straw path of sticky yellow-green sludge that lined the entrance to the chicken coop. The straw was supposed to absorb the droppings, but in this heat, vile-smelling poop would congeal around the straw, becoming so slippery it inched up the sides of her muck boots and even onto her calves. Her hair, usually Shanty-Irish coal-black, had picked up dots of chalky poop.

As disgusting as the chicken yard was, it wasn't the main reason Celie hated working with the chickens. The hens weren't so bad. They'd pretty much scatter themselves as she walked and scooped, but the roosters were nasty in general and apt to develop peculiar vendettas. When they weren't fighting each other, they might get

---

[1] For all headnote citations, see Works Consulted.

1

a notion to come charging across the yard for no reason other than meanness and a craving to poke a hole in something — another chicken, a dog, or the hand of the fool holding out scoops of poultry feed. To protect yourself from these devils, you had to stare them down first, eyeball to eyeball, before they got themselves going toward you. Celie was pretty good at this, but there was one grizzled old bird she could rarely outsmart. Frank had dubbed him 'The Old Dastard.' (Mom had tried to make him change the name to Mr. Dastard, her futile attempt to reign in Frank's talent at finding words that were not-quite-swearing.) The evil-spirited rooster would wait around corners until some unwary victim made the mistake of crossing through the yard, rather than going around. Celie was sure the bird knew when his target couldn't see him coming, which gave him a running start. Wings in an awkward, flapping mess, he would heave himself up into the air, his beak aimed toward the victim's head.

Of the three children in her family, she was the one least likely to take chances. People mistakenly thought of her as bold because she had what Daddy called "the Irish gift of gab." Today, however, she was in the right mood to fight with a rooster because everyone else had gone off the farm, leaving her to care for all the livestock. In addition, she faced the indignity of having to make dinner for her father, brother, and male cousins, whenever they all got back from hunting rabbits in their cousin's woods. Normally, she'd be with them, but on this day, her ill-tempered uncle Bob from Philadelphia had shown up to tag along. Uncle Bob had some lame-brained notion that girls couldn't be trusted to use guns. When Daddy informed him that Celie was quite a fine shot, Uncle Bob had escalated his argument. "Girls with guns are just plain bad luck, Guy. I'd be too nervous to shoot straight."

Celie wasn't sure which felt worse, missing out on the trip or being stuck cleaning the chicken yard. She was furious that Daddy had been taken in by such a lame excuse. She'd glared at the red pickup truck as it wound past the cucumber vines and disappeared behind the rows of tall corn stalks, sending it her strongest possible negative energy. She hoped to influence Providence so that Uncle Bob might trip and break something – an arm or a leg — or maybe he could be in the wrong place and take a butt full of buckshot.

She grabbed a shovel and started walloping oyster shells to bits to scatter along the feeding grounds, a chore that suited her mood perfectly. She glanced up from time to time, basically keeping an eye out for Old Dastard. In the bare edge of her line of sight, at the darkened edge of the woods, she saw people, five or six of them, coming across the fields on foot. She stopped hacking the shells to get a better look.

There was an old woman, short and stooped over. Behind her came two young men, one tall and skinny, the other short and pudgy, bouncing along and poking each other. They're just boys, she thought as she saw one of them take a tumble and spring back up. Trailing behind the three of them was an old man wearing a straw hat, a wide-brimmed Panama, holding hands with a young girl who was taller than he was.

They came through the soybeans and crossed over to a field of cucumbers, fitting themselves carefully between the rows. The way the mid-morning sun was pitched, aimed at their eyes, it was unlikely they could see her yet. They'd stopped, all of them bending down to look at something on the ground, conferring about it, when Celie dropped her shovel, shed her apron and walked toward them, her hand extended.

"Howdy, how you all doing?"

Right away, she realized that by approaching them from behind, she had just about scared them to death. Not that they would stay startled for long at the sight of a grinning ten-year-old girl.

"We – why, just fine, ma'am. Uh — Miss," said the old man. "And it's a fine farm you have here. Yours?"

"My Dad's. I'm just in charge today."

"Seems it's in good hands," the old man said, hooking his thumbs through his suspenders and leaning back on his heels. The woman who'd been in the lead before, now stood behind him. She was exactly his height and both of them had dark brown skin, wrinkled with age. Except for the man's hat and pipe, they looked like twins.

The woman yanked off the old man's hat and mumbled something Celie couldn't make out. "Oh, that's right, old woman," the man said when she'd finished whispering. "I got to apologize, Miss, for meeting a lady with my hat on. My name's Isaac Jackson."

"I'm Celie Mowbray, nice to meet you. The sun's so high you probably should put your hat right back on, though."

He did so, then put his hand on the old woman's shoulder, guiding her forward. "This here's my wife Minnie. This fine-looking little gal here, holding on to my hand, is our niece, name of Ava Skipton."

'Little' Ava was the tallest of them all, slim and with the darkest skin Celie had ever seen. Her face looked like it had been chiseled from stone, all angles and lines, except for the lively eyes shining out. Usually, Celie took note of what other girls wore, but not with this girl. Her clothes were insignificant (a word Grandmom Mowbray used to describe garments which she thought were too plain.) No matter what clothes Ava wore, they would look insignificant next to her glorious face and piercing eyes.

"How do, Ava," Celie said and stretched her hand to where Ava could reach it.

"How do," Ava said back, her eyes almost meeting Celie's.

Celie turned back to Isaac. "And the boys?"

Isaac rubbed his chin with the palm of his hand and tilted his head sideways, as if trying to figure out which boys she meant. Meantime, that pair had run off and sat themselves down in the dirt to play a silent game. Even poking and scuffing about, they had yet to make a peep.

"Boys?" Isaac lifted his hat, scratched his head, and snugged the hat back in place. "Oh, I clean forgot – yes. They're a pair of boys alright."

"No – I mean what's their names?"

"Names? Oh, well, nobody makes no mind of their names," he said good-naturedly. "They're just a coupla' boys like to hang around."

Celie didn't believe this for a second. Here was a story. She was dying to know the reason Isaac didn't identify them. Probably to hide them from someone – a mean parent? A truant officer? Her imagination soared. She wanted to learn more about Isaac and Minnie, and most of all, to learn about the girl who seemed to be her own age.

When they'd finished shaking hands, Ava had kept her hand holding Celie's. She accepted the girl's gesture as a pure sign of friendship, unbound by the usual social customs. It was a gesture that said, I like you and I hope you like me. Maybe just being in a new place, she imagined, Ava had to act on every chance for friendship.

She'd soon find out. She was already thinking of this family as hers, like when you are the first to spot a new kid at school and introduce yourself, and then you have a responsibility to keep looking out for him. She'd "found" a family out for a walk and was lucky enough to have been outside when they passed by.

Isaac's next words sliced through her daydream. "You think your Pop needs help with the picking? I see you got cucumbers about ready."

This was the question she should have expected, of course. Her stomach sank. It wasn't an enchanted encounter after all. *Me and my silly daydreams. Always thinking there's magic of some kind when the real business of life is so often just practical. Find a way to get food for your family. That done, next comes shelter. No time for strolls through woods and farms just to say hello.* She felt foolish and moved her mind to where it should be, to business. She said, "you must have heard we lost our crew last week."

"Yes'm. Friend of your Pop's told me to come on over, get to know each other a bit. It's me and Minnie and Ava here – maybe twelve, fifteen others. We got a late start this season and just got up here yesterday. We got a good truck, too ... had to send my folks out in it for wood, in case we'd be staying outdoors tonight. You reckon your folks will be back this evening?"

"My Daddy will — and Mom ... my mother and my little sister are visiting family, but she'd never forgive me for my bad manners. I didn't even offer refreshment, and all of you out here in the hot sun. Do you think that...the no-name boys over there ... might like to come up to the house for some nice cold tea?" She smiled at the boys and they returned wide grins.

Celie felt dizzy with excitement, partly from the excuse to have left the chicken yard, but mostly because it looked like they'd get some labor for the crops. Pop would want her to move forward in the deal, he was that short of help since their one hired hand, Big John, had busted his leg and was laid up for the summer.

"You got any year-round help?" Isaac must be reading her mind.

"No sir. One hired hand, but he's laid up."

Isaac hesitated and then asked, his voice soft, "That hired man. He got family needs taking care of?"

"A wife, Willi, and two kids, almost grown. My dad's got them covered. If you come tomorrow, you'll meet Willi; she's helping my Mom make the pickles. She'll also be picking with us when the crops come, to earn some extra." As was usual for her when she wanted something badly, she'd begun chattering. "Their cabin is right down the road. One of my uncles owns it and he'll let them stay free until Big John is back on his feet."

6   *Fox: The Last Skipjack*

Isaac breathed out easy and his eyes opened wide. He said, "Well that'll be fine, then. Reckon we can work together real fine, your pop being a man like that." He had put the smile back in his voice.

Celie was charmed. A barrier had been lowered, a friendship made. With family to feed and his own living hard to find, he refused to take advantage of another man's bad luck, even a man he didn't know. He was more like her daddy than he could possibly know.

"Ain't my business, Miss, but your daddy must be something special. To get by with just his family and one hired hand to work a farm this size."

Celie thought for a minute before answering. She didn't want to come across like she was bragging. Sister Mary Emily called this, *the sin of pride.*

"My dad has been moving more to grain crops. He and his brothers have a harvester and they rent it out. It was my dad's idea and it pays for the bad times." She watched Isaac process the economic upshot of such a thing, a farmer who could make his land pay in the winter.

Her gabbing, what Grandmom called her blarney, had been partly to put Isaac's family at ease, but mostly to cover up her uncertainty about the right thing to say to protect Daddy's interests. She wondered ...

Oh my God – her manners! "I almost forgot our drinks! While I get them, won't you please come up on the porch and sit?"

"That's mighty nice," Minnie answered, "but if you don't mind, these kids'd just as soon run around in the grass. Ava might like to walk up with you."

Celie had nearly forgotten Minnie. The social question Celie just asked must have crossed into her realm. She said, "As to me and Isaac, we'd be dearly pleased to pick a spot of shade under that big old oak tree over there. To us, it's coming up on the best part of the day."

Celie ending up bringing out two trays, one with iced tea, the second with peach pie. She made them all sit while she served them, Ava quietly helping. When they'd all finished, she excused herself, put on her coverall and boots, and aimed herself back toward the chicken yard to finish her work.

"Hold on a minute!" Ava said, with no dialect at all; her accent as smooth as that of any white town kid. "I'd be pleased if you'd let me work with the chickens and maybe get the eggs for you. I miss my chickens back home."

Celie helped Ava suit up. As she tied the back of the apron, she thought her eyes must be playing tricks on her. Now that the sun had shifted and cast her in shadows, Ava's face was highlighted with intense shades of deep blue. Again, Celie felt she might be looking at a statue. Maybe one carved out of ebony. While she'd never actually seen any ebony, it just sounded right. She'd never been so close to anyone with skin so black. Her hunch was that Ava probably didn't have a single drop of mixed blood in her, unlike most of the folks around here. Celie's own great-grandmother had been a full-blooded Nanticoke Indian, which was originally listed on her birth certificate as Mulatto, as had been the law at that time for all persons of color – no distinctions in those days. You were white, or you weren't. The family story was that when she married Celie's great grandfather (a white judge), her birth records and even her first name were altered. Only their wedding portrait, showing her leather dress and her long shiny braids with feathers woven in, gave away the truth. That and the name on the back of the photograph; "Victoria Mowbray" had been written across her name, "Littlefeather," which had been eliminated both from the picture and from history.

There was a sudden scuffle over in the long grass by the tool shed, the two boys fighting. Isaac grabbed them by their collars and held them tight. Both boys reacted quickly, one coiling back his right arm and holding it across his face like he expected to be hit, the other folding his arms over his head and rolling into a ball.

"Lord help you, Jim," Isaac said, putting them both down and patting their heads good-naturedly. "Ain't nobody gonna hit you around here, or Tom either." Word by word, Isaac's voice had gathered sadness. The no-name boy (named Jim) was sobbing like a baby.

"Yessir."

Isaac laid a hand on his shoulder. "None of us ever gone to beat you, no matter how dumb-ass you are. Isaac'll see to it. Now stand up and be proud."

Jim sniffled and scrambled up, but he looked more sorrowful than proud. Minnie poked a finger into Jim's arm muscle, patted Tom's head, and grinned at them. "We've been feeding you boys long enough to get some of our outlay back – don't fold up before we get at least one season's labor." Minnie's teasing seemed to loosen up the boys. Even then, with them smiling a bit, they were two of the scaredest boys Celie had ever seen.

Ava had gone into the chicken yard while Celie was watching the human drama with the no-name boys, or else she'd have warned Ava about Old Dastard, who now came hop-jump-sailing from behind the barn. He'd angled himself straight toward Ava's shins. Celie didn't have even a second to warn her. Darned if Ava didn't have that feed bucket in front of her legs before Old Dastard got within three feet of her. His beak bounced off the steel bucket, flinging him back, landing him upside down on the ground. Ava picked up the rooster and smoothed his feathers, set him on his feet, and made clucking sounds.

"You're not so tough," she crooned, and the bird simply walked away, calm as an old hen. Ava looked up and winked at Celie. "I'm pretty good with chickens," she said, smiling. Celie found herself once again chattering like a magpie, while Ava picked up one hen, then another, like they were pets or something, stroking their feathers until their eyes closed. With the chickens done, Ava crossed back along the lawn to Celie, with not a particle of yard waste outside the boundaries of the apron.

"Your family been farming here for a long time?" she asked.

"Not so long. My dad comes from carpenters; my Mom's kin were coal miners up north." She bit her tongue to avoid adding that her mother had studied music at University for a year, just before falling head over heels for the charmingly funny farmer she met at a bar. "*The sin of pride*," again. Instead she said, "There were too many brothers for Daddy to work in the family business, so he took up farming. You from around here too?"

Ava's eyes narrowed. "Sort of. Long, long time ago." She'd kept the friendly tone, but her face had closed up and Minnie, listening in, reached over to pat Ava's shoulder. Ava relaxed and said, "Minnie is my aunt. My mother is … still on her way from Florida, where I'm from. Minnie and Isaac will take in anybody's child."

Minnie had already turned her attention to the pile of dishes, giving them a hosing before stacking them on the porch step. From there, she moved on to the kindling pile, rubbing her hands briskly, like you do when you're about to grab an axe and chop.

"Hold on, Ma'am – Mizz Jackson," Celie called.

"Just need to call me Minnie. Mizz makes me feel like an old woman."

"No need to chop. That's my brother's chore."

"My way of thanks for the pie," she said. Celie wanted to argue back but knew it'd be taken as ungrateful. She watched the old woman's swift, strong strokes, like she only wished she could do. She took a harder look at Minnie's wiry body. She was by any standard, a bent-up old woman but her strength hadn't left her. She had dozens of small scars on her arms and hands and on her wrinkled face, the latter so jagged they distorted the shape of her brow. Celie couldn't help but wonder who – or what – had put them there. She tried to imagine her as young and beautiful, tried to picture Isaac as a jaunty young man bringing her a handful of flowers. She couldn't. As with her own parents, it wasn't possible to see any of them any other way than they were now.

It was pitch-dark by the time Daddy came home and he and Isaac worked out a contract. Isaac signed "ISAAC JACKSON & FAM" in neat block letters and then tipped his hat to Celie – nobody else, just her – before gathering his folks and leading them back through the fields, staying between rows, like when she'd first seen them. She badly wanted to go with them and help them settle into the camp to make sure their cabins were clean and that there were enough cots and blankets, but it couldn't be. It wouldn't be tolerated by either of their two families.

Celie believed there was something special about Ava. Something between them would go past the usual criteria like who their kin was or where they were born, or the color of their skin. She knew she wouldn't be allowed to ignore those things for long, but she and Ava, coming into each other's lives today, had felt a mutual connection. She was sure of it.

Chapter Two

By 1954, US migrant workers constituted one-tenth of the total labor force in agriculture, approximately one million adults. More than 150,000 children under the age of 18 traveled with them. Most children, sometimes as young as 5, worked along with adult members of the family. State school-attendance laws didn't apply to migratory children. If by chance, a school was nearby, they could attend, if the state law allowed. No arrangements would exist for them if they weren't near a school. (Maryland Advisory Committee)

Ava

As much as Ava loved the beach in St. Petersburg in the winter, living in Florida was always pure hell in summer and at first, she was glad to be north. She'd grown bored to death with her work of gathering shells on the beaches in St. Pete's, polishing them, and adding paint before selling them to tourists. What was important, though, was what had been happening to her sister, Sari. Kids around their beach cabin had grown merciless, taunting her almost daily with filthy chants about their mother, Venus. (Ava had long ago stopped calling her mother Mahm, like she was supposed to.) One of the rhymes was, *Sari, Sari, quite contrary ... we know why your mama ain't married.* Another was, *Roses are red, Yo mama's a witch, give her a quarter and she'll be your bitch.* And some were much worse.

Ava had run out of lies Sari would believe about Venus's parade of men, and Venus acted like she didn't even care if the girls knew what it meant.

Thank God they'd got a break from all that. Uncle Isaac had talked Venus into traveling with his crew from Florida to Maryland's Eastern

Shore. The minute they'd joined Isaac's crew, Sari had begun acting cheerful again. Even Venus seemed happier, probably because of being close to her sister. Aunt Minnie acted more like Venus' mother than her sister, and it had made a difference. This was the longest Venus had ever lasted in the same job. Maybe she was actually changing.

Ava felt deeply grateful to Minnie and Isaac for taking them on. Really. But the job itself was far worse than working on the beach back in Florida. There had been at least a spark of creativity in painting and displaying shells, but there wasn't a single good thing you could say about picking crops. To add to her trouble was Summer-in-Maryland, which turned out to be nearly as hot as Florida, except with heavy air that stalled, dead-still, above the fields. Not that there weren't plenty of rivers and streams around, but they were all lined with thick rows of trees. What little moving air might be above the river couldn't penetrate the trees. White people swam in the dirty rivers and set up games and picnics on the rocky river banks, calling them "beaches." The only thing the river was good for, as far as she saw, was flooding the air with humidity. Venus had begun talking about staying here for the icy cold of winter. Ava had seen snow only once, when they were staying in Virginia, and she hadn't liked anything about it.

Ava had begun to find ways to get out of steady picking. Errands for Isaac. His eyes were failing, and she was a good reader, so she took on his receipts and crop records. On the days when there was nothing to do but be in the fields, life was a misery. She took too many breaks and often got caught staring off into the trees.

Today Sari asked her, "why you always stand there lookin' at nothing?"

"I'm trying to imagine what it will be like if we stay the winter like Venus keeps saying. When it's always cold and the trees lose all their leaves and the grass turns all brown and dead."

"Like I said, lookin' at nothing. You gonna get us fired, you keep wasting so much time."

Sari was wrong about that. Guy Mowbray was the man who maintained the tenement camp where the workers lived. He was what Isaac called a Saving Grace, a good man with a nice family, who laid in far more furniture and supplies than the law called for.

The Mowbray house stood white and stately in the distance surrounded by a huge yard inside a white wood fence. They kept their house as polished as a new coin. Ava would stare at it, imagining a dozen rooms filled with treasures.

Even though she and Celie had bonded, right from the first, she wasn't sure which she wanted most, the house or the people who lived in it. It had worried her that she might have been drawn to Celie mostly because she could provide a way out of these fields. She would have hated herself if her reasons were that shallow - if she was that much like Venus.

By the end of the season, she'd learned, thank God, that it wasn't true. Ava's fondness for Celie was unmistakable. She'd begun to feel differently about a lot of things she'd taken for granted, like even mealtime. Minnie cooked with love, the table was full of laughter, and the food tasted better than anything Venus had ever provided. The different music thrilled her, all the folk stories and songs from old times she'd never heard when living with Venus. Reels with old and young folks together, although she didn't like how the music mellowed as the crews moved north. Up here, the folks sang mostly spirituals and never jazz, like they had in St. Pete's. Their drums came out on week-ends, if even then. Mostly they produced smooth harmonies, drifting out soft and sweet, as if they were part of the air.

Mornings at the camp were a trial, even under Minnie's watchful eye, an even harsher reminder that she didn't belong living with this much forced closeness. Minnie soon taught her to sleep with her clothes folded under her, so she could get into them quickly and in silence, covering up before boys got wind of her movements and tried to examine her body as she dressed. Minnie said, "Just keep away from them, much as you can. You gonna be a real beauty, I'm afraid. Too bad you ain't plug-ugly like me."

Ava thought Minnie was probably right; good looks seemed to be more a trouble than a blessing. Best thing was to avoid the kids her own age. And if she could, avoid Venus, too. Get dressed, then grab up somebody's fussy baby, feed or rock it until time to load up, so her mother would let her alone. She'd just sit, rocking, daydreaming of a day when she could go even further north. A place where she wouldn't hear only spirituals any more. She would listen to jazz and — and *John Jacob Jingleheimer Schmidt* and *Frère Jacques* in rounds, like Celie and Hannah and the other white kids sang. Some place where she could laugh out loud anytime, for any small reason that came into her head.

After a while, she was going to the farm with Isaac twice a week, sometimes three times. The girls were usually inside the white post fence, out of the way of pick-up trucks, tractors hauling harvesters and plows. She'd once thought it ridiculous how Celie's mother babied her kids like they might break. She had made fun of them to Sari, calling them 'china doll girls,' but she never said a thing like that to Isaac, who wouldn't stand such disrespect.

When she realized how the white girls smiled and laughed all the time, especially with their father, how they dropped everything to follow him, no matter where they were and what they were doing, she let go of her cynicism. She saw a kind of love she longed to understand more about, since she had begun to feel it with Isaac and Minnie.

Ava groaned aloud. She'd just knelt on the dry ground to reach a bean pod and her knees were on fire from the hot soil. She wrenched the huge cluster of string beans from the vine, ripe ones and tiny shriveled ones all together, and then tried to stuff it into her basket before a grown-up could see it.

Sari's husky whisper came from the side somewhere, "You cheatin'. I saw."

"Shush," Ava warned. "Mahm's not even looking, so be *quiet*, for the Lord's sake!"

"Shouldn't say Lord's name."

"I said *Shush*, hear?" Angry as she was, she knew Sari was right. It would hurt the whole family when they poured out her basket and saw a haul loaded with beans that were wrinkled with age, and skinny, pint-sized pods with their stems still attached. Money would be subtracted from their take.

But Ava was too mad to care. "Let me alone," she snapped.

"Ava, what's wrong with you?" Sari asked, her whole face a frown. "Why you wanna' get us all in trouble? Pick right, OK?" She pitched her voice down to a whisper again, "You want some of my money?"

Sari being woeful made Ava feel like someone had just kicked her in the stomach. She almost gave in and abandoned her plans to escape to the river where she could at least cool her feet. She said, "It's nothing about money, Sari. Don't be like Mahm, thinking everything's about money."

Ava stood up, hands pressing in at her waist, massaging the crook in her back. Each day she'd been with Isaac and Minnie, she had loved them more, but she knew she didn't fit into this way of life. It was one hardship after another, like her back aching every day now.

"Isaac was supposed to take me with him," she told Sari.

"Ava. Get to work," came her mother's voice from four rows over.

"My back's killing me, Venus," she yelled back.

"Something is killin' all of us. Nothing wrong with you. You're just getting a woman's body is all. Get picking."

Ava bent down behind the stalks separating her from Venus. She rustled the vines and pretended to pick. Suddenly Venus was right next to her. "What you think I'm blind all of a sudden?"

"No ma'am."

A tear started down Ava's cheek as she reached into her basket to pull out the bad beans. She swallowed the urge to cry and picked as steady as she could, until she felt a hand on her shoulder. She knew without looking that it was Isaac.

"Ava. Need me a strong girl to carry some things for me up to the house."

"Yes boss!" She yanked the cloth covering her hair and used it on her face so that dirt and sweat and tears were gone with one swipe. "Venus, I'm going with Isaac," she sang out, dumping her own basket into Sari's, hoping the unexpected bounty would make her sister happy. For some reason she hadn't figured out, Sari loved to pick — counting out every bean as if she was collecting treasure.

Ava settled in next to Isaac, her hand on top of his to help him steady the wheel as he drove. He didn't like people to know about his palsy, inviting a trusted few to ride with him in case he couldn't still his hand when he needed to. She adored him for trusting her ... for needing her.

****

Isaac's truck pulled up at the white gate to drop her. She hadn't heard a word he'd said to her since the second she'd spotted Celie and Hannah huddling in the soft, green grass of their front yard. As they got closer, she could see little piles of pink and white and pale blue. Next to Hannah was a miniature wooden trunk, still closed, but with bright ribbons trailing from its corners. Ava's heart raced as she realized that the girls had brought out their dolls!

Isaac patted her shoulder, but she hardly noticed that either. Her mind was floating with images of little pastel dresses with ruffles and soft, silky slips to match. Tiny booties that looked like cotton balls. She didn't even hear Isaac tell her to 'enjoy her time' and she hadn't a clue as to when he said he'd be back for her. When she reached the gate, she stood as still as she could manage, eyes on the carved wood arches and curlicues of the gate, hands at her sides. Her body shifted from jittery to paralyzed and then back again, as she waited to be asked inside the fence. She would be, of course, but she mustn't take it for granted .... It was bad luck ....

"A-va," Hannah squealed. "Hurry up. Look, we got a new doll! And Celie – "

"Hush, Hannah. Don't ruin it," Celie scolded.

Hannah clapped both her chubby hands to her mouth obediently, but she couldn't stop herself from bouncing up and down a few more times. By the time Ava was inside the gate, Hannah's fists had been replaced by a grin; she'd dropped her fists so she could hug Ava.

"Can I tell her?" she begged. "Let *me* say it, Celie."

Celie looked as vexed as a kicked rooster, arms folded, head tucked under. This led Ava to forget everything except helping Celie. She could see Celie was torn between two powerful wants–indulge her little sister or keep hold of the surprise she'd planned?

Ava said, "Tell you what, Hannah — how about you say one part and Celie say the rest?"

Hannah squealed with delight, "Yes, oh yes! My part is ... my part is that the new doll has something to do with you, Ava. And ... and —"

"Fine, you told your part," Celie said. "Now go find Tiger and bring him back here. He's going to be the carriage baby." She gave Hannah a boost up and over the fence.

Hannah scampered off to find their huge orange cat, who was so fat and lazy he'd allow himself to be dressed in an infant's christening gown, tucked into a doll carriage, and pushed around for at least a few minutes before he caught on he was captive. After that, Hannah would be occupied with rescuing the dress from a running cat, leaving Celie and Ava time to talk about things they liked – boys, parents, life.

When she'd first seen Celie and Hannah together, Ava had thought they were twins, despite their difference in age. They had glossy black hair, were the same height, and when they laughed, they wrinkled up their noses and flashed their clear blue eyes in the exact same way. But now, having learned all their mannerisms, she was amazed when people would mistake one for the other. Celie had a heart-shaped face compared with Hannah's rounder one. Celie always acted excited and talked fast, like now. Clearly bursting with pleasure, she couldn't help but embellish the details of her surprise.

Even when she wasn't excited like this, Celie's face moved constantly, her expressions always part one thing, part another. There was a portrait of her in the family hallway – a school picture of a posed, smiling Celie. Ava hadn't recognized her even after she was told that the flat-faced likeness was really, truly Celie. In addition to the liveliness, Celie was loaded with Irish freckles, so much a part of her face that in summer, she looked like a polka-dotted girl.

Today, there in the shade, the way the mimosa tree bathed her skin in shadows, her skin had blended into alabaster – at least the way Ava imagined alabaster looked when she heard about it in Minnie's bible stories. As eager as she was to learn about the surprise, she was moved by the sudden realization that Celie was becoming beautiful. She interrupted her to say it. "Just look at you! The color of your skin is just about perfect. White but not white-washed, maybe from the freckles. You're still a white girl, but your skin isn't dead-looking like most of them."

Celie sat unmoving, her face stunned. "What do you mean?"

Ava touched her fingers to the girl's wrist. "You look like marble or something. There are times I'd give anything to have skin like yours. To be white like you."

Celie jumped to her feet, doll things flying everywhere. She said, her eyes filled with tears, "Don't say that! Don't even think it! Ava, how can you ever wish away your own color?"

Ava felt horrified. She'd spoiled Celie's joy in her gift. She wished she could take it back. Maybe if she turned it into a joke? All she could think of was, "I didn't mean to make you feel bad. You just looked pretty then, that's all I meant."

Celie slipped back down to the ground, her movements still slowed. She lifted the trunk lid with both hands and took out a creamy white cardboard box, handing it to Ava in slow motion. "Open."

"If you don't want to give it to me because I said that –"

"Just open it, Ava. When you see what it is, you will fall down laughing because of what you said. We both will."

Ava was almost afraid to lift the lid. Besides, she was so rarely given any kind of surprise gift that she wanted to draw it out, same as Celie had been doing. The lid up, she found a wad of pale pink tissue, layered in folds. Gently she slid the tissue aside, one layer at a time. It was a doll! A dark-skinned baby-doll. You couldn't really call her a black doll, because she had a white baby's face with slim, oval, pale-blue eyes and a tiny upturned nose. The skin coloring was the only thing different from the rest of the dolls. To Celie, though, it was a black baby. Celie was trying to honor Ava's color and at the same moment Ava had seemed to dishonor it.

Ava threw back her head and laughed, long and so joyfully that Celie seemed to have forgotten her sadness already. They grabbed each other's hands and danced in a circle, and when they fell down in the soft grass, they laughed even more. After both girls caught their breath, Ava undressed the new doll slowly while Celie sorted through the clothes in the trunk, pulling out a ruffled white dress, matching white pantaloons, and a flannel bib with *"Tiny Tears"* embroidered in pale pink.

She said, "You can take whatever clothes you want for her, but I thought you might like church clothes to start."

Ava was stunned. Somehow, without visiting the migrant camp more than twice, far as she knew, Celie had learned that the black girls wore white to church. This dreamy girl who could be as ignorant as a motherless lamb when it came to the adult world, was able to see things that were invisible to most white people.

Celie said, "If you're worried somebody will … you know, take her from you, you can just leave her here. In the playhouse would be good. You could come play with her there whenever you want." Celie had figured out that Ava couldn't just walk home with a black baby doll any old time she wanted. Celie somehow knew that Venus would never let her keep the doll. You gotta' love a girl who could read your heart, even if she hadn't yet learned that looking black was more than just a color.

Afterward, as she trudged toward Isaac waiting in the truck, her feelings skipped along wildly. For years she would think of this doll, as imperfect as she was as a prototype for a black child, as the most perfect gift she'd ever received. The doll was a reminder for Ava to believe in her own beauty. She wished she and Celie could keep this feeling of being as close as sisters. She didn't dare expect this much, but she knew Celie believed it. It would have to be enough to sustain them both.

Ava had been kicking stones to slow herself down when Hannah shrieked out, "Wait! You almost forgot *my* present." The little girl ran up, breathless and near tears.

"Just because Celie gave me a present, doesn't mean you have to think up something too, Little Thing."

"But I had a present *first*! I had.... Ask Celie.... I had this present for *days*! I been keeping it inside Tiger's carriage, so's I'd remember."

This wasn't a tall story, Ava knew, because of Hannah's face, which was open and full of light. Hannah was clutching a flat tin box that had once held licorice, and she thrust it into Ava's hand. "It's not candy anymore, though! Not like the box says," Hannah cautioned. "I mean just 'cause a box says candy doesn't mean you're supposed to eat what's in it."

"I know." Ava was trying not to laugh aloud at Hannah's gravity. She lifted the lid. Inside was a dead starfish, shriveled to the size of a cookie. She knew in an instant what it was. She'd seen starfish, dead and alive, every day back in Florida.

"It's magnificent," she said and kissed Hannah's cheek. She may have had to leave the doll behind for Celie to hide, but she could take the starfish with her.

****

What you think you're doing with that?" Venus asked when she overheard Ava telling Sari about the starfish. "What kind of ideas those white kids trying to give you?" She made a grab for the tin box.

In the meantime, Minnie, while she was many inches shorter than her sister, had moved quickly to push Venus aside before she got her hands around Ava's treasure. An angry Minnie was not a force to be messed with, not even by Venus.

Minnie's voice shot out across the camp like the blare of a trumpet. "You think you might *like* somebody wanting to share the world with Ava. You think you'd appreciate those girls' kindnesses to her."

"Well, I don't."

"Why not?"

"What good it do Ava – what good in trying to give her what she don't have now?"

"Because she *already* has what you don't have. Instead of begrudging her, you should be glad she has it."

"What you talking about she already has? What's she got that's so special?"

"Hope. And those lil' girls over there at the boss house, they give her even more of it."

Chapter Three

Green Point is a recreational park covered by massive pines and cedar trees, along an expanse of sandy beach. Many of the roads leading to it bear Indian tribe names - Nanticoke, Algonquin, Shawnee. The remains of an ancient Indian Town found near the water included five wigwams, one wooden house with a glass window, and a few buried ceremonial blades. It was all that was left of the Nanticoke [aka Choptank] tribes, once the largest and most powerful in the east. (Eshelman)

1957

On June 3, 1957, Celie turned twelve, the same age Becky Miller would have been if she'd lived until the end of the summer. Celie always wished that she'd met Becky when she'd still been alive.

June 3rd was also the last day of school and the first day of summer, a great day in any kid's life. With all *A's* on her report card, Celie was an academic star in her own family and the picnic was both her reward and her birthday present. Mom had made Celie's favorites, fried chicken, potato salad and lemonade. They were all loading up the back of the Ford station wagon with food, towels, sand toys, bathing suits. And the red and white quilt of course, to hold their spot on the beach.

"Where we going again?" Hannah asked as she shoved her feet into sandals with fat straps. Hannah liked to ask things again and again, just to hear the words. She was seven now and still such a baby.

"Wrong feet dopey," Celie fussed, dropping her school books on the step and switching Hannah's sandals so they were right. "You know where. What do you think the food basket is for?"

Mom was cheerful, always a sign it would be a good day. She said, "Frank can build you girls a sand castle – he's so good at it. You can use your buckets to bring him the water."

"Only if I'm not diving," Frank said. Like the rest of the high school kids, he'd had the whole day off from school and was way ahead on his day-dreaming. He'd just finished his swimming and lifesaving merit badges and now practiced diving whenever he could, determined to qualify for a lifeguard job at one river or another.

The car was loaded, and Frank started a silent race to the car, winning it by allowing the screen door to swing back against Celie's face. She had the sense to wait until Mom was out of earshot to seek revenge. "What makes you think they'll have a diving board?" she whispered. "Most rivers don't, you know."

Celie winced against the coming punch, but Mom was not out of earshot after all and stepped in. "This one does, and they also have an Indian burial ground where kids can look for arrowheads."

Hannah, who always felt left out, interrupted. "Do they have swings? And ice cream?"

"Probably both, right Mom?" offered Celie, eager for peace and wanting to get going. It was time to claim seats, the best being the one right behind Mom's head where she couldn't turn and see what you were doing.

"You in front," Mom told Frank. "I need you to navigate. Celie, you sit behind Frank, so I can keep an eye on you in the mirror."

Annoyed all over again, Celie began picking on Hannah. "If you want ice cream, you'd better have raided your piggy bank."

Celie, a spendthrift like Mom, could never pass by anything for sale without wanting to buy it, but Hannah was a saver like Daddy and she almost never parted with a nickel. She was sure to have come out of the house dead broke.

"I didn't," Hannah said, her eyes tearing up, her hands pressed hard against them to stop any leaks. "I bet I won't want any ol' ice cream." She dropped her hands and began hugging her Raggedy Andy by the neck with both hands, as if gripping him might keep her tears back and her money safe.

"You *will* want some. You think I'll go all soft and buy it for you, but I won't." They both knew Hannah would find a way to get ice cream anyway. People were always buying things for "your sweet little sister."

The trip to Green's Point took almost half an hour, enough time for Celie to feel guilty about Hannah's pouty mood and fix it. She tickled her belly and under her armpits, and soon they were singing *Frère Jacques*. They sang one round after another, trying to harmonize at the top of their lungs out the window, which Celie had to admit, took away some of the effects of their blended voices. Frank had hunkered down, his nose buried in comic books, like he always did when his sisters sang.

The last few minutes of the ride, they were too excited to sing anymore and even Frank was restless. "Hey girls, let's play a game."

Celie ignored him, but Hannah said, "OK."

What a chump, Celie thought. Still annoyed at Hannah's being such a tightwad, she didn't jump in to protect her.

"You got a nickel?" Frank's voice was crafty. Surely the little cheapskate would notice.

"No – but Celie does. Give him a nickel, Celie," Hannah begged. "I promise I'll pay you back." Celie had spread herself across the back seat, lying so she could see only the top half of the landscape, calming herself by reading billboards – *Pabst, Schlitz, Barbisol*.

"Nope," she answered. *Esso, Pepsi, Dairy Queen*. "Just don't play his game, Dummy. You'll lose." Celie leaned up on one elbow and glared at Frank. Mad as she was at Hannah, she hated it when Frank tormented her. "Tell her the game," she said through clenched teeth.

"We flip a coin, you see," Frank said, eyes flashing. "Heads I win. Tails you lose." He snickered while Hannah sat back quickly against Celie, shooting her thumb into her mouth. She looked confused. Celie whispered in her ear, "Don't be so dumb."

Mom always knew when to intervene. "Frank, stop it or I'll turn this car around."

Hannah's eyes teared up and Celie whispered, "Sssh. She's just saying that to shut him up." She tickled Hannah into a fit of giggles. By then, Mom had slowed the car to a crawl and Celie realized they were on the long dirt access road to the river. Their wheels slipped into two deep ruts in the sandy soil – a record of the hundreds of cars full of families looking for a parking space. With the windows all down, the air was suddenly saturated with the scents of cedar and salt from the brackish water that swept into the marshes surrounding the river.

"We're here!" Hannah shouted and began bouncing on the seat.

Celie almost joined her but remembered, just in time, that she was now officially in junior high school. She planted her feet squarely on the floor so that only her toes betrayed her, tapping along with Hannah's bounces. She edged toward Hannah's beach-view window, perching herself above her shoulder so that both their heads poked slightly out the window.

"You girls keep yourselves all the way in this car while it's moving," Mom warned.

"Okay," they said in unison. Hannah pulled herself back inside and Celie used the moment to shove herself into the gap where Hannah had just been.

"Hey," Hannah objected, and Celie gave her a quick elbow in the gut as a warning to shut up. Hannah dropped to the floor and curled up, no doubt sticking her thumb in her mouth, like a little bird, Celie thought. She had no regrets about her maneuver. After all, she was the one with all *A's* and a birthday. She deserved a full view.

She breathed in huge gulps of fragrant air. Charcoal smoke was now mixed in with the cedar and salt. The Lion's Club Chicken Barbecue, she would bet. There was another strong odor, one she could both taste and smell, something she didn't recognize. Something sweet and bitter, pungent but not totally unpleasant.

Frank was excited too, despite his trying hard not to show it. He asked, "What smells rotten?"

"What do you mean?" Mom asked.

"I smell something rotten. Probably dead bodies that didn't get buried deep enough."

"Oooo!" both girls squealed, as expected. Over-reacting to danger was one of the main ways they communicated with their brother. Mom chuckled a little and said, "Don't be ridiculous. It's probably seaweed. Or maybe some fish got caught in the seaweed before the tide went out."

"See, like I said, dead bodies." Frank's face was triumphant.

"That's enough of that. Look for a space I can fit this beast of a car into. And don't anybody go running off when we stop. I need all hands to help."

Celie took the beach blanket, the digging toys, and a small ice chest, while Hannah filled her arms with towels.

"Don't strain yourself," Celie whispered. Hannah stuck out her tongue, but only after she'd looked to see that Mom and Frank were well ahead and busy balancing the huge picnic hamper between them. Hannah was the best of them at not getting caught.

They passed rows of charcoal fires, their grills loaded up with sizzling chickens in various phases of doneness. Celie's stomach rumbled but Mom's fried chicken was just as good, maybe even better, and she was content thinking about that and the ice cream after. They passed badminton nets and croquet wickets set up on the grass; beach balls were everywhere, and Celie could hardly think of what she wanted to do first.

Mom was waving crazily to someone over at the picnic pavilion area. Millie Harper, Mom's best friend and her son Eddie-the-wimp, who cried at everything, even bugs.

Celie whispered to Hannah, "Oh for God's sake. We'll be stuck with Eddie-the-wimp. I'll have to find a way for us to lose him."

"Me too," Hannah said, her reply to almost every opinion Celie gave.

By the time the food was finally arranged according to some configuration in Mom's head, Celie was starving. They all were. They ate greedily, and Mom kept telling them to slow down or they'd get a cramp. This made Hannah jumpy and she asked Celie, "What kind of cramp?"

"Mom has this thing about stomach cramps that drown people, or at least she thinks so."

"How do you get them?"

"I'm not sure. All I know is you have to wait a half hour after you eat before you go into the water."

"And that makes you safe – the half hour?"

"Sure, dopey. It makes you perfectly safe," she lied. If Hannah got too scared, she'd whine all afternoon.

After lunch, Mom walked them down to the beach, arranging their toys and towels on the quilt, which had been spread out and anchored with rocks. She slathered Coppertone on both girls' already-freckled shoulders and backs, their legs, and even the tops of their feet. "Irish pale skin," Mom muttered as she spread and rubbed.

"I'll make you a deal," Mom said when she'd finished. "You girls play on the beach after Frank builds the castle. I'll come and take you in swimming in a while. For now, only go in far enough to fill the buckets. Not one step farther. Not even up to your ankles, understand?"

They nodded, trying to look serious while Mom gathered up her things and went back to the food pavilion. With any luck, she'd be content to stay up there and chat with her friends.

Frank, meanwhile, had decided to make a huge sand shark instead of a castle. It was much bigger than life-size, he told them. They kept bringing him water until it was nearly done, then sat and watched him add the finishing touches. Rows of teeth, fins.

"We love it," they yelled as he swaggered around his sculpture, admiring it.

"Oh no. Here comes Eddie," Hannah warned. Without even checking to see, Celie threw herself down flat and pretended to be asleep, hoping Hannah would copy her. The next thing she knew, they'd both fallen asleep for real and Hannah was shaking her awake.

Eddie-the-wimp and Frank were gone.

"Celie! What about the ice cream?"

"Fine. You must have money hidden somewhere; you always do. Even a nickel would help."

"I forgot. Really."

Celie sighed. "OK, we'll go see how much it costs."

They opened their towels and wrapped them around their waists, aiming for a sarong effect like the high school girls. On Celie it looked pretty good, but Hannah still had what Mom called baby-fat around her middle, so she looked more like a fat little penguin. It was all Celie could do not to laugh as they walked to the soft-serve stand.

Scanning the price board, Celie realized she didn't have enough money for even a small cup of vanilla. "We can't afford *any*," she told Hannah.

Hannah was screwing up her face to cry, but Celie punched her arm in time to stop her. "Look!" Right behind where they were standing, the Lion's Club had just opened a tub filled to the top with smoky dry ice, with dozens of ice-cream bars nestled deep inside. And they were free! A Lion volunteer would reach a hand down into the swirling miasma, ignoring the signs marked, "Dangerous, do not touch," and up would come little blocks of ice cream wrapped in foil. Three flavors — vanilla, chocolate, strawberry.

Celie stood in line and got two bars. The red-faced volunteer puffed out instructions, "Keep it in the wrapper while you eat it and don't throw your wrapper on the ground, OK?"

Celie nodded but Hannah said, "I wanted just chocolate."

"Holy cow, Hannah. This is all they got. And it's free." Celie could count on that word, *free*, if all else failed. There's nothing a skinflint likes better than something for nothing, she thought, as she ate her own bar in about ten big bites. Hannah licked hers slowly, saving the chocolate for last. By the time she got to it, tiny streams of chocolate were dribbling down her chin to her elbow and onto her belly, and she was a sight! Celie laughed out loud and Hannah looked sheepish but said, "I *like* it melted."

They tried to clean off her front with little napkin squares that must have felt like shaved sandpaper, seeing as they were turning Hannah's skin bright red.

"We'll have to rinse you off in the water instead," Celie told her.

"We can't! I'll get stomach cramps," Hannah wailed, but followed.

"No you won't. Ice cream is a liquid. It doesn't count as food."

"Cross your heart and hope to die?"

"Sure," she answered. "Don't be such a baby." Celie was lying again but some part of her *kind of* believed it.

After she'd washed Hannah's stomach, she built her a little sand castle but when she looked up from it, Hannah was gone. She wasn't on the quilt; she wasn't anywhere. Celie felt frantic, until finally, up by the sand fence, she spotted a bright yellow bathing suit under a mop of shiny black hair. Hannah was at least a thousand yards away, walking on a sand dune festooned with dozens of dangling coils of seaweed. Frank was with her.

Celie ran toward them, yelling, "Hannah, what are you doing?"

"Looking for bodies," she answered, her face solemn.

Celie glowered at Frank, once she was sure he was looking at her. "Good show, Bro. Did you hear what she just said?"

"So? Hey, not *my* fault. She's the one who wanted to see dead bodies."

"Right. You try telling that to Mom."

"Hey, don't say anything, OK? I'll take you with me to the movies on Saturday."

"Don't worry. I won't say anything." She tried her best to sound gracious. "You don't owe me anything back. All I want is for Mom not to worry."

His face reddened so much she couldn't even see his freckles. He hated to carry debts, no matter how small. "You want me to take Hannah back down?"

"Oh sure, and while you're being so helpful, be sure to tell her to go down the road a few miles so she can find some pirates, OK?"

"Ha. *HA*. I'm going snorkeling. Don't tell Mom that either."

He shot off. A flash of a tall, skinny body in scuba goggles and rubber fins. He was obviously fed up with them both and willing to risk Mom's wrath rather than put up with sisters. Celie would remember afterward that she'd issued a silent but very heartfelt wish for him to get into trouble, as payback for being mean to Hannah. She'd also remember hoping he'd stay there for just a few more minutes, so they could keep exchanging insults. She'd had a couple of real doozies ready. But she was too mad to follow him, and besides, there were boys her age all over the place, which could be much more interesting. She envisioned herself marching down the sand bank, heroically leading her little sister. (Scarlett O'Hara bringing Melanie Wilkes back to Atlanta.)

Unfortunately, the sand was deep and didn't provide good footing. By the time she'd stumbled down to the bottom of the dune, she was panting, while Hannah's face was rosy with excitement, her dark hair framing her face so that it shone like a star.

"I found lots of dead bodies!" Hannah chirped, holding out her bucket with a dried-up fish of some kind, some old oyster shells, and other shells that were probably just stones. Everything was ensnared in slimy tendrils of seaweed.

"They're lovely. But you weren't supposed to leave me, you know."

"I didn't go away. I could see you every minute."

Celie didn't argue back only because of a ruckus brewing down at the shore edge. The life guards were shouting for somebody. "Becky! Becky! Where are you?" Becky who? Nobody she knew.

She poked Hannah. "You hear that? Those are life guards calling for some kid who wandered off and whose Mom is probably having a cow right now, worrying. It's thanks to me that they aren't shouting out *Hannah*, too."

Maybe it's thanks to me, she thought, but Mom wouldn't see it that way. Grabbing her sister by the shoulders and turning her so she'd pay attention, she said, "Listen, don't you dare say a word about going up to the dunes with Frank."

Hannah looked puzzled. "Why not?"

"Mom would have a cow about me letting you wander off, that's why not! In fact, we'd all be in trouble."

"But I knew where I was the whole time, Celie. I wasn't being in trouble, honest."

Celie knew Hannah believed in her own safety. She'd even read somewhere how little kids could never imagine they might die. She wouldn't push it. All she needed was for Hannah to swear she'd never been away from her. She made her practice saying it right a few times, until she was satisfied Hannah actually believed the words she'd been rehearsing. The secret to being a good liar, she thought, is lie to yourself first and then just keep practicing.

Celie pulled Hannah into the sand and began covering her feet and legs, planning for them to take turns until Mom came to take them swimming. Her plan collapsed within seconds. Something all around them was very wrong. The lifeguards now had a megaphone to call for Becky. And here came Mom, actually *running* toward them, one hand clamped over her mouth. She grabbed both girls, hugging them to her and saying the same thing over and over, "It's not you. Thank God, it's not you."

When Mom let them go she asked, "Where's Frank?"

When had they last seen him, which direction ... and Celie felt a huge wallop of guilt. She should say where he'd gone, but she'd promised him she wouldn't. In the end, seeing Mom's face like that, she had no choice. "I think he took his scuba mask and stuff to the diving rock." She knew even as the words left her mouth, that she'd made things worse.

"Did he go with anybody? Who was his buddy?"

"Eddie-the...um, Eddie."

"Eddie! For God's sake, he couldn't be the buddy of a water dog! I specifically told Frank *not* to go diving without a grown-up. You heard me tell him. I did tell him, right?"

As Celie nodded, Mom crossed her arms tightly, which she only did when she was worried. "Celie, go to the edge of the water. See if he's out there but do — not — go — into — that — water. Hannah, you sit here on the quilt and don't move a muscle. You got that?"

Hannah's thumb was in her mouth and she nodded, then yanked out her thumb to say, "You know, Mommy, Frank goes in the water by himself all the time."

Celie tried to think of a quick way to shut Hannah up but couldn't, not with Mom on high alert like that. Mom was saying, "No, he doesn't. He always has Bobby or somebody with him."

Celie knew for sure this wasn't true, but she wasn't about to let Hannah educate Mom on Frank's real habits. She yelled, "Hey, Mom – the diving rock is empty! He probably went to the campground. You told him about those arrowheads, remember? He's probably there."

Mom started to answer but was interrupted by a roar of voices — people appeared all around the lifeguard stand, then began running toward the river, pointing and yelling.

"Why are they hollering?" Hannah asked from behind her thumb, and that was when Celie spied Frank out in the river, walking toward them.

"Look Mom! I see Frank!"

Mom turned, hands crossed against her throat as she looked to the spot where everyone was pointing. Celie expected Mom to smile once she saw him, but instead she froze in place, just for an instant, then grabbed both the girls by their arms, nearly dragging them all the way back to the picnic pavilion, saying, "We need to hurry, OK?"

When they reached their table, Celie asked, "What's the matter? Why aren't we waiting for Frank?"

"Frank's just fine. He'll be here in a minute. In the meantime, you two sit right here and don't move til I get back, Ok?" They nodded, and Mom was gone.

Hannah let loose what they'd both been feeling and began bawling, "What happened? Celie, I want Mommy!"

Celie didn't know what to answer. All she knew was the chaos surrounding them – adults shouting and children crying and car engines starting. She decided just to hold Hannah and rock her while she tried to make sense of things. If there was danger, why wasn't Mom putting them in the car, like the other families were doing? And why had seeing Frank scared Mom out of her wits?

She looked over their things, which looked perfectly normal, picnic baskets packed up, dry clothes piled on the bench, ready to change into. With a start, she realized she had missed an obvious clue. Millie and Eddie were both gone.

Hannah, maybe sensing Celie's growing panic, began wailing again. Celie grabbed her and gave her a shake. "Stop yowling."

"I'm s-s- scared."

"So who isn't? If you want me to find out what's going on you're going to have to quiet down, so I can go ask."

Hannah sniffled loudly, hiccupped once, said "OK," and stuffed her thumb back in her mouth. Celie made her curl up on a beach chair and covered her with a huge towel. Walking to the edge of the pavilion, she stared toward the part of the beach where she and Hannah had just been sitting. She could barely see the bright red border of their quilt, still laid out, even though all the other beach blankets had been taken away. A jumble of strangers surrounded it, but there was no sign of Mom or Frank.

She simply had to find out what was going on.

"Stay there until I come back for you," she ordered Hannah. "I'm going down to find out what happened." She wished she knew for sure if Hannah had heard her.

Chapter Four

The largest of the Eastern Shore rivers, the Choptank, winds for 68 miles from its non-tidal, freshwater beginnings at the top of rural countryside, down to its brackish mouth, over a mile wide, at the southern crook of Cook's Point in Dorchester County. The river is wild and isolated in parts, bordered by marshes in some places, and lined with old-growth forests in others. It is 'mother' to countless lesser rivers, coves, and creeks, all of them home to an amazing abundance and diversity of life. (Leatherman)

Becky Miller had walked through the river until it was all the way up to her waist. She'd been following a very long eel, and after that, a handful of silvery crappies swam by, nearly bumping her arm. She could feel little flutters as their fins whipped the water. At almost twelve years old, she felt brave for trying to touch live fish. She wondered what else could be down further. The river water was murky, but here on the sand bar, the water was shallower and clearer. She had a new scuba mask and had heard it sometimes let you see things that were all the way on the river bottom.

She pulled her mask down over her eyes and ducked her head under, crossing her fingers, wishing for oysters or mussels. Within seconds she'd spotted a scattering of oyster shells. She picked up a large half-shell and a reasonable-size whole oyster and tucked them into the pocket of her bathing suit. She found another small oyster that fit under her bathing cap, one for her baby sister, Emily. She'd get Pop to open them. They'd found a real pearl once, not very pretty, but she loved it as if it had been fit for the Queen to wear. (All the pictures of the new Queen Elizabeth showed her wearing pearls.)

Her stomach had started to hurt again, like it did almost every day now. She hadn't told anybody, worried they'd make her stay home from the picnic. She hadn't been able to eat though, slipping off while her friends and her family were eating lunch, not wanting to lie to anybody.

Another cramp, sharper now. Maybe she should go back to shore, despite her disappointment with just three shells. If she could just find a mussel shell, or even a sand crab. It was possible she was only inches from the real oyster bed. She slipped forward slightly deeper, an inch at a time, making sure her feet stayed firmly on the sandbar. She bobbed her goggled head in the water and then out, in and out, laughing aloud at how silly she must look.

Another pain knifed her belly and in an instant, her laugh changed to a cry. She felt her body folding in half. Grabbing her stomach with both hands, she tried to uncurl herself, still not believing the pain had increased this fast.

Must – stand – up, she thought. Usually she could make the pain pass just by breathing in and out a few times, but the more she struggled against the knot gripping her belly, the more it cramped, until it was holding her so tight she could barely even move her legs.

What worried her at first was that she might have to hop all the way back to shore, coiled up like that, looking stupid. Long seconds ticked by, and with the spasm not letting go, it struck her that she would have to yell for help. Somebody would have to come and get her.

Meantime, she'd be OK just by staying on the sand bar. With water that wasn't even all the way over her head, nothing really bad could happen, right? Just stay on the sand bar and not let herself go off the shelf.

Stretching her neck back, she could easily lift her face out of the water to where the air was, just above the surface. A little rest and then the next time up, she would breathe once, twice, and yell "help" before letting her head fall back under. By then the pain might let go....

****

Celie passed the picnic grounds, where most of the families had cleared out. The only people she could see were on the campground, people whose tents wouldn't pack up so quickly. She approached a man helping a little girl put on her sneakers.

"Hi, I'm Celie. I'm trying to find out what happened out there because my sister is real scared. Do you know anything?"

"Yes," said the father in hushed tones, holding his hands over his daughter's ears. "A child was found unconscious on the bottom of the river. A little girl."

Not Eddie then, Celie thought, relieved. The lifeguards had been calling for a girl named Becky. No one she knew.

The mother of the family got up and took Celie by the hand, guiding her away from her own children. "The little girl was found by a teen-age snorkeler ... an eagle scout, they say. He accidentally stepped on her. They say he just scooped her right up and hauled her to his own blanket back on the sand. Laid her down and began artificial respiration and everything. A real brave kid. They're not sure he was in time, though. I think now they're all waiting for the ambulance."

She was talking about Frank! The drowned kid they were all talking about ... she'd been found by Frank!

She had promised Mom to stay with Hannah, but there was no way she could just go back and wait without at least making sure Frank was all right. If she ran the whole way to the beach, she could slip in between people, just long enough to see that Frank was OK, and be back with Hannah before Mom knew.

****

Celie got close to the crowd, close enough to see Mom and Frank standing at the edge of their quilt. Frank was shivering, Mom's arm around him, both of them staring at the quilt center. She could just glimpse a girl her own age, lying on her stomach. A man with a Lifeguard shirt was trying to make her breathe on her own, pushing on her small back with his large hands, over and over. Celie could see water pooling beneath her mouth, water out - air in, and she felt relieved.

She had to be alive. She just had to be. How could somebody her own age drown in water shallow enough to walk in? She wanted to stay until the girl – until Becky – recovered, but now she had to get back to Hannah. For the first time in her life, she did something completely unselfish. It had nothing to do with what anybody else thought. Not with being punished, either. Not even with going to hell when she wasn't in a state of grace. She decided to go back to Hannah because that was where she'd be most needed. It didn't make her feel any better, but it did feel right.

****

The drowning had been two days ago, and Celie didn't feel like the same person, as if she'd started the summer as one girl and would come out of it another. It was close to midnight and she was lying on her back, eyes wide open and staring at the ceiling. She wished she hadn't gone down to the beach that day when Mom and Frank were gone so long. Now, every time she let her eyes close, she saw the drowned girl, lying face down on their quilt, her short hair wavy as it dried, the pink gingham bathing suit crisscrossing her back, her right hand still tightly clutching an oyster shell.

There was a spot on Celie's ceiling that had allowed in water during the last hurricane, a tan spot with deep brown edges that had shaped out an elf's hat. A long, thin blotch reached out from the top of the stain, like a feather. She stared at it until her eyes got blurry. In her head were some lines from "The Brown Dwarf." *"How fair she seemed among the trolls so ugly and so wild! Her low, sweet voice, her gold-brown hair. Her tender blue eyes. ..."* Celie kept thinking about the once-beloved little girl who would never again know love. Mom had told her she needed to stop thinking so much about her, but if people forgot the little girl, it would be as if she'd never lived, wouldn't it?

She heard the washer starting downstairs. The machine leaned on the same wall where her headboard was. When she wanted, she could hear nearly everything that went on in the laundry room and sometimes the kitchen. She hadn't told Hannah this secret yet because she was the kind of kid who'd worry about the things she'd hear. Celie had come real close to telling Frank once, just because she wanted to show off how clever she was. Luckily, she'd held her tongue. Frank could be heartless, and she was positive he would have someday used her trick against her.

Against the buzz of the washer was the sound of Daddy coming home. His loud voice told her he was upset about something. She would bet her lucky rabbit's foot that he had new information about Becky. They already knew she'd lived near Bridgeville, Delaware because this morning, her family had driven over, baby, Grandma and all, to thank Frank for trying to save their daughter. Celie had been desperate to go out to the car and meet them.

"Can I go? I won't say a word. Please, Mom, I'm old enough."

"Not this time." Tucking a flyaway curl back under the black velvet ribbon she wore as a headband, Mom brushed a hand across her bangs to settle them. She shot a look at Celie. It was what Hannah called her 'tight face,' and it meant she better not say another word.

Celie had to watch from the window while Daddy shook hands with the father and hugged the mother and Frank did exactly the same. Mom hugged them all, even the Grandma and the baby. When her parents came in, they told her bare basics, name and age, and then clammed up tight the whole rest of the day. Even Daddy, usually a pushover around his daughters, held his finger to his lips, a silent *shhh.*

Celie had her back-up plan, the listening wall. She laid her ear lightly in place to create a small pocket of air, then cupped her hands along her ears to amplify the sound waves.

Daddy was speaking. "Why didn't they miss her for so long?"

Mom's voice came up the wall, clear and strong. "They'd just finished eating. The adults sent all the kids off to play while they cleaned up. Becky's mother wasn't there, you know. Apparently, Becky was a friend of the family's little girl. They had no idea she had a stomach ulcer – who would think that about a child? I don't think they even knew she'd gone off until they heard the commotion and began counting heads."

"My God," Daddy said. "Dear God, how do you get over a thing like that?"

"I don't think you do. Anyway, Millie and I were cleaning up our tables and she went into a panic because she hadn't seen Eddie for a while. I told her he was with Frank and the girls...at least I thought he was. I was already on my way to check on them anyway, so I hurried that along. Millie went out to the cars to search there."

Another long pause, dishes clanking. Celie heard the tea kettle whistling and could picture all the steps, Mom putting together two cups of instant coffee, Daddy's with milk and sugar, hers black. Since there was an apple pie, she'd slice him a piece and ask if he wanted ice cream.

Daddy's voice next. "No, just the pie."

Then Mom, "It was a good thing I went down to the water because it turns out I was wrong. Eddie wasn't with the girls and Frank had gone off with that damn scuba gear of his."

"Son of a gun." Daddy's voice was shaking; she could tell even this far up the wall. She knew how much he was afraid of the water, but she didn't know why. Maybe it had been something like this? Had he found a drowned kid when he younger?

Mom was talking again. "I should have known he'd go off like that. Diving was all he talked about the whole way there."

"Don't tell me he took Eddie with him out in the deep river!"

'No! Thank God. Eddie was perfectly safe, out by the swings. He'd be the last kid to go into the deep water. And the girls were right where they were supposed to be the whole time. Sitting on the quilt just playing."

Which of course, we weren't, Celie thought. Not until just about a minute before Mom came to get us.

Daddy was asking, "So Frank saw the little girl while he was diving?"

"No. Much worse. He was walking to the big rock and he actually stepped on her. He pulled her out right away and got her to shore in less than a minute, it seems. No one could have got her out any faster than he did."

"At least there's that. Thank God."

"Yes, there's that."

"So, what do we do? About Frank, I mean – I don't know what to do to help him."

"To tell you the truth, he's not as upset as you'd think. He's not a kid anymore, I guess. I'm not saying it doesn't upset him. That's why he's huddled up in his room. It's just that I think he'll get over it and be OK."

"You're right. He will. There's something tough inside that boy. Maybe too tough, I don't know. I worry more about what he'll do to the world than I do about vice versa."

Celie had no idea what Daddy had meant. She wrote it down, word-for-word, a note tucked into her diary to figure out later. She lost the note but figured it out anyway the first time Frank was arrested for setting a fire at the school. That night though, the lesson to be learned was that the rivers they all took for granted were much too treacherous for swimming. They were all looking for reasons other than water to explain things. The stomach ulcer was not the cause – it was the river that had killed Becky Miller. This was the third time Celie had been around a river drowning, all three times when people were supposed to be having fun.

She just didn't get it. Why did folks keep trying to swim in fast-moving water with whirlpools and stuff, where the bottom dropped off in places you couldn't see and where there could be blue crabs or eels or even water snakes? She shivered, thinking that maybe next time they all went swimming, she'd stay home with Daddy.

The talking downstairs had stopped. Even though she wasn't sure exactly why, she finally managed to close her eyes without seeing Becky.

She woke up the next morning to the spin of the washer. It was before dawn, still barely light outside. She decided to sneak downstairs to see why Mom was washing stuff so early. She didn't get all the way to the kitchen, though, because in the corner of her vision as she passed the porch, she picked up movement outside.

It was Mom, hanging their quilt on the clothesline. Washed last night and again this morning. She figured Mom must have washed that quilt four or five times by now. How many times did it take to wash away a drowning?

I should go help her hang it, she thought, but instead, she just sat on the top step looking out the window, watching each clothespin go up. Plain wooden clothespins, gripping the points of each red calico eight-pointed star. Then Mom sitting down in her white wooden lawn chair, in front of the quilt Grandmom had sewed, her eyes on it as it wafted like a flag in the crisp morning breeze. Mom watching the quilt and Celie watching Mom.

****

Usually the summer ahead was a glorious thing to think about, a time filled with boats and water, swimming and fishing. But not today, not for the rest of the week, and maybe not forever. Today,

Celie was glad to be able to stay in the house, even to do dishes. Cups done, plates next, and as always, a few minutes lost in daydreaming.

Her kitten began rubbing the backs of her ankles, its purr loud enough to nearly drown out the 'tap-tap' that came from outside the porch. Was it a real knock, or just wood scraping wood from a screen door that no longer hung square in the frame, a door so loose that even a steady breeze could set it to rattling? With her imagination, she always had to stop herself from making something out of nothing. She plunged the stack of big plates into the scalding hot water, suddenly in a hurry to get the chores down so she could occupy her brain with reading or grooming the horses, anything to forget what happened at Green's Point last Friday.

There was a second noise, a definite *TAP*. Shaking the soap suds from her hands, she moved to where she could see the plastic Felix the Cat with his clock face and side-swinging tail. Eight a.m. Too early for either Isaac or Ava. Must be a dog wanting in, and it was too hot already to leave a dog outside.

"Hold on," she called and aimed her dripping hands at the over-sized apron that Mom made her wear even though it was way too long for a twelve-year old. The rough muslin hurt the second it touched her throbbing skin and she decided to air-dry her hands because she still had the pots to do.

She did a quick turn to side-step the stupid apron hem as she crossed the door jamb but snagged one of the dangling ties with her big toe and tripped anyway.

"Fiddle-dee-dee," she yelped, trying her best to sound like Scarlett O'Hara.

Her bare feet stuck with every step across the closed-in porch. Daddy had just finished laying the vinyl floors in his makeover of the milkhouse-turned-porch. This time his idea was to make it a combination laundry-playroom. It was one of his never-ending improvements meant to convince Mom that her house was as good as any of the houses in town.

When it was this humid, the vinyl floor idea had already showed itself to be a bad one. Mom, like her two daughters, rarely wore shoes in summer; she said, "The tile feels as tacky as it looks." The old wood floors, now hidden beneath the gluey layers of plastic, had felt cool and silky-smooth on the soles of her feet. At least that was the way Celie remembered them.

She regained her footing and tried to see through the patched screen but couldn't make out any shape at all. It must be Isaac after all, she thought, since a dog would have been leaning hard enough against the screen to curve it inward, as if the owners inside might feel its weight and respond sooner. Isaac would do just the opposite, hunkering down to make himself invisible. Isaac's humility was a part of his skin by now, along with his blackness and the sweat that beaded up perpetually along his back and his arms. And the straw hat which she'd never seen him without.

"Isaac? Is that you?"

"It's me, I'm a mite early." He moved a couple inches closer but didn't climb the steps, which would have put him level with the door. All she could see was his hat.

"How you doing? Come on in."

"No need. Just came to pick up what your Ma ask me to. She here?"

"No, she isn't. She wanted to get to the Acme before it gets too hot."

"That's right smart. Well, you tell her I said 'morning' and that I'll stop on by later."

"No wait, I have the bag ready. She left it for me to give you. *Please* come in for a minute. It's too hot to stand out on the step. I'll get you some nice cold tea."

"That'd be nice."

Celie knew he would hover just outside the door. Even as well as their families knew each other, he'd never come all the way into the house without Dad or one of the uncles there. No black man would, not even a sweet, harmless old man in his fifties, (or was it his sixties?) who walked with his back bent over halfway. Isaac's shoulders bent down even when he danced. Celie smiled, remembering his dancing a few days ago, when she'd rode along with Daddy to take supplies over to the migrant workers' cabins. Isaac had been doing a reel by the campfire, spiraling around, swinging his wife Minnie up in the air like she was a feather. She'd wondered then if he was as old as she'd thought. People in their sixties couldn't dance like that, could they? Not that she'd ever ask.

She poured out the iced tea, mixing in some extra sugar and squeezing in near half a lemon. All the field hands liked their tea loaded up the same way kids drank it, more like lemonade, the way anybody did who spent long hours in the hot sun.

Holding the glass tight with one hand, she moved slowly, enjoying the coolness while trying not to slosh tea on the already-sticky floor. With the other hand, she was dragging the heavy burlap sack from the hallway where Mom had filled it last night.

Isaac had sat on the bottom step to wait. He had the unique privilege among the crew of staying seated in the presence of the family. The honor came to him not because of his age but because he was Field Boss. All the rest of the migrant workers, women, children, even the old folks, would have stayed standing in the dirt drive, no matter how fierce the sun might be. Even the young'uns would stay upright, feet scuffling dirt to churn up little clouds of dust, their eyes aimed downward and their straw hats in hand. It was tradition.

Isaac stood up when he saw the overstuffed sack, reaching for the cord without touching her hand, and dragging it smoothly toward him. He waited for Celie to hold the tea out to him, taking it carefully, again without hand contact, as was the custom for any black person when dealing with anyone who was white. It made Celie furious to think about it, but she was helpless to change anything, and she sure didn't want to embarrass Isaac by challenging his choice.

He had guzzled the whole glassful down in one long chug.

"Wow, you sure were thirsty! How about some more?"

"I don't mind."

By the time Celie returned with his refill, Isaac had sorted the sack's contents and was nodding and smiling at each item of clothing or bedding. He crooned, "Yessir or um – hmm," as if everything there was precious and irreplaceable. "Never seen one as handsome as this," he said about a corduroy shirt outgrown by her brother and unseasonably dark and thick. "It'll fit our Gabe just fine." He caressed a dresser scarf with lace edging and then held up a large plastic hand mirror with silver backing that was scaling off. "My, my," he said, "Minnie's gonna love this."

Celie tried to smile but she felt oddly embarrassed, ashamed that this jumble of throwaways, cast off by her family, was being prized by Isaac. She wasn't sure why she suddenly minded. Was it just because she knew Ava and Sari so well? Or because for the first time in her life, she wondered if his flattery was sincere. She would need more time to think about that. But not now. Isaac had reached the quilt, and this was all she would be able to think about for the rest of the day.

The quilt was a very fine one. The squares and circles had been cut and sewn together by hand into perfect eight-pointed stars, created in Grandma McBride's tiny, even stitches during the first year of her marriage. It was still almost perfect despite its age. Isaac fingered the quilt and his eyes grew wide - with appreciation? Disbelief? Or maybe both? Everyone around these parts knew the value of a hand-sewn quilt in top condition. Isaac held it up and asked, "You sure about this one here, Miss Celie? You might want to just check it with your ma first."

"I don't need to. It's the main reason ... you're meant to take it. I'm ... sure." Celie had heard her voice growing prickly as she'd pushed out each word, one by one, past a hard lump stuck in her throat. Isaac raised an eyebrow and kept it there, a question mark that made her look away. She helped him fold the quilt edges together, her eyes on the quilt rather than on Isaac, her lungs easing air in and out evenly, until she could relax her throat and swallow. By the time she looked up from the neatly folded quilt, she had pushed her mouth into a wide grin. Isaac was such a kindly soul that it was easy to smile at him. He seemed to relax, or at least had resumed his nods and smiles, and the difficult moment had passed.

Celie had hardly thought about the quilt today, so the strong feelings surprised her. She'd thought that her sorrow had settled last night when they'd reached agreement about the quilt's fate. You don't destroy a beautiful family heirloom just because it's seen tragedy. Daddy said that Isaac would make the best possible use of it, because "that's what Isaac does. He finds and rescues treasures."

She and Hannah had wanted their parents to tell Isaac the whole story of the quilt, but Mom and Dad voted against it. Hannah had jumped over to their side at the last minute, the little rat.

Frank might have sided with her, but he'd been excused from the vote and had gone to bed early, so it ended up three to one. They wouldn't burden Isaac with the quilt's role in tragedy. The treasured quilt would be given to Isaac free of heartaches.

God knows, it was a relief she didn't have to tell him the rest. She hoped she'd never again have to talk about the day of the drowning. As soon as he was gone, she squeezed her eyes hard before attacking the last of the dishes. Sometimes squinting could make a terrible thought go away.

Chapter Five

*Secretary, at the head of the Warwick River, was settled by Europeans
arriving in Maryland in 1634. For 300 years, its waterfront buzzed with
boats bringing fish and crabs, skipjacks bringing oysters, and with farmers
bringing fruit and vegetables to the canneries. In 1674, Captain Henry
Trippe won a war that pushed the Nanticoke Indians off their land. With
his reward money, he built a fine home, which was eventually used as
the Rectory for the Our Lady of Good Counsel Roman Catholic Church.*
(Owens)

Being Catholics living in a Protestant town, Hannah and Celie
knew what it was like to feel like an outsider. They'd never even set
foot in Daddy's church, Grace Baptist, having been told by Maryanne
Moxie that they could go to Hell just by sitting inside (if they died
without confessing it). They went to Our Lady of Good Counsel
Church ten miles away in Secretary, a community made up of fishermen and the industries that served them. Mom had told them all
about the watermen and how they lived, about their skipjacks and
fishing boats, about the men who were mostly Polish or Irish or Italian.

On Sundays, they got to play with kids they didn't get to see anywhere else. After Mass, Mom always stayed for charity work while
the kids all played. They'd run through the grass next to the river,
in and out of the church hall, and could even go up and down the
church aisles if they were careful to make the sign of the cross and
genuflect.

Anywhere except the rectory, where the priest lived, and the river,
which was forbidden to everyone. A single, thin strip of sandy beach
bordered a huge, shifting sandbar, making the swirling water above

45

it unsuitable for docking boats or even for swimming.

Our Lady of Good Counsel Catholic Church sat just above the War-wick, surrounded by thick rows of evergreens. Sailors coming in and out of the harbor could get just close enough to see through the trees to the back hall of the church where their wives and kids so often gathered. If they kept looking toward the top of the trees, they could see the steeple and the right edge of the cross. Religious or not, all the Catholic men made the sign of the cross in respect for the Sunday mass they'd miss again.

"I thought it was a mortal sin to miss Mass," Hannah asked one day as they watched the fishing boats heading out.

"The Blessed Mother will forgive them," Mom said. "After all, she was the mother of a fisherman."

On warm days, the kids played near picnic tables behind the kitchen, with whatever games had been donated to the church, at the least, a giant box of Tinker Toys, a roll of tattered newsprint paper and about a thousand mostly broken crayons. The toys were often ignored in favor of wind and sun and running around like crazy in your shirt sleeves, when it wasn't freezing. On those days, someone's mom would bring out fresh cookies piled high on a huge platter, some of them still warm.

The summer after seventh grade, Celie had found a serious boy-friend. She began spending all the free time on Sunday sitting and talking with Dale Kent, leaving Hannah on her own. Celie and Dale didn't even come in for the cookies.

Hannah was playing jacks with her friend Penny when the cook-ies appeared. She always sat as close as she could to the cookie tray, enthralled today with little white snowballs floating atop the choco-late chips and ordinary oatmeal. (Mom did not bake. Cakes, pies and cookies were delivered by the Bond Bread man)

"What are these?" she asked Penny, who shrugged her shoulders.

"That's one of my mom's. It's called an Italian Wedding Cookie," said a new girl with dark thick braids and flashing brown eyes. "I'm Madeline DeGenoa. My mom's a baker. Which is your favorite?" Madeline was reaching for a Pecan Sandy.

Hannah's eyes were fixated on those amazing white snowballs, completely round, with a thick coat of powdered sugar. They looked as light as a feather. She took one, first tasting it with the tip of her tongue, followed by a nibble on one side. Finally, she popped the whole cookie into her mouth and closed her eyes. It was crumbly rather than chewy – little clumps of fluffy crumbs melting in her mouth.

"I love it," she said. Hannah had the same instinct to break traditions as Celie did. She was intrigued by anybody different and especially anybody looked down on, like the Italian shopkeepers, the Jewish department store owner, the rugged watermen. And their own mother, of course. Hannah had overheard the Hurlock librarian call her Mom, "that girl Guy married, you know, the Catholic from Pennsylvania."

She also knew that Mom took her outsider status personally. When Miss Hilda from Sadhoff's Department Store told Mom, "We're both in the same boat," Hannah put it together; it was about religion. In Hurlock, a town of Baptists and Methodists, Mom was the only non-Protestant besides the Sadoff's. By living on a farm, the whole family, even Daddy, was assumed to have nothing in common with the watermen. Being Catholic, it was assumed Mom would have nothing common with the Protestants (even though she'd married one).

It might have been confusing, except that Celie had told her, "being an outsider is always so much more interesting." Hannah made up her mind to find out more about people whose lives she couldn't imagine, which is how she developed a crush on a boy named Jesse Wanex, the only son of a skipjack pilot.

She'd met Jesse in Catechism class. He spoke with great pride about the skipjacks, the oldest kind of oyster dredging boat on the Chesapeake. Their romance seemed to proceed in slow motion, since Church was their only connection. Then, the elementary schools were consolidated, and the Hurlock school bus swung wider to pick up Secretary's fourteen kids. The girls from church were at school every day. Madeline DiGenoa became Hannah's best friend. (The fact that her mom was a superlative baker may have had something to do with it.)

Hannah had expected to see Jesse more, never imagining he wouldn't come to school. She hadn't known that boys in fishing families were water-bound, coming to school irregularly and never in fishing season. When they did show up, they wriggled in their seats and tapped their feet and seemed pre-occupied. Yet, Jesse had somehow let Hannah know he was interested, waving at her those few times he came to church, and once leaving her a note with a sailboat sketched on it. When she asked him about it, he told her about skipjack sailing and why he loved it.

Sometimes she would walk out on the piers after church, trying to imagine her future life as a fisherman's wife. The smell of saltwater and seaweed was pleasant enough. She imagined she'd be eating fish most days instead of just on Fridays, and that would be OK too.

There was just one problem — they'd probably have to live right on the water. Celie had developed such a strong fear of water that it had begun to affect Hannah too. When Celie had nightmares and talked in her sleep, Hannah would hold her hand until the next morning, and then they'd talk about the people they knew who'd drowned. More than once on her walks to the waterfront, Hannah found herself staring into the Warwick River, looking for lost faces in the seaweed.

She'd have to get past this difficulty somehow, after they were married. Meanwhile, she often gazed out for long minutes toward the Bay where the waves broke as they hit the river. She was hoping to catch sight of Jesse's skipjack zigzagging through the water, but she never did. By the time she got to junior high school, Jesse had stopped coming to school and church both. Hannah tried to get up the nerve to approach his sister, Lacey, to ask about him. She'd heard rumors at the church that his father was sick, with Jesse already having to manage the family's livelihood. By High school, she had lost track of him. The one thing she knew for sure was that if the active skipjack fleet in Maryland was dwindling, like her teacher said, it would make Jesse even more determined to preserve their family legacy.

*****

The day of Jesse's thirteenth birthday, he woke up to the sound of a pair of gulls shrieking, squabbling over a fish. He hugged the sides of his pillow to muffle his ears, but the racket was even worse that way. Throwing off the pillow, he reached under his bed, feeling for something he could use as a guided missile. His room held only his bed and a small dresser with his socks and the clothes he wore to church. Sometimes, things could roll under the bed, and he felt around, hoping.

He was in luck. His fingers curled around a stone the size of an egg. Groggy as he was, he rolled off his mattress toward the wide-open window, let out a whoop and aimed at the gulls, his hand releasing the stone in one smooth motion. It went sailing over the heads of the birds, missing them by ten feet, not close enough to even slightly disturb their tussle over breakfast.

"Go on!" he shouted, but they kept on squawking. He was thinking about a second rock until he got a good look at the birds. A big creamy-colored male and a smaller, scruff-feathered female. The male, of course, was going to win. The female had known it all along but with chicks to feed, she had to try to hang onto at least a chunk of the little bay anchovy it had taken her so long to catch. Stupid birds fighting over fish-bait, he thought but watched the battle until she had given up her prey and gone swooping down to the water to search again.

Jesse was almost back asleep when he thought he heard a creak on the stairs. He didn't register that sound for what it was, his father's boots on the steps, maybe because the sound was muted by his mother's pink carpet. Maybe it was just that he wasn't awake enough to consider that the boots could be headed for him. Or maybe he was wondering how things would change, his being thirteen. He was dreaming - a flock of gulls that were escaping a giant fish –

He didn't finish the dream because he woke up skidding across the floor. His father had rammed his shoulder into him, rolling him off the bed, and sending him the whole way over against the brick wall.

"Get your ass up, damn it. I shouldn't have to haul you up in the morning like youse some damn little kid."

Jesse gave a grunt as an answer, fearful of using real words lest he pick the wrong ones and earn himself a whack.

As his father disappeared back into the hall, he scrambled up and began rubbing a sore spot on his head, as if that would help anything. It was already forming a knot that would press against his watch cap all day and give him a headache. He cursed aloud at his own stupidity. He deserved the knot. If he'd had half a brain, he'd have rolled out just as the blow hit, controlling the fall and saving his head from the bricks. He was starting to fight just like his little sister — all reaction, no offense.

Having slept in his clothes, all he needed to do to get ready was pull on his boots. They were downstairs, just inside the kitchen door ... but what if his father was still in the house? He crept to the top of the steps, for once grateful for carpet that could mute his movements. He put one hand against his mother's cabbage rose wallpaper, leaning, listening for Pa. He might need a diversion to avoid another walloping. Maybe grab up his little sister and sit her in his lap? He waited two minutes, then three. He couldn't wait longer. "Ma," he whispered down the stairwell.

Nothing.

"Ma?" he called, louder. Still no answer, except the clanking of dishes and pans, a sound as promising as a spoken invitation. He sprinted down the steps, stopping at the kitchen doorway, just to make sure that only his mother and his sister were inside.

"Hey Jesse," Lacey chirped. Jesse moved to the table, straddling his chair and beginning to wolf down a bowlful of cold leftover grits. Ma turned to watch him, smiling.

Jesse plunked down the empty bowl and gave a high sign to his sister. "Hey, Lacey." He could see she wanted to talk and he wished he had more time.

"Happy birthday," she sang, and he grinned back.

"Eggs in a minute," Ma said, all business. They both knew he needed to hurry. Lacey knew it too and she jumped up to help as best she could, setting a mug of hot coffee down next to him. The mug was almost too big for both her hands and steaming hot. She was already like Ma, whose hands were as oblivious to heat as fiberglass.

"Careful Bubby, it's hot," Lacey whispered, her mouth close to his ear, as if she were telling him some great secret.

"Thanks, Half-pint," he whispered back, tousling her hair, then reaching around her and rifling through the bread basket in search of a leftover biscuit. His mother had finished cracking two eggs on the edge of the iron skillet. She somehow managed to catch his eye so she could toss him a hot biscuit. He winked at her. The three of them listened to the eggs sizzling in the hot fat, easy in each other's company, although you could never relax in the morning in this house. Pa was never good in the morning.

And then he was there, outside the back door, yelling, "Hey!" Jesse froze for a fraction of a second. He started to get up, but Ma shook her head, *no.*

"He'll be there in two shakes," she said to the door.

Pa was just outside the door but hadn't opened it. Jesse couldn't see him but knew he was staring at his mother, who still hadn't turned from the stove.

Pa said, "Didn't you hear me, boy? I said. *Hey*."

"He heard," Ma said. "I just started his eggs."

"He don't get to eat. He decided he'd rather have beauty sleep then breakfast. Let's go."

Again, Jesse started to get up, but his mother's hand was swift to push him back down. She said, "I'm the one let him sleep extra. It's his birthday."

"His birthday?" Pa's turn to hesitate a second, then, "if the boy expects to have any more birthdays around here, he better get up on time."

Ma's black eyes shot sparks. "He's gonna eat. He's twelve years old and he can't be out on the boat all morning without food."

He saw Lacey mouth the word, "Thirteen." Lacey would never speak aloud with Pa that close.

Ma never missed anything. "Thirteen, I mean." Ma said.

"I said he don't eat. He's got thirteen years of lazy-ass habits that gotta stop."

He could hear Pa raise up his body inside the plywood door frame, his wool shirt catching a nail, one rubber boot squeaking against the uneven door jamb. He was big enough he could nearly fill up the door space. As usual, he moved no further into the kitchen. The kitchen was Ma's territory. Lacey had disappeared, no doubt to hide in a closet. Smart girl.

There stood Ma, no more than 5'3" high and willow thin, but she stood up tall as she could and kept cooking, turning his eggs with a brisk flick of her wrist, looking straight at Pa while she did it. Looking him right in the old eye.

She folded her hands into fists and shoved her knuckles against her waist, one fist with a spatula sticking out of it, as dangerous-looking as any weapon Pa might have on him. You had to give Ma credit. She was the only person on the waterfront with guts enough to stand up to the old man.

"I say he eats," she said, reaching over to get the pan, then sliding the eggs onto a plate.

She smacked the eggs down in front of Jesse, jangling his utensils, now hidden under the plate. Ma stood there, hands on her hips, signaling for him to eat, but he couldn't, and it had nothing to do with his buried fork. It had to do with which of his parents was going to win. He sat still as a stone, waiting for somebody to make the next move. The oddest vision popped into his head. It was of the three of them stuck inside the huge portrait of the Holy Trinity up at Our Lady of Good Counsel. Three figures painted into position at each point in a triangle, forever locked together at equal distance, united every minute but never touching, Father, Son and Holy Ghost.

Pa made the first move this time, slamming the thin wooden screen door shut as he turned around and stomped off, wordless. He hadn't even bothered to cuss, but Jesse could hear him dragging his bad foot, a sure sign he was furious.

He wouldn't take the time to dig out his fork, upending the plate and downing both eggs in one gulp. He took a second to kiss his mother while she was shoving two wrapped egg biscuits into the pockets of his sweatshirt.

"Thanks, Ma," he said.

"Keep safe," she answered, "Happy Birthday, son."

"Keep safe," echoed a small voice from the hall closet.

Jesse ran across the quay with his boots half on, half off, thinking how they'd all come out of that battle lucky. When Pa got dug in like that, any outcome was possible. He thought back to the clean, win-or-lose struggle between that pair of gulls. He wished his parents could do that, just give in, one or the other of them. Instead, they argued about him daily, sometimes more than once a day. Mostly Pa got his way, but sometimes Ma stood her ground, like just now.

The only person who never won was Jesse. He felt like one of those rubber clown dolls you see at a carnival. It pops down, up, down, and then back up again no matter how many times you whack it. The face of the clown always has this shit-eating grin on it, like it's great to spend your existence being shoved from one side of the floor to the other.

"A real dumb-ass, all right," he thought. Not the clown. He was trying to imagine the face of the idiot who had dreamed up such a stupid toy. Some guy without enough sense to draw a believable face. That damn clown smile was even lamer than the idea of a toy that could never win or lose. What the hell was the point?

He was aboard and ready to cast off the moor line. Big Bill, his cousin, was retying the jib while his son, Little Bill idled in the push-boat next to them.

"Just about ready to cast off, Pa," he called down in the cabin, but no answer came. Jesse didn't dare go below. Better to stay aft until Pa told him otherwise, and he expected that would be soon. Birthday or not, Pa would stay on his ass all day, more so than anyone else on the crew.

But he was wrong. As he fiddled with one dredge and got ready to check the other, he realized that Pa was drunk already, which meant he wouldn't come aft until at least noon, and probably not even then. Big Bill would be the only one to go below to the galley and bring up soup and coffee and ham sandwiches to feed them all. But for them to even get on the water today, Jesse needed Gabe to round out the crew — two to sail and two to dredge, and so far, Gabe was a no-show.

Jesse went to the portside edge and looked out over the docks, past gulls in small groups circling overhead as they rose to fly out with the boats to sea, where full nets made fishing easier. He looked out past the boats in drydock, past the pleasure boats idling near the Waterside Inn, his eye stopping, as it always did, at the telltale single masts and huge mainsails of other skipjacks. This harbor had almost no working skipjacks anymore. It was like they'd become the clown at the party, their whimsical figureheads and painted trailboards a source of amusement to tourists.

Before the oysters thinned out, Pa had been the fastest oysterman ever to captain a skipjack. He'd made his own sails and built parts of his boat himself. Before his injury, he had loved to tell stories about sailing before they changed the rules, before watermen were given only two days a week when they could dredge under power, and how having to depend on fair winds had made their harvests uncertain. The way Pa told it, you could tell he missed the old life, no mistake about that. He was a real sailor, only truly happy when working the jib of the *Lacey Jean* against the wind on the open sea. Jesse and Gabe talked about it a lot, how different Pa got when he talked about the old ways on the old boats.

There was a shout from one of the piers and Little Bill yelled up to him that Gabe had been spotted. Jesse turned to see Gabe, running like his feet were wings. Jesse waved wide, his way to signal Gabe that Pa wasn't on deck, and Gabe slowed his pace to an easy trot, his skin catching rays of morning sun so that he stood out in contrast – black against the graying docks and pale fishing boats.

"Can you wait?" Gabe yelled out, as if, ridiculously, Jesse would leave without him. Must come naturally to Gabe, this fretting about being left behind. Only a handful of watermen hired black helpers. Jesse looped the moor line over the piling and did his best to look patient. It was his job to look after Gabe because he had no family at all. He'd found Gabe early one morning, nestled against the hull under a cardboard lean-to, fast asleep. They'd fought hard. Gabe was twice his size but was on his way to losing, having been caught by surprise. And besides, he was the trespasser.

Just short of flattening him, Jesse had asked, "What do you want?" Kind of a stupid a question to ask a homeless kid who sleeps under your hull at night. As soon as he caught his breath, Gabe had answered, "I'm hungry. I'll work for it."

They'd ended up shaking hands. It was right around the time Pa had hurt his leg, so he hired Gabe for the summer, paid with oysters, no cash, like most oystermen. He could work with hardly a word and Pa had liked that. He also worked as if he knew what people wanted from him without them asking, and Jesse liked that.

"Morning!" Gabe was huffing as he climbed aboard. "Your Pa still below?"

Jesse nodded and yanked in the tow line, eager to get under way. He waved at the push-boat to get started, almost happy. They could work clean and easy without Pa staring at them. He pulled out one of the biscuit sandwiches to hand to Gabe. Gabe ate in a hurry, a few crumbs sliding down his oilcloth jacket. He asked, "Old Man started in with the hard stuff already?"

"More than started," Jesse kept his voice low, so he wouldn't be heard disrespecting his Pa by the two Bills. Anyway, it wasn't contempt he felt. He felt glorious.

The boys punched each other a couple of times, drank some coffee, and then Gabe lowered the center board. Little Bill's pushboat gave the first shove and the *Lacey Jean* began its zig-zag progress toward the oyster beds. Gabe and Jesse would do all the sailing today, stopping only to help the two Bills when they pulled up the dredges, then culling oysters until their gloves shredded and their hands grew raw and their backs throbbed with the strain of tending dredge and sail. Jesse would be whistling the whole time and sometimes even singing, overjoyed to be out in the open sea, with the old man out of it.

Later in the afternoon as they finished the last bed, the northwest wind kicked up, snapping and fighting the sail. Jesse nosed her into the wind to give Gabe and the sail a rest before heading home. All the men watched a great blue heron head toward the mouth of the river near Cook's point, headed toward Tilghman, signaling the changing seasons. The sun hit the waves and turned them the color of the sky, kind of a burnt coral now that the sun was low. The wind had subsided until it hardly swelled the sail at all. Jesse signaled Little Bill to lower the push-boat and take them in the rest of the way.

The Skipjacks might be nick-named 'clowns of the harbor,' but he loved the *Lacey Jean*. Today out on the sea, while he'd been watching the waves break and splash over her sides, barely rocking her despite their force, Jesse had been hit with a sudden flash, right along with the cold sea spray. As if it had been written there in the sky, he grasped the point of the absurdly stubborn clown doll. He'd always known the logic of picking yourself up again when you get knocked down.... Who didn't? What he had understood, finally, heading toward harbor, him grinning at Gabe and Gabe grinning back, was why the damn thing kept smiling. It was that no matter how many times you hit the floor, you know there'll come a time when people will get tired of hitting you. All you have to do in the meantime is act like you don't care. Later in life, he would learn the word he wanted that suited him and Gabe, the clown, and the skipjack. The word was paradox.

Chapter Six

The true soul of the Chesapeake region, they say, is the bay itself, the water. The estuaries, where ocean salt water mixes with fresh river water, produce salt ponds and marshes, and incredible diversity of fish and fowl. People would say, "the water feeds the people on every level." Generations of plucky, stern watermen with ancestors they could trace to the early 1600s, all chose a harsh, dangerous life harvesting crabs, oysters, and fish. (U.S. Department of Agriculture)

Ava had always believed the camp folklore about how Isaac had rescued Gabe. Supposedly, when Isaac learned that his nephew was living in Secretary with a skipjack family, he'd driven his dilapidated truck right onto the wooden pier in broad daylight, down to where they moored the working boats. Rather than go to Captain Wanex's house, he left Minnie to guard the truck, went to the top step of the boathouse, and let out a single whistle, long and low. Gabe had come running, it was said, leaving behind everything he owned and throwing himself into Isaac's arms.

When Ava asked Isaac about this version of the story, he laughed, insisting that nothing of the kind had happened. Sure, he drove up close to the houses. Having just heard where his only sister's son was, there was no way he was gonna leave him there. As a black man with the intent of taking a valued worker off the docks, he sure couldn't go poking his nose inside houses and businesses up and down the waterfront, now could he? Even with a woman along. Even if the boy he wanted was his own blood nephew. Ava preferred the rumored 'fable' version because it made Isaac even more of a hero than usual.

Isaac so often took in half-grown kids that the presence of a new boy on the crew mid-season had been no surprise to anyone on the crew. Hattie's greeting to Gabe had been, "New boy, huh? He looks on the scrawny side to me. May need to get some meat on him, before he's any good to us."

"Boy's strong as an ox and smart as a fox," Isaac had replied proudly.

Within no time, Isaac was always with Gabe or Ava; often it was both. At first, the teens didn't take to each other, although Ava acknowledged that Gabe did Isaac good. He followed Isaac everywhere, determined to learn everything possible. When Isaac would reach for something, Gabe was there to hand it to him. Before Isaac even knew his legs were aching, Gabe would have a stool or a barrel near him, a resting place for a tired old man. Isaac had given the harder, longer hours to Gabe and it was understood that Gabe was in line to take over.

Celie had asked Ava if it bothered her having a new 'brother' about to take over as boss.

"It's nothing much to do with me. I still got the receipts and business papers to do. I still go around with Isaac on errands. Where he needs Gabe is the field, and that's where Gabe stays. I'm glad he has the help. Besides, Gabe is like the son Isaac never had."

Celie said, "Maybe Ava, but you're the daughter."

Isaac was a good 'father' to the pair. In return, they worked harder than anyone, which didn't always please him or Minnie.

"Too many of our folks never got time to be young. Not gonna have it with any young'un's we're blessed with." He and Minnie sent every child on the crew on regular excursions. Isaac would tell them, "Do a favor for an old man. Don't do nothing except a whole day's good times."

****

From what Celie could see, it appeared Gabe didn't know what to do with himself when he'd been instructed to take time off. Ava must have felt sorry for him because she started bringing him along instead of Sari on the days she came over to play with Celie and Hannah. Celie tried asking Ava about why Sari stayed behind, but Ava would change the subject and Celie decided to leave it be.

Before long, the four of them comprised a kind of 'gang,' four congenial kids who together, were bolder and braver than any of them would be alone. One day, they were searching out an almost-hidden, fast-running stream that made a great sound, like a waterfall, when they heard Daddy calling them. They waved to acknowledge him, expecting they were about to be redirected. The four of them dropped down to the rich, dark earth of a newly plowed field to wait for him, taking turns writing messages in the soft dirt.

"I've been looking for you hooligans," Daddy said, breathless but smiling as he handed clean burlap sacks to each child. "The trout are running."

"What trout?" asked Hannah but Daddy just smiled and led them to the stream that bisected his fields. It was a stream they knew well. Someone long ago had built a wooden footbridge across the slippery rocks that lined the edge of the water. The girls had been forbidden to so much as dangle a toe in it, and they'd never even been tempted. Today, here was Daddy himself leading the way off the bridge, onto the stream edge, barefoot, weaving himself between the rocks and on down into the water. Celie was clearly fearful. Daddy held her one hand while Ava took the other, both of them hanging on so hard Celie started feeling ridiculous.

"I'll be OK," she said, sticking her big toe in the water. "It's freezing!" she declared. She kept expecting Daddy to say, "That's in far enough," given how he was afraid of the water like she was, but he didn't. Instead, he let go of their hands and said, "Go on ahead, then. In you go Ava. You too, Gabe. Step sturdy as you go, eyes on the water the whole time and then do exactly what I do."

Once the four of them had planted themselves like pole-beans around Daddy, she made herself stop worrying about where she was long enough to look at the water. Unlike the rivers and the ocean she was used to, this water looked crystal-clear all the way to the bottom. A white froth layer churned in places where the stream rushed over the rocks.

"Look," Daddy said, pointing to the movement of the water, and then Celie realized what they were seeing — long, silver-gray fish, one on top of another. Thick layers of trout, heading somewhere in a hurry. Using only his bare hands, Daddy reached in and grabbed one slick trout after another, holding each one tight with two hands as he tossed it high on the bank and into the grass. "Hold tight even after he's out of the water. Hold until the second you see the spot where you want him to land. Release him too soon, and he'll flip-flop himself right back in the stream."

One by one, Gabe going first, they learned how to reach in and grab a slimy, wiggling fish and 'land it' with their bare hands. When they had collected what looked like a mountain of trout, they climbed back up and began filling the burlap bags.

"I thought you were always a farmer, Daddy. When were you a fisherman?" Hannah teased.

"Oh, I've been called a lot of things one time or another," he said, his eyes twinkling as he rumpled her hair.

It was hard to imagine how anything could have been more fun than that day, each kid with a sack of fish to take home, and then, the picnic. Mom had sent tomato sandwiches which they ate greedily, juice dripping down their chins. Still bare-handed, they ate chunks of watermelon, just cut and even drippier. Just watching Daddy pick out the watermelon was magical. Following him through the watermelon field, they would all crouch down on their haunches to watch him feel each melon, as if seeing him at eye level was a key part of his choice. He had a way of touching the outside skin, sliding his hands to the ends and giving a light tap against the blossom end, until one melon suited. To "cut" it, he would drop it straight and fast onto a rock, and it would split perfectly down the middle, rosy red and loaded with dots — the black seeds they would then use as bullets to spit at each other.

As they sat around their own 'kids' campfire that night, Gabe said, "Your Daddy has the hands of an artist." Gabe had built up the logs of the firepit, stoking the initial flame high, and was now tossing on chips of wood to keep it going.

"Artist? He can't draw a lick!" Hannah protested, poking the fire to stir up the flames.

"There are all kinds of artists," Gabe answered.

Celie liked thinking of her father's skills as 'art.' She and Hannah believed he'd been born with knowledge others spend a lifetime learning, like how to take apart and repair a cistern. And build a barn, tame a stallion, pull a stuck calf from a birthing cow.

He'd been meant to become a master carpenter like his father. Woodworking had been passed down, father to son, since the days of shipbuilding on all the local rivers. Since the years when Harrison Ferry and Sherman's Landing and Cook's Point had been boat-building docks. She didn't know if this kind of talent could be born in, but it sure was mesmerizing to watch Daddy build things. He could hammer in a four inch nail like he was sliding a knife into butter – one light *tap* to position it and then two quick strokes to drive it home. It was practically musical. *Tap, clop, clop - tap, clop, clop,* one after the other without missing a beat.

Celie had asked, "How'd you learn that, Daddy?"

"Pop took me everywhere he went. Worked me hard too, hammer in my hand when I was five, and I loved it."

****

When the campfire was over, Celie took Ava to her room to show her Daddy's family in the photo album.

"There aren't any of his mother," Ava said.

"I know. One time I asked him where his mother had been when he was small. He stiffened up and didn't answer. In fact, he never says a single word, good or bad, about her."

"Your Daddy doesn't like to think about his mother, same as me."

"I think I know why. Uncle Elmer told us that Gramma Mowbray kept him tied to a table leg for most of the day. Grandpop rescued him by taking him along to work with him – as soon as he turned five."

Celie stood up, poising herself to tell the story. "Guy Mowbray's apprenticeship was woodworking. His father had also tried ice cream production, ice delivery, door-to-door sales and then back to woodworking – furniture and houses from the ground up. Woodworking was the family trade since the 1600's, but it wasn't what Daddy wanted. One night, he supposedly told his parents he was leaving home to find a farm. He was nineteen. His father tried to convince him to stay and work at the furniture factory in Seaford. And to save for a house. But Daddy didn't want a house, he wanted a tractor. He took his wife, his baby son, and a couple pieces of Grandmom's old furniture and he moved them into this drafty house on a Friday. The next day, he headed out to the fields, leaving our Mom with a colicky new baby and the wind — wind that blew dirt into every corner of every room. Daddy loved every inch of that dirt." She flopped to the floor and caught her breath. "And here we still are."

"I don't understand." Ava said. "He was a great carpenter and he loved wood-working. And he had a family. Wasn't the factory a better job?"

"Daddy might have loved wood, but he loved dirt more," Celie said, as if this reason was enough to explain everything.

Ava had heard this sentiment many times, up and down the Eastern Shore, right about the same time she was coming to hate everything about the fields. But now, listening to the story Celie told, she wondered if they felt the same way about their land as she did about the sand beaches of the Florida Coast, especially sand that was wet and alive with tiny mollusks.

The people here managed to love their Tidewater land, even though it was brackish and lay only inches deep over clay and rock. Even though their too-salty topsoil got scraped away by winds every winter, and even though most of their farms were chopped up by stands of pine, and swamp marshes, yielding too little space to provide a living.

"When a man down here wants a farm, he usually gets one," Celie explained. "Most often, he gets it from family, and it passes on and on. Some people can trace their roots back to the seventeenth century. Or they got their land from a great-great-grandmother who was a Nanticoke Indian, like mine."

Ava never did understand the yearning to own land, but she understood ancient roots and she knew plenty about big families. She knew that as youngest of eleven children, when Guy Mowbray chose to farm, his family would lack the resources to help him. Without land to inherit, he'd have to strike some kind of deal to rent acreage. For him, it was 285 acres of bottom land with no buildings except for a ramshackle white-painted clapboard house. Like most independent farmers, he would have to borrow money from his landlord or the town bank to buy the first year's seed and a tractor on installments. Or the landlord would rent him the tractor and take a bigger cut of the crops.

"What about your Mom?" Ava asked. "Did it take her long to get used to it?"

"She hated it. It was almost winter when they moved in and she was freezing. They had one wood stove in the kitchen. She says she had to wrap baby Frank up in layers of wool to keep him warm. I believe she made up her mind to never forgive Daddy."

"For making her move to a farm. I can see that."

"No. Not for that! For his good humor."

Ava made a face. "That's just mean. Didn't she have a right to hold a grudge? New baby, and having to cook, sew and clean, and those layers of dirt – wet dirt – that cover every stick of furniture like a curtain. And after Frank, there were only you two girls, not really proper field help. Your brother and Dad mostly do everything. And, besides, your brother hates farming."

"It's true. Frank has to tend all the livestock so that Daddy can spend every daylight hour on his tractor, plowing furrows, chopping weeds. Up and down, circling the rows, back again."

Hannah, who eavesdropped whenever she could, joined in from the other side of the door. She said, "Daddy's always singing, happy as anything, and Frank's yelling at the milk cows to hurry up."

"Your mom must like *something* about it, to stay as long as she has," Ava said, watching Celie shove a bath towel under her bedroom door to block off Hannah.

"I think she's as bound to her world as Daddy is to his. Her by duty, and him by love."

"Not true," came Hannah's voice, now muffled. "She loves to cook and tend the garden and think how much she loves all the animals. She gets up in the middle of the night to bottle feed lambs. Nobody ever asked her to do that. But she won't admit even for a second that she enjoys anything."

Ava expected Celie to fuss at Hannah, but she didn't. Instead, she seemed about to cry.

Hannah's flattened voice said, "Tell her."

Celie opened the door, yanking Hannah into the room and pulling her down next to her. She said, "It's a family secret, never said aloud by anyone."

"You might as well tell me," Ava declared. "If you don't, Hannah will."

Celie sighed and moved closer to Hannah. "It's this. Our mom hates to be touched. I can only remember once when she hugged any of us – the day she thought we might have drowned. She doesn't even touch Frank and she adores him. But Daddy ... well you know. He hugs everybody. Sometimes in the kitchen, when Mom looks happy,

Daddy will try to touch her, like, while she's picking up his dishes. He'll say something like, "that was delicious, Mom-mom. He tries to hug her or kiss her cheek. He just can't seem to understand that look on her face."

Celie choked and couldn't go on, so Hannah said, "The second she feels him touching her, she shrinks back as if Daddy's hands are claws trying to slash her."

"Hannah! Don't be so dramatic," Celie said.

"You know I'm not exaggerating. Mom starts shivering... just like a raccoon caught in a trap. Like she's thinking about chewing off her own arm to get loose."

Ava now guessed something about their Mom that they hadn't–that their mother must have been sexually abused as a child. In Ava's world, even good men take what they want when it comes to women.

She didn't want to sound insensitive. She said, "Your Daddy is a joyful man, but he must ... doesn't he ever get mad at her?"

"Not as I ever saw," Celie answered. Hannah chimed in, "Joyful, yes! I like that word. And warm and loving. Hugs for everybody in the world, even people he doesn't like. He sings all the time. He sings when he plows and even when he's just walking to the barn."

Celie said, "His love of music is what took him to the tenement campfires. To listen to ballads and watch the southern reels. Without the migrant work force, Daddy says, this kind of music never would have made it as far north as Maryland. Do you remember how he used to bring me to visit you at night?"

Ava nodded. "And then it was just you alone. He stopped coming."

Celie said, her face reddening, "My fault. I just wanted to go more often. Daddy said no, it would get in the way of y'all's privacy. One day I stood my ground. I said, 'You pretend you have business there but you're going there for fun, just because you like the music. Why can't I?'"

Celie's tone darkened. "He thought it was his secret. I let on that I knew it and it hurt him. He told me to go on ahead then, go when I liked. I had never heard his voice sound like that. I felt terrible and I still do. It was something I'd wanted so bad that I was willing to disrespect my dad to get my way."

Ava whispered, "Whenever you uncover people's secrets, even if your intention is innocent, you take away their pride."

Ava had a secret of her own. Celie's confession about her parents had made her feel less shameful, although she wasn't sure why. She'd almost said something about what had happened to her and why she knew about their mom. She couldn't tell the whole secret of course, nor could she figure out how to tell only a piece of it, so she said nothing at all.

Chapter Seven

The Bay and its adjoining rivers had once boasted some of the finest oyster and crab grounds in the watershed. Then, a combination of over-harvesting and habitat destruction almost totally wiped out the oysters. As tides changed, sea nettles became a constant visitor in the Bay and its rivers. They would drift in by the thousands, each with a sting that would be rated as 'moderate' to 'severe' and lasted for hours. (U.S. Department of Agriculture)

Dale Kent was sweet, gentle, and funny, and Celie loved him. The summer after seventh grade was going to be a misery. She would see Dale only at church, since their circles never crossed anywhere else. Desperate, she begged Frank to start dropping her at the movies when he went out on Saturday nights. He agreed with an exchange of favors. (She would lie if Mom ever asked whether Frank had stayed in the theater.)

She and Dale arranged to meet on every second or third Saturday night. It would have to do. The first movie was *The Blob*, which scared her half to death. Dale grabbed her hand and held it for the rest of the movie. Next came *The Oklahoman*, and then *Tammy*, with Debbie Reynolds. Right during "Tammy's in Love," Dale asked her to go steady. She agreed, of course, meaning that night, they exchanged school pictures.

She pasted his into the front of her diary and began writing about him every day. She couldn't wait for the beginning of school when they would be in the same home room – the alphabet insured it – Kent and Mowbray.

****

67

Dale almost made it through the summer. With school about to start, his family had decided to pull together one last-minute Labor Day picnic at Trappe Pond. The sea nettles had been thick as glue in the warm, salty river water all season, staying on throughout most of August. The kids were frantic from missing out on a whole summer of swimming.

"A day at Trappe will put them in a better mood to face the school year," said Dale's older brother, Bill, a school teacher with a new baby and an over-tired wife.

Dale, the younger of Ruth Kent's sons, had a swimming merit badge needing completion to earn his Eagle Scout award. He had been a very welcome late-life child, adored by his older brother. Bill took him everywhere, even after marrying Jana. Now with the baby in tow, Bill and Dale could give Jana a break from the baby's colic.

The family had probably packed for their outing in a rush, people said. After all, it was a Sunday, and it was also the day before Labor Day, with the grocers and cafes all closed. You'd have to leave right after church to have any time at all for a decent outing.

Now that the jellyfish had cleared out, the river bank would be over-crowded with picnickers fitting in the last trip of the season. The Kent family, as it happened, had to spread their blanket a good stretch away from the water's edge, but Bill said the baby needed to be in the shade anyway.

Ruth always remembered her own version of that day. Everyone in the extended family had been teasing Dale about his new girlfriend, Celie Ann Mowbray. The young pair had always hung together at church as friends, but lately she'd seen them holding hands in a different way.

It tickled Ruth, this puppy love, and she'd taken Dale all the way into Easton yesterday, so he could buy Celie a silver friendship ring, a slim band with an all-over ivy pattern carved in.

"How do I know the size?" Dale wondered. He'd wanted the ring to be a surprise. His own hands were big for his age and not a good comparison. The jeweler told Dale he had a football player's hands and the boy had blushed with pride.

Dale decided to use his little finger as a sizer. He would wear the ring to church tomorrow on his pinky and Celie would notice it on him. Kind of a tease before he gave it to her, the kind of humor Celie loved because she said it was like her dad's and brother's.

"She can always exchange the size," the jeweler was saying somberly while he polished the $3.00 ring, as if it were his prize sale of the week. He had winked broadly at Ruth Kent and she had given a slight head-shake (don't!) while praying that Dale hadn't seen the wink. He was a shy boy, yet he wanted so badly to be like his gregarious father and his brother Bill.

The jeweler talked hurriedly to cover his blunder. "You sure you don't want it gift-wrapped? No? Here, I'll send along the box – it has a real velvet lining, you know, and girls just love these little boxes." This pleased Dale and he kept the ring in its box until it was time for Mass.

As they always did during the recessional hymns at the end of Mass, the teen-agers slipped out and gathered on the front steps to gossip. Dale took Celie aside and gave her the ring, luckily without anybody else poking their nose in. The ring fit her perfectly, Dale told Ruth, and they shook hands, mother and son, two like-minded conspirators.

After that, the details jammed together. Ruth could never remember whose idea it had been to assemble a picnic, but she gladly threw together ham sandwiches and packed them into a basket with last night's fried chicken, half a watermelon (wrapped tightly in foil), biscuits, newly dilled pickles, and plump, ripe peaches, the last of the season. She filled the gallon thermos they used for Dale's Boy Scout meetings with sweet tea, squeezing in two lemons and tucking in another bag with a sliced lemon for Bill, who liked his tea loaded with lemon.

Ruth had decided, in the end, not to go along. There were two bushel baskets teeming with peaches that were going soft. This was the kind of detail she could recall clearly, her thinking they needed to be blanched and frozen since she didn't want to make jam or pies with them. As she worked through them, tossing the pits into a lidded bucket so the dog wouldn't eat them and get poisoned – was it arsenic? ... Later she recalled the instant she'd changed her mind, thinking how Bill dearly loved her peach pie, although he never said so in front of his young wife. Jana had barely learned to cook and then the baby had come. She would make pies after all, two of them, and Billy could take one home. Poor Jana was having such a hard time nursing, and they needed all the cooked food people would send.

Ruth had always heard horror stories of people who had huge

fights with their loved ones before disaster struck, and how they could never get over it, even many years later. This didn't happen to her. She had stood watching her family as they drove away, feeling happy and satisfied with the bountiful summer crops, with Billy's marriage, with the sweet temperament that Dale was developing. She hadn't had a single unhappy thought in her head. Even when the ambulance went screeching by, headed toward the river, it never occurred to her that the disruption had anything at all to do with her contented and well-ordered life.

She couldn't say she ever really got the details straight about what actually happened. The only part she could remember was her husband coming home in the truck all by himself, no boys, no Jana and the baby. She had no memory at all for the words he spoke to her. The funeral had been a nightmarish blur, more like a bad dream than anything really happening. People would come up to her and try to tell little stories about her sons, but she would shut them all down – quickly, cleanly, permanently. There was only so much a mother could bear.

She knew, of course, that both her sons had drowned. She knew that Dale had gone under first, disappearing without a sound, caught in a whirlpool while standing on a shifting sandbar. Billy dove in for him only seconds later, reaching his brother's arm and holding on tightly as they were drawn down by the undertow, into a hidden mass of swirling seaweed. Some time had passed, not very long, before a friend rushed to them and cut them loose with a scout knife. Someone had begun artificial respiration while their bodies were still warm, they'd told her, and then the firemen got there with pumps and tanks of oxygen. They all tried so hard, they said. Their efforts were heroic, they told her. What did that matter? No amount of air breathed into them could make their lungs expand and contract on their own, or get those sweet, loving hearts to beat again.

****

Celie was asleep when Daddy came upstairs and woke her. She'd gone to bed early, so she could have time in the morning to fiddle around - maybe try on a few outfits in case she needed to sew something before the first day of school.

"Wake up, Celie. I have something to tell you."

His hands on hers had felt ice cold. She bolted up into a sitting position. The cat that had been asleep on her stomach, tumbled sideways and onto the floor, yowling his dismay.

"Daddy! Why are you ... what's wrong?"

"I have bad news."

"Is it Frank?" This fear response was automatic, with a boy like Frank in their family.

"Not this time. It's your friend Dale Kent. I'm afraid they lost him."

"Dale *Kent*? What do you mean? Lost him where?"

"I'm so sorry. He drowned today swimming at Trappe Pond."

"It can't be, Daddy. I just saw him at church this morning!" She looked at her father's face, this beloved face that hadn't looked this sorrowful more than half a dozen times in her life, and she knew it was true.

Daddy told her as much as he'd learned, which was far more than Ruth Kent would ever know. About how Dale had yelled for his brother, bobbing up exactly three times, like in a movie, how on his third yell his brother had reached him and everyone on the bank had cheered, now that it would be all right, but then the only thing that followed was eerie silence. The stillness of the water above the spot where they'd been struggling just seconds ago, had made it all seem unbelievable.

Daddy didn't short-cut the details, instead allowing her to direct things by asking questions until she had no questions left. She swallowed his answers, one at a time. Swallowed her memories of Dale and her feelings about him, allowing them to sink to the bottom of her belly where they could churn, disconnected from her head and heart, her own private drowning. Later, she completed the separation by dropping the ring down the sink and visualizing it floating out to the river and into the demonic tentacles of the seaweed.

After Dale's funeral, Mom kept Celie home from school for two weeks to help with the canning. The idea was supposed to be that chopping and blanching vegetables and stuffing them into jars was better medicine for Celie's ailing heart than letting her tackle school. Her parents also kept her engaged with life, letting her keep all of the kittens in a new litter, giving her a young foal to train. Still, she felt disconnected from her own life. She lived in a community where water defined most people's lives, and she'd now become so terrified of water that she wouldn't go in it, or on it, and sometimes not even near it. It was so bad in those days that when Daddy installed a shower in the bathroom, she'd felt panic when the water hit her face, skipped dinner, and sat in her room with the door closed.

Maybe that's why Frank asked her along on a squirrel hunt. The invitation had been tossed at her offhandedly, but she had a sense he was valuing her in some way other than as a target for pranks. She said yes in an instant, even though she'd never shot an animal in her life, preferring rocks and bottles and trees for her targets. She left her gun behind, figuring she could just walk along, looking for things for her nature scrapbook, like bird feathers and snake skins, odd-shaped stones, anything to add to her collection.

It ended up being a trip where her collection grew by one Irish Setter. The dog had taken refuge in one of their corn fields, somehow managing to find a nest of dried cornstalks and to burrow into it. The part of the dog that was still above-ground was barely visible inside the thatch of stalks that had been overlooked by the John Deere Harvester. It would have been a great hide-out except for one thing; the dog's long coat was the color of a campfire. The sun had worked its way through the stalks and Celie could see the dog was trembling from her muzzle all the way down to the tip of her feathery tail. The quivering sent her silken fur rolling ... wave after wave of tiny radiating highlights. Celie was mesmerized by the sight of her.

"Frank. Come look at what I found," Celie called. Frank was way ahead, as always, but now bolted back to where she was pointing. Before she could even finish the sentence, he had his rifle cocked and aimed, ready for the emergency.

"Don't shoot for God's sake!" Celie yelled and reached her hand up like a fool, grabbing the barrel to shift it away before he could pull the trigger. She had a fleeting vision of Mom's face, just as her hand closed around the barrel, with Mom's voice saying, "For God's sake Celie, are you crazy?" This made her let the barrel go, but by then Frank had at least stopped for a second to look at what he'd wanted to shoot.

"Oh, man," he complained. "It's just a dumb old dog." He set the rifle on the ground and leaned inward to see better. "Come on, boy. Come out."

The setter hadn't moved, except for the shivering, which never let up, as if full-body shaking was her natural state.

"What a beauty," Celie whispered. "Call her again."

Frank tried a sharp whistle, then yawned and shouldered his rifle. "Not coming out," he pronounced, ready to move on now that there was no snake or other varmint to kill. "Let's go, Pipsqueak. You've always whined like a baby for me bring you with me, so now that I have, keep up."

He was right about her always begging to go along, Celie thought. However, despite his acting like it was such a hardship, the truth was Frank loved any audience willing to admire his skills. At fourteen, Celie was still enthralled by her brother, almost mesmerized actually, by the worldly ways his four added years gave him. Maybe she would even have given in and followed him up the path, if he hadn't added another smart-ass exaggeration.

"Anyway, the dog's probably been shot already."

"Why do you say that?"

"It's a hunting dog, stupid. An Irish Setter. Must have been out there in the woods with those hunters we heard this morning. This kind of dog doesn't run off unless it's been hurt. They're going to come looking for it sooner or later. Besides, hurt dogs don't like strangers."

Frank knew a lot about dogs, especially hunting dogs, so usually Celie listened to him. She wasn't going to this time because she was sick of him always knowing everything, and also because of the dog herself. Not just the beauty, but all that raw fear. Fear like that does things to people who are able to see it. Her response was to be hooked for good.

Frank had seen the fear, too, but his reaction was to head away from it and toward the woods, his eyes scanning the brush piles for rabbits and quail.

"Leave the dog and come on," he called over his shoulder, his voice harsh with dismissal. "There's nothing you can do." It occurred to her that Frank was always like this around strong feelings, his own or anybody else's.

Celie didn't move. She knew that her mulishness, on top of the dog's panic, would be eating at Frank and he would take a stronger stand. As expected, he upped the ante. Moving in her direction he said, "Look, that thing will bite you if you even go near it. You'll get blood poisoning."

That thing? Really? She felt her mind close against him. It wasn't just his overstating things; she was used to his Irish blarney. It was his calling the dog 'it' that riled her. No matter what he said or did now, she would not back down. She said with forced nonchalance, "You go. I'll stay here and figure out how to help her."

"There isn't anything you can do, *bozo*. You're just being a...." She knew he'd intended to step up the level of insults and wondered why he'd stopped himself mid-sentence like that. She wouldn't figure out until weeks later that it was because of her turning down his invitation to follow him for the first time ever. Meanwhile, she slid herself along the cornrow gully closer to the dog by jamming her feet deep into the loose soil for leverage. She had literally dug herself in.

Frank was used to getting his way with his sisters just by demanding it. When that didn't work, he used bullying, which usually kept them in line. When Celie still hadn't budged, out came a new tactic, bargaining. "Look, how about I promise to call the sheriff's office the second we get back to the house, OK? They'll be out here in no time. They'll bring along a vet or something. We gotta go before you do something that scares the dog even more. You could make it worse, you know."

Celie was still watching the dog, chin in hand, holding herself as still as she could for just the reason Frank had said — not to startle her. With the narrow head and flanks, she was definitely female. The dog was very gentle, not just shy but truly sweet-tempered. But even though there was no blood visible, the dog was quivering with discomfort.

She said, "I think she hasn't been shot. She's not bleeding."

"OK, so the dog is just scared, then, see? It'll be fine until they come looking for it, and they will, you know." Still at a distance but just inside her line of vision, she saw him tip back his cap and fold his arms, staring at her in the same way she'd been staring at the dog.

"I didn't say she was fine. She isn't. She hasn't heard a single sound we've made. I think she's deaf."

"How in the world you think you know that?"

She wasn't going to tell him how she knew, how she'd noticed a nose that was over-engaged in sniffing, nostrils flaring wide, muzzle aimed high to catch maximum scent; and how she hadn't responded at all to their talking, not even when Frank had yelled. And her eyes; Frank would never have noticed that they weren't right, that they were probing, desperate. They weren't the usual working dog eyes –

they were trying to make up for what she couldn't hear.

For once, Celie was the one who knew stuff and Frank was the observer.

Celie prepared herself to touch the setter. She stood up and gave her body a hard shake, willing all the tension out through her fingers, wiggling them until they felt loose. She dropped to the ground and in a squat, she crept, an inch at a time, toward the dog, her hand extended low, palm up.

She began to croon just above a whisper, mostly to relax herself since the dog wouldn't hear anything. "Hey lovey, how you doing? It's OK." She had reached her face.

Frank was so used to running things between the two of them that he couldn't keep out of it. "You aren't supposed to touch it, lamebrain. It will bite you, whether you're helping or not. What? You expect it'll understand that you mean no harm?"

"She. It's a she and she isn't going to bite me," Celie answered, relieved to notice that her voice sounded as calm as she was feeling. Her brother might know a lot, but he had no heart to go along with that great big brain.

"The most important thing about this dog is clear as rainwater. She's desperate for contact. There's not even a hint of a threat on her face." The dog's silky ears hung loose and easy, almost touching the ground even with her nose aimed high in the air. "She trusts me already," Celie finished.

She found herself thinking of Daddy and all the times she'd watched him examining farm animals for wounds. Like that morning a pack of dogs had hunted down the sheep just as they came out to pasture and had killed some of them. They'd all run outside in a frenzy when they heard the barking, trying to figure how to help the sheep. Daddy was the quickest, moving through the flock, sliding his hands expertly through their thick fleece, somehow holding each one still long enough to fill the wounds with styptic powder. He'd saved half a dozen ewes from bleeding to death in that half hour. Frank and Celie each took away something different from that tragedy. Frank learned survival of the fittest and Celie started a mental encyclopedia of search and rescue data. Something else, too, came to each of them after that horrible morning — Frank would never try and touch a dog in pain, not even a buddy, whereas it seemed Celie couldn't keep her hands off them.

"I don't know how you think you can know all that stuff," he said now.

"You have to sit and let your eyes adjust to the darkness in her shelter. You can see her body beneath this ... this magnificent coat."

Celie could almost hear Daddy's voice telling her what to do. She had a leftover peanut butter sandwich in her pocket. Pulling off a chunk, she pierced it with her thumbnail to release its smell. For the first time, the dog moved purposefully, the curled edge of a fat tongue reaching out. The food was magic. The dog let go of her worries and allowed Celie to slide her fingers slowly down her long body. Celie felt for cuts, bruised muscles, smashed bones, but all she found was silky fur, and beneath the fur, lean muscles and long, thin bones. As Celie slid her hands along shoulders, back and haunches, the dog's trembling stopped. She laid her head against Celie's arm and seconds later, the dog's eyes drifted closed.

"She doesn't have an ounce of fat anywhere," Celie said, looking over her shoulder at Frank, who was squatting behind her but still keeping himself apart, out on the trail.

"And she's sound asleep. She hasn't been hurt anywhere, other than the deafness."

"Gun went off too close to her," Frank mumbled. "Could be temporary, but probably not. I guess the owners will tell us."

"Those hunters won't be telling us anything. They had their chance with her and this is how she ended up. Her name is going to be Redsy and she's coming home with us for good. Give me your gun strap. I need it for a leash."

Celie knew that this time, he wouldn't argue. If there was anything Frank liked better than shooting small animals, it was conspiracy. He handed her the strap and Celie eased Redsy to her feet. The dog was trembling again but didn't resist the leash. She seemed almost content to be walking next to them as they headed toward home.

Frank didn't say a word the whole way. Celie figured his mind was busy trying out versions of the story he would concoct so that Daddy wouldn't look for the dog's rightful owners. And probably dreaming up another story for the hunters in case they ever came looking for Redsy. She knew Frank would make it all work. He was as good at lying as anyone she'd ever known. This left her free to do what she did best — reversing a creature's fortunes.

She pushed away a mindful of images of all the harm humans can inflict on each other and on innocent animals. She focused her mind on Redsy, because when you rescue a dog, you have to think about that one dog only. As they took Redsy the rest of the way home, she noticed that she and Frank were walking at the same pace for a change.

Chapter Eight

In the mid 1950's, there were 33 migrant camps on Maryland's Eastern Shore. Less than half of them qualified as "good." "Good" housing for a family of four-six typically consisted of rows of unpainted, 9 by 12 ft, cabins, with one or perhaps two screened windows (no glass) in each unit and with unfinished interior walls. Each cabin had at least one bunk, a table and chairs, but probably not electricity or running water. The bare earth around them would be home to the camp's central cooking facilities and privies. Most camps had no trees, leaving the cabins fully exposed to the sun. (Laurent Dubois)

The morning they lost Minnie had begun with a clear and beautiful dawn, cool for August. The sky was filled with color as Isaac and Ava drove to town with a load of trash that had to be dumped before breakfast. They drove slowly both there and back, savoring the smell of the air and the short respite from hot weather.

As Isaac's truck came lumbering into view of the camp, they saw Gabe in front, trying to run interference against the women folk, who were converging on Isaac's truck. Gabe was trying to shush sounds of opposition rattling amongst the older women, and they were pushing back, a sure sign something was very wrong at the camp, giving him no time to savor the fact that the boy had built a basketful of confidence since he first came.

"Y'all just stop all that," Gabe was saying. "The boss is here, but he couldn't have done a thing anyway. This was God's work and that's all. Get ready and go on to work now."

Gabe's strategy might have worked if Isaac had stayed in the truck, but he'd seen that whatever was wrong went way beyond objections to the boy's orders. He limped forward, his hand on Ava's shoulder for balance, a lucky thing since the women began shoving up against each other, jockeying for access to the 'real' boss. "That boy too big for his britches," he heard Venus whisper to Ruth. He also heard, "Minnie ain't moving, boss. We didn't know what you'd want us to do. Gabe kept stirring everybody up, maybe because he didn't know where you were."

Minnie ain't moving.

Isaac hesitated long enough to get the work on track, the one truth that always came first. "Shame on y'all. You know where I've been, every fan-dang one of y'all. There's only one thing for you to do; get to work. Now hush up and do what Gabe tells you, so I can see to Minnie."

Isaac pushed his feet toward to where Minnie was. Was it possible his wife might have passed over before he'd even lit out this morning? He might have risen and dressed and kissed the cold cheek of a woman already gone to a higher rest.

His legs felt heavier the closer he got to his shack. It was the same as everyone else's except for cardboard sign tacked above his door, "ISAAC," marking his status. Ignoring the pain in his hips and legs, he knelt down next to the cot where he and Minnie slept and checked for her pulse, just to make sure. You never knew with old folks, since when they went to sleep, they often looked like they'd never rise again. Plenty of mornings, she'd lay there so peaceful — he'd touch her cheek 'til she would open her eyes and give him that little sideways smile. On those days, she'd looked exactly like this. He almost believed if he touched her cheek in just the right way now, he could wake her up.

Isaac tried to picture her as he'd last seen her yesterday. All that would come to mind was Minnie as she'd been years ago, middle-aged and holding young-uns in her lap, smiling her contentment. Was that the last time he'd really looked at her close – had he really missed the tracks of their aging?

He saw Gabe and Ava, waiting for orders outside the door. Isaac needed a minute to prepare himself for what came next. He looked out over the camp at everybody who wasn't picking that day, little kids and a few old folks, all standing there, silent, waiting for him to say what to do. He looked down at his own right hand, still gripping the burlap sack full of goods he'd brought from town. Gabe touched his hand where it clutched the sack and tugged, trying to take it from him, but Isaac's fingers seemed to be frozen there. He stared at his fingers as if they weren't actually his.

He watched Gabe's hand prying up the fingers one at a time, breaking his grip, until finally, he could let the sack go. Gabe ran off, tossed the sack in the wagon, and then came springing back on his long, straight legs, while Ava held his hand. Even now, boy's trying too hard to get in my favor, Isaac thought, remembering without wanting to, how he'd acted in the exact same way around Amos, the boss before him. He envied this young man his sinew, his strong bones and teeth, but he didn't envy that eager face. Not that aching wish for time to move forward toward this or that.

Isaac used Ava's shoulder as a prop to push his back up straight and get himself taller by four inches, but Lordy that did hurt his spine. He wasn't sure why he wanted to feel as straight as he could when he asked Gabe, "Who was it found her?"

"Hattie brought her some tea and grits when breakfast was nearly over. Nobody'd seen her up yet; that's why Hattie went. Then she came and got me. Before I looked inside your cabin, boss, I made sure the crew got ready to work but they didn't want to walk all the way, so they moved out slow. Me and Hattie were gonna be the only ones to stay back. I kept her to help with the ... you know, boss."

"Why Venus and Lucy still here, then? Should be in the fields too, especially with us being short Minnie, you, and Hattie."

"You know that answer, boss."

Gabe had been hinting for Isaac to give him the right to demand obedience from even the most hard-headed of the women.

Isaac told him not to be so quick to chew fire. Folks always misbehave around a death, and Minnie was important to them. Tough times for the next few days. Maybe he'd go on and bring up the boy now, since Minnie....

Isaac knelt next to her, at first just listening to the silence. He had her right hand between his, holding it the way he'd done every morning for near sixty years. "Time to pass on the burden?" he whispered to Minnie. "That what you been telling me, old woman?" Her hand felt cold, but her hands had been cold every day for the last ten, maybe fifteen years. It was easy for him to pretend she was still with him.

Outside his wall, he heard Venus and her friend Lucy, still out there, cackling. A pair of wretched hens too old to lay eggs, too tough to turn into stew. He snapped at them, "Get to the fields." He could almost feel Gabe's eyes flashing approval. For sure, he'd seen Ava was holding Gabe's hand and he wished he could finally appreciate their closeness, but his mind wouldn't leave his cabin.

By the time he stood up from Minnie's side, only Gabe, Ava, and Hattie were left outside. "What you want us to do next, boss?" Gabe whispered, a tender sound, given his often clumsy eagerness.

Isaac gestured for Gabe and Ava to pick up Minnie. Meanwhile, he took Hattie's hand and together, the two old friends led the way to the giant oak tree at the back of the campground property. Gabe followed silently, carrying Minnie like a doll, Ava trailing behind him. The four of them eased her on to the patchy grass, and then he realized he couldn't allow Minnie to lay in the dirt – not yet.

"Gabe, go back and get that flat box I keep under my seat. There's something in there to keep Minnie off this ground. Meantime, Hattie and Ava, y'all go to the big wagon and get out Minnie's church dress and some shoes. Ones to look good; doesn't matter if they fit perfect."

By the time Ava brought Minnie's white church dress and some nearly-new shoes that would fit good enough, Gabe and Isaac had unfolded the large, hand-sewn quilt and spread it on the ground next to Minnie's body. Gabe had the sense to turn his back while Ava and Hattie washed and dressed Minnie, fixed her hair, made her right. Isaac was pleased the boy had respect.

Despite the fact of Gabe not being quite ready yet, seems old father time was pushing them both forward, ready or not. It was Gabe, alone, who picked up and laid down the frail body in the quilt center. Isaac saw the boy's face was tight; his mouth thin and drawn, the serious face of a boy doing a serious task. No excuse for holding him back. He patted Gabe on the shoulder before nodding to Hattie to begin a mourning prayer. Hattie had chosen one from the old days.

Oh, saints an' sinners will-a you go
See the heavenly land

I'm a-going up to heaven for to see my robe,
See the heavenly land.

Oh, yes, I'm going up, going up,
Going up all the way, Lord,

Going up to see the heavenly land.

They wrapped Minnie in the quilt like a newborn babe in a bunting, her face showing full out, in service to the living, who would want to kiss her goodbye.

"Now what, boss?"

"Me and Ava will go on to Frampton's Funeral in Federalsburg. They take coloreds and treat 'em right. If you'll just get her into the truck for me, you can go on to the field and still get in near a day's work. Good you're there to watch over. Anybody gives you trouble, you just say Isaac said so." He was relieved that Gabe did his best not to show off too much pride at being put in charge of the crew for a day.

Isaac took Hattie's hand. "Meantime Hattie, I need you go and find Mr. Guy at the big house and tell him what's what. He's got the right to know."

"I'd just as soon go to the fields with Gabe, Boss while you and Ava gone. Take my mind off and all."

"*Won't* take your mind off! Ain't nothin can do that. Besides, you're too old to be much use picking anymore. You'd for sure starve, if me and Gabe stop looking out for you."

Hattie smiled, a rare sight since she'd lost most of her front teeth. It shamed her to show people. She mostly kept her lips puckered to hide her gums. But not with me, Isaac thought.

Hattie said, "Reckon you right at that, boss. Most important thing is ... do right by Minnie. If you're not the one tells him, should be me."

She reached her bony arms down to give him a hug. Isaac hadn't realized until now, that even Hattie was taller than him. Just when he let his body slump down, that is.

Isaac sent Ava to gather some of Minnie's things. Finally, he was alone, sitting beside the body of the woman he'd loved for all but the first four years of his life. So long he couldn't think of her as a separate human being. She was part of him, as he was of her. He touched her cheek, then the frizz where once there'd been long, thick curls, and last of all the hands that had made his food and sewed his clothes and bathed him when he was sick.

Beads of sweat began to drip from Isaac's face onto Minnie's arm. He used the edge of his sleeve to dry them away. *No use in sentiments.*

What his own Pappy had taught him and what he taught his own young'uns. *No use bellyachin'.* A man couldn't stand on the banks of the river, crying for what he left behind on the other side. Isaac began to sing the old spiritual ballad that Minnie had loved best.

> *Steal away, steal away, steal away to Jesus;*
> *Steal away, steal away home;*
> *I ain't got long to stay here.*
>
> *My Lord, he calls me. He calls me by the thunder.*
> *The trumpet sounds within-a my soul;*
> *I ain't got long to stay here.*

Minnie had once heard Mahalia Jackson sing this hymn in a park in Georgia, folks all gathered together inside a huge tent just to pray and hear gospel songs, one after another. This was the only song Minnie had taken away and she'd sung it every day, as if it was her only wish – to cross the river and be out of the world Isaac had provided her.

He sang it now in a voice still rich and mellow, and he kept singing until the ache in his back moved to his belly and to his throat, releasing the tears, and then ... all he could do was lie next to Minnie and sob.

Chapter Nine

"Must be 10,000 stitches in here," exclaimed Venus. They were all at the crematorium, waiting for the funeral director to finish talking over the last details with Isaac. Venus pretended to tuck in a wisp of Minnie's hair and was now patting the quilt wrapped around her sister.

"Leave the quilt be, Venus," Hattie said.

"She's my own sister. A blood relation. I get to touch her if I want to. And know what else? I get to decide some things, too."

"Decide what? What you talking about? Isaac decided about that quilt already. He wants it for Minnie's rest."

"This here quilt may look dang near perfect but it's bad luck. I don't want to see my sister's soul stuck on the wrong side of the river just because of this quilt. I won't have my only blood sister keeping company with the devil in her journey over Jordan."

Hattie considered for a minute, touched the quilt lightly, then pulled back her hand as if the quilt was made of fire. "Bad luck, how?"

"Been cursed."

"How can you know that?" Hattie could barely see Venus's face in the dark of the anteroom and she couldn't decide if the woman was teasing or serious. All these years and she still couldn't figure out what Venus was up to until it was too late. Too late to see Venus' hand sneaking into the till at night, too late to keep her from luring people's husbands into her bed, even Hattie's own man...

Venus's voice had dropped to a raspy whisper. "That lil' white girl ... the one drowned walking in the river that summer. I know you heard about it."

"So what?"

"When she passed on, she was laying on this very quilt. Why else you think Mr. Guy's woman sent a quilt like this out of her own house?"

Hattie sat back with her eyes closed, buying what time she could to think. It was never a good thing to go against the boss, but if the quilt was cursed, didn't she owe it to Minnie, her best friend in the world, to remove the presence of the devil – or anything else that might imperil her immortal soul?

Venus began to unwrap the quilt.

"Just you hold on!" Hattie was exasperated. Venus might be Minnie's sister, but unwrapping her wasn't right. She pulled the edge of the quilt back in place, "I need to think more on it."

Venus moved in, very close, her breath hot and smelling of alcohol. Hattie wondered where she'd found liquor, with the funeral not over yet. She narrowed her eyes to take in Venus's face and posture, as if by staring at the woman she could for once, make sense of her. Or at least buy more time to make the right choice for Minnie's soul, and for her own.

As it turned out, more time didn't matter, as was always the way when Venus wanted something. Venus moved even closer, her lips now touching Hattie's ear, her voice thick with menace, "I tell you why. She *threw it out*. She *knew* it was cursed, that's why."

Hattie felt desperate, now certain she was being railroaded. She said, "could be you're right but could be somethin' else. Like ... like it coulda' been just kindness."

"Kindness? You crazy? Well you can think on it all you want, gal. I ain't gonna let this here evil quilt go into the funeral fire with my sister's remains. If it was to catch on fire the same time her body does, it'd take her soul straight on to *eternal fire*."

Hattie's desperation dissolved, and fear replaced it. Everybody knew that Venus was closer to the ways of the old country than anybody. If a woman needed a curse removed or wanted a boy to love her lil' girl, she went to Venus for an amulet, or God forbid, a voodoo doll.

Come to think, Hattie mused, she was near as scared of Venus as she was of Isaac. She swallowed the knot in her throat and said. "Go ahead and do what you got to. You going to anyhow. Just so you remember I ain't got no part in it."

"You don't got to have no part in it. All you got to do is just keep your big mouth shut."

There was no doubt about that, Hattie thought. Isaac would have had to pull out her fingernails one by one before she'd say a word.

She left the anteroom quickly. If she stayed and saw Venus actually take the quilt, the good Lord might think she was in cahoots with the evils of the world or even worse, the evils of the dark forces. She shook her head as she walked to the truck, thinking how the one thing she knew for sure was that Venus stood for both kinds of evil.

Best to stay out of her path for a while.

****

"Try not to act like you're here to have fun," Celie warned Hannah for the third time in fifteen minutes. Celie had managed to talk Mom into letting the girls go to Minnie's funeral, provided they would act right. Somewhere in her negotiations, Celie had said, "I'll keep her outside until the luncheon starts. She'll think it's a church social. She'll be good as gold if she knows there's food coming."

Hannah had been just close enough to hear everything. A spark set her off. "I want to go to the party if Celie goes."

Hannah hadn't even looked up from her jigsaw puzzle and she was chewing toward the center of a Tootsie Roll Pop.

Mom said, "I swear, Celie, someday you'll talk the salt right out of the sea. All right, go. I guess you're both old enough. And Hannah, it's *not* a party. It's a funeral reception. You need to act with respect."

Hannah nodded as respectfully as she could, given she was biting through the last of the hard sugar to get to her taffy center.

When they arrived at the funeral home, most of the woman and girls were out back, messing around with food. Celie grabbed Hannah by the hand and hauled her off to a tree next to picnic tables loaded with tea, lemonade, cakes and pies.

"Yummy!" Hannah declared. "Let's see what they have."

"Not yet. We're supposed to wait here and be quiet until the service ends and not bother the ladies laying out the food."

Celie was headed to the big willow tree when she spotted Ava, curled up against its huge trunk, her head buried in the lap of her dress. "C'mon, Hannah. There's Ava."

Hannah bolted over to Ava and plopped herself down directly in front of her, curling up like a kitten. At first, she just laid a hand on Ava's knee and sat humming a tune. A minute later, she dug into a ruffled pocket on the front of her dress and pulled out a nearly clean Kleenex. With astonishing delicacy, she drew it across Ava's forehead, down both her cheeks, then along the fold between her chin and neck. Ava lifted a face that was streaked with tears. Lightly, Hannah stroked her cheek.

Lying next to Ava was a cardboard church fan with "FRAMPTON" printed in gold letters. Pictured on the back was a sad white family, their hands folded in prayer, the women holding white lace hand-kerchiefs. Their short, blond bobs were draped over with a layer of black netting that stopped at the edges of their starched collars. Hannah picked up the fan and wafted it over Ava with wide strokes, her song changing to a made-up jingle, "You feel better now Ava? Does that cool you, cool you, so fine?" Celie would always remember the little girl's tenderness to Ava, her instincts tuned to what was most needed. She started to complement her, but Venus appeared suddenly within the archway of the back door of the funeral home. She was dressed fancy for a funeral. Fancier than she'd seen on any woman in her whole life — a forest-green velvet dress with a wide satin border. Her hat was made entirely of matching green feathers.

To Celie's dismay, Hannah called out to Venus in her always-exuberant way, "Hi, Miss Venus! Wow! You sure look pretty! What you got in the package?"

It was too late to stop her now, Celie thought, and besides, she was curious too, about the brown paper parcel Venus was carrying, a package tied tightly all over with string.

Taking long strides, Venus came right to them, swaying as she walked. Celie thought she seemed much too lighthearted for someone just about to leave the funeral of her only sister. Venus handed the package to Ava. "You and your sister got to hold onto this. Don't let nobody else try to take it. Don't you open it, and don't go nowhere til I come back and get it."

"What's in it?" Hannah asked again. "Is it a present for Ava?"

Venus narrowed her eyes slowly, maybe surprised at the audacity of this child. Then it seemed she almost welcomed the challenge of sparring with the white boss's nosy daughter.

"Why that's Minnie's soul," she answered slyly. "Ava and Sari been blessed enough to be able to take care of it a while. But nobody else can touch it, 'cause they ain't been blessed, you see? The ol' Devil would just spit out fire, if somebody else tried to open it. Or if they tried to take it away from Ava."

Ava came alive. "Venus! Hannah is just a kid, younger than Sari. You watch what you say, you hear? If she was to tell Mr. Guy what you already just said, I'd have to back her up."

Venus's eyes shifted from one white child to the other and then over to Ava, who shoved both hands on her hips and stood up straight.

Venus said, "Yep. I reckon you would. My own flesh and blood child …and…" She stopped, stumbling on a tree root and landing on the ground beside Ava and Hannah, who both stooped to help her up. Venus began humming a lullaby, her voice sweet and hypnotic. Sliding herself between the boss's two daughters, she patted both their heads and then stroked Hannah's soft, dark hair before retying the bows on each of her silky pony tails.

Celie recognized the tune. A sweet spiritual that old folks sang to babies to sooth them. Ava was anything but soothed. She said, "Venus, stop it."

But Venus kept on. "Hannah, you'd never say anything bad about old Venus, right honey? We're good friends and good friends don't talk behind each other's backs. You got enough cake, girls? Or some punch? Lots of good treats."

Celie doubted even Hannah was foolish enough to fall for such an obvious bribe. In fact, being a spoiled little urchin who worked the edges of all her relationships, Hannah was already looking for lines to slip between. She reached her hand to the top of Venus's head, patting the green feathers that anchored the hat. Drawing out a second Kleenex from her pocket, she wiped Venus's face as she had done Ava's. She said, "No cake, thank-ya, ma'am. I just wanna' sit with Ava for a while, case she needs me. I'm her good friend, and Sari's too. We love them, me and Celie. We'll take good care, don't worry. As good a care as their own Mama."

Celie's eyes flew open wide and so did Ava's. Did Hannah really know that Venus was not a good mother, or was this just another of her little flirting games? It wouldn't have mattered, Celie decided. Venus knew so little about real love that the whole thing sailed up and out, way over her head. Later Ava would tell her the same thing, "All Venus hears is what she wants to hear – which meant that she found no enemies sitting next to her under the willow tree."

Still, something must have got under her skin. Venus had looked directly at Celie and said, "Y'all got a third death on the way you know. Happening soon. Works in threes."

Celie waited until Hannah was out of earshot. "What did she mean, Ava?"

"Pay her no mind. She likes to get a rise out of people is all."

"All I can say is it worked. Sure sent a shiver up *my* spine."

"Forget it. She's hoping you'll spend fifty cents and come ask her to tell the future."

Celie shuddered. "No thanks. How much would it cost for me to get her to un-tell it?"

But by then, Hannah was skipping toward Venus and they decided to grab her and get her as far away from Venus as they could.

****

Venus slipped away from the funeral crowd, having fixed it so she could disappear without being recognized. A simple shedding of a dress and hat. She rolled them into a ball and stuffed them into a trash bin. She had to chuckle.... People wouldn't recognize this Venus, Venus traveling, the one that didn't want attention. She counted on that. Dressed in her plain brown jacket and pants she looked androgynous.

The person she was most avoiding, Isaac, had gone back inside. Not that she was afraid of that old man. What could he do to her now? Not a dad-blame thing. She didn't care enough about anybody he had his hooks into, except maybe Sari. She'd wanted to take the child along for comfort. Then the damn kid began crying out in her sleep, just about every night. Where Venus was going, a child crying out at night was a serious liability. Too bad Sari didn't have Ava's tough hide. Too bad Ava had her head up her ass.

Besides, she needed someone to watch over her interests. If she took her fortune along, it'd be stolen from her in no time. Couple of the things there would sell for a right pretty penny. And there was something else: As long as her girls were with Isaac, he'd always take her back.

All that was in the future and she had to think more about now. Now that there was nothing to hold her here, with her sister dead. No one left to give her a break, a nickel, a cup of coffee in the morning to wake her up. Time to move on, by herself this time, the only person she was sure she could truly count on. Now that she'd left the package with Sari, no more business to finish. Out of this damn backwater and good riddance.

Chapter Ten

Small family farms with natural cover between properties never really had a chance on the Eastern Shore. Most soils throughout the region are not continuously saturated nor naturally fertile. The nearly-level soil near the Marshyhope Creek is of a type that has little use unless it is drained regularly and heavily cultivated. Unfortunately, poorly drained soils occupy more than 60 per cent of the land in upper Dorchester County. (U.S. Department of Agriculture)

Celie knew, as most people did, that Guy Mowbray wasn't a great success as a farmer, even compared with other struggling farm families. In addition to his loans, the land he'd chosen to farm was poorly drained and nearly untillable, at least when he started out. But money wasn't the way Celie's parents counted their blessings. If there were times there were no store-bought clothes, Mom could sew just about anything. In the years when they lived from crop to crop, literally counting out pennies by the time spring came, they ate what Mom had preserved. In a good year, Daddy could squeeze out enough profit to upgrade his machinery.

Sitting around the kitchen table planning out the next year's crops, Daddy had once told Celie how he wished that before he started out, he'd known how much damage a landlord could do to a family's self-respect, all the small ways a greedy man could keep his tenants trapped in poverty. When he had planted his first year's seeds and worked every waking hour, sometimes even in the dark, he did it without knowing that in addition to rent, his landlord could claim a share of anything that grew, anything from bales of hay to fresh-cut flowers.

"It might have gone on that way forever," Celie told Ava, "except for the county flower show."

"That's a joke, right?"

"Oh no. It's real. The landlord's wife, Mrs. Elkridge, came for Mom's peonies every spring. She'd say something stupid like, "You just can't grow a thing in my postage stamp yard." This was supposed to explain her ravaging our garden. Mom always smiled and treat her like a Queen. The older we got, the more we knew how it bothered her to lose those peonies. We thought it might change when Mom's friend Isabelle LaForge got all fired up watching the peony raid and tried to convince Mom to stand up for herself."

Hannah said, "Isabelle was furious. She said, 'I never saw anything like this in the free world. Does that woman think you're a serf?'"

"Did they stay friends?" Ava usually imagined the worst in any family story.

"Sure," replied Hannah. "They were all playing duplicate bridge and Mom ignored her and just kept bidding. You had to ignore her since they were communists. Different standards."

"Quit saying they were communists," Celie scolded. "You don't know that."

Hannah made a face. "Well anyway, we always cried. Mom's peonies were her babies. She tied little strings around them, so they wouldn't fall over. Stuff like that, and she never cut them, not until that woman came to get them."

"We had to watch the same horrible scene every year," Celie said. "We made a pact we'd stop her someday. I kept a secret document in my diary with her mannerisms and habits and even her horrible clothes."

"Her clothes? How could clothes stop her?

"They couldn't, I guess. It just made me feel better to make fun of her ugly shoes that tied all the way up to her ankles. And her silly lace collar pinned to her dress with safety pins. And that dress! Black rayon pulled tight all over. She looked like one of those dummies boxers punch in the movies."

"More like sausage casings," Hannah said, her eyes brightening at her own joke.

Celie winked and said, "Good one. The dress ran straight up and down but she had a belt anyway, sitting at least an inch too high. Or too low. She had no waist and didn't seem to know it. We figured it must be because of the corset underneath, but since Mom never wore anything like that, we never knew for sure."

Hannah added, "We wouldn't have minded her so much if it didn't make Mom act so pathetic. Mrs. E. would drive up the dirt lane in her big black Ford and not even get out of the car — just sit there waiting for Mom to come out and see what she wanted. Like the Queen or something. She'd say about three words we never could hear, then the fakey grin, and then off she'd go."

"While Mom got ready for the peony massacre," Celie said, fists clenched as she talked. "Mom would slice down half her flowers, one at a time using her kitchen scissors. She'd pile them into buckets of water, with wet newspaper all around to keep them safe on the ride to town. We were never allowed to help. Mom wanted those peonies to look just perfect.

"And we had to look perfect, too!" Hannah grumbled. "'Put on your Church dresses,' she'd say in that voice that meant business. She'd make us wait on the couch, totally stock still so we wouldn't muss the dresses."

"While she loaded the flowers into the car," Celie continued. "So many buckets we had to sit in the front seat, which wasn't easy since we had to practically suspend ourselves in the air to keep our dresses from wrinkling. Mom hauled the peonies in by herself. Mrs. E. *couldn't* help because she was too busy 'arranging' them in vases on her dresser tops and her sideboards and her corner tables ... she jammed them everywhere. While we sat on her hard chairs in our Sunday clothes watching that woman treat Mom's flowers like they were hers."

Always ready with details of the food situation, Hannah said, "She gave us tiny little square mints the size of Chiclets. 'Just help yourselves,' she'd say and put a teensy little candy dish next to us. As if a stupid ten-cent box of candy was some big deal."

"Tell her about the cakes," Celie said.

"Oh my!" Hannah sighed, dreamily. "The cakes! I'll try not to drool while I talk. Out in the dining room, in the middle of her big fancy table, under one of those big glass dome things, there was always a giant double-layer cake. I used to imagine what kind of cakes they were and what they might have tasted like. Because we were never offered *any*. Not once." Hannah sighed again, her eyes wistful. "They had little swirls of velvety frosting, all across the top and all around the sides. Like ocean waves...."

Ava smiled, as Hannah's voice trailed off. Everyone knew about Hannah's sweet tooth. If anyone even mentioned cake around her and there wasn't one, out would come the cake flour and superfine sugar. Never a box mix, even when she was a teenager. She made cakes three fat layers high and decorated with something fancy, like orange syrup or whipped cream or coconut ... or all three.

"You can thank Mrs. E. for every one of my cakes," Hannah was saying. Which had to be true, since as far as Ava knew, their mother was a plain Irish cook who never baked a cake from scratch in her life.

Celie said, "I always wanted to yank those scissors out of Mom's hand and tell her, 'No cutting! Go back in the house and read your *Book-of-the-Month*.' And Hannah would call up Mrs. E. to tell her we'd be keeping every single one of the peonies from now on."

Ava said, "Well, it's a good story even if it does have a sad ending."

The sisters laughed uproariously. When Hannah caught her breath, she said, "Tell her about your revenge."

"I can't really take all the credit for it. In a small town, justice tends to occur naturally, well, mostly."

"Especially if you give it a push."

"Actually, I was patient. I bided my time for a change. It just so happened that my 4-H club hosted the county fair last year. I saw that Mrs. E. had entered some hybrid peonies, which of course Mom had created. All I did was put a short note on the judges' table."

Hannah said, "The Old Bat would have won, too, but after they read the note, the judges talked to Mrs. E and found she didn't actually grow them. Or any peonies, ever. After she left the booth, Mom's name was put up instead, and Mom won. She said, 'It's a varietal I call *Celianna*,' and everybody applauded, but she was embarrassed."

"And then, you asked me why Mom wasn't happy, remember? I told you she was happy; she just didn't know it yet. Then you punched me in the arm and told me to stop being splenetic."

"Splenetic?" Ava asked, laughing.

Hannah said, "I study 'It Pays to Increase Your Word Power' in *Reader's Digest*."

"I racked my brain trying to remember any other words from that issue," Celie said. "I picked *obviate*, but I don't think I've ever thought of a way to use it."

"You haven't," Hannah said. "Anyway, last fall, the Elkridge's raised our rent. Celie was furious when she found out, weren't you, Celie?"

"Yup. It challenged my victory. But Daddy told me, 'It's OK. We'll be better off.' I didn't believe him, until this spring. The 'crop-lifting' – Frank's name for it – has stopped completely, including the peonies. Mom has started singing in the garden, and she still does, by the way."

Ava said, "That's what they call a victory worth any price."

****

Ava had come to appreciate the teasing, loving banter of the Mowbray family. Her own sister had always been more like a dependent than a sibling, even before Venus left. During her time in the tenement camp, Ava hadn't socialized with anyone besides her sister, and Minnie and Isaac. When folks came in from the fields in the evening, Ava would disappear, getting both her food and her fun elsewhere. She was careful not to let on how much time she spent at the Mowbray house. They all resented her enough already.

When Gabe came, she knew how badly Isaac wanted Gabe and her to be brother and sister, but Gabe was so different from her. Within days of his arrival, he knew everyone's names, habits and quirks. For instance, he knew that Ava left early and came back after the fires were low. He certainly knew she stayed up nearly as late as he did, but she'd never told him a thing about where she was going. He'd never asked, maybe respecting that whatever she was doing was her business. She was aware that as soon as he'd seen how things were for Isaac and Minnie, he'd started crafting a plan to get them out of migrant life. It was the kind of thing she knew but didn't say anything about. That's how she was like Gabe. How anyone else lived life was nobody's business.

****

Gabe's plan was simple. He would go to school, get good grades, and excel at academics and at all school sports. He would learn basketball, football, baseball, and the rules of team play.

He had practiced and studied until he knew he was fit to take the entrance test for Mace's Lane, the colored high school in Cambridge. He was not only going to get in, he was going there as a star. After that would be a scholarship to a competitive college, than a degree that would lead to a good salary.

Ava came back to camp one night at one a.m., her usual time. Gabe was sitting by the remains of the campfire, reciting American History facts, eyes closed so he could concentrate.

"What you practicing?" she asked, seeming to be sincerely curious.

He opened his eyes. "History."

"What, for Church or something?"

It was early enough in their relationship that everything was still a negotiation. He must have noticed she'd dropped her dialect, since he did the same. "I'm taking an equivalency test on Friday. Going to school in Cambridge this winter if it suits Isaac."

"You're trying to get into Mace's Lane? Don't you have to be a county resident to go there?"

"Well, well. I'm surprised you know about that."

"What — girls are supposed to be stupid?"

"Don't lay all that on me. I don't expect you to understand anybody different, is all."

"What makes you think you're different from me?"

"Nothing makes me think it. I don't think anything about you. I don't know you."

"Well that's the smartest thing any boy ever said to me. Maybe you got a brain in there after all." She laid down the bag she always carried and sat cross-legged in front of the fire.

He said, "No need being mean, Ava. I'm pretty sure I never said or done anything to you to warrant that."

"You're right. I'm wrong. I apologize for jumping to conclusions just because you're a guy."

She reached out a hand to shake. Instead he took it and patted it for a second, the way Isaac did with the crew. He was glad she didn't take her hand away. Instead, she said, "Nothing in this world I hold more in disrespect than judging a person for how they look. My apology is humble and sincere, and I hope you accept it."

"I do," he said and kissed her hand lightly, a move meant as brotherly affection.

A truce was all Gabe had hoped for, but by the end of an hour, they had built the beginnings of a deep, lasting trust. He didn't know whether it was because they were now in the same "family," or if it was as uncomplicated as their mutual dislike of migrant life.

It didn't take long after that for Gabe to discover a bond that ran much deeper. Venus had come back to the camp, early one morning, to drag Sari from her bed. She danced her around like a frenetic puppet on a string, but it was her behavior toward Ava that chilled Gabe to the bone. Venus directed a stream of venom toward Ava, the worst he could imagine, and he'd seen plenty of troubled relationships. Worse than Jesse's father when he was drunk and mean, hurling insults at his two children. It was then he realized how he and Ava were more the same than different. You could always recognize when another person was a motherless child.

Chapter Eleven

Tenant farming is a system of agriculture where a farmer pays rent to the landowner. In sharecropping, the farmer also needs to buy supplies and equipment for their crop, as well as to find or borrow the funds to feed their families until harvest time. In return the landowner keeps a share of the tenant's crops. When expenses are factored in, the debt can exceed the sharecropper's return. Tenant farmers and sharecroppers are significantly poorer than their landed neighbors. While tenant farmers are usually better off than sharecroppers, most are only one bad crop away from slipping into the cycle of debt. (Reid)

Sometimes Celie wondered if, in her own way, she didn't cause her parents as many headaches as Frank did. Ava had been the only girl her age for miles around, and they'd played together as much as they wanted. Celie had refused to let invisible boundaries dictate the where and how long of her friendships. She planned to be Ava's friend forever. Maybe ignoring boundaries was as natural a part of her character as Daddy's refusal to become a carpenter when he wanted to be a farmer. At least that's the way she saw it.

She was always pushing people together, whether they wanted it or not. Last week was a perfect example. She and Hannah had been headed to Nick's Luncheonette to buy comics, a trip they took on most summer Saturdays. Celie had been ready to go since breakfast. She stood outside Hannah's door, jingling quarters together, to encourage Hannah to stop dragging her feet.

Mom was guzzling the last of her coffee when Celie managed to pull Hannah into the kitchen. Mom smiled at them and held up a finger, meaning, *ready in a minute.*

Celie elbowed Hannah.

"Can we bring Ava and Sari along?" Hannah asked.

Mom's face clouded for a second. "Celie, did you put her up to this?"

Celie flushed at being found out. Of course, she had. Since Mom almost never said no to her youngest child, Frank and Celie used Hannah to negotiate for everything. They'd assumed their parents didn't notice.

Hannah was a sport. "No. It was just as much my idea this time." Mom was visibly agitated, though — whether because of the trick they'd tried to pull or because of the prospect of bringing two colored girls into a white luncheonette, Celie wasn't sure.

Mom's Catholic status had led to snubs that got under her skin bad, and they could usually count on her to side with the underdog. After a few seconds, she nodded yes. Celie took off across the cucumber field to invite the girls, practicing what she would say to Willi, slowing down when she realized that Hannah was barely keeping up.

They arrived out of breath and stood smiling at Isaac, who was sitting on Willi's porch sipping coffee. He smiled back and unbent his body, one joint at a time, so he could stand.

"Can Ava and Sari come to town with us?" Celie and Hannah asked in chorus.

Isaac's eyes twinkled. "Well. Let's see. Venus has gone off for a while, so we can't ask her. Could ask Willi, but she just got in from her shift and has gone on to sleep. That leaves me to ask, only right now, I happen to be out on errands. So, I guess Ava and Sari are the only ones left to ask."

They laughed loud enough to bring Ava and Sari to the door. As they were leaving Isaac said, "Just a caution. Y'all need to be careful of what places you go into."

"We know," Celie answered, not wanting to think too carefully about what he was warning about. Riding to town, the four girls stayed huddled in the back seat of Mom's car, orchestrating their buying plan. It had been a good year; each girl had a crisp one-dollar bill to spend in addition to any savings they'd brought. If they used the whole dollar on comics, they could buy four each, a treasure trove of reading when you factored in trading. Or there could be fewer comics, and more money for ice cream....

Hannah was the biggest problem, Celie thought. She'd developed an unexpected taste for dull stories with real-life heroes – biographies and such.

"You can get them in the library, Hannah." Celie argued as they walked into Nick's, trying hard to negotiate civilly.

"Nope, you can't. Besides, I like to read things that are real life."

"Why? You always know the ending ahead of time! Paul Bunyan finds a big ox, George Washington nearly freezes to death, Davy Crockett loses at the Alamo. It's *history* – we're supposed to be getting *comics*. Like in *fun*."

When Hannah stopped arguing back, Celie realized there was no winning this, which, as often happened, made her even more long-winded, until her arguments started sounding ridiculous even to her.

Mom's voice jumped into her head, saying, "You just like to argue." Was that true? She didn't think so. The way she saw it was that people often made decisions without enough evidence, so if she gave them more facts, then....

Her attention was diverted by what was happening to Ava, who had just put her money down on the counter. Mr. Nick, the proprietor, had a crabby look on his face. He was one of the biggest racists they knew, but Daddy was well-liked in town, so Mr. Nick signaled to his daughter to work the register. Ava paid and left the store quickly, but Celie's skin prickled long after she was gone. The more she thought about it, the more she suspected that Mr. Nick had almost asked Ava to leave.

Meanwhile, Hannah had paid for her stupid books, like *Clara Barton, Army Nurse,* and was already halfway up the street. Who knew where Sari was? Celie was alone with the racks and her own temper.

Thanks to Hannah, she'd need to be even more discriminating. Two *Archies*? No. One *Archie,* a *Sugar-and-Spike,* a *Wonder Woman* (her favorite), and a *Superman* which Frank would devour when he came home on leave.

Mom was always still at the grocery store or bank or something whenever they finished. Their routine was to walk to Wright's pharmacy at the corner of Main Street and the railroad tracks, where they'd buy penny candy. If there was enough left, they'd get ice cream sodas. Mr. Wright made a whopper of a fountain soda, loaded with ice cream.

Still cranky when she got to Wright's, Celie was open for trouble. Let somebody have told Ava she couldn't sit at the counter, for instance. It hadn't come up, maybe because Mr. Wright had hired an elderly black woman to work the fountain. Miss Nettie, she was called.

Miss Nettie didn't make eye contact with Ava. She took her order and filled it, collected the change and deposited it in the register. They all finished their sodas without incident, but as they were leaving, Miss Nettie chased out after Ava and took her aside.

Celie's body went rigid as she watched Ava's face from a distance. Should she go over? No, Ava was on her way to them in less than a minute.

"What did she say?" Celie asked, squeezing her fingers too tightly around the handle of her bag.

"Nothing. It's OK," Ava said but her eyes were aimed at the ground.

"You might as well tell me. You know what a pain I can be."

Ava took a deep breath, still not looking up, and said, "She asked me, 'What the devil you think y'all doing, Little Miss Uppity? Why you got to make trouble?'"

"What did you say back?"

"I said, 'You have a nice day, Miss Nettie.'"

Celie's chest muscles knotted, her hands forming fists that she shoved against her waist to contain them. She wanted to scream, but she swallowed, trying both to calm herself and to find the right words, somewhere in between outrage and support.

Ava said. "Drop it, Celie. And drop the Superman routine, OK?"

"Super Woman. And I *can't* drop it. What she said was outrageous. I know you couldn't be rude to her, but couldn't you have said something clever?"

"Like?"

"I don't know, like 'Seems like the only trouble is coming from in here.' Or, 'Ma'am, I think it's your boss who's the trouble.'"

"Easy for you to say. It'd be much worse me saying anything. You don't understand what I'm up against."

"You're right. I don't!" Celie said dramatically. She dropped her bag at her feet to hug Ava. "Why doesn't it make you *mad* to be unwelcome in a store just because of your color? And don't tell me you're used to it."

"Of course I'm not used to it! It makes me furious. But I can't go around with a chip on my shoulder all the time. Not everybody can be as brave as you."

She should have said rebellious, not brave, Celie thought as they walked to meet Mom. If she was brave, she'd have gone back and said something to let both Mr. Nick and Miss Nettie know that not everybody saw things their way.

Celie was still stewing on the short ride home, when Mom said, in an annoyingly offhand way, "One or both of you girls is going to have to babysit for Hap and Janet tonight."

"Pass," Celie and Hannah said in unison.

"No, you don't. And Ava, don't you and Sari try and get them off the hook."

Everyone maintained the awkward silence until Ava and Sari were dropped off at Willi's.

"Why do we have to?" Celie asked two seconds after the car door closed. She was still ready for a fight with somebody, even Mom. Normally, any opportunity for extra spending money was a windfall and she'd have jumped at it. But babysitting for toddlers? As much as she'd once loved dressing and babying her dolls, the idea of being responsible for the lives of real children was terrifying. She'd made up her mind to find other ways to earn spending money and so far, things had worked well. Why give in now?

Mom said, "I don't want an argument about this. They've been waiting all year for this dance. Their babysitter was *LeeAnn Bailey*," she added with unnecessary (Celie thought) emphasis on LeeAnn's name. Celie groaned theatrically, which showed she knew she was going to lose this.

LeeAnn was a girl in her class, a bit 'slow.' A girl who struggled to keep up with academics and found other ways of expressing herself. She'd just run off with the high school football captain, a graduating senior named Jed White, who everybody agreed was a total hunk. No one knew if they were married yet.

As soon as she got into the kitchen, Celie saw that Hannah had wasted no time in sneaking her math workbook on top of her bag of comics. Magically, there was a pencil in her hand and she was writing in the workbook.

Celie's plan was to distract her mother in a different way. "Poor Hap and Janet. It's a shame they'll miss the dance, but I guess if you decide to have kids, that's the way your life is."

Mom didn't even swerve. "Your friend LeeAnn is... I mean *was*... a cheerleader, wasn't she?" Mom asked provocatively. Mom is fully aware, Celie thought, that I have nothing in common with LeeAnn except that.

"I'm a cheerleader too, Mom, and you know it."

"That's different – you aren't *that* kind of cheerleader."

There was no use in trying to follow Mom's reasoning. It would only get worse. Celie groaned again, plopping down at the table and burying her head under her arms. This time she was only slightly exaggerating her distress, since she could now actually see herself as a helpless hostage to whining toddlers with a never-ending list of wants. Debbie and Ronnie Jackson were aged four and two. Or maybe it was three and one. It made no difference how old they really were, they were horrible.

"Six o'clock," Mom said and headed into her garden, the one place where no one would dare disturb her. The negotiation was over.

Hannah didn't even look up as she said, "You knew you were gonna have to do it, Celie. Why fight?"

"Why do I have to be the one?"

"Because if you aren't, Mom would end up going over there herself. And she'd make me go with her. And I *have* to wait here because Rick is going to call tonight at exactly 7 o-clock. I've already worked it out with every neighbor to keep the line free. Do you want to be the one to totally ruin my future marriage?"

"Marriage? Hannah, you're too young to even have a boyfriend. And I thought you were going to marry Jesse?"

"That's not the point and you know it."

"Well, tell him to call you earlier. Or later."

"He's got to do the milking earlier. And his parents … look, just give up, OK?"

Celie looked at her sister's baby face and thought, I'm sunk and as always, the last one to know it.

Mom offered to drive her to town, but Celie would rather ride her bike. She'd feel less trapped with her own way out of there. She used the State road that crossed through shanty-town on the left, the pickle factory on the right, then across the tracks and behind Main Street, to the back of Hap's house. This avoided the center of Hurlock, bypassing the lovely white Victorians that lined both sides of Main Street. Especially the house of the horrible Elkridges and their disgusting nephew, Rodney, who had moved in with them over the summer and was starting the new school year with her. Celie would do anything to avoid laying eyes on him. He had just joined her enemy list.

It had seemed out of the blue. All the way home on the bus one afternoon he kept staring at the library books in her lap, probably the one called *The Souls of Black Folk* by W.E.B. DuBois — a book that tried to look under the skin of people and find the thing that connected them. But Rodney wouldn't read books like this. Maybe he wasn't happy knowing anybody who did.

Next, he had barged into a story Celie was telling on the bus. She was just arriving at the punch line, "So Daddy was running and waving good-bye at us and blowing us kisses. We were trying to warn him that Prancer was right behind him, ready to ram him." She waved her arms now, for drama. "Then wham! And Daddy was so mad. He yelled, 'Whose idea was it to put these damn sheep on my farm, anyway?'"

Everybody started laughing, except Rodney, who said, "It's not your Dad's farm. He's just a sharecropper. It's more like my farm than yours since I'll probably get it in my aunt's will."

Celie looked straight into the eyes of her assailant. Tall for his age and beginning to display the muscular build of an athlete, Rodney sat with his arms splayed loosely on the backs of the seats, classic bully-style, hogging what should have been four desirable seats. She'd never noticed it before, but his skin was tan in an unhealthy way. Not from working outdoors, more like the bile-colored skin of people who were ill. If he was sick, she didn't feel sorry for him.

"So why you keep calling it your farm?" he insisted, tapping his fingers on the seat back.

Holding his gaze, Celie's aim was deadly sharp. "Because our Dad isn't a mean-assed old drunk who runs off with a waitress. And because you don't own *anything*. Just because your aunt took in your sorry ass doesn't mean you're in her will. How about you just ask her?"

She was fully aware that her words were just as cruel as his. When she calmed down later, she would give herself the excuse that she'd been ambushed. A giant red cape had been whipped across her face and her reaction was no more intentional than it would have been for a charging bull. When she'd thought about it even more, she would be as pained by her own brutality as she'd been by his. For now, though, the monstrous word *sharecropper* still reverberated, having latched itself inside her brain, and now hanging on with its claws. Her only relief had been to plant, within Rodney, a similar many-clawed monster.

For her whole life, Celie's concept of her parents had been as farm-owners. Daddy was renowned for his love of his land. He volunteered at the Farm Bureau; he sent soil samples for testing to the Agricultural Bureau and fed his soil fertilizer to keep it alive. Not many hours went by that he wasn't thinking about his farm.

Even more upsetting to Celie, if that was possible, was that Rodney had started squeezing his fists in and out repeatedly, as if he was trying to think of who he could belt. Earl, their closest neighbor, was sitting next to him and was quick to take Rodney's side, chanting, "sharecropper, sharecropper." He held a bony fist up to Celie's nose, which was laughable, given that he had no visible muscles and was a mental weakling to boot. She said, "Earl, sit down. Just be glad Frank's not around, or your head would already be coming out the other end of your body."

What else had she said on that ride? Probably a lot. All she could really remember was how she'd just kept scowling at Rodney, trying to think up something even more hurtful, silently daring him to move. He was still in his James Dean pose, but his face was bright red, his eyes puffy with rage.

When she was positive she'd reduced Rodney to a quivering lump, Celie turned to comfort her sister, sitting motionless except for big fat tears rolling down both cheeks.

"He's wrong," she whispered. "He's a liar and an ignoramus." The rest of the ride home, all five minutes of it, had been a nightmare. Only a few kids remained at that point on the bus route; all of them had sat like rocks until Celie and Hannah got off.

They walked from where the bus let them off more slowly than usual, their hands laced together. Just as they got to the porch, Hannah whispered hoarsely, "Are we, Celie? Sharecroppers?"

"Of course not. We're *tenants*. Loads of people around here rent their land."

"But if we don't own like, even our *flowers* – "

"Forget what that jerk said. He's scared and mad because his parents left him. That's what makes people mean. When they lose something important."

"But you didn't really tell him he was *wrong*. And Earl and Jennie were mean too. I thought they were my friends."

"Earl and Jennie are real scared, too. Their dad just lost their equipment mortgage."

"How do you know that?"

Celie hadn't told Hannah about the listening wall. "I just do. Both their tractors were taken away by the Bank."

Open-mouthed, Hannah just stared. Mortgages were one thing; almost no one ever had the money to go out and actually *buy* a tractor, and they all made payments. Even big farmers like the Nickersons ran huge equipment debts. Every farmer, from migrant worker to corporate partner, shared a common terror — what a bad harvest could do to their finances. With both tractors gone, Lloyd Jencks couldn't even plant next season's crops, even if he could afford seed. He'd be coming home every night drunk and furious and he'd be pounding on his wife and kids. Celie had actually seen the bruises on Helen and her daughter Jennie, but she didn't want to scare Hannah with this much detail.

"Don't worry, Hannah. They'll figure out something and Daddy will never let it happen to us. We're *not* sharecroppers."

But probably, we are, she was thinking. The way Rodney's aunt had helped herself to their produce and flowers whenever she'd wanted.

She felt something slip away from her sense of security. She remembered what Ava had once said about the farmers of the Eastern Shore. "I always used to feel bad about being poor all the time. Then I learned how poor the rest of y'all are. Just a tractor payment away from ruin."

As much as she had loved farm life, Celie resolved never to live it. She'd go to the city for college. If she ever came back to the Eastern Shore, she'd live in Easton or Cambridge.

****

Homework?" Celie asked, laying a hand on her sister's shoulder a few days after the school bus showdown.

"No way. I'm reading *Pride and Prejudice* for fun. I like to try and figure out how those girls could stand each other. The oldest one's unmarriageable, the youngest of all with three or four boyfriends and no chance of marrying any of them until she got to the head of the line. It's a wonder they didn't poison their older sisters more often."

"Go ahead," Celie said, smiling. "I won't even try to stop you."

Hannah put down the book. "You do know I'm kidding."

"Of course. But *I'm* not."

"Celie, what happened today?"

"Nothing specific. I guess it's just a tough year. I'm trying to figure out a way to hide the fact that I'm Frank's sister until the teachers know me better." Celie was reluctant to complain about school in front of Hannah. But her reaction to the incident with Rodney on the bus had made Hannah feel more protective.

This year she had new teachers, all of whom had known Frank. Miss Smith, for example: "Lilian Ann Mowbray. *Frank's* sister?" In Miss Smith's eyes as she looked over her pince-nez, was her wish to get a better view of Frank Mowbray's relations. And then Mr. Moore: he had kept a scowling face, only at her, from the beginning to the end of Chemistry.

Her imagination had painted a Scarlet "F" on her back. She believed she was seeing her brother through the eyes of Authority. All she said to Hannah now was, "I liked it better when the teachers knew me since I was five."

She gave a light tug to her sister's long pony-tail, a signal to go back to what she was doing. Celie needed to be alone with this unexpected cloud on her reputation. If she could think of a way to remove the shadows now, they'd be gone for Hannah too.

A solution presented itself in, of all places, the seating arrangements. Alphabetical seating put her between Nadine Jeffers and Carol Muller, mild-mannered girls and honor roll students — and Baptists, like Daddy. When they started a Home Economics club, Celie became Treasurer. By Christmas, she felt accepted for who she was, rather than who she was related to. Still, she stayed on the honor role for insurance and was always extra nice to everybody, right up until she left for her senior year work-study program at Cambridge High School. There, no one had known Frank at all.

In fact, she'd been wondering if she knew him. She saw a chance to find out when he came home on leave before his two-year "secret" assignment to Formosa. She corralled him by going into his room at an ungodly early hour.

"Go away, Pipsqueak. I'm asleep."

"I know. That's why I'm here. I want to ask you something when you're too sleepy to spin your bullshit stories. And no listeners to impress."

He grinned, his eyes still closed, the smile being a kind of homage to her for being able to outmaneuver him.

Celie said, "It's about Mr. Moore. He asked me how you were, but he flashes me the evil eye every day. I'm sure he doesn't like me, but he gives me A's I don't deserve."

"Good." Frank said and laughed loudly, although it was more of a snarl. He said, "He hates my guts and vice versa."

"Why?"

"Because he's a mean man who likes to hurt people? Moore punishes kids just to see them squirm. Not because of anything they've done."

"That just tells me why you hate *him*."

Frank yawned and sat up, one eye still closed, the other peering at her cautiously. Celie hadn't really got a good look at him since he'd finished military training. He now had a stubble of a beard that wouldn't have filled in fully if he'd grown it out. His face was still blanketed with freckles, like hers, but his skin was roughed up by sun and wind now and was no longer delicate, no longer the skin of a boy. He's toughened up on the outside, too, she thought. She waited while he stretched and began rubbing his scalp as if to smooth his hair, although it was now a stubble that matched his beard.

What a contrast he presented, Celie thought, his bare chest profiled against the backdrop of blue wallpaper with little cowboys swinging lassos from ponies. He pulled his face into the one she'd seen so many times, the expressive countenance of a raconteur. With his little-boy ponies there in the room with him, she had never liked him so much.

His eyes fairly sparkled as he began. "One day Old Moore called me into his office for a beating. He had out his leather strap, a thin one he could keep rolled up and invisible in a pocket, although the thinness was more because of the way it operates. It hurts more when it slices into your skin. Plus, he could maneuver it to make narrow welts on your legs that would heal up by the time you got home.

"Anyway, he calls me in and shuts the door and takes off his glasses. He would squeeze his eyes into slits, like a snake. He had that mean little smile on his face."

Celie shivered. She'd seen the smile in class. The kids all talked about it.

Frank continued, "He'd roll and unroll the strap, over and over, taking his time until he could see fear. He figured the more he fooled with the strap, the more his victim would worry. I never let him see anything even close to fear from me. Not once."

"He hated you because you refused to look scared?"

"I honestly think that would have been enough of a reason, yes. But it wasn't the reason. I don't know what was different that day, but when he told me to sit, I refused. He started cracking the strap in the air. It got closer, then it touched my face. Maybe that was what pissed me off — I had a date that night with Charlene Jackson and I liked to look good for Charlene. The next time the end of the strap got close to my face, I grabbed it. Pulled the damn strap out of his hand, rolled it up and stuck it in my pocket. Moore started to swear. It was just after lunch and he had a piece of spinach or something stuck between his teeth. While he was yelling, he spit the spinach out and it landed on his chin and stayed there. All I could see was a ridiculous man with green food on his chin trying to scare the Beejeezus out of a kid. I pulled out the strap and began flicking it at *him*. I said something like, "You want this back? Come take it from me." I made the strap get closer and closer to his face and he stopped screaming and just stood there. He was shaking all over, with his face purple, and his eyes actually tearing up."

"You scared *him*?"

"Scared maybe. More like confused. He was the one everybody was supposed to be afraid of. Maybe he finally figured out I never would be. He turned around and went out and slammed the door."

Looking at Frank in that second, Celie understood how the man had felt. Frank was wearing the exact same smile he'd just described in Mr. Moore. She swallowed. "And that was the end of the strap, then?"

"Not quite. See, that's the best part of it. I used to put the strap in different places he couldn't get to. On top of the lockers so he'd have to get a ladder, but it'd be gone when he got back with it. Once we hung it from the gym ceiling, holding that strobe thing at the prom. Moore stopped trying to reach it after that, but we never stopped moving it around, because we could see it always got a rise outta him."

Knowing how Frank couldn't resist embellishing his stories with blarney, she had to ask, "Is this all true?"

"Every word. Ask Bobby. Or Ralph White. Anybody. They'll back me up."

She wanted to hug him or shake his hand or something, but decided it wasn't a good idea. Instead she said, "Well thanks, that helps. I hope you go a little easier on the Air Force."

He ducked back under his pillow and she went downstairs to help Mom make breakfast. All the way down, she was remembering the time she and Frank had reached their own understanding, the one that made him stop torturing her and Hannah.

Frank had been given the milkhouse-turned-porch, which he'd turned into a laboratory, his privacy guaranteed by blackout curtains on the window. His first project was to build a working electric chair. He invited Celie and Hannah, one at a time, to "come in and have a seat." He'd leave the room on some pretext, but really it was to press a shock button.

They had gone into his laboratory gladly, fully aware he was up to no good, but curious to see his contraption and always grateful for any kind of attention from him. Celie received the jolt first, whispering to Hannah that it was uncomfortable but not really painful. By the time Frank had finished talking Hannah into the seat, Celie had a brainstorm. She slipped into his control center and reversed the wires so that when he pressed the 'shock' button, the current had come to him instead. Hannah had burst out crying, maybe from expecting a shock that didn't come, or maybe just afraid he'd be mad.

Celie held a finger to her lips to signal Hannah to stop crying. "Watch," she mouthed. She engaged the wires again and Frank gave a little jump. He scratched his head as he walked toward her, looking completely confused. As soon as he got a look at Celie, standing next to the controls in her Wonder Woman pose, he burst out laughing.

"That's a good one," he said. Then he said it again.

Celie nodded back, acknowledging the tribute. It was the last practical joke he ever played on his sisters.

Chapter Twelve

According to the (Maryland) Governor's Commission on Migratory and Seasonal Farm Labor, "as many as 7,500 migrants come into Maryland each year to harvest crops in orchards, in the tobacco industry, and on nursery farms." They were part of the "Eastern Stream" of migrants who were on the Eastern Shore of Maryland from late April or early May to late October. (Maryland Advisory Committee)

1960

In the three years since Minnie had passed, Isaac had come to feel twenty years older. While his wife was alive, he hadn't noticed how much she helped him get through his day. Why else would he be finding even the simplest tasks so hard now? Hauling himself out of bed in the morning, getting himself dressed and undressed, hoisting himself to the running board and behind the wheel of his truck?

He was leaning more on the younger folks, not that he ever felt really comfortable doing it. He was supposed to be the one folks depended on. It's the way his own pappy had done — every decision had to be run by Pappy John.

When it had been Isaac's time to take over, he'd run the crews with a velvet hammer, the way Pappy John taught. "Let 'em know you love 'em like your own young'uns, but if they step outta line, down comes the hammer. Knock 'em back in line without you hurt anybody. After a while, they know the hammer is to keep them safe. Keep them from throwing away what they earn."

Isaac had operated that way most of his years as boss, but lately it was getting harder. He was older or maybe just tireder. Whatever the reason, he'd been looking forward to the day Gabe would take over. When he'd realized that this day wasn't going to come, he'd been surprised how his heart was so much lighter, and he couldn't quite grasp it. Hattie brought him a cup of coffee, and he looked forward to talking it over. They went outside to watch the work around them.

"Gabe's awful distracted lately," he said. Gabe was weeding the camp's patch of rhubarb. The pair of them turned to stare openly at the young man working in the garden, moving through it easily with his lean, muscled body. His face glowed, his eyes alive with things he wouldn't tell any of the grown-ups.

"See how he is?" Isaac elbowed Hattie as she bent to yank some Lamb's Ears invading the lettuce. "We're staring at him and he don't even notice. Something big on his mind."

"Yup," she said. "Restless. All boys his age is restless."

"Maybe yes, maybe no…"

"What? What do you mean with them maybes?"

"There's a spark in this boy. The same one I saw in Pappy John, and my Grandpappy."

Hattie grinned. "Oh yes, indeed. Now your Grandpappy was one right beautiful man. He got a lot of mileage outta them looks. I reckon Gabe will too."

"Not working the land, though. The boy likes his schooling too much."

Isaac sat down in a sturdy rocker that Gabe had procured for him. Hattie stopped pulling weeds and perched on the tree stump next to him, fanning herself to keep away mosquitos, and said, "Where you suppose he got that from?"

Isaac said, "Not from my side. Grandpappy said fifty times if he said it once — get you a trade, boy. Only way to get through life without the boss man's boot on your neck. His looks and all took him far, but I like to remind folks how Grandpappy learned to shoe horses when he was six. That's what kept him his own man all his life."

"Then how come his own son went to the fields anyway?"

"Him and my Mama, too, God bless her soul. And then down to me. I started filling baskets with my Daddy when I was a bitty thing. Can't say why, Hattie. I reckon only God knows the answer to why a man chooses one job over another."

Isaac uncurled himself from the chair. The rockers on the bottom made it a true gift from heaven, except getting out of it took some doing. He walked the four inches to where Hattie was sitting with intentions to help her up. It being a Saturday before a holiday, Labor Day, he'd given everyone an extra day off. He and Hattie were going to ride into Cambridge to visit some cousins and, hopefully, finish arrangements for Gabe's schooling. He hadn't got around to mentioning this part to Hattie.

He helped her up, or maybe she helped him, and they moved slowly to the campfire. Hattie was murmuring, maybe to herself, or him, didn't matter which. Isaac settled while Hattie made instant coffee.

Hattie asked, "So where does Gabe get all that pride from? After his Pop died, he worked on the docks and then came here to the fields. And still he's prideful. Maybe that's what keeps him from being a good field boss."

"Even the easy parts, like keeping the women from wandering off when they're supposed to wait for the truck."

"Um – hmm. I heard you scolding him about that."

"You heard me ... but he couldn't. Said he couldn't understand the harm. I told him how each morning they'd go a little bit further. One inch, then another. How there's a lot to keeping them in line."

Isaac remembered how he'd felt, sitting next to the boy while he was wolfing down his second huge bowl of grits and gravy. He didn't like giving what was, for him, a long lecture. And when he ended with, "You got to stay tough, even on little things," Gabe had answered, "I've known that for a long time now, boss."

He'd filled his dinner bowl a third time. Isaac had draped an arm over the boy's broad shoulders, which he could manage only when Gabe was sitting. Gabe's body had gone rigid under his touch. For a second, Isaac felt hurt, but he hadn't loosened his grip. He had to make the boy understand that the power being given him could be taken back just as quickly.

"So you know already, you say?" he'd asked gently.

"Yeah, boss. I know enough to get the fields done and the beans in. I'll grant I don't know why it is they're never happy."

Isaac had looked close to make sure the boy wasn't just making fun. "So what you think's gonna get you that?"

"I don't know, boss," Gabe had snapped, standing up without finishing his food, raking his thatch of hair with one hand and shoving away his bowl with the other. Isaac had expected him to be either humble or restless, but he hadn't expected him to be angry. Did Gabe think Isaac was trying to dampen the fire that had burned in him since the day he met him? Didn't he know by now that Isaac wanted that fire, had counted on it?

No use to have fire, though, if you don't know how to use it. Isaac was thinking of a way to say all this, but Gabe had grabbed his jacket and walked off in a huff. Only to turn back after a few feet, head bowed in respect, the way he should.

"My night out ... that still ok?"

Isaac had nodded and waved Gabe away, keeping his face set, withholding his too-easy smile. Wondering if he was the problem, driving the boy too hard. He'd wanted him to step up before the whole crew guessed the depth of his own weariness. The boy was too young to know how easy it was for an old man to slip away from his own life. At his tender age, Gabe would never put Isaac's weariness together with the other half the story, about how getting old didn't mean Isaac was glad for a younger man to take his place. All it meant was that old men slip away, no matter why or ... what happens after.

Hattie set down her coffee and said, "I been thinking a lot about this. You and me, we're too old to keep running a crew North, then South, then try to work peanuts, then onions, then back North again. Some crews around here are deciding it's time to stop. Get work in one place or another and stay all year round."

"Where'd you hear that from?"

"The Minister – some of the folks in church. Doesn't matter. Point is, maybe we should think on it, too. Give you and me a rest and the boy his chance for his schooling."

Isaac heaved a mighty sigh. "Minnie always did say she couldn't bear for us being planted in just one place, like a tree." He was glad they were sitting side by side, so Hattie couldn't see his eyes filling up. A man needs his self-respect.

"Um-hmm," she said gently, adding some more sugar and stirring it for him. "You're right. What Minnie wanted was to be always moving. That's something you no longer got to worry about. Now you can decide for your own self, and the young'uns."

She hadn't mentioned, bless her, about his body failing him so much. She could see how bad his fingers were, each knuckle fiercely resisting any attempt to bend it. She was the only one who knew how his soaking them or liniment didn't do a thing, and how even Venus's voodoo herbs hadn't made a difference. But she didn't know that he'd gone to that white horse doctor over in Preston, a kindly man who suggested icing them. That had lessened the pain a lot, but it didn't help the stiffness or make it so he didn't have to hold everything with two hands. Bless Hattie for not saying that no crew would work long for a crippled old man. They'd figure his brain had gone as lame as his legs. Instead, Hattie was helping him the way Minnie would have done, pushing him to where he had to go.

He said, "I ain't against our staying put and letting the young'uns get their schooling. And as to us, if the old way of life is gone, we'll just have to find a new one."

"Gabe won't go off without your blessing, Ava neither, even though this work's never been right for either of them. You always saw that in Ava; how come you don't see it in Gabe?"

Isaac cleared his throat. "I do see it. I know the only thing in the world he loves is books. Talks all the time about if he could just go to Mace's Lane."

Isaac had talked to Edward Tate about letting Gabe stay in town and work at his restaurant. He would tell Hattie this, but he might not mention that he wasn't totally selfish in keeping the boy close to him. Only Isaac knew that Gabe's love of books had come from his real pappy, before the drink got him. Isaac had just wanted to make sure the good Lord had given Gabe the books but spared him the love of the bottle.

He'd known since Minnie's funeral that Venus wasn't coming back to stay. He had already talked to Willi Barclay, Guy Mowbray's neighbor. She'd just lost her husband, Big John. He'd asked for an exchange of favors, since Willi would be needing extra help—a girl maybe to live in. Sari needed a woman's attention, too young to have her own Ma gone. Ava would stay with Isaac to help him close down the camp when the time came, and then, maybe go to school with Gabe.

In truth, he was eager for all the children to learn more about the new world, whatever it held. Sari could stay with Willi, get a woman's touch in her life. With Ava and Gabe at Mace's Lane, Isaac could find a place to plant his little patch of potatoes and cabbage, crops for all year round, close enough to check on them all now and then. Maybe even go with Hattie to church and sing Minnie's hymns for her, until his own time came.

Willi had said, "I can take one girl. Probably rather have the younger one."

Meaning Sari. Isaac had replied quickly, "That's real good, because I sure couldn't stand to part with my Ava."

****

Ava had been grateful to Isaac for making her feel like she was the wanted one. Maybe he thought that Sari was already too damaged. Was he thinking there was still hope for Ava?

When they were riding back to camp the next day, she asked, "Why me and not Sari, Boss? Why you look out special for me?"

"You really wanna' know?"

She thought she'd nodded "yes," but she wasn't sure she'd wanted the answer then. Seeming to sense that, he didn't give one. After a few minutes of mutual silence, she asked, "You think Sari will be all right with Willi?"

"Best thing for now. Have to just wait and watch."

She wished she knew if he believed it, or if he was instead, just trying to comfort her.

It wasn't until months later that he'd answered her question. They'd been planting his new garden — peas, carrots, lettuce — Isaac leaning on his walking stick, reaching out once in a while to poke in a wandering seed. He said, almost as a stray thought, "Ava. You remember how you ask me why I look out special for you?"

"I remember. You didn't answer."

"Wasn't sure you really wanted to hear it. Hard message for a child. Then I got to thinking what Minnie would've said. She'd always told me, "That witch Venus has taken a grudge against her own child." I asked her why, and she told me that Venus doesn't need a reason. She knew Venus likes it when folks are all agitated. No reason for her to love Sari and not you. So we took you, gave you love she didn't give."

He grinned and reached for her hand. "Love is the one thing me and Minnie always had plenty of."

"I'll say," she said, squeezing his hand.

"Another reason, Ava. We both saw something special in you. Gotta give that specialness a chance to grow."

****

As it turned out, Venus didn't completely disappear. Her next appearance came several months later. Although she didn't really blame Venus for it, Celie always thought of that day as a turning point for all of them, and not in a good way.

The day before the crisis, they'd been making plans to bring dinner to Willi's house and all eat together the following night. Celie and Hannah had brought in a huge just-cooked ham and were sliding it along the table when Celie saw the distressed look on Ava's face. "Ava, what's wrong?"

"There's news about Venus and I have to tell Sari."

"Bad news?"

"Depends. Venus took a place in New York. She says she's going to stay there. Nothing about bringing Sari. I think it's her way of disappearing from our lives."

Ava picked up a bowl of scrubbed potatoes that needed peeling. Celie handed her a peeling knife, the only helpful thing she could think of, since there wasn't a helpful thing you could say about having a mother as cruel as Venus.

Hannah had been completely unnerved by Ava's news. She asked, "What do you mean disappear? Do you know where she is? Or when's she coming back?"

Ava snapped at her. "Don't you know what disappear means? No, I don't know where, and as to when, the answer is never."

Celie took a breath, determined to hang on to her temper. How dare Ava treat Hannah this way, after all she'd done to help Sari settle in at Willi's? Ava had become increasingly testy with everybody, but up until now, she'd exempted Hannah from her acid tongue.

Celie thought of a dozen ways to snap back at Ava, but she'd promised Mom to stop fighting Hannah's battles for her. She'd sworn not to say things to bail her sister out. However, nothing had been promised about not using her face to radiate fury that would be as loud as a shout to Ava. Which is what she did.

And then she realized that Ava hadn't really answered Hannah's questions. Maybe the sniping was to distract them from trying to find out more. Ava must know that no one was looking for Venus; Isaac was an old man now who lacked the energy it took to hunt down a woman who didn't want to be found.

She'd have a talk with Ava when she was less irritable. For now, she just cut the ham into thin, even slices and hoped that Hannah wasn't too hurt.

The next day, Celie saw just how complicated things were for Ava. Willi and all four girls had been sitting companionably on the porch all afternoon. A lovely summery wind was blowing, cooling off the porch. Celie had brought ham sandwiches for lunch, and now they were all shucking peas, listening to Willi's stories about when her own girls shucked peas here and the games they made up with them. It seemed to Celie that Willi was going out of her way to make Sari feel at home, and Ava was funny and cheerful.

Then Venus arrived in a thunderstorm of wrath, spewing out unintelligible swear words. She grabbed Sari roughly, and without explanation, hauled her inside the house. Hannah sat frozen in place, Willi looked stunned, and Ava's face was flat-out furious. Celie tried to feel nothing except awareness of all of them, so she could know who to help and how. Poor Ava, she thought, every trace of anger toward her friend now completely forgotten.

From inside came arguing, then yelling, then Sari screaming. A door slamming and Venus flying out again, down the walk, and then gone, without a word more to anyone. Celie stared at Ava, still with no idea what to say.

It was Ava who reacted first. "Sari will think all this is her fault. I'll tend to her and try to have her ready by supper. Thank y'all for your patience."

Willi patted Hannah's hand and said, "You girls take the peas over to your mama, so she can go on and make the soup. Come on back around five-thirty to six."

Hannah sat, still frozen.

Willi said, "It'll be alright. Go on, now."

Celie had to tug Hannah up, to bring her out of her trance. She stayed silent all the way home.

Hours later, Mom was still trying to explain to Hannah the different ways mothers love their children. They'd reached the point where

Hannah was rolling her eyes, as if to say, "Why does she think I'm such a kid?" Celie winked back and began pulling chickweed from the strawberry patch, a spot where she could keep both Hannah and Willi's cabin in view.

Around 3:30, Isaac's truck arrived at Willi's with Gabe in it. Celie watched him carry a series of boxes into Willi's house. Ava came out and helped, with Sari trailing behind, carrying nothing. Celie thought Sari looked droopy and sullen, even from across the field.

Maybe she'd added that last part from her imagination. She decided to help Mom roll the dumplings for the pea soup – something practical to keep her imagination in check.

Around 5:00 on Felix the Cat's clock face (you had to guess now that the second hand had been bent sideways), Hannah tried to sneak off the back porch toward Willi's. She'd made a bad job of it since Mom caught her right away and called her back, saying the most honest thing she ever heard Mom say to her 'baby.'

"You go when you were asked for, not one minute sooner. Their mother has left them. It's the hardest thing a child could ever face. Those girls need time alone to think."

"How long do you think before she misses them and comes back … just to see them?" Hannah asked, her voice trembling. Celie reminded herself, again, why Mom babied Hannah. She was a true innocent, unable to believe that a mother could leave her own children forever.

Isaac would always worry about his kids. It was natural, but Gabe would do just fine, as would Ava, who was more grown up than any girl her age should be. When it came to Sari, well, Celie couldn't think how Isaac, or anyone, could make things right for that girl. The sound of her screams at Venus that day would stay with Celie for a long, long time. Venus had left a hole in Sari as big as a canyon.

****

At 5:30, Gabe came over, saying he needed to borrow a couple of boxes. Mon told him, "Sit and have some sweet tea. I have a pie – cherry. How they doing?"

"Sari can't stop crying," Gabe said with a sigh, collapsing, clearly glad for the chance to speak openly. "She's afraid to go anywhere at all except the front porch. Afraid Venus will come back and not be able to find her."

"And Ava?"

"You know Ava, more upset for Sari than for herself, and worried how Isaac will react."

Mom said, "Ava knows how Isaac frets because he can't keep up with the girls now that Minnie isn't here to help him."

What Mom means, Celie thought, is that Isaac's arthritis has become unbearable. He has worn out his body. She knew a doctor at Cambridge hospital who could help, but she didn't know if he would take a colored patient. If not, she'd get Daddy to drive Isaac to Baltimore. She loved this old man like a grandfather, in fact more than she had her own grandfathers. Grandpa Mowbray had died before she was born. She remembered Mom's father, Pop McBride, as a cold, hard man, gruff and impatient with his grandchildren. Young as they were when black lung disease took him, what they remembered most was his awful temper. His photograph, a permanent hallway feature, showed a man with an unmovable face and a straight, stiff body.

"A portrait that could hold up the roof single-handedly," Frank joked.

Chapter Thirteen

Voodoo (Voudon) is a West African spiritual system brought west with slaves when they came to the US. Variations involved at least 100 divinities (Voodoos) that could be asked to intervene on behalf of ordinary people. People sought help on a variety of issues — to be cured of a disease, find a job, find a spouse or have a child. Herbs could be used to cure the sick or even to poison enemies. (Laurent Dubois)

Ava sat cross-legged in the middle of Sari's bedroom, stacking books alphabetically, watching Sari try on clothes. Her mind was searching, as always, for something she might say to get her sister to connect. Anything that might cut through that bored expression, Sari's latest mask.

Voices approached from outside and Ava glanced at her watch – 5:30 – dinner time.

"We got supper," Celie called out as she rapped hard on the porch door. "A big pot of pea soup and dumplings!"

The front door latch barely worked, like everything in this place. Ava could hear Celie give the door a mighty shove. Then she and Hannah were inside, chattering like a pair of birds as they carried food to the stove to reheat. She could also hear the sound of wood being chopped and knew Gabe was out there, helping the best way he knew.

"Where's Sari?" Celie asked over her shoulder as Ava joined them in the kitchen. A thin voice floated out from the closed door of Sari's bedroom. "In here."

"We got your favorite soup," Hannah called to her. "And guess what? I helped make it." Sari opened the door a crack, grasping the edge as if she wasn't sure whether to open wider or close it back.

Hannah skipped to her and touched her hand the way she always did, working her magic, crooning, "All day *long*, I couldn't wait for *you* to taste it and tell me if I made it good enough."

A minute went by and Sari was still half in, half out. "I'm sure it's good. How could you do anything not good?"

Ava caught the misery beneath her words, but Hannah would take it as spoken, never one to doubt people's intentions. How simple life can be if you live in the here and now. Even Sari, damaged as she had been this day, had softened under the little girl's loving attention.

To Ava, the first half of the meal was melancholy rather than comforting and not just because of Sari. Everybody but Hannah acted as if under a burden. Ava had to admit her recent moodiness was part of it. It hadn't helped that every day, they all kept food coming to a kitchen that was a calamity. The plates they'd just pulled out to serve the supper were badly cracked. Celie had been making a list of some kind, no doubt planning new dishes.

Mid-way through the soup, the chair Gabe was sitting in suddenly gave way and shattered, just from the weight of his well-muscled frame. He gave a mighty laugh and they all joined in, which led to a conversation about how the world looks to them as full-grown, versus back when they were little. Then Hannah told a story about how their Irish Setter kept stealing the new kittens one at a time to clean them with her fat tongue, returning and exchanging them until the Mama cat gave up and stopped fretting over it.

Ava had winced at the theme of the story – mothering. Thankfully it seemed that Sari hadn't noticed. Sari was actually smiling by the end of the meal. Afterward, Gabe moved the furniture around in Sari's room to give her more space while Ava and Celie cleaned up, tossing at least half the dishes into the trash.

One of the many ways she and Celie were alike — they were more comfortable with clean-up than cooking, both able to find peace in putting things back in order. Hannah and Sari had disappeared outside until Sari poked her head in to say, "Hurry up, you two. Gabe's got a fire and I got a game for us. Soon as the fire's going good."

Ava was relieved about the campfire, their favorite way to spend evenings for as long as they'd known each other. It should mellow out even Sari. When they were younger, they'd pretended to be settlers, or Indians, or explorers. As they got older, they told stories. Celie was the best of the storytellers, Gabe wasn't so bad when he had the time to relax and enjoy himself. Sari could tell amusing tales, but they always had a dark message. She knew Celie worried that Hannah could be disturbed by Sari's taste for the macabre.

By the time she and Celie got outside, Gabe had the fire at a steady burn. She was happy to stare at it for a while, and Celie had the same idea. They watched the flames lick the air and listened to the pops and crackles that burst from the long crevices in the cracks of the logs. In the meantime, Sari and Hannah were all giggles from the game they were playing. A silly game, as it turned out, but one that perfectly fit the lightened mood that had taken hold of the evening. Ava tried to remember the last time she'd heard Sari laugh that way and couldn't.

"What's this game of yours?" Celie called over to them, obviously charmed by their laughter.

"Fortune telling." Sari answered mysteriously. Ava bristled at the tone, not at all deceived by its apparent playfulness. She'd heard it a thousand times from Venus when she was using what she called her 'special magic.' Sari was lightning-quick to pick up the effect of her tone on Ava and she rushed to soften it. "Some girls in town taught it to me."

"What girls in town?" Ava was still suspicious.

"Outside the library at that little playground. They saw me on the swings and asked me if I wanted to learn."

Ava told herself to stop being so skeptical of every word out of Sari's mouth.

"This foldy thing is called a cootie catcher," Sari explained. "You write fortunes on the flaps. See M.A.S.H. here at the top? That's the first category: what kind of house you'll have when you grow up, Mansion, Apartment, Shack, House. Every flap is a category."

"Such as?"

"The boy we'll marry. Next one, the number of kids you'll have. Then, the kind of job your husband will have, and this one is — uh –"

Hannah jumped in. "The kind of car you'll drive."

"I know the categories are pretty stupid," Sari said. Again, that sly smile. "We could change them. We could predict the year we'll die, or something like that." An owl screeched right as she finished the word 'die,' and Ava couldn't withhold a shudder. Sari seemed determined to add an element of fear to the game.

Ava said, "Lighten up, Sari. Let's just keep the categories the way they are and have some fun. Any other rules?"

Hannah was dancing with excitement. "Yes, we left out the best part. Each answer has four choices — three good ones – and a fourth one you'd hate to come true; else it would be too boring."

They'd played the game for almost two hours, first writing fortunes for each other and then for everybody they knew, giggling like when they were little. Gabe smiled benevolently but declined to join in, instead sitting with his book under the porch light, attracting mosquitos and slapping at them when they bit through his shirt. It would never occur to him to go inside and read when he could sit under the stars with people he loved.

"Stir up the fire Gabe, so we can do one more round," Sari ordered while Hannah yawned loudly.

"I'm afraid it's time to get Hannah home," Celie said. "She's asleep on her feet."

"Now you're the one who needs to lighten up," Hannah declared, opening her eyes as wide as she could. "We might not be together like this for ages. Maybe not 'til Thanksgiving."

Ava realized that Hannah must feel lonely, by herself with her parents in the big house. She thought of a way to make them both happy. "How about one more round, free style, only we just say the questions. Writing them takes too long."

"I'll start," Hannah said. "The beginning part is, "I want to marry a man who – and then you finish with your answer. You first, Ava."

Ava was surprised how quickly an answer came to mind. "A man I can respect and look up to."

"Like Isaac, you mean?" Celie teased, and they all screamed with laughter, even Gabe, who couldn't help but pay attention to that.

Ava said, "OK, I'll add a qualification – a man who's also my own age. I can't imagine Isaac ever being young and attractive, but Minnie must have thought so once. OK, next is Celie."

"Someone who loves animals, definitely. A man who takes care of others. Maybe a veterinarian or … a doctor would be OK."

"Why not a farmer?" Ava knew that Celie had a wild crush on a farmer's son down the road.

Celie gave her a friendly shove. "Troublemaker. Well then, he'd have to give it up and become a veterinarian. Sari's turn."

Sari's mood had inexplicably darkened. "Why marry anybody? I'll play the field."

Hannah pressed. "That's not a fair answer. You *have* to pick somebody."

"Ok, then. I'll pick … a man who's rich. Filthy rich. Rich enough to buy anything and anybody I want, no matter what it takes. My ideal fortune would be … well, a fortune."

A curtain of menace, almost physical, dropped over them. Ava could sense they all felt it. Sari's pessimism, her contempt for what was ordinary, her outlook so hardened at the age of fourteen.

Ava stood, ready to douse the fire as soon as Sari finished her sentence, when Sari's attitude shifted again. "I always used to … I hated going back to Florida, didn't you Ava?

"Uh-huh," Ava said, feeling tentative. "I hated leaving Celie. Not just that, I hated leaving the feeling of being safe here."

Sari said, "I used to fantasize that Isaac would let me and Ava stay with your family, Hannah. Maybe not in the main house but in the back carriage house, while Venus was away — until Venus … until …. " She stopped. Even the crickets seemed to stop and wait for Sari to finish the sentence.

What can I say to her? Ava wondered. That each time Venus goes off, the time gap before she returns will surely grow longer? That I am sick of making up excuses Sari might believe? Or that I feel relieved that Isaac asked for help from Willi to help raise her?

Before she could say anything, Gabe spoke up, maybe thinking he was being fatherly. "Being here with Willi has been a blessing, Sari. You have to get over Venus, like Ava has. You can get real schooling here, and it's good for Willi too; she needs a helper around. You should appreciate how your being here is good news … for all of us."

Ava wanted to kill him. How in God's name could a mother abandoning her children possibly be seen as good news? Gabe always had to pretend there was a silver lining in everything. On top of that, she was deeply skeptical of what was in Willi's heart, and she hated the scornful way she talked to people. Why couldn't he see that?

Celie jumped in with the intention of leading them down a side path of distraction, a move that was pure Celie. She said, "I just wish that Ava and Sari would come to my school."

"Celie, *stop!*" Hannah scolded, always ready to collude with her sister in a distraction. "You know Ava can't go to a white school.

How could you forget a thing like that?"

Celie reddened, but not with humiliation ... with fury. "I haven't forgotten anything. And just why can't she? Is there some kind of law?" Her tone was indignant.

"Of course there's a law." Hannah answered.

"And what is that law, exactly?" Celie pressed.

Hannah backtracked. "OK, so maybe it's just ... what people want. You know what I mean. There are boys' schools and girls' schools. Catholic schools. People go to schools for their own groups."

Gabe's face was hard to fathom. Ava expected he'd say some pie-in-the-sky thing, but he shocked her. "I'm not so sure about that."

"About what?" Ava asked, appalled. "Not sure there are different schools for different groups?"

"I'm not sure there's a *law*. Celie may be right. I'll look into it. Meantime, no use for us to fuss at each other about this. None of us ever made any law like that."

"What difference does it make? Law or not, Sari and I can't go to a damn white school!" Ava snapped.

She hadn't meant to let her temper escape like that. She stood and brushed bits of grass from her clothes, as if to dismiss both her mood and the conversation.

"I bet you could," Celie insisted.

Ava was exasperated. It was time to get everyone back where they belonged. She said, "Maybe I could, maybe not, but I agree with Gabe about one thing. No use arguing. Time for bed."

But Gabe was now the one riled up. "You all playing a game with your futures and all you can think of is husbands, cars, stupid stuff. Why don't you set your heart on things that matter?"

Ava rallied. "Like what?" Gabe's acting smug and superior thoroughly pissed her off. "The job you do and what you get paid, matters. Having children matters. What else should we have put that's important enough for you, Gabe? Name of the college you wish you could go to if you weren't black? You're the one who's never happy with what you got."

"Let me just tell you about that," he said, his voice strong with emotion. "Isaac tried to bring me up as a man like him. He taught me well, but it was something different than what he thought he was teaching. He made me want to be the best I can be. So, every time I look up ahead, I see something higher – next time I look, I see something higher than that. As long as I see there's more ahead, I'll keep reaching. Why not reach for a better school than the one I got?"

"What do you do when there's nothing any higher?" Sari asked, in a voice so earnest it was almost shocking. A voice Ava hadn't heard in years. When she looked at Sari, she saw eyes that had picked up the last of the firelight and glistened with tears.

Gabe said, "I'm not sure yet. The things I have now — used to be I couldn't even dream of them. Then one day I had them. You don't have to know everything ahead of you to keep aiming for it. Just look at the women who raised me. Minnie, Hattie, Aunt Evelyn. Good women. They say prayers every day their whole lives and what do they pray for?"

Ava said, "I don't know. For mercy, I guess."

"Forgiveness?" Celie suggested.

Gabe smiled at Celie. "We sure can tell which of us was raised Catholic. No, and not yours either, Ava."

"For God," Sari said.

"Close. They pray to be in heaven. With all their hearts they beg for it, and not a one of them there has ever seen heaven, I promise you."

Gabe turned and took Hannah by the hand to walk her home. Sari stretched out in front of Willi's new television and was immediately asleep. Celie pointed to the kitchen, nodding at Ava, "Let's finish it. We'll have it sparkling by the time Willi gets home."

They sorted out the few unbroken plates and bowls and stacked them in Willi's cupboard. They scrubbed the cupboards and shined the chrome on the small appliances. The kitchen looked almost well-ordered.

"How did Willi let things get this bad?" Celie asked.

"I reckon she's just old." Ava had stopped counting how many piles of unsorted junk there were throughout the cabin.

"For a woman who cleans other people's houses, hers couldn't be much worse."

Ava cringed. "Just because it's the only way she can earn a living doesn't mean she has any kind of values about cleanliness, Celie. It's just work for her, not a lifestyle. Besides, the last thing she wants to do when she gets home is to keep cleaning."

Celie almost dropped the wet plate she was holding. "Wow. How stupid of me. I never looked at it that way." She was blushing, having once again tried to bear fault for the world's bigotry. As if in not catching every little nuance of prejudice, she was guilty for the way things were. Ava thought about saying something to let her off the hook, but why should she? She was tired of saying things to make white people feel better.

Celie was still fumbling for words. "Well. All I mean is do you think Sari's all right here? Willi's got some problems and I wonder if she puts too much work on Sari. I don't know how else to put it."

Ava was stunned for a second. Nothing like being hit back with the weapon you just laid on the table. She said, "With her living in a pigsty you mean? Don't mince words now."

"That's not at all what I mean. I was thinking that the main reason Willi took her in was to have her do most of the housekeeping. Are you OK with that?"

Ava nodded, chastened, but Celie wasn't done. She said, "I know what I was hoping, and it was that Willi would be more maternal. Isn't that what Isaac had in mind?"

"Not necessarily. Isaac usually knows what he's doing. If Willi had tried to mother Sari, she'd have bolted out of here in a heartbeat. Sari wants privacy and a safe haven. That whole mother thing – when it comes to Sari, there's no use to try and figure it out."

"Not that much to figure. She wants her own mother, not a substitute."

"Yes. She has her very own mother, doesn't she?" Ava said, trying to keep the sarcasm out of her voice. "Just because Venus isn't visible doesn't mean she doesn't influence every move Sari makes. Sari is the one child that Venus might have wanted, and she does love her in some twisted way. They used to find a way to connect with each other."

"Sari was happy then, with Venus around. Do you think she can ever be happy here? Or will she spend all her time waiting for her mother?"

Ava was slow in answering. "I think she's mixed up. I think she's feeling lost without Venus. My hope is she'll get excited about school again and get settled into some kind of groove with Willi. I made Willi promise to make sure she gets on that bus every single day and I made Isaac promise to keep after Willi. Maybe with structure, attention by the teachers and … you know, normal school ideas … her thinking will straighten out … away from that mystical mumbo-jumbo Venus used to feed her."

****

Willi was almost back to her cabin after a killing work day. She had stepped on a tennis ball when cleaning the Wilkins's poolside. Damn kids, leaving their crap everywhere. She should give that woman a piece of her mind about what is and isn't cleaning. But she wouldn't. It could cost the job. Everybody wanted these rich people jobs lately. Besides, she'd have been limping anyway, tennis balls or not, with her bones all hurting steady, day and night.

She wasn't sure how she felt about Sari being in the bedroom where her own darlings once slept. She sure did miss her own sweet girls. It pained her to even think their names, they both across oceans with their husbands, one in Japan, one in Germany. Too far away to get to hug her Grandbabies. God knows how old they'd be before she ever saw them.

She had hoped Sari would be a comfort because she could sure use a comfort. Especially without a husband's good earnings. She could soon give her some of the jobs with the spoiled kids dropping shit everywhere and dogs running after damn tennis balls.

The cabin was pitch black. The girl would be asleep. She heard breathing from the living room and could just make out a shape on the couch. The older girl, curled up asleep, worrying about her sister for one night before going back to her own life. Maybe she'd seen what Willi had, that Sari was a becoming a little 'touched.' Venus's crazy magic had done something to her. She hoped she hadn't made a mistake and taken the wrong girl after all. Sari was quiet and pretty, whereas Ava was all mouth – she must be eighteen now, and with an even bigger mouth — while Sari was still quiet, but with a hard edge to her prettiness

Lordy, she didn't want to have to deal with that big mouth tonight. Just pick up her feet and tiptoe past the couch – never coulda' took them both, fussing, making all kind of noise. Even her own sweet girls had drove her crazy like that. Truth was, she wanted quiet even more than she wanted help.

Just take a quick look at her ... looks small and alone in that big bed. No sign of strangeness in the sleeping face now. Looked like a lamb, didn't she? And a mighty fine little worker. Throwing herself into any task, like it was all she ever wanted to do her whole life. She was glad for the help of a decent worker, now her arthritis had got so bad. Even if the girl was a little touched.

Sari rolled over in her sleep, then settled. Yes indeed, a pretty little thing. Oh, Lordy, she'd meant to ask Ava to start teaching the girl to cook.

Chapter Fourteen

Tidal marshlands are subject to flooding by brackish saltwater. These soils are quick to form swamps and except for small parcels, are not suitable for farming. Nearly 95 percent of tidal marshes are subject to salt water encroachment. (U.S. Department of Agriculture)

As the summer of 1960 ended, Celie was glad school would be starting soon. All the time she'd been with Ava, doing chores next to Ava, last night and this morning, she'd longed to talk about her problem, but Hannah kept hanging around and Celie didn't have the heart to send her away.

Mom's pots were all in their right places. Celie picked a subject she knew was worrying Ava. "Funny how two sisters can be so different. I don't mean you and Sari, I mean Venus and Minnie. Minnie was a true angel and Venus..."

"You can say it. My mother is a devil," Ava said matter-of-factly. "But you of all people should understand that. Look at Frank compared to, well, compared to all the rest of your family."

Hannah said, "I think he actually *likes* to be in trouble. It's the only explanation."

"You just say that because you'd rather eat ground glass than get in trouble." Ava said, laughing.

"If there's no trouble, people like that don't feel anything at all." Celie was remembering the electric chair incident in a way she could only describe as illuminating. She was able to appreciate this side of Frank, maybe because she'd won a few skirmishes. Sometimes she even liked him for his cleverness, but despite her admiration for his bravado, the kind of boys she dated were the opposite. Squeaky clean and sweet as strawberry jam, boys Ava had dubbed "terminally innocent."

Ava said, "Can you imagine what it must be like for girls who fall for Frank?"

"No thanks," Hannah said.

Celie said, "In one of my classes there's that thing about nature versus nurture."

"What – you mean like the bad seed? I don't believe in that."

Ava said, "Of course you don't, Hannah. You and Celie believe love heals everything."

"I don't really," Celie said. "My brother is the way he is because it's the way he *always* was, not because of anything anyone did to him."

"I think that about Venus too. For some reason, she treated me and Sari totally different. I worried she'd ruined her. I'm still hoping Sari can change."

"I hope so, but Frank won't. I love my brother, but I'd never go out with a boy like him. He's such a liar."

Ava laughed. "Honey, if you want truth, I'm afraid that leaves all boys out. Even the babes-in-the-woods boys you like. You gotta pick out the ones that lie a *little* less than the others."

Celie knew Ava wasn't joking. "What about Gabe? You think he's honest. Don't pretend you don't."

"That's because we're friends, not lovers." Ava's voice was bland and impersonal and yet Celie flashed bright red with embarrassment. The feeling was so strong and unexpected it took her breath away. Here Ava was talking about sex, and she was thinking about Gabe.

Thinking of him this way was the main reason she was in such a hurry to get the summer over with. Something had changed between them, something very confusing.

It had started a few weeks ago when Isaac announced his retirement and Mom broke tradition — permanently it seemed. That part was lovely. She invited Isaac and his family for a little celebration of his moving to Maryland. They were all nervous, none of them really comfortable in the living room, even Mom. Gabe fiddling with his collar, Ava tapping her foot, Celie pacing. Mom kept running back and forth with trays of tea and cookies and the tiniest sandwiches Celie had ever seen. Since when had Mom started making tea sandwiches?

Isaac was the only one who'd looked normal. Sitting in the decal-covered rocker, he'd looked more comfortable in it than even her Grandmother had in the days when she'd lived in it. Isaac brushed cookie crumbs from his shirt into his hand and dumped them into a neat pile on his napkin.

"My folks all wanting to settle in one place, now. I've decided, time to catch up," he explained as if the whole thing was his idea. "Minnie came to me in a dream and said she don't mind I settle down, long as I keep an eye on all the young'uns."

Ava had said, "Play something." Celie was flabbergasted when she realized she was asking Gabe, not Mom, to play. Gabe had looked at Mom with a raised eyebrow, and she had nodded back an enthusiastic yes.

Isaac said, "that'd be nice."

Did everybody but Celie know that Gabe played piano? He slid along the piano bench, settling his feet on the pedals, and began touching the keys, skimming his fingers along like they were dancing. He punched out two tunes, short and quick, as if they were just a re-hearsal. With the third song, a Rachmaninoff piece that Mom loved, Celie knew it was the 'real' piece. She watched as Gabe disappeared into that space where you go if you're good enough at something to become one with it.

Everyone applauded with delight. Celie said, "Wow! I can't be-lieve it. How in the world could you possibly have learned that?"

"What? To play a white man's instrument? Ever heard of *Jazz*?"

"I ...I didn't mean it like that!" Celie could feel her face blaz-ing. Isaac frowned and started to stand. Ava, visibly mortified, said, "Gabe! Why are you being so rude? She didn't mean anything close to that and you know it. It was a compliment. She was honoring you, not insulting you."

The fact that Ava took up for her had smoothed things over for the moment, but Celie stayed miserable for days after, her emotions ranging from elation to despair. She kept picturing Gabe in profile at the piano. Then, at last night's campfire, when he'd sat off by himself reading, she'd nearly gone crazy. Aware of every single word and every move he made, she'd had no idea what she wanted from him, and today was no different.

For some reason, picturing him at all made her miserable with her own image. She found herself changing clothes three or four times a day. With school starting tomorrow, and Gabe gone to Mace's Lane, she hoped things would go back to how they used to be.

****

"You taking the bus to school tomorrow?" Mom called up to Celie. It was the third week of school and Celie had yet to regain her social bearings.

"OK if I drive? I have cheerleading practice. Jane and Donna asked me to meet them for a hamburger afterward at Moxie's, if that's OK."

"What about me?" said a plaintive voice in the hallway. Hannah was thirteen, but she could be as pouty now as when she'd been six.

"Mom!" Celie said it like a pronouncement, then waited for Mom to do the right thing. This year she was determined that some of her friendships would stay hers alone, separate from a little sister who'd become very clever at worming her way into any party or sleep-over Celie ever tried to have.

"I have a right to go to Moxie's if I want," Hannah said.

"Mo-omm!" Celie added the extra syllable to let Mom know she was exasperated.

"Calm down, Celie. Hannah – do you have a ride home from there?"

"Sure. I got a sister with a car," Hannah said, trying to be funny, her face a roadmap of defiance. Celie felt elated and tried not to let it show. Nothing got Mom's goat more than one of them taking her consent for granted. Celie tried to look innocent as she waited for Mom's reaction.

"Well if a bomb blows up the bus," Mom began, "it's good to know you'll have a back-up. But, since your sister has already made her plans, you'll need to ride home on the bus and take your chances you'll get home safe."

Celie gave them both a quick kiss and was able to get out before the fireworks started. "Remind me never to have kids," she said to herself for about the fifth time that week. She spent the next hour scripting a dialogue with her best friends. She had to try it out and the last person she wanted to hear was Hannah.

She'd say, "Would you ever go out with a Negro?"

No. She'd say, "Would you ever date a black guy?"

No, she wouldn't say that either. In fact, she couldn't find any words that didn't sound awkward. Better to wait until it came up in conversation.

Which of course it never would. In the early 1960's, the great racial divide between blacks and whites had grown worse in Dorchester County than anywhere else in the state.

****

Celie slept in the next Saturday morning, cozy under a plush blanket and her two favorite cats. The first month of school was always exhausting. By the time she meandered into the kitchen, Mom, Daddy and Hannah were all sitting there like statues, Daddy's face somber, Hannah's head buried in her hands, Mom sitting serenely, hands in her lap.

"Hello ... all of you. Is this some kind of intervention? Did I do something?"

"Celie, it's something serious," Hannah said. A sob came out on the last syllable and then she was bawling.

"There was a car accident after the game last night," Mom said.

Celie's mind raced, wondering who. "Who, for God's sake?"

"It's the Nickerson boys."

Todd Nickerson had been a good friend, since birth, practically. He was the oldest of four boys who were boisterously in love with rural life. She'd gone out with Todd a few times, enough for him to share his dreams for the future. He had a scholarship next year to the University of Maryland, and then he planned a revolution, a modernization of his family's enterprise, Stillwater Farms.

Please, God, don't let Todd be the one hurt.

She put her hand in Daddy's, as ready as she could be to face it. "Which boys?"

Daddy put his arm around her and around Hannah, who was still bawling, and said, "All of them. They were coming home from the game last night, and it was – they were hit by Rodney Elkridge. Rodney was drinking. He crossed over route 50 into their lane. All four brothers and their friend Ralph – he'd hitched a ride – they were all killed instantly.

Another senseless tragedy killing off kids. She had learned to brace against the news of children taken by the dangers of farming and fishing, but for some reason she still found it impossible to grapple with tragedies that happened when people were supposed to be having fun.

She didn't even ask about Rodney. She didn't care. No, worse – she hoped he was dead – an instant, childish reaction because her brain refused to accept what had happened, right? But hours later, she still couldn't take the high road, and weeks later, she still resented his being alive. She and Rodney finally had something in common. They would both spend the rest of their lives wishing that he'd died in the wreck that killed his friends.

January 1961

Celie's work-study assignment at Cambridge Hospital was to prepare and distribute career day orientation booklets. She didn't have to stay for the whole event. She did the work half-heartedly, still too gloomy about the Nickersons to think in terms of career futures, especially her own.

The recruiters were late. A radiator malfunction had stalled their bus and Celie was asked to stay and make sure they got situated. With time on her hands, she filled out the questionnaire needed for the interviews and penciled her name into time slots.

The cafeteria filled with doctors and nurses, crisp and white, sitting at tables loaded with brochures and health care propaganda. She could have gone home, but they looked so eager that she decided to complete her scheduled interviews.

"So then, what might attract you to a career in nursing, Miss Mowbray?" asked a nurse-recruiter.

Sizing up the woman's starched cap and stiff shoulders, Celie decided to talk about efficiency. And then, inexplicably, she didn't.

"I'm in a nursing prep program already. I like it, but regular nursing doesn't seem like it'll be enough. I don't know a solution, yet. To me, serious healing starts after the body forms scars — even after the patient is home. What good a nurse could do about this kind of healing, I don't know yet. I know it can't start until you can count *all* the battle wounds in front of you."

The nurse sat up, her face shifting in surprise. "Your family is military, then?"

It was Celie's turn to be surprised. The nurse's face had opened a little, into a smile. Celie smiled back and said, "No, not that kind of war. I grew up here. Farms and rivers were the battlegrounds I experienced. Kids getting hurt going about their ordinary lives."

The nurse cocked her head and put down her pencil. "Yes," she said, her voice now warm and almost collegial. "How very insightful of you. I've often felt that way too, given how many young people never make it through high school on this side of The Bay. One thinks of the tidal basin as being a place of tranquil beauty, but it's a hard life when you make your living with nature as your partner."

Celie felt like she was outside herself looking down. She heard herself say, "It's not just the work that kills them, don't you see? It's the way they play, too. Car crashes, boat accidents, stupid stuff. I sometimes think the boys around here would be safer in a foreign war, instead of staying home where they can drink and drag race and dive into rivers."

The nurse picked up her pencil and reset her face. "Have you given any thought to a specialty? Maybe community or emergency medicine, for example?"

"I'm not familiar with those fields. "

"Well, Emergency Medicine .... After the *Korean Conflict*, we founded concepts like *triage* – you may have heard it. It puts professionals other than doctors right on the front lines. Community Medicine brings help home from the hospital with the patient."

"They both sound fascinating."

"Think about it. Come see me when you begin your training. I'll be interested in what you decide."

But Celie didn't need to think about it. Community nursing. The decision had been brewing for years. Becky's drowning, then Dale's. Other kids, too young, cooking and caring for livestock while their parents were out plowing or fishing to earn a subsistence living. Kids who ran in front of their fathers' tractors or fell off the beds of pick-up trucks, just not knowing any better.

Todd's loss had smashed the lives of a dear family. God knows if those parents would ever recover. But because of Todd, something in her self-awareness had shifted. A door left open, and if she walked through it, she might make a difference in how people took care of themselves day to day. She couldn't wait to get started.

****

"It's a career search internship to see if I would like community nursing," Celie explained to Ava as she climbed behind the wheel of the Ford. "We're going to a farm."

They were on their way to Toddville in the lower part of the county, once a thriving farming and fishing community. It wasn't any kind of farmland Ava recognized. The land was too saline for crops, and yet interspersed between cordgrass marshes and salt ponds, were fields that must have been there for hundreds of years. It was as if the bay and the freshwater rivers were engaged in a death struggle over the land.

"When their tomatoes and cantaloupes failed, the last few farmers planted soybeans, then, as you can see, corn," Celie said.

"Which seems to be failing too," Ava answered. There were underdeveloped corn stalks everywhere, standing knee-deep in small ponds filled with blue-green algae, salt grass, and ducks. Oak trees had given way to loblolly pines. A handful of white cedar stumps stood as markers where farmed uplands had lost the battle to the advancing marshes.

Ava asked, "So tell me about this community nursing idea. Is that where you go around giving shots to kids, so they can go to school?"

"No, that's the public health nurse. I don't know exactly what I would do yet. It's a career program, where we go to find out. Don't you have something like it at Mace's Lane?"

"Sure, Celie. They take us to rich women's houses and see if we'd rather scrub their floors or watch their kids." Ava crossed her arms and slouched down, unable to look in Celie's direction.

For some minutes, they rode in tense silence. Ava could feel Celie's eyes burning a hole through the side of her skull and after a few minutes more, she swallowed her pride. "I'm sorry for the sarcasm. We don't have much beyond the basics at Mace's Lane, but it's certainly not your fault."

She turned to see if Celie was OK and was surprised to see tears on her cheeks. She felt just awful. Well, of course she'd made her cry. Why did she keep forgetting Celie's enormous capacity for suffering? Her willingness to seize people's troubles and wear them like a coat? What were those Catholic priests thinking, when they laid their shit on girls like Celie?

"In a way, I think it *is* my fault." Celie was already in the middle of a long apology. "I take so much for granted. I can't believe I forgot how different it is for you and Gabe."

Ava heaved a dramatic sigh and patted Celie's hand lightly, mindful of the gearshift Celie was holding. "For God's sake, Celie, everything in the world isn't your fault. Why should you feel responsible that the Board of Education can't ever seem to find any money for us? I get so mad sometimes, it's like I'm mad at everybody, but it's *not* your fault."

"I wish I could help. I just don't know what ...."

"Look, I'm truly sorry for the sarcasm. Someday you'll find a way, or I'll find one for you. For now, just go on being Celie."

Celie's face relaxed but a telltale furrow remained above her eyebrows. Ava had known that look for half her lifetime. She'd wounded her friend. She was caught in a conundrum, deeply sorry, but at the same time, still annoyed at the lack of parity between their schools. She'd made it into an emotional dilemma between them, which wouldn't help anything. Once again, she needed to move on and fret about it later.

They had reached a cabin in the middle of several scattered acres of barely tillable soil. Dead cornstalks lay flat, their roots buried in saline ground water. A tiny rowboat was stuck forever in one of the ponds.

"Who lives here?" Ava asked.

"A widow with four children. The woman was arrested for nonpayment of taxes and couldn't afford to raise the two hundred dollars bail money. She asked to have somebody check to see where her kids were taken, since no one seemed to know. Social services hasn't had time to follow up, so they sent it over to us candy stripers as a practicum."

Soggy mud was sucking at the car's tires. "I'm afraid to drive in this," Celie said and stopped the car half a mile from the house.

"We can get there if we walk up that little hill," Ava said, pointing past the barbed-wire fence.

They picked their way through patches of salt grass and got to the front "gate," a scraggy affair to which a cardboard sign had been nailed. It announced, "Auction of Premises."

Celie said," This is dated three days ago."

"Aww. Looks like they've lost their home completely."

"A lot of that going around lately."

"Do we have to go all the way inside?" Ava was trying not to sound as if she hoped the answer was 'no.'

"That's the assignment, to check out the house for a note or any sign of where they took the kids."

They had to hopscotch through the sand and grass and approach the house from behind. As they rounded the corner to face the front of the tiny cabin, Ava was shocked to see Celie suddenly sprint forward and throw herself on the front porch. When Celie sat back up, she was holding the hands of three filthy, crying toddlers who must have been sitting on the cabin steps. There was no adult in sight.

"What's your name, sweetie," Celie was asking the biggest child. "Can you tell me what's happened?"

"Name is Ruth. Bogey Man came and took Mama."

Ava and Celie exchanged a glance over Ruth's tiny blond head.

"Baby be screamin', when Bogey Man take it offa' Mama and give it over to Carol Ann and me. Then Mama gone."

"He ain't been back since," added the smallest of the toddlers, a little boy not much higher than Ava's knee.

"What did he think would happen to the kids?" Ava whispered to Celie. "And then somebody came here to put up that notice, what, three days ago? They could hardly miss the presence of three little children."

Celie was rifling through her day-bag, and crooning, "Come on over here, darlin.' I got something to eat." In a louder voice she answered Ava, "I don't know. As to the sheriff, I'd say he didn't much care what happened to them. His job was to arrest the mother for whatever financial crimes destitute women with small children commit."

"But this is a *white* family."

"I can see that, Ava. Hand me that bucket please, or better still, bring it to me full of water."

When Ava returned with the water and a handful of nearly clean rags, she said, "I'd assume that if they found a white woman on hard times, they would help her out. Or if they couldn't be bothered directly, at least call county services, or a neighbor. How could this have happened? How could they just leave these kids here to wait for their mother to come home?"

Celie had begun to wipe the children's hands and faces with wet rags. She asked Ava to go back inside and look for any sign of food, and maybe some clean clothes. Ava could hear Celie talking to them as she searched the kitchen for food, and for clues as to how long since their mother had been taken.

"Ruth ... do they call you Ruthie? Ruthie, how long has it been since the Bogey Man was here?"

"Cain't say."

"Twenty suppers," piped up the other girl in a surprisingly strong voice. Carol Ann, wasn't it? A pint size version of her big sister, both of them with masses of soft yellow curls.

"Nuh-uh, more," Ruthie said. "Don't you 'member? We jes' stop *countin'* on twenty."

Ava had finished poking around in the kitchen and she called to Celie," I think it's more like a month. There's a grocery receipt here with a date of four weeks ago. Probably the last time their Mom bought –"

She stopped herself, realizing her speculation would upset even kids that little.

There wasn't a scrap of food anywhere. She filled another pitcher with fresh water and took it out to them. Celie was scooping water with her hands and dribbling it on their tongues a little at a time. Next, she took a Clark Bar and a peanut butter sandwich from her bag, breaking off pieces the size of a dime.

"In just a minute, I want you to eat this real slow. Little bites. Like this."

"Like this?" the boy asked, taking a tiny piece of bread and looking up at Celie with earnest brown eyes. Ava noticed the boy had different looks from the others, olive skin and jet-black hair. A different father, she thought automatically.

The kids were heartbreakingly obedient, nibbling the food fragments, their eyes on Celie for approval that they were doing it right.

Celie said, "Ruthie says they had dandelions for breakfast. They've eaten every living thing they could find, including grass."

After they ate, Celie asked them in a gentle voice that Ava had never heard her use before, "So where's the baby now?"

Ava shuddered violently, shocked at herself. *A widow and her four kids.* How could Ava have forgotten there was also a baby?

"Sleeping." All three kids had answered at the same time, using the exact same voice intonation. They had rehearsed their answer. That meant — another chill ran up Ava's back and she saw Celie's face wash over with anguish.

Celie stood up slowly, still holding Ruthie's hand. "Sleeping where?"

Or at least she'd started to ask it, but the words got caught in her throat and it was Ava who finished the question. "Where, darlin?"

Ruthie and Carol Ann pointed inside the cabin, but the boy shoved his hands tight against his ears.

"In the other room?' Celie asked.

"Yep. In Mama bedroom. Where she sleep with that baby."

Celie left the children and walked to the back of the house to a tightly closed door. She had one hand on the doorknob, the other over her nose and mouth, when the little boy screamed, "Don't! We cain't wake the baby! Mama said! No, no, NO!" and he collapsed, choking with sobs.

Celie ran back to comfort him. "It'll be Ok, Jack, shhh!" By then, Carol Ann and Ruthie were wailing too, and Celie's lap was again full of filthy, bawling children. Celie kept wiping grime from their faces as she tried to calm them.

Ava took a huge breath. It was up to her to go into that room to look. She had never been so terrified.

Before she even got to the door, she picked up the putrid smell that must have stopped Celie. As she eased the door open, the stench mushroomed — the most horrific smell of her life. She would never forget it. She spotted the cradle right away.

She went back to the kitchen and soaked a large rag. A mask for her face to let her get close enough to that cradle to look inside. She held her breath, tied on the mask, and eased the door open.

The walls inside were decorated with thousands of tiny flowers, seemingly drawn by hand. There were two small windows bearing lace curtains, filthy, but finely woven and also sewed by hand. A bright morning light shot into the center of the room. An unthinkable setting for what lay ahead, Ava thought, and inched forward.

The inside of the cradle was still and silent. An empty baby bottle lay at its bottom. Two glasses of water, still full, sat upright by the baby's head, as if that close, the water might somehow end up in her mouth. Most heartbreaking of all was a paper straw, taped to the baby's cheek.

High above the baby's body, on the hood of the cradle, the children had dangled bits of colored paper, attached to the hood with scotch tape, paper clips, anything that would stick, a way of distracting the baby as they ran out of ways to ease her crying.

Ava somehow found the strength to look at the still, gray face but she didn't remember what she did after — or maybe Celie had done everything after that point. She remembered thinking, hoping, the baby had died quickly. She also remembered that she couldn't stop shaking as she went to get Celie. Later, she'd be ashamed that she hadn't been able to bring herself to touch the little body to feel for breathing, that even though Celie had her hands full with the three older children, the living children, she'd said, "Celie. You have to go check. I just can't touch her."

Then she was sitting on the kitchen floor, shivering, her arms wrapped around her knees, waiting for Celie to verify the baby's death — *signs of life*. Asking herself, how could this happen? over and over, until she felt her return to sanity. The most important thing, she realized, was doing something useful for the surviving children. They must need so much, physically, emotionally. And still she sat, waiting for Celie.

Celie had crossed herself before going inside. When she came out, she crossed herself again as she headed toward Ava, saying, "We'll need to call that Sheriff. The Bogey Man. I wish to God there was someone else to call, since he's the one who created this horror."

Ava was amazed at how composed Celie sounded, and she was determined to be more helpful. She had an idea. "There is something else we could do. We could call the County Coroner. Do you know who it is?"

"Sure. It's my uncle. Dr. Hastings."

"You don't mean the horse doctor?"

"He does both. I guess there aren't that many questionable deaths around here so it's not a full-time job. What a great idea. One of us will go get food, call the coroner, and get a real social worker out here. The other will stay here with the children. Which job do you want?"

Celie barely had the words out before smacking her palm against her forehead.

"What's the matter with me? We don't have that choice. Sorry

Ava, I wasn't thinking. I know what you'd rather do, and I wish I could spare you having to stay here, but I guess I'm the ... uh ... best one to raise alarms." She didn't say the obvious, *because I'm the only one who's white.*

Ava nodded and then tried to widen her heart to take in these miserable children. At least act with some of the warmth Celie had shown them. The least she could do while Celie arranged for the dead child was bring a bit of comfort to the ones still living. She had meant to ask Celie if she'd covered the infant's body, not that it mattered. It was some archetypal notion that had grabbed her, an urge to keep the dead covered.

While she waited, she sang all the songs she knew and told all the stories she could think of, hoping it would soothe them. As the sun waned, the kids began shivering. She nestled them against each other and wrapped them in a large, nearly-clean blanket, and held them against her on the grass, in the remaining sun. She couldn't bear to be inside that awful cabin. For God's sake, why didn't Celle come back? How much longer could it take? At least the kids were all asleep. It was nearly dark when Celie arrived with milk, cereal, and more peanut butter. Together, they fed the children until a police car with two social workers arrived and relieved them.

"I couldn't have done what you did, Celie," Ava said when they were on their way home. "When I saw those kids, I wanted to feel pity but all I felt was disgust. And that poor baby.... If I had been there alone, I doubt I would have even gone in to check. I'd have waited for the authorities."

"It's easy to criticize yourself if you ask, 'what-if.' You don't know what you might have done if you'd been alone. And hey, maybe I wouldn't have been so strong if I hadn't had you there with me. We faced it and we got through it, which is all that matters. Except, of course, that the mother's in jail somewhere and doesn't even know it yet."

"Yes, that matters, and so does holding the Bogey Man accountable. Won't somebody do that? Have him arrested or something, since she was a white baby?"

"That's the second time you said that. Why do you keep saying 'since she was a white baby?'"

"For God's sake Celie, you know why."

"Yes, I do. Do you?"

Ava looked into Celie's lovely sky-blue eyes, the eyes that always seemed as if they could see all the way through her. She felt exposed. She knew Celie couldn't read her mind, but for that moment, Celie had seen something ugly in her and it had surprised them both. Celie had seen the beginnings of something Ava had been feeling for months now. Anger that had been growing, and maybe the beginnings of her own racism.

Chapter Fifteen

Every black teenager in Dorchester County attended Mace's Lane, an underfunded and understaffed all-black high school in the heart of Cambridge. (Levy, *Civil*)

Gabe had loved Mace's Lane even before the first day. He loved the idea of it. Learning was a journey that could take him anywhere he wanted to go. He had a passion for geography that was often directed toward places he'd never been. That day Jesse had found him sleeping under the skipjack, Gabe had been scheming to hitch a ride that would take him away from where he was, from here to – anywhere.

He was voracious in his consumption of maps and travel books. While he was a generous book-lender, he didn't lend out his travel books. These, he kept hidden. Likewise, he kept his knowledge of exotic places entirely private. He knew he should share his ideas with his classmates who, like him, dreamed of faraway places; but he couldn't, not even with Ava. It was as if saying his dreams out loud would weaken his chances of ever reaching them.

Besides, as a boy who'd had practically nothing he could call his own, he now owned the whole world. Egypt, Africa, the Galapagos. He wasn't sure he wanted to go to places like Germany or Austria, but even so, they were his for the taking. He'd lie awake at night and imagine the way the Aegean Sea looked, how it differed from the Nile or the Dead Sea.

There'd been a library book once, called *Animals of the Galapagos.* He memorized the names of the animals Darwin discovered there, keeping the book hidden under his mattress, even though everyone knew he had it.

The irony was that he longed to have someone to talk to about things he couldn't master on his own, like evolution and Mendelian genetics, but that would have meant sharing his dreams. He stubbornly stayed his own worst enemy, bottling up his questions, unanswered, and keeping himself captive to his own stinginess. He never felt greedy in any other way, and he hoped he'd change someday; but if he didn't, well ... then he didn't.

Most days Gabe went straight from ball practice to his job at Tate's Emporium. Isaac had insisted Gabe find a place to stay in town. "Not going to have you hang around my place taking care of me. I got what I need here. Besides, life is supposed to change. New replaces old; old gotta' let go. You go make a new life that takes you where you want to go."

Gabe would never give up spending long hours in the old man's company. They'd found him a cabin for rent less than half a mile from Willi's. Between them all and with Guy Mowbray's expertise, they had refurbished the cabin with new floors, insulated walls, and an oil heater that needed just a kick or two now and then to work just fine. Most important to Isaac was being close to Sari, having a cot for Ava or Gabe to use, and as much garden space as he could manage.

Gabe loved the quiet time with Isaac, reading or sometimes just sitting, but as usual, Isaac could always find a way to plant new seeds in Gabe's thinking.

Like the day he'd said, suddenly, "Right now the way you look reminds me of when you were a boy, always sitting in corners or behind trees. What were you thinking, off to yourself like that?"

"About what I was reading, I guess."

"*Mmm.*"

"What's that mean, boss?

"Means *mmm*. Every *mmm* don't got to mean somethin'."

"You forget I'm not a little kid anymore? I learned a long time ago that with you, *mmm* never means just *mmm*."

Isaac laughed, took off his hat and rubbed his head a bit. "Well you sure got my number. All right, time for something's been on my mind. When you're looking so alone like that, like now, I wonder if you might be thinking about your papa and mama — maybe why they left you alone."

"Boss, I promise you. I'm never thinking about that."

"*Mmm.*"

"There you go –"

"No, I just mean *mmm* this time. Wondering how could that be? Wondering why you never asks me about them. Naturally curious boy like you, asking about everything – except that. It's not normal."

Gabe put down the coffee pot he'd been fiddling with and poured Isaac a cup of hot coffee. He stirred in some sugar.

"*Mmm*," Isaac said, grinning. "This time means, *just the way I like it.*"

Gabe flashed a smile back and patted the wiry, grizzled head. He said, "I'll tell you the truth about it, Boss, if you promise to keep it secret." He waited until Isaac nodded agreement. "OK. I reached a child's kind of peace about my parents. I made up a story a long time ago – that my parents died as missionaries back in their own country—"

He cut himself off at Isaac's raised eyebrow. "You want to know which country, right? Different ones based on stuff I read about. Nigeria, Zimbabwe. The last couple of years it's been South Africa. Wherever it was, they always started out doing the same work, bringing God and medicine to little children, especially orphaned children. If people ever asked me about my parents, that was what I said. Got so I almost believed it myself."

"And now?"

"Now what I believe is that I'd rather have a little boy's story than the truth."

"Well that's that, then. You don't want the truth, no problem. No reason anybody gotta shove it down a boy's throat. I'm just making sure that far-away look I see, ain't something bad, like you wishing away your own past without even knowing what it was."

Gabe stopped in the middle of scooping sugar into the bowl, lowering the scoop slowly. "All right. You've hooked me. I guess with me in high school and all, it's time for me to know the truth about who I am. Do you really know? Well, of course you do, or you wouldn't be dropping all those hints."

Isaac said. "Do you remember the man you called Pop? Well, he wasn't."

"He wasn't what?"

"He wasn't your pop. He took in your Mama and you when you were a baby. He treated you both fine, but when she died, he gave you to cousin Evelyn to raise with her young'uns. But Evelyn got on hard times, so Pop came back to get you. You must have been about eight by then. Minnie and me wanted you bad, but it was his right and we let him do it, and then we wished we didn't. He kept you a while, and never told us — but when you were about twelve he took you to the docks where the old skipjacks sail out from. Hell of a thing, leaving you alone there, not knowing a soul. Minnie never did forgive that."

"I wasn't alone. Jesse found me. Gave me food, a skipjack job. A place to sleep."

"Like I say. All alone. He could've called me, or even Evelyn. All of us would have took you."

Gabe poured more coffee and drank it down quickly to loosen his throat so he could speak. The rush of emotions had been sudden and unexpected.

"I was pretty hurt back then. I thought he was my father. Why'd he let me call him Pop?"

"Lot of reasons. Your Mama had you call him that, for one. Another reason, he hoped if you did, maybe you wouldn't ask the truth about your real daddy."

"You know that truth, too. Will you tell me?"

"Um – hmm. I'm working up to it. Give me a bit of patience, boy. It ain't easy, even now."

Gabe tried to quiet his own fidgeting but couldn't. He heard boys yelling outside, starting their pick-up stickball game in the empty field between Willi's and Isaac's. If he had any sense, he'd go out there and join them, and just stick with his missionary story. But his feet were rocks and his legs wouldn't bend. In fact, he could barely breathe. He guessed there was no going back now.

Isaac walked to the window and waved at one of the boys. Gabe smiled, thinking how Isaac had always been a magnet for boys on the loose.

Gabe asked, "The reason why – the man I called Pop — gave me up. Was it because of something I did?"

"'Course not. It was all in Pop. He used to say he was scared to death he'd get mad at you for some reason or other and just spit the story out. I told him, 'Well so what? If he asks, just tell him.' What good is it to tell lies just to make somebody feel better? Sooner or later, the truth comes along in place of the lies, anyway."

"That's who you are, truthful and straight. I'm like you, Boss. I'm not like — whoever my real father is — any more than I was like Pop. Telling me about my real father couldn't have turned me into a man I never even met. I don't believe in inherited personality."

"Well, ain't you the fancy talker?"

The fact that Isaac's mood had lightened must mean the worst of Isaac's revelations were over, that whatever his father had been, or had done, couldn't be all that horrible. Or else Isaac wouldn't be smiling.

Isaac said, "Pop was afraid *for* you, boy, not afraid *of* you. He was not a strong man and he truly didn't know what to do with a boy. And you looked so much like your mama. I think seeing you walk and talk hurt his heart. Says he thought you'd go right back to Evelyn from the dock. Minnie and me always did wonder that too."

"I knew Evelyn was even worse off. She didn't need another child."

Isaac nodded and returned his gaze to the boys playing outside his window. Gabe made himself wait patiently until Isaac was ready to unload the rest of the burden he'd carried around so long.

Hefting himself up, Isaac limped to the sink and began rinsing dishes. It pained Gabe to watch Isaac grasp plates and cups with fingers so gnarled they stayed bent in half at the knuckles. He forced himself to stay still. Isaac always needed to keep himself busy when he had things on his mind.

Isaac said, "Your real daddy was sent to the State Penn before your mama even knew of you. Never came out of that prison. Your mama'd would have rather died than tell him about a baby he'd never see."

"Prison! What in God's name did he do?"

"Well, he was a hard man by then, for sure, but wasn't any one thing he did. He fell in with a bad crowd. One of them shot a bank guard, killed him. Your Daddy's worse problem was liquor. Start out with a shot glass and hold it up, like he had to look it in the eye to get it down. Then gulp the whole thing, making a face every time, like it didn't taste right. Same with the next drink and so on, until he'd fall flat on the table."

Isaac stopped rinsing things and sat. "Me and Minnie had enough of watching your childhood get taken from you. We couldn't leave you with that white family, with that hard man, that Boat Captain. Man like that makes you doubt yourself, just like had happened to your daddy growing up."

"Ok, go back. My real Daddy killed somebody – that was why Pop couldn't keep me?"

"May or may not be him that pulled the trigger, nobody knew. Anyway, Pop's problem was something else." Isaac raised himself up straight like he did when he had anything important to say. Gabe flinched, knowing how much that hurt him.

Isaac said, "Your Daddy was a white man. He was a skipjacker. Grew up right on those docks where Pop dropped you off."

A shot straight to the heart. Well, he'd ask for it. He stood up to stare at himself in the mirror. "My skin … my skin is black as yours, Boss. I don't believe it."

"Believe it. Blackness ain't a thing you water down, father to son, to son. It don't work that way. A lot of our people been mixed with white folks, but it's not written down. Not even talked about. You can't tell –"

"I know." Gabe pulled Isaac to him for a long hug. He knew it was true and more importantly, just as suddenly as it had shocked him, it suddenly settled everything. He had just one more question for now. "She wasn't raped. I mean did she choose this man to…"

"She was married to that man, son. Loved him until the day she died."

"Maybe the real reason, then, that Pop let me go? She loved my real father still?"

"No. I ain't gonna lie. It was him being white that got to Pop."

So him having white blood had been so hateful to his stepfather that he'd abandoned the child he'd helped raise. Color – race – was so powerful it could make people hate each other, could make a man turn a blind eye to a boy he'd once loved. Or maybe he never did love him.

He kissed Isaac and then unpacked the things he'd brought, putting them all away. The rest of the pie, some fried chicken Edward Tate's wife had made, a loaf of bread from Edward's bakery. He tied the cord on his duffel, now with only his books in it, and hoisted it over his shoulder.

"Thanks for telling me, Boss. I need to think on it a while. I'll be coming out here on Friday. Maybe work on that roof a while."

"You sure in a hurry to get outta here now, all of a sudden. You alright?"

"I'm fine. Why you think I'm not?"

"Hmm – well, guess I can't see any way you could be, after learning such a big thing."

"You don't always know everything, Boss. Just most of the time.
You want me to finish these dishes?"

"Nope. Ain't dead yet." Isaac held on to Gabe for a bit, then
started toward the window. When Gabe was gone, he stayed at the
window, watching him walk down the dirt road, toss the ball a few
times to the boys and then turn and wave at him once more.

After Gabe had gone, Isaac sat in his chair, waiting for Ava. She'd
promised to be there by supper and Isaac told her they wouldn't need
to cook anything because of what Gabe had brought.

Meantime, Gabe was thinking how amazing it was that Isaac, as
much as he'd faded physically, could still know so much about everything, especially about how much Gabe could take in one sitting.
And knowing how to make things all right, no matter how hard the
message.

Even more amazingly, Isaac had given him what he needed to be
freed from the shackles of his childhood for the first time in his life.
The next day, he began sharing his travel books with his classmates.

****

When she arrived home, Ava wanted to talk more but could see
how tired Isaac was and began to help him up from his chair. It pained
her to watch him spend nearly three minutes twisting his body up to
get on his feet. They held hands until he got to his bed and she helped
him take his shoes off, then tucked him under his comforter.

"This room feel colder than usual?" he asked. She told him she
didn't think so.

"Maybe fall's come early? Or maybe I don't have the flesh to keep
my own self warm anymore."

She laid an extra blanket across his shoulders and another over his
feet. She wondered if he went to bed with his clothes on every night,
and if so, whether it was just to keep in the heat, or more because his
buttons were too much a trial to his ever-more-brittle fingers.

One thing the fingers could do, though. Through the slightly open
door, she saw his hand on Minnie's pillow, petting it gently, back

and forth, as if Minnie was there, just like he'd done when she died, and probably every night since. A small gesture, revealing such a powerful emotion that it took her breath away. She was more envious than sad, knowing there would never be a soulmate like that in her own life. Venus might be gone, but she'd cursed both her daughters before leaving. Hadn't she?

Chapter Sixteen

The Phillips Packing Company had once been the largest cannery in America, employing one-fourth of Cambridge's residents until the day it closed. Thousands more farmers and fishermen had depended directly on Phillips to buy their harvests. Indirectly, everyone from local restaurants to beauty parlors had relied on the patronage of Phillips employees. (Levy, *Civil*)

When the noon whistle sounded at the old pickle factory, it could still stir up action in the community, even after it had shut down. The town still reacted to the whistle by locking their doors, opening the windows to let in a bit of air, turning the lights off, or on, if they worked the next shift. At Finnegan's Music store, the manager hung his sign, "Back in ten minutes," on the door and tucked his head against his shirt to grab forty winks. People stretched and shifted in their seats at Mace's Lane High School, Wise Oil and Fuel, the Dairy Queen.

It was Monday, May 18, 1962 and Gabe had just sat down to his history class at Mace's Lane. The topic was *Plessey vs. Ferguson* and equal rights. Two of his buddies were already asleep, heads propped, chin to chest, but Gabe was the opposite of sleepy.

"The concept is 'separate but equal,' which theoretically could exist, but in reality, does not."

Gabe had been at the school for a year, staying midweek with Edward Tate and managing stock for the aging businessman. Who was he kidding? Edward Tate was paying his way. Here was another man like Isaac, only the community he supported was much larger. He thought of Edward as the mayor of the Second Ward, where all the town's black people lived.

Gabe had loved everything about school, until this political science lesson, which had sealed a growing determination in him. After finishing his day's work at Tate's, he drove out to talk with Isaac and Ava. The next morning, first thing, he got Ava from her classroom and they went, hand in hand, to the guidance counselor's office.

Gabe began the meeting. "Ava and I want to transfer schools."

It was first period and the beginning of a very long day for Mrs. Emery. She was already exhausted from yesterday's undone work and hadn't even finished her breakfast yet. She wasn't able to stifle her yawn as she asked, "Ok. Where?"

"North Dorchester."

"To North...." She sat up sharply, fully awake. A fly buzzed around her uneaten egg sandwich and for once, she ignored it. "That's a white school."

"I hate to disrespect you, Mrs. Emery, but no, it isn't. It's a public school. Folks here in Ward Two pay taxes for that school. Any of us kids want to, we can go there. And we want to."

"But why? Why, child, would you want to?" Her eyes darted to Ava who kept her head down and was silent. Mrs. Emery came out of her seat, something she rarely did when talking to students. She stood, arms crossed, eyes narrowing behind her cat's eye glasses. "You've been talking to those Freedom Riders, haven't you?"

"That's not why."

"Then why do this?"

As a matter of fact, he *had* been talking to people and a couple of them might have been Freedom Riders. He and Ava had tried to hear some of the speeches of this new movement, speeches by people trying to fight segregation at white businesses up and down Route 50, including Cambridge. The rumor was a big march was coming soon, maybe this summer. They'd learned that college students from all over the state, both white and black, would be coming to support local black leaders trying to win civil rights for black citizens. Some of those activists were called Freedom Riders. He admired them, what he knew. Around here, though, news of their movement was scarce.

He and Ava both wanted to be involved, but they both worked far too many hours to afford time for rallies and sit-ins right now. They'd just found another way. They were going to enroll in a white school. Not so much to "make a statement" as to better themselves.

They'd thought hard about how they would answer "why," what they'd say to teachers, friends. Their answer had been Isaac's idea.

"It's ten miles closer," Gabe said, raising his eyes to meet Mrs. Emery's.

She mouthed the words of his answer, as if to make sure she'd heard right. She opened a metal file drawer, fiddled inside for a minute, yanked up forms, and handed them over. "For your parent or guardian. Mr. Isaac Jackson is what — your stepfather?"

They nodded.

She looked even more skeptical, if that was possible. "Your – stepfather – has to sign it."

"Thank you," Gabe said. "How long will it take? This fall?"

"I ... it should be. I hope so, but I never tried to do something like this before."

"As long as you promise you'll do your best, we can wait."

"If your stepfather signs, it's all I need. As for doing my best, you won't find me standing in the way of any student in my school who wants to ... well, I was going to say 'try to move ahead,' but Gabe, Ava, are you sure this is a way *up*? It could be nothing but trouble."

"Trouble, we expect." Gabe glanced at Ava, who was frowning. He said, "I'll speak just for myself. I got trouble now. Everything in life worth doing is trouble."

"Ava. What will your mother say about this?"

Ava finally had something to say. "If she was around, which she isn't, it would be what she said about anything I ever wanted: 'That's plain wrong.' She thought I had wrong ideas about everything. I'd sure like to find a place where people will see that I'm not the useless girl my mother thought."

Gabe added, "We have to give ourselves a chance at life before we blame other people for holding us back, Mrs. Emery. You see?"

"I see. No, let me change that. I see trouble everywhere. I hope you haven't been influenced by the wrong people ... ones giving inflammatory signs to kids. They scare the dickens out of people and I don't just mean white people. Black people have got even more reason to be scared. Ask your stepfather, if you don't think I'm right."

Ava spoke up, "We know you're right, without asking anybody. The signs are supposed to make people uncomfortable. Comfortable people don't change things."

As the door closed behind them, Mrs. Emery attached a note to their file, saying that their reasoning, while admirable, sounded a bit too rehearsed for her comfort.

She shook her head back and forth, too upset to eat or even get back to work. In this day and time, you never know where the bad influences on children came from. Those so-called Freedom Walkers and their followers were turning up everywhere these days and confusing her students.

****

Gabe was surprised at how easy it had been to talk Ava into the change in schools. At first, he figured she went along just to keep him company, and then he saw she was keyed up in a way that even he wasn't.

"I'm more a renegade than you'll ever be," she teased. "I'm going to love bucking convention. I can't wait to walk through a gauntlet of shocked white-girl faces." He didn't answer that his reasoning followed a different course because he didn't want to dissuade her from going with him. The truth was that he didn't think much about the white faces. Instead, his aim was at what the white faces were studying. He had one advantage over Ava, he'd admit. He was now a fine, well-rounded athlete. Sports should protect him from the worst types of harassment.

****

They'd given Isaac his fondest wish. Ava and Gabe were finally brother and sister. By the time they'd walked hand in hand into Mrs. Emery's office, they were a team. There had to be two of them, they'd reasoned … well, Gabe had reasoned, and then persuaded Ava. Someone to wave at, speak to at the new school, in case nobody else would. There had to be someone there who could convince you that you weren't crazy for doing this.

The first day of school that fall had been surreal. Later, they both remembered it as an overcast day, the kind that threatens storm but delivers nothing except more dark clouds. A perfect backdrop for what happened inside the school — not a single student had spoken to them. At lunch, the white kids kept two to three tables of space on all sides around them.

In the weeks after, when harsh verbal exchanges had taken hold, there were many days both Ava and Gabe would have gladly traded for that uneventful first day. Ava wasn't going to be able to finish out the first fall term. She'd hoped to last until Thanksgiving, but on the day before the holiday break, a horrific turn of events sent her home feeling defeated. By the time she got on the school bus, she was so distressed she was shaking. She even thought about scrapping her weekend stay with Sari, another source of hostility that had become almost too much to bear.

As soon as they found their seats, she told Gabe what happened. "In the morning, it was just the usual insults and catcalls, occasional swearing, and then suddenly it turned to something uglier and more … personal. Instead of just, 'Hey Nigger,' they got crude and threatening. Philip Stern said, 'What color your pussy, nigger girl? How about you show us? We never seen one yet.' And worse."

Gabe's face, usually the paradigm of self-control, showed dismay at first, then rage. "I'm sorry, Ava. I would have never imagined this kind of abuse. We'll have to find a way to —"

She stopped him. "Doesn't stuff like that happen to you?"

"Not that vulgar. Hateful, yes. Threats to beat me up."

"You never told me about them."

"I guess I was trying to spare you. I thought it was just me. It's been worse for me, too. For instance, yesterday, after basketball practice, there was a drawing taped to my locker. A stick-figure man hanging from a noose. But I never had anything disgusting. We have got to do something."

She planned to do something, alright, but she wasn't ready to tell him yet. She let him talk for a while as he tried to make sense of why things had escalated.

"It seems gender specific — death threats for a boy, rape threats for a girl. Not that it makes me understand why they do it."

When the bus dropped them at Willi's, he said they needed to figure out how real the danger was. They talked and thought and talked more, sitting at the edge of the road, until Ava realized an hour had gone by.

"It's getting late," she said. "Let's walk. Sari's expecting me, not that she's glad to see me anymore."

Ava decided to wait until tomorrow to tell Gabe she was quitting NDHS for good. It would take the rest of tonight's energy to deal with Sari. They stopped at the porch steps because by now, Gabe was fed up with Sari's insolence and he preferred not to come in.

Ava said, "Thanks for listening so long. You always make me feel more settled once I can talk things through. I'll call you later. Where will you be?"

"Isaac's. I've been patching things up for winter. Got to work more on the windows before it gets too cold for the caulk to dry. When rains come in heavy next spring, every leak would be a misery."

"You're a blessing to him."

"Other way around — he's a blessing to me, and so are you. You've helped me stick it out at NDHS. I need this school for college ... the sports, of course, but the academics even more."

"You mean you're getting a scholarship to college?"

"Pretty sure."

"Sports or academics?

He laughed. "Languages, and I don't mean Latin or French. The one that lets you talk with people of any color or education level. I used to think that sports would be what would save me from the worst bigotry, but they haven't."

"You know, the way they applaud you on the court and all, I kept thinking it was easier for you. You know, because you've got something they need. You're saying it doesn't help?"

"It helps when I'm on the court or in the field and sometimes in the locker room. I'm tolerated by some people, but there are plenty more that show me pure hate. The more I succeed, the more they resent me. In hallways or the cafeteria, it's sometimes pure hell — well, you sure know what I'm saying. Even those who aren't hateful treat me like a leper. They don't want to get too close. I just keep saying my poem every single day — to remind myself of my strength. I have a copy taped up everywhere."

She nodded. She knew the poem, "Invictus," by heart thanks to him.

He said, "I keep thinking it has to get better. And to be fair, there are some white boys who reach out to try to set an example. Paul Medford, Steve Reed, Charles Adkins. I wouldn't call them friends exactly, not like Celie is to us, but they stand up against the bigots. Just them walking next to me cuts down the comments."

They were still standing at Willi's porch. The air had chilled and Ava was shivering. Gabe handed her his jacket, his letter jacket, and she realized how much progress he'd actually made, despite the shared misery. She had not made that kind of progress.

"I was naïve when I asked you to do this with me, Ava. I didn't know it would get so bad."

He'd given her the perfect opening and she had to take it. She made sure she could see his whole face. "You'll make it Gabe, but as for me ... I've decided not to go back. Not even for another day."

"I don't blame you," he answered.

His clear, simple reaction was unexpected. She said, "You're kidding? I thought you'd be disappointed in me. I had promised we'd do it together."

"Good Lord, girl! We *did* do it together! Starting something like this, you have to take it day by day. I'm fine with you leaving, Ava. You've been my buddy all the way. Like I said, a blessing. If I can make anything easier for you back at Mace's Lane, let me know."

"I'm probably not going back there either. I can get a GED and do the new jobs program out at the State Hospital. Celie told me about it. Or, I have an aunt in Baltimore I could stay with. Take a couple of education classes, maybe try for a job teaching."

Ava knew they were losing something important between them, as he went one way, she another, both of them trying to create a place in a part of the world where they weren't wanted.

Gabe was halfway down the path when he turned to ask, "What will your Ma think if she comes back and finds you gone?"

"She was never any kind of mother to me. Like you, I answer to Isaac. Anyway, I don't expect she'll ever be back. Now *that's* what I call a blessing."

"For you, maybe. What about Sari? You gonna just leave her for Willi to raise and that's that? And what about Isaac?"

Ava told herself to overlook his critical tone, given it was the same way she felt herself. She said, "I'll always take care of Isaac, like you, but Sari doesn't want a caretaker, certainly not Willi. I hate leaving her where Venus can find her so easy, so after I get settled somewhere, I plan to bring her with me. She'll like the city, although the idea of keeping track of that little airhead in a big city is another kind of burden."

She wasn't going to tell him yet about her taking a job with the Black Caucus in Washington. After all, the position might not come through.

"Maybe Sari could stay with Celie in Cambridge until you get situated? It's a good community. They'll look after her."

"Celie's got enough burdens in her work-study program."

"She's always got time for us."

"Look Gabe. I'm not going to ask Celie to keep track of Sari and don't you try and push me to." She braced for a fight.

"Wouldn't think if it." Gabe grinned and yanked her single long braid, like he'd done with her pigtails when they were kids. She allowed herself a moment to feel grateful for him in her life before going in to face Sari.

Chapter Seventeen

Willi's cabin was dark, except at the door edges of Sari's room. Ava could hear her moving around inside. "Sari? You here by yourself?"

"Of course. Willi works 'til ten – who else I got?"

"You got me, that's who," Ava said, easing open the bedroom door. "Unless what you really mean is, you wish you had Venus. You're better off without her."

"Don't say that!" Sari whimpered.

"I'm sorry that hurts you. It'll hurt you more by not seeing the truth, that you can't count on her for anything."

Even in the dark, Ava could see Sari's eyes were shiny with tears.

"Where you been, Ava?" Sari sobbed, opening the door the rest of the way. Ava could tell she'd been crying for quite a while, and answered, "You knew I was at school. Sari, why you still miss Venus so much? She was horrible to you, and she got worse every time."

"She gave me things, that's why. Nice things."

"You don't mean that dumb mirror? Minnie gave that to you, not Venus."

"Not that! Something better. A special thing."

Ava didn't like the look on her sister's face. It was cunning, the way Venus had looked every day of her life. Whenever she saw that expression on Sari, she wanted to smack her. Instead, she kept her voice sweet and said, "Can I see it?"

Sari reached in her pocket for her treasure and held it high in front of Ava. Her smile was slick, her eyes piercing. She must have been wanting to show her this for weeks by now. It was a ring, gold, polished to a muted sheen, framing a huge stone that had to be a gemstone ... the way it was set with prongs, and the cut of it, the way all those little angles flashed light. A clear green stone, an emerald maybe? Where would Venus have got hold of an emerald? She kept her voice calm. "You know where Mahm got it, Sari?"

"Umm — think she bought it in town."

Ava's hackles rose. She took some easy breaths to regain her composure. "Think again. This is way too expensive for her to have bought herself."

"Maybe somebody give it to her."

"Nobody around here has that kind of money, even if they wanted to give her something like this."

"Well, maybe she got two jobs?" Sari's eyes were scheming, her lips pressed into a thin line. Ava grabbed her by the shoulders and shook her, hard. "Sari, don't be such a stupid girl! You're lying. This is a rich woman's ring and you know it. This ring is big, big trouble. We're going to have to get it back to its owner."

"No-oo!" Sari screamed and began to run, but Ava was fast and caught up to her easily. Still, she wasn't prepared for the intensity of Sari's fighting back and was knocked to the ground by a wallop on the head. Then came a tight kick to the groin. She screamed out, "Gabe," at the top of her lungs, hoping that, by some miracle, he was still close enough to hear.

He was there in less than a minute. Between the two of them, they pinned Sari to the ground. Ava saw that her lip was bleeding and patted her sister's mouth with the edge of her sleeve.

While Gabe was still holding her down, Ava put a finger in front of Sari's face, risking a painful bite but determined to get control of her. She had to. Like Sari had said, she didn't have anybody else.

"You have to quiet down. You'll wake up the neighbors ten farms over. Do you want a bunch of white people all coming up here with shotguns?"

She felt a twinge of guilt at implying that any of their neighbors would ever fire shots near Willi's house, but only a twinge. She had to do whatever it took to stop this tantrum.

"You said I was stupid!"

"I'm *not* sorry about that. It's stupid to lie to me. Show Gabe the ring."

The thought of being able to show off her treasure seemed to be just what she needed. She held it high. Even in the near-pitch darkness, the ring flashed its sharp light.

Gabe let out a low-pitched whistle. "What kind is it?"

"I think it must be an emerald," Ava said, "but I'm guessing. Sari doesn't know or won't say."

"Your Mahm give this to you, Sari?"

Sulky silence.

Gabe relaxed his grip some. "Expensive ring like this as a gift to a kid?"

"Venus wouldn't give away anything worth real money," Ava answered. She probably told Sari to keep it until she comes back for it. She uses Sari like a bank."

"That right, Sari?" He pulled her up and into the light, so they could both see her face. Sari nodded, her face distorted with misery.

"I guess we should tell Isaac," he said, but he sounded as doubtful as Ava felt. She'd made up her mind. "No. He's the last one we'll tell."

"Why?"

"Isaac is an upstanding man, which makes it certain he'll do everything wrong. Can you picture it? An honest black man deciding he has to make things right? What's he do?"

"Calls the police?"

"Yes. He goes to the white police and tries to hand over a stolen ring. He can't say where he got it because he doesn't want anybody else in trouble. What would the police do?"

Gabe didn't need more than a second to answer. "He'd be in jail. No matter what he said, he'd be blamed."

"Right. Now, how about a *good* idea instead?"

Gabe reached his hand over to Sari, who so far, had kept the ring in a tight grip. Her eyes looked deadly as Gabe said, "Give me the ring."

Sari kept her fist clutched but couldn't prevent him from prying the ring loose. Through clenched teeth, Gabe said, "Actually, I do have an idea. I can get it into the police station, without them ever knowing where it came from."

"How?"

As dark as it was, Ava saw he was grinning. He looked so damned innocent, even when he was scheming like a fox.

He said, "They have a night depository."

Ava sat on a log and pulled Sari down next to her to make sure she stayed put. "Wouldn't there be security lights near it?"

"Usually, but all the station lights got knocked out when that last bus full of Freedom Riders came through. Nobody's replaced them yet. I'll wait until about three a.m. The night watchman goes to the coffee shop then and waits for his shift to end. Nobody will see me."

"What about the National Guard?"

"They don't want their heads busted in either. They usually stay out of the shadows."

"But wouldn't somebody eventually try to find out where this ring came from?"

"Maybe. Right now, they got their hands so full of student demonstrators tromping up and down the streets, they can't get to the normal stuff." He put an arm around her shoulders and whispered, "It'll be OK. I promise."

"OK. Ok, thanks."

"I have to add one 'except.'" Standing under the stars and in the shadows, he looked as tall as the loblolly pines behind him.

"Except what?" Ava felt Sari's body tense again and she tightened her grip.

"Except if Venus hurt somebody to get this ring off them."

Sari managed to jerk free and leap to her feet, preparing to scream, but Gabe wrestled her back down and clapped his hand over her mouth. Ava grabbed Sari's hands and held them behind her back.

"You got to chill, little girl," Gabe whispered in Sari's ear. "I haven't heard about any injured rich white woman lately. I'm just telling you why you got to keep your mouth shut. Unless you want to spend the rest of your natural life in a white man's jail."

Ava braced for a scream, but Sari stayed frozen in place. Gabe seemed to have hit on the right trump card; Sari's dread of being locked up.

Gabe tucked the ring into his shirt pocket and gave Ava a final kiss on the forehead, then laid his forefinger against Sari's mouth. "Not a word to a living soul. Got that?"

Ava had never heard gentle Gabe use such a menacing voice. Sari nodded. They sat listening to Gabe's footsteps crackling across the pine needles and fading out. Then all they could hear was crickets. Sari held her hand as they walked inside.

"I'm in big trouble, ya' think?" Sari asked, the sneaky look completely gone from her lovely face, which gave Ava a shred of hope.

"I don't know, but I tell you what, baby sister. If I hear you've said a single word to anybody about Gabe taking that ring back, I'll wring your neck."

"But what if Mahm comes for the ring?"

"You say somebody broke in here and stole it. She'll believe that, right enough. That's how she got it. Try to forget you ever had it."

Ava took her sister to her room, lying next to her on her bed, afraid to leave her. The specter of Venus was always in this room, ready to wreak havoc. She kept trying to imagine how the ring could have been lifted from its owner, unknowingly, and never missed. Venus must have left some kind of trail, which might be the reason she'd left so abruptly. Maybe it would keep her from coming back. As mad as she'd been when Gabe had suggested it, it was true that her staying away would be the best thing for everybody. Sari might even get her head straight, with time away from Venus' mixed-up ideas.

Sari fell asleep and then Ava realized she'd forgotten to ask something important. She'd have to wake her. "Sari, wake up. I need to ask something. What else did Venus give you to keep?"

"Nothing." There was that damn devious tone again.

"For God's sake, don't lie to me. I'm trying to keep your little ass out of reform school."

Sari stood up in a huff, signaling Ava to step aside. She lifted her mattress up on its end, pulling out some kind of coverlet. When she spoke, her voice was plaintive rather than cocky.

"Why I gotta give this up? Nobody'll miss it. Everybody thinks it's burned to a crisp."

Ava shot out her hand to touch the silky cotton. It felt familiar. It looked familiar, too –

"Oh shit." She didn't know what else to say. It was the quilt Isaac had wrapped Minnie in to bury her. How in the hell had her devil of a mother managed to steal it from her own sister's body?

She lay down next to her sister again, this time covering Sari with the quilt and tucking it around her. She vowed to let her keep the quilt. Sari's life was so empty of anything from Venus. The quilt served as an illusion of a mother who might have once loved her. Little enough to spare and it sure couldn't do Minnie any good now. She'd think of something to tell Isaac, if it ever came up.

When Willi came home, Ava said, "You have to help me make sure that Sari finishes high school. If you run out of money, just ask and

I'll send you more. You need to promise me."

"Well, that lil' girl does like her spendin' money." Willi flashed a smile that displayed a brand new gold tooth. When had she got that?

Ava said, "You let me worry about getting her the money. You just get her onto that school bus every day."

Willi promised, and Ava talked herself into believing it, but the new gold tooth stayed on her mind for weeks after. Gold teeth and emerald rings – she wished she'd had time to stay and make sense of it all.

Chapter Eighteen

Early Spring—1963

Across the peninsula, Celie was on her way to class at Cambridge General Hospital. Her senior-year nursing internship included a number of classes right in the hospital, which meant a daily drive to Cambridge. With Frank not home anymore, Daddy transferred to her the title of the Falcon. At first, she'd been deeply disappointed. She wasn't sure what kind of car she'd seen herself driving, exactly, but it wasn't a boxy two-door hardtop Ford with a manual transmission. She might have spared the car a bit of sentimentality, given that it was the car she'd learned to drive on, but it didn't come close to feeling protective.

Her attitude began to mellow when Daddy went through the ownership manual, pointing out the main operating and maintenance features. By the time he'd finished, she found herself marveling that she could understand a machine this complicated. Her friend Scott gave her a pair of fuzzy dice for the mirror. Gabe Armor-all'd the upholstery. By mid-summer, she'd named the car Betty, in honor of Betty Crocker, the cookbook that had been her graduation present from Aunt Margaret.

"I'll never even open this cookbook," she told Hannah. They were lying on the living room floor in front of the circular fan, cooling themselves off from an insufferably long-lasting heat wave.

"I'd rather be the worst nurse in the hospital than the best cook in the Betty Crocker kitchen. Some good should come of this book – why not a car as its namesake?"

Naming the car was just a joke, until she realized how well the name fit. A down-home, wholesome, practical vehicle that would provide reliable and maintenance-free transportation. Within days she was babying the car like an old friend.

Then, disaster struck. "Betty's been killed!" she wailed. Someone had crashed into Betty in the hospital parking lot, crumpling her whole rear end before fleeing the scene.

"Totaled," said Mr. Jensen, the State Farm Agent. "Totaled," Daddy repeated.

"Murdered," Celie sobbed.

"Celie, it's just a car." She was in the kitchen and Hannah was doing her best to comfort her. "I mean I know you loved it, but you can get another car."

Daddy said, "I'm afraid I can't afford another car right now– "

Celie said quickly, "No, it's OK, Pops. I'm good. I don't really need a car. They have student quarters three blocks from the hospital. I can stay there and walk."

"I'll fix it," Frank said, ambling into the kitchen, still in his P.J.'s. He was home on leave and she and Hannah hardly recognized this new Frank. He was still funny and charming, but he'd stopped teasing them. He engaged in deep conversations with Mom and Daddy that lasted until bedtime.

"You should let him try and fix it," Hannah said that night as they rolled their hair with fat pink sponge rollers.

Celie grabbed a roller and began twisting a handful of hair ends around the foam. Supposedly her hair would flip up, like Jackie Kennedy's.

"I'm not sure I should let him. Good grief! Hannah, look!" Celie held up some very straight hair strands. "I'd have to wear the rollers all day for this hair to even begin to change direction. And as to Frank, why would he want to fix my dead car?"

"It's wrecked, Celie, not dead. It was never alive. And the answer is he loves working on motors. Remember when he took your little toy ringer washer apart and got in trouble?"

"Only because he still tells the story and calls me a rat fink."

"The point is the mechanical thing. He likes it. And maybe he just wants to help."

"Well that would be a first, but if you think so, let him take it. Then you take the car if he gets it to run. It's my chance to convince Daddy I need to stay in town, so make sure it isn't fixed until I'm settled in my room there."

Car-less, she'd established a walking routine that ended up with what Celie believed had been arranged by destiny. There was a garden behind the church Ava went to, and Celie would often sit and eat her lunch there. That's how she struck the deal with Reverend Hiram Benson at the St. Paul AME Church.

"Hello! You must be Celie. I notice you like to sit out here on nice days."

"Oh! Yes, I do. Is that OK, Reverend Benson? Ava mentioned me, I guess?"

"The answer is, it's more than OK. I love to see it being used. And yes, Ava more than mentioned you. She talks about you a lot. You're a nurse now?"

"Nursing student still. I hope I may be lucky to get a job back here when I finish, though."

"Ava said something about community outreach of some sort?"

Celie explained the details of her plan to bring follow-up services to those in the community who might need a helping hand to complete recovery from illnesses or surgery. At the end of her description, she asked if the Reverend might help her identify those who would benefit.

"Your program sounds wonderful. I'm positive I could help with some names. I feel like I've been blessed to run into you today."

"Gosh, here I was thinking I was the one blessed! That program will fulfill a long-time dream for me."

****

The dreams of many people in Cambridge, including Celie's, were about to encounter a hurdle as they were swept along by the Civil Rights Movement. After the closing of the Cannery, there had been no new jobs to replace the old ones. In Ward Two, where the entire black community of Cambridge was housed, disrepair became the norm for homes and businesses. 'Rich' residents like Edward Tate reached deep into their pockets to help folks out until a permanent solution – new jobs — could be found.

Demonstrators came to Cambridge for a few rallies and sit-ins. Then, early in 1963, there were violent incidents in the Second Ward. People got hurt and fires were set. This was happening too near her hospital for Daddy's comfort. The report was aired on national TV on January 10. Daddy was on the phone five minutes after the end of the eleven o-clock news, calling her home until things calmed down. She couldn't argue him out of it.

Celie dropped off her luggage and went straight to Isaac's, too fuming mad at Daddy to stay in her parents' house more than she had to. News clips of the riots filled Isaac's TV screen and for the first time, the gravity of the situation hit her. "This looks serious. Did you know about this before it happened, Isaac?"

"Ava said a little bit of something. It was Edward Tate told me more. He's mighty scared."

"Is Gabe involved? He works so close to that school they set the fire to…."

"Gabe's not in it at all. He wanted to, mind you. Lots of feelings about folks that lost their jobs. I told him, don't mess up your future. He told me right back, how getting rights for folks is his future. But he's been keeping away from the street, only because Edward asked him to keep the Emporium safe. He says he owes Edward a lot."

Gabe also had serious doubts, Celie found out later, about the Freedom Riders. He told her that too many of them were white. Celie had flinched and asked him why that should matter. Wouldn't white support be seen as a good thing? He didn't answer, instead saying that he didn't really have time to talk about the politics of it all. She didn't understand his reasons, but she was relieved he wasn't going where there was shooting. At the same time, her distress about the worsening problems in Ward Two had become her daily bread and she was itching to get back there.

Another emotional conflict with Gabe in the middle of it. She should be used to that by now.

Chapter Nineteen

The falling-down black elementary school, a constant foil for unrest, had been torched, as predicted. Also burned was a church and a community hall. The embers and smoke swirled to the streets and chased away the rioters, leading some fools to suggest the fire may have been a good thing. The next day, a baby died of asphyxiation from smoke blowing in through his window. People stopped saying the fire was in any way a good thing.

Weeks went by and people kept getting hurt. Some black students were arrested. Most of Gabe's friends had escaped harm owing to Reverend Benson's sharp eye. When white boys with guns were spotted in the Second Ward, he would gather up his flock and kept them in the church hall until the unrest ended. By summer, National Guardsman lined the streets and there was no plan to remove them. Martial law had come to Cambridge.

****

Something had changed Ava. She had scolded both Gabe and Celie, furious at them both for "playing it safe" during the downtown fighting.

They were all at Isaac's, determined not to argue loud enough for him to hear. Gabe had explained as calmly as he could. "I did my part, Ava. The Emporium is more than one family's livelihood. Edward holds that community together and I was there to protect him."

Celie sat listening, fuming, and didn't explain a thing to Ava, partly because she was mad that Ava implied she didn't care. Besides, who was Ava to scold anybody, given how she was neglecting her own sister? I should be the one doing the scolding, Celie told herself. She left all this unsaid. When Ava was on the warpath, it was best not to expose any vulnerability. She picked up her things and walked home.

A few days later, Celie had calmed down enough to telephone Ava, wanting to smooth things over, but still not trusting her temper face to face. Ava pounced, with what felt to Celie like accusatory questioning, and then Celie's thin veil of patience fell away.

"Where was I, you ask? I was busy living a 17-year-old life," she snapped. "Saying goodbye to my friends, keeping my grades decent, getting into nursing school. You know, the normal stuff for a kid my age."

"The normal stuff if you're white, that is. I don't have that luxury. When you heard there were riots, did you even check on Gabe or me to see if we were there – and if we were OK?"

Celie didn't tell her that of course she did, that she'd been scared to death for them both. That she'd sat with Isaac and watched the events unfold, talking with him until she could find her own understanding of what they now called the Civil Rights Movement. She was struggling to figure out her role in it, but everything she could think to do was seen as wrong by somebody.

She planned to explain to Ava, even apologize, but wherever this blaze of anger in Ava had come from, it was burning so hot that nothing Celie could say would get through. She hung up her end of the phone with a decisive *thunk,* vowing not to try and prove herself solely to please Ava. Gabe had his path, Ava had a different one, and she had a right to her own.

Celie was trying to feel self-righteous, but the truth was she didn't know what she thought about the Freedom Marches or even Civil Rights. Her problems were more immediate. All her patients kept getting poorer and sicker as time went on. She was doing all she could to make their lives better, and it didn't always work.

She gave Ava time to cool down before calling her again. Right from the beginning, she'd screwed that up. She made the mistake of asking Ava if she was ready to talk about things civilly, at which point Ava hung up on her.

Probably I deserved it, Celie decided. She stopped calling Ava and wrote down what she felt in several long, painfully polite letters, which she sent. They remained unanswered. As the stand-off dragged on, she focused everything she had on work. She still wrote everything down in great detail in a series of long letters to Ava, but she stopped mailing them.

April, 1966

When Celie finished nursing school, she was elated to find a job at Cambridge Hospital. Somehow, she had to tell her parents she would be living in town, rather than on the farm. On her way to see them, she decided to stop by Isaac's first and ask about Ava.

When she did, Isaac hemmed and hawed and changed the subject. He looked sadder than he had in all the years she'd known him. It was clear to Celie that it pained him to talk about Ava and she sure wasn't going to push him.

But she was alarmed and went to Sari's to ask if she knew how to reach her sister.

"I don't hear from Ava much," Sari said. "When I do, she doesn't tell me what she's doing, and she sure doesn't talk about you. Why the hell would she want me to tell you what she's doing?"

"I didn't ask you what she's doing. I asked you if you knew how to reach her."

"Maybe Gabe knows. He'd tell you anything, right?" Sari asked cunningly. Celie turned away from that wily face, more upset about Sari than about Ava. She made her some soup, straightened up Willi's kitchen, then wrote down some phone numbers where Sari could reach her. "I put some money in your cookie jar. Call me any time you need anything. I'm going to Ava's church now to look for her — you need a ride there?"

"That'll be the day. I got my own rides when I need them."

Reverend Benson was warm and welcoming. She was thrilled to be able to tell him that her new job would include the home visits they'd started to plan three years before. He opened a drawer in his beat-up wooden desk and pulled out a marked-up church directory.

"All done. Here are the folks we talked about. I put a check mark next to the names of folks who can't get all the way to the doctor – and a star next to those who just won't."

It was a good bargain because he told her what he knew about Ava, including how she helped at the church regularly. He probably didn't intend to let it slip that Ava was involved in some controversial activist groups. He looked stricken as soon as he'd said it.

"What groups? Do you know?"

"Might be those Black Power people. To hear Ava tell it, they're going to change life for the folks here. Edward Tate says we got a lot to worry about if we let those activists back in Cambridge. I got to say, Ava doesn't sound like Ava anymore. Worries Isaac to death."

Celie's new apartment was on the edge of Race Street. Not just close to the Second Ward, but right in it. One of her white friends called her and asked how she could "live in that hell hole." Celie had an urge to say something snarky like, "If I lived where you do, I'd die of boredom." Instead she said, "I love my place. Come visit."

Mom disapproved, not of the neighborhood, but of Celie's living alone in town, even Cambridge. It wasn't what a young single girl should be doing. Celie asked Daddy what he thought, and he said, "whatever Mom says."

Celie had a flash of insight. Neither of her parents knew the first thing about how to interact with adult children. Their own parents had slid into the shadows after their kids grew up. She was going to have to teach them how to stay in her life. Daddy would be easy, so she decided to tackle her toughest customer first.

At first Mom made up excuses not to come see her in town, until Hannah literally pushed her through Celie's door one afternoon. Mom was dressed to the nines, a houndstooth suit and spiky high heels, like she was going to church. The minute she crossed Celie's threshold, she looked uncomfortable. Celie hoped Hannah knew she was expected to stay, too.

Hannah said, "I'm just along to make conversation," which translated, meant, "to keep you from opening your big mouth and arguing with every little thing Mom says." Celie got the message. Right now, Mom was eyeing the curtains, fingering the rolled edges, raising her eyebrows. Hannah placed her index finger over her lips and Celie took a deep breath, pretending not to notice Mom's examination. "Iced tea or coffee?" she asked, forcing a smile.

"Your coffee is so strong. Maybe hot tea. Only if you have it."

Celie bristled. It was all she could do not to say, 'If I have iced tea, it means I have hot tea too.' "I'll have it in a jiffy," she said.

Mom said, "The doctor says coffee is bad for my heart."

"What's wrong with your heart?"

"Nothing. My heart is fine." *Classic Mom-speak.* Celie raised an eyebrow at Hannah, who now had two fingers on her lips to go with her raised brow. Meanwhile, Mom was turning up curtain hems. "I used to sew all your clothes, you know. Dresses from feed-sacks, can you believe?"

"Yes, Mom. You told us." Celie flinched at her own words, while Hannah cleared her throat, which meant 'shut up, Big Mouth.' Celie pulled out an assortment of teabags and a box of loose tea, arranging and rearranging them until the water boiled.

Mom was still talking feed-sacks. "Dad was so bad at picking out the colors – he always went for yellow and red – and plaid. He thought little girls liked plaid."

"I remember flowers," Hannah said.

"That's because the feed man liked me." Mom was stacking a pile of magazines, or pretending to. She produced a wicked smile. "The feed man would trade out the sacks Dad picked for the more feminine fabrics."

Celie had a vision of her mother when she first came south from Philadelphia, a dark haired, blue-eyed, 4-foot-11-inch pixie of a girl. She remembered how people, men particularly, had treated Mom special. How their family always seemed to have extra jelly donuts from the Bond Bread man, when the rest of the neighbors claimed he was out of them. Her mother flirting for favors. Imagine that.

****

Celie knew that Ava visited Isaac and Sari often, without communicating with Celie. Weeks went by and Gabe told her, "Be patient. She'll come around."

And then one Saturday, Gabe called to say he'd like to bring Ava to dinner. Celie was thrilled. She took a cab to get to the seafood market and she made their favorite foods — crab cakes, coleslaw and beer. She laid everything out on a card table and located four folding chairs (one came from a neighbor).

The meal began delightfully. When Celie passed around paper towels for napkins, they began a jovial discussion of dinners at Mom's house on her 'mahogany' table with Grandmom's Irish lace tablecloth and embroidered linen napkins. It was shaping up to be an agreeable, nostalgic evening. Gabe was gracious, and Ava was funny, like in the old days.

Then everything fell apart.

****

Ava judged the timing was right. She'd wanted them both to feel at ease before she brought up the list. Her chance came when Celie explained how she tracked patients in the community. "I know everybody between Race and Pine," she was saying proudly.

Ava said, "Wonderful. Could you look this list over and see if there's anybody I may have left out?"

Celie skimmed the list. "This is just about everybody in the Second Ward. All of the young adults and most of the older ones. Why do you need a list like this?" She looked confused, which Ava had expected. Gabe did too and that was a surprise. She thought he'd get it right away.

"My job is to discover how much prep work needs to be done here and report back."

"To who, Ava?" Gabe asked.

"The Black Caucus. Who else?"

Celie and Gabe jumped to their feet at the same moment, Gabe asking, "You ... what ... give out information about our neighbors' personal lives?"

Celie was saying, "Prep work? You mean it's a list for strangers to use? That's outrageous. I won't help with that."

Ava decided to deal with Celie first. Gabe would understand.

"You, Celie? Not help me? What a surprise."

Celie ran out of the kitchen in tears. Ava had expected Celie's anger, but Gabe's response shocked her. His eyes were blazing with disapproval and maybe even contempt.

He had made her promise not to bait Celie with history or politics, where Celie was at a disadvantage. He'd asked her not to criticize Celie for her simplistic do-unto-others point of view. She'd almost succeeded, hadn't she? Except for that *one* little snipe.

She said, "Doesn't it ever occur to her that she's part of a cultural conspiracy to keep her sick patients exactly as they are? Or that the engine it takes to really change things, is the work of people like me?"

"It was a cheap shot," he growled, "and she didn't deserve it. Besides, how do you expect to win people over if you belittle them?"

Ava could hear Celie sobbing in the next room. Gabe was right, of course. She'd been trained not to aggravate, if there was any possibility of changing hearts and minds. Persuasion, not accusation, was the formula. It seemed that more and more, her passion for change was coming out as anger.

"Damn it, Ava!" Gabe continued. "They teach you to mow down anyone who disagrees?"

"I'm not doing anything that hasn't been done to us. Celie's golden rule – right? Treat people the way they treat you."

"Golden rule my ass. She never said anything like that and you know it. You're punishing Celie just because she's vulnerable to you. Because she loves you. Hell, Ava, who in your life could have taught you to punish the people closest to you? Anybody come to mind?"

Ava felt sick. Talk about cheap shots. He was implying she was like Venus because – well because it was the only way he could hurt her, right? She opened her mouth to zing him back, but he'd gone into the living room. To comfort Celie, no doubt. Ava stayed in the kitchen finishing the dishes, a task she could depend on to comfort herself.

****

When Gabe got to Celie, her eyes were so clouded from crying that she couldn't see. She bumped a stack of magazines, sending them helter-skelter. Reaching over her to help retrieve them, his hand brushed hers. They stood up in slow motion, mesmerized by their feelings, ending up face to face, poised as if for a kiss. When Ava came into the room, they were holding hands and staring into each other's eyes.

Ava jumped all over them, her hands pushing Gabe's shoulders from behind. "Are you two crazy? Gabe, Celie? This thing – whatever it is – can't go *anywhere*. Don't you know that?"

Gabe had shoved Ava's hand off his shoulder to push her away from him. His fury seemed directed at Ava, or so Celie hoped, but defeat lodged in his hunched-up shoulders, and he had tucked his head against his chest. He stood for a minute, looking at them from one to the other, and then he went out, letting the door slam shut behind.

Despite her fury just seconds before, Ava was completely calm, like the old Ava, straight-talking but empathetic.

"Celie, you need to understand, that kind of relationship with you would destroy him. Gabe comes from nothing. I mean really — no one and nothing and yet he's had the strength to build a life on solid ground. He's going somewhere bright and good. Unless somebody comes along to sidetrack him from his future. I'm not talking about somebody bigoted and hateful. I'm talking about somebody like you."

Celie wanted to shout something like, "Don't be so dramatic," or "You should know I'd never hurt Gabe."

What she said was, "I know." As angry as it made her, she knew, deep down, that Ava was right. She was crying hard, hands to her face, and then on Ava's shoulder as Ava moved to hold her. Then Ava was crying too, the pair of them hanging on to each other as if they'd just been saved from drowning.

Ava said as she left, "You need to get your head straight, Celie. I mean it. You could get Gabe hung from the lowest branch of the nearest tree, and I mean literally, not figuratively. Promise me you'll stop this."

Celie didn't think she could keep such a promise, even with Ava's tears still wet against her cheek. She felt sad and guilty, but she hadn't really changed her mind. The feelings between her and Gabe had sprung up full-blown, and this time there was no going back.

She replayed what had happened, over and over. His hand skimming hers while reaching for a book, an ordinary movement, a light bump. In that electrifying instant, a yearning that had once been barely simmering, had boiled up so fast it had rocked her body and brain, and ever since then kept her conscience on a roller-coaster ride. That night she dreamed, as usual when she was upset, that someone she loved was drowning.

The next morning she felt even worse. She'd been transformed in a single day. She was ready to shove aside all that she had wanted and planned for years. She'd been reduced from a busy, multi-faceted nurse to an obsessive nut with one singular purpose, to be with Gabe. There was no way to explain this cataclysmic shift to Ava or anyone. She couldn't even make sense of it herself. She couldn't stand being without him but if she spent time with him, it would distract him from his own schooling.

The stone foundation Ava had described depended on his focused spirit. If he stumbled, he might never get back up. It was what life was like if you were a black man in the 1960's. Him trying to move forward and her hanging on to him and dragging him back. Wherever she followed him — college or job — they would face bigotry. If they were knocked off course, she'd find a way back into her old life. But for Gabe, it would be the end. Her world was a danger to him and always would be.

That's what Ava was trying to tell her, and she'd dismissed it, telling herself that Ava was always expecting hazards. Telling herself that Gabe was too cautious, that he moved too thoughtfully through his life, testing his position in it. She believed that whenever Gabe had to push against walls that white men put up, she could help push them down.

No use saying any of this to Ava; she knew every word of what Ava would say. Even when she was this furious at Ava, her voice was there in her head, helping her make sense her own life. Saying, this time, *he'll succeed only if you don't distract him. You can't let him love you back.* Oh and one more, *you wouldn't be able to live with yourself if he couldn't reach his dreams because of you.*

Celie had spent a lifetime rejecting decisions based on race and gender, or any prejudice. How could she now deny her own feelings because of other peoples' bigotry? It wasn't right. Of course Gabe would be able to see it. All she needed was to script it out.

"Gabe, Ava's wrong. It'll be different if we go to a big city, like Washington or New York. People there are more accepting."

Picturing his face and his laugh, and most of all his charm, she asked herself, how could anyone not like him? She tried to imagine them together in a bustling apartment complex where nobody cared what anybody else did – they'd be left to themselves. Ava's argument was, "the kind of equality you dream of is at best, twenty years – or more like fifty years — off." She would prove Ava wrong. As soon as they all calmed down.

Who knows what would have happened, she always wondered, if she hadn't experienced what was to her, a personal Armageddon one afternoon? It was a gorgeous day at the end of the summer of 1966. Gabe was wrapping up his semester at Morgan State, she was finishing her Nursing internship. And Ava – God knows what Ava was doing, something with militant black armies, probably. She'd read about Black Panthers and it had scared her to death to think of Ava robbing a bank. They'd all stayed busy after their blow-up, postponing serious conversations and in fact, personal relationships of nearly any kind, as they studied and worked.

On a whim, Celie had jumped onto Gabe's commuter bus from Cambridge to the room he rented near his campus in Baltimore. Sitting next to him, she felt angry eyes all around them. Her own eyes dared any other passenger to say a word. It reminded her of those times back on the county school bus when one injustice or the other, one bully or the other, had made her mad. Back then she would stand up, certainly not tall, but with her hands on her hips and her eyes flashing danger signals. In those days, she might mention Frank, to remind them she had power behind her threats. Now, even without Frank to back her up, she still felt that power.

"We shouldn't sit so close," Gabe said, bringing her back to today — a bright day on a commuter bus in August, 1966. He was trying to look composed, but the beads of sweat on his forehead told her he was bursting with emotion. "Are you going to go all the way to my campus?" he asked, in his strong, beautiful voice.

He's hoping I'll say no, she thought, immediately grief-stricken. A lump formed in her throat at the thought of never hearing that voice again. She tried to sound light-hearted, brushing back her bangs and giving him a wink. "I'd like to, but only if you're going there."

"It's not a game, Celie. This is serious."

"I couldn't be more serious."

"You can see them, can't you? Those men over there would kill me if they could. This is just a hint of what it means, me being black and you being white. Did you forget that when you decided to come on this bus today?"

"You never forget it, so how could I?"

"Of course, I never forget it! The minute I *do* forget it, call it race or color or whatever you want, this thing that matters more than anything else I ever do, or think, or try to be …. If you're black and if you forget they're not, even for a minute, they slaughter you. If I were a doctor, some of the white patients would say, *I don't believe that colored guy really finished medical school.* Others would let their appendix burst before they'd let their lily-white skin be touched by a black man's hands."

Celie was shaking from head to toe, her feelings so strong they threatened to propel her out of her seat. She couldn't let her emotions skyrocket like this.

"Aren't you being ... isn't that a little paranoid? Sure, there are lots of miserably small-minded people on the Eastern Shore and everywhere, but if we're careful, play it low-key for now, we'll go away from here when you graduate —"

"To where?" he interrupted, his voice so harsh her heart skipped beats. "Go away to where, exactly?"

His voice, so clear and serene, and usually such a comfort, had frightened her. She scrambled for an answer that wouldn't sound lame.

"To a ... a city. New York. Or California ... someplace where it doesn't matter about race or color – "

"Celie, stop." He had dropped his voice so low she could barely hear him, yet the words shot through as if he'd aimed a bullet at her heart. "There *isn't* any such place. And besides, I'm a soldier now, like it or not. I've had my eyes opened to the way things are for my people. I won't shut them again. All the things I'm doing now, my sports, my college, they don't count for anything."

By now, she was livid. "That's bullshit! Your college matters. Your career matters."

She wanted him to add, *and you matter, Celie.* When he didn't, her brain tried to drive out her wounded pride, to give her the room to think straight. Why hadn't he said it? Had his feelings about her changed that much?

It hurt too much to ask him. A man whose heart she knew like her own ... a heart that, right this moment, made her afraid. She turned to see his face. What she saw was that he was in as much pain as she was. Words between them now would just create more pain.

It was blistering hot on the bus and a slow trickle of sweat had formed on his forehead. She wanted to reach up and redirect it before it went into his eye, but she didn't dare. He hadn't even noticed the salty sweat, barely even blinking against it as he said, "The things I do now aren't really what matters. I do them just to tally up credentials. When I graduate, I plan to go straight to Alabama. A minister in Montgomery is organizing peaceful protests, Martin Luther King. I'd like to join his group – the Southern Christian Leadership Conference. If they take me, I won't be coming back here to live."

"I see."

"No, you don't. You think you do. I know you love me, in a way.

You're a great friend to me, but you don't really know what it's like for me. Or my people."

"In a *way*? In a *way* I love you? I've loved you one way or another since the day I met you. I've been there for you, whatever you went through. And don't forget who I am! A Roman Catholic kid in a Baptist town. They used to call Hannah and me 'bead-mumblers.' Since I was nine, Jimmy Pitt would tell me I'd go to Hell unless I converted and got re-baptized."

"Celie." His face was tight, his voice heavy with sadness. "It's not the same."

"Why not? Or what about me being a woman? Just ask Ava. We're supposed to be nurses or teachers, right? Type and make coffee. All of it, color, gender — it's all about the same thing, about prejudice. Exclusion. You aren't the only people on this earth who suffer, you know."

"Maybe you're right. I know you're right. I can't say that anybody else has it any easier than us, but the rights of black folks is my mission, and it always will be. Even if they didn't take me in Atlanta, and I came back to the Shore, I'd teach at Mace's Lane, not North Dorchester. I'd be a history teacher, a coach. Run for town council in the Second Ward. I'd try to do for other black kids what Isaac did for me — bring them along to be proud."

"But that would be great for me too! I could *help* you...." A sob slipped out with the word 'help.' She wanted to scream for letting that damn sob escape. It told her that, in the deepest part of her mind, beneath her awareness, she already knew she was losing. *What to say, what to say — for God's sake?*

But Gabe brought things to a close before she could think of a thing. He laid his hand on her arm and her nerves throbbed with that touch – not with pleasure but with irritability that bordered on pain, and she recoiled. He didn't even seem to notice her flinch. "Celie, please just listen. Can you listen?"

She nodded, moving her arm away from him. His touch made her feel too vulnerable.

"With you along, the whole community would hate you, and they'd hate me. Not just the white people — the black people would hate us too. We'd spend all our time, maybe for our whole lives, struggling and fighting how they all see us ... until all the joy would be gone from us." He swiped his forehead with his sleeve. The line of salty sweat she had wanted to wipe away for him. How dramatic a small gesture could be when everything had changed.

She opened her mouth to argue and all that came out was, "But."

He grabbed her hands and held them tight against his chest, forcing her around so that she had to look at his eyes. "There is no *but.* I've agonized over this for days ... for weeks. All our good feelings would be destroyed, one at a time, until they were gone ... gone from *you*, gone from *me*, and gone from *us.* I don't know how long it'll take for our two worlds to get right with each other, Celie. I don't know how long before my heart stops aching every time I think of you. But I do know that for now, my dearest girl, we both got to go our own way."

Hours later, she could hear his voice as if he was still next to her. His voice saying, not "I love you Celie," or not "just give me time to think," but lines from a poem: *"In the fell clutch of circumstance, I have not winced nor cried aloud. Under the bludgeonings of chance, my head is bloody, but unbowed. I am the master of my fate, I am the captain of my soul."*

He'd given her "Invictus." She couldn't even remember if he'd said anything else before he got off. She only remembered how her stomach felt. Like those boys on the bus with the hateful eyes had kicked it. All the way back to Cambridge, she sat huddled on a seat in the corner, not caring how many stares she drew.

When she got home, she crawled under her covers, her head pounding. A kind of haze sifted down over her thinking so that there were no clear thoughts, just fuzz. Was this shock? The cloud over your feelings before the real pain hits, like when Dale had died, and the Nickerson boys. The truth would sink in soon – that whether he was right or not, Gabe had made up his mind to go on alone and there was nothing she could do to change it.

When she woke up and he'd been gone for a few hours, she had accepted it. He wasn't coming back, not the Gabe she knew. What was worse was that he had essentially taken Ava with him because she could never hope to talk to Ava without Gabe as an intermediary. Two of the people she loved most in the world had walked out of her life, just like that, one of them disappointed in her, the other rejecting her relevance to his life.

No, Celie, not just like that. It would be self-deception to paint herself as an innocent victim in all this. She had spent her whole life minimizing their troubles, their racial burdens, telling herself that if she treated them equally, lovingly, it would be enough to keep them close to her. She'd failed to acknowledge a significant part of them, the losses they suffered every single day, by virtue of their being black. All the no's and slights, the snubs, the insults they suffered, one after the other, day in and day out. Her reaction had been all words and feelings, no action. She thought of herself as being nearly as out of touch as the white politicians who pushed white culture down black people's throats, demanding they fit in, rather than trying to understand what was real for them.

A sudden flash of insight, why it was that her black friends made fun of the white kids at those first Cambridge rallies, those who had carried signs, even endangering themselves to show they "understood." As sincere as they were in wanting to make things right through solidarity, this wasn't what the black community had needed white people to do. They needed them to make things right for real. Was this why Ava had started seeing her as an enemy?

It was time to dress for work. She got out of bed and made herself a cup of strong coffee, drinking it down while it was piping hot, like Gabe always did. She could feel the heat all the way down to her stomach. She wanted to be fully awake and aware of every movement she made, so she would hang on to this lesson. *A lesson is no good unless it actually changes you.* The words of the Sisters in Catechism class. *God doesn't care what you intend. He cares what you actually do.*

Years ago she'd sworn never to forget that lesson.

But there was nothing she could do, was there? Nothing real. She couldn't change politics or make people more accepting. Was she just supposed to give Gabe up? Let Ava slide away?

It would take more than a night or two to solve this. She washed her face and pulled on her nurse's cap, straightened her skirt. Standing before the mirror, she checked to make sure she looked presentable and got ready to reset her mind for work. But not until she told the reflected Celie, "I don't have a notion of the right thing to do to win them back. But I do know one thing. They'll never stop me from trying." She realized that she finally did sound like Scarlett O'Hara.

Chapter Twenty

In the 1930s, Cambridge attracted some of the greatest names in music to the clubs on Pine Street, including Ella Fitzgerald, Cab Calloway and James Brown. But that all changed when the packing companies lost their wartime contracts, and the employers left Cambridge. By 1967, unemployment averaged 30 percent for whites, but soared past 70 percent for blacks. (Levy, *Civil*)

May, 1967

Dear Ava: Willi don't give me my mail. Send letters to PO BOX 642 in Cambridge.
PS. I could use some more money. Sari.

Not even *Love, Sari,* Ava thought. Ever since Ava had joined the SNCC, she'd only been able to get home once a month. Sari's letters, when they came, had grown increasingly cryptic and Ava could no longer get a sense of her sister's state of mind. The last three weeks, neither Willi nor Sari had answered their phone. They had never once used the number she'd left for them to call collect.

Sari must think of herself as an adult who didn't need Ava anymore. All right, then, Ava wouldn't send a dime until Sari called her. She dashed off a post card saying just that.

Four days later, her phone rang at 11:08 p.m. A collect call.

"Hi, Sari. Where you calling from?"

"Home. Where else?"

"I can check it, you know."

"Fine. I'm out with a girlfriend, OK? We stopped at a pay phone. Why you on my case? I'm doing great, except for being broke all the time, so you can just stop tracking me."

"You're doing great at Willi's? I don't believe it."

Sari's answer had been a derisive laugh, and that's what decided Ava to get an assignment back home for whatever period of time it took to get her sister straightened out. She hadn't been able to keep a proper eye on Sari, and obviously, neither had Willi.

The time had never been right to bring Sari to Baltimore or anywhere else. Ava traveled all the time. When her East Coast assignment had spread to the Midwest, even keeping a place in Baltimore had become impossible. She was always too engaged in important events for anything other than lightning-quick visits that had started to end badly, driving home how far apart she and Sari had grown.

She could go on for hours giving reasons for how it happened. When she learned Cambridge was being targeted for a big event, she'd pleaded, "Let me be the one to go there. I know the folks there better than anybody you could send. More importantly, they know me."

The assignment had seemed simple. Straightforward. Talk to old friends and neighbors, parishioners, business folks, see how open they were to being active at a rally. She hadn't felt guilty about this — after all, it was for their own good. It was just logical.

Like leaving Sari behind had been logical, too. What chance would her sister have for a better life if she'd discovered the darkness in Ava's soul? Logic was the way she kept emotions under control, the way she kept them hidden from Sari in the little time they did spend together.

She packed for a few weeks stay and caught a bus to Cambridge, cleansing her mind of ill will so she would be open to Sari, so she could fairly assess what her sister needed. Just sizing things up, no scolding or recriminations. What was it Isaac had always said? *Living in the past ain't really living.*

Isaac was the one topic she let herself feel guilty about. It had been — could it have been a year? — since she'd spent any real time with him. She mostly kept up with him through Gabe. While Gabe hadn't joined the SNCC Caucus, he was active in the NAACP and she saw him often. The first thing she always did was ask after Isaac, right? The last time he'd answered with a sad shake of his head. She'd been afraid to ask what it meant.

All right, then. She'd neglected Isaac, and despite her "logical" reasons, Sari, too. As long as she was facing the truth, she had plenty of remorse about Celie, too, for judging her harshly, almost on purpose, so she could pull away from her without feeling guilty. Celie had continued to reach out to her and, to her shame, she had ignored her. In the way you ignore your right arm as your left arm begins sawing it off.

Just before boarding the bus, Ava put a message on Celie's fancy message machine, confident that Celie would play it over and over, maybe not even erasing it. Her forgiving nature would motivate her to make peace.

All the way across the nearly four and a half miles of the Chesapeake Bay Bridge, a huge gray cloud hovered overhead, crossing the water with her. She hoped this wasn't an omen of what she'd find on the other side. With all the reasons she could list for it being time to come home, none of them gave her even a minute's consolation.

Close to town now, she could feel the cloud's heaviness pushing her deep into her seat, as if the gray mist had worked its way through the metal roof. Maybe when she got there, she'd go straight to the window and buy a ticket back home.

As the bus discharged its passengers, she was shocked, as she was every time, at the obvious segregation. All people of color in one tiny corner of the station, away from the main seating area. How did she always forget this? And yet it was why she'd been sent home.

She was eyeing the ticket window, still tempted to get out of here, when a streak of energy came rushing over from the white side of the terminal. Celie, her arms and her heart wide open, as if no time and no harsh words had ever passed between them.

"Ava! You're even more beautiful! Please come home with me. I have an apartment near the hospital and right next to your church. I can drive you out tomorrow to see Sari and Willi. I took the whole day off. We'll go wherever you want, or you can just take my car, if you want. Please say yes!"

No scolding about the Prodigal Child. Not even the mildest rebuke for being absent for the best part of two years. How could she refuse?

"I'll be happy to come. Except, could we see Sari tonight? She hasn't been returning my phone calls and Willi sounds exasperated. I could stop in and see Isaac, too. How is he? I wish somebody would talk him into getting a telephone."

"But he *does* have a ... " Celie began, but then quickly shifted her sentence to answer Ava's question. "He's fine. Old. Tired. But plugging along every day like always. Sari goes and sees him, Gabe too, and I do."

"Oh, good. So, it's just me, then, who abandons people?"

Celie ignored her and hoisted Ava's backpack onto her own shoulders, bouncing off toward the exit. "This way," she called, turning and walking so that Ava could only keep quiet and follow, which she did. Ava felt an odd combination of gratefulness and resentment. Around Celie, nostalgic feelings had returned already, replacing anger with amusement. Just go along, all Ava's internal voices agreed. It's useless to fight all that good-natured enthusiasm.

It hit Ava that she, on the other hand, had changed for the worse. She had left here wanting her resentments to have life, wanting her anger to be what motivated her. She had called it her dark passion, that hidden side of herself that was so ugly, so distasteful, she never brought it to light. She'd been certain that Celie could never understand this side of her, that no amount of empathy could make the darkness in her soul comprehensible to anyone, especially to a white girl. Even one like Celie.

The post-Victorian building where Celie lived had been refurbished during World War II to house war widows. Ever since, it had served as a haven for young working women. Miss Roundtree looked after the building and its inhabitants as if they were her own daughters. Celie loved her landlord's hominess, she told Ava, but her main reason for choosing this apartment was for its "character." The stark, clean, white of the hospital made her sad, she said, unless she could get a break from it.

Celie's décor resembled the inside of a Victorian doll house. She'd brought along all the stuffed animals from her childhood, arranging them along the furniture, on the bed, even propped on floor cushions, as if they were children, lined up, waiting for the mom to come home. Celie had named every one of them during her childhood and she still referred to them by these names.

Cape Cod curtains draped down the windows, billowing ruffles of aqua-blue nylon that would have looked odd next to the industrial-grade slatted blinds, except that Celie kept the blinds pulled up so high they were invisible. She'd even hidden the cord ends. Ava had once accused Celie of living in a fantasy world. How very unfair. Even though she might be a champion daydreamer, she chose to work in an impoverished community, treating the sickest and poorest people in the County, her good cheer as much a part of her uniform as her starched whites.

Ava was ashamed at how easy it had been to dismiss Celie. Frivolous and simplistic, wasn't that what she'd said? She'd been wrong. Celie had built this little nest to restore her soul, so that she could plunge every day into the darkest places people could fall into. She didn't know why she couldn't keep hold of the enduring nature of Celie's goodness. If she couldn't do it with Celie, she would never succeed with Sari, especially since who knew *what* she'd find when she went to see her sister. It sure wouldn't be goodness.

She settled into Celie's second room, furnished sparsely, a folding bed and a small nightstand. It suited her fine. She had almost called Sari to let her know she'd be coming tonight, except that would have defeated her purpose of seeing how Sari was *really* doing. Celie was bustling around, setting out towels and water and a basket of toiletries. Ava had forgotten how gracious Celie was to everyone, how much she tuned into what people needed.

Celie said, "I need to take some things over to Mom before my shift tonight. Can I drop you off?"

"Yes. To Willi's since you're going out there. My plan is to see Sari before she has a chance to expect me."

"Sure, but, uh ... Ava, are you sure she'll be there?"

"She lives there! She has to come home some time."

"Well, she comes to town a lot in the evenings. Her job is here. And sometimes she stays in town when her shift ends late. You may do better to try Tate's." Celie's voice had dropped its good cheer and she sounded nervous.

"Tate's? Are you crazy? She's way too young to go there. Edward Tate would never let her even walk into that place at night."

Celie began spitting out words like someone would steal them all if she didn't get them out fast enough. Ava's hand went out, an effort to slow her down, but it didn't work. Celie flung out the last piece of her message.

"... and we all keep tabs on her as much as we can, but she's impossible and anyway, instead of going all the way to Willi's and getting stuck there, just try her at Tate's."

A quick kiss, and she was gone, leaving Ava alone with her heavy heart.

****

Celie wanted to bite off her tongue for dumping such a harsh message on Ava so soon. She had talked too fast and too much for all of her life. Sometimes she would get to the end of a sentence at such breakneck speed that the words came out literally one on top of the other.

"Slow down," said just about everybody she knew, at one time or another.

"I'm trying to," she would say back. She'd tried to explain that the words came out so fast because of other people, not her. She'd be telling a story or giving directions and would see the light go off in a listener's eyes. Or somebody's smile would go flat – the listener was losing interest! She had to rush the rest of the words before she lost the listener completely.

By the time she'd got to nursing school, she no longer gave that reason, because she no longer cared that people couldn't keep up with her – with the obvious exception of her patients. When she was on duty, she didn't sound like the same person. Her voice was decibels lower, a soft, pleasing drone, words to sooth and comfort. Even when she was scolding a patient for something serious like squirreling their pills into their cheeks, she would sound approving.

"That's a nice idea, Mr. Jones – it will dissolve more slowly there in your cheek, which is good for your stomach. You might feel even better if you swallow it the rest of the way down, though. You'll sleep more, and we can get you home sooner! That's it – take a sip – now another – open and let me see — nicely done. Hmm? Sure. I'll be happy to sit with you a while. No, I'm never too busy for you. Besides, I'm so glad you thought of it — my feet are killing me."

The truth was no matter what she felt like when she got to work, she seemed never to get fatigued, never to need a rest, never to feel anything bad at all. Her face beamed its light down every hall, shone into every doorway. Sometimes it was the only face in the room with the slightest bit of hope or joy.

She knew the patients loved her, and she loved them too. Except for the one thing she lacked — even a shred of romance in her life - Celie was happy.

Chapter Twenty-One

In the post-World War II era when Jim Crow laws were first being challenged in the South, the Aunt Jemima label continued to present the image of a happy slave or servant on breakfast tables nationwide. In the mid-1950's the company opened the Aunt Jemima restaurant in Disneyland, where Aylene Lewis was hired to portray Aunt Jemima. Many premiums at the time were aimed at children and teenagers. (Rothenberg-Gritz)

Staying with Celie even for a few hours had affected Ava more than she could have imagined. The cleanliness, Celie's light-hearted chatter, and the sunny atmosphere, had already boosted her mood. This wasn't the mood she needed for confronting Sari. Still, she had reached a balance in her own temperament. Love and toughness both, but most importantly, listen before you say a word.

The last time Ava had gone to Willi's cabin, she'd suspected that Willi was drifting into a dark and shabby place, overwhelmed with tiny problems of daily living she couldn't overcome. Having Sari there was supposed to have been a help to her, to help pull her up from the loss of a husband and kids who'd moved too far away. All she had to do in return for help and company was keep Sari in school. Ava had trusted her. With Celie's news about Tate's ringing through her brain, she knew that it had been her own need that had motivated her to leave Sari behind.

Sari was spending her free time at Tate's.

The way Willi had been telling it on the telephone, Sari showed no signs of ever moving out. Was she being dishonest? No, Willi was probably telling the truth about that part - Sari hated change so much that once she was settled in somewhere, she would dig in tight. And Willi would do her best to keep her there. Sari was the kind of girl

Willi would hang on to, a child who wasn't quite whole, who couldn't function without some kind of jury-rigging. It wasn't that Willi could ever think of Sari as a substitute for her own family. It was that even when raising her own kids, she'd jammed her house full of other kids, pets, junk. She couldn't get along without a collection of half-broken things to care for.

From outside, the cabin's windows were anything but inviting. The café curtains Celie had put in the front were no longer there. Ava knocked lightly, then harder, then pushed open the door, calling Sari's name. No answer.

She scoured the rooms, hoping for signs things were OK, but saw that instead, things were worse. Cheap posters jammed corner to corner, ceiling to floor. Piles of clutter carpeted the floor of the living room and she had to walk on her toes to avoid stepping on things.

Sari came home an hour later. "Oh, you're here," she said and plopped herself down in an upholstered chair in front of a TV set that was tuned to something called *American Bandstand* with rock and roll and flashing colors.

Ava was on her own to find a place to sit. Praying for patience, she looked for a chair or a stool or even a corner of a cushion. She found a spot on a chest next to the TV, which seemed to be damaged, too — the color wasn't right. All the dancers were wearing body make-up that was an unpleasant variation of marmalade orange.

"Do you want me to fix the color?" she said but stopped herself mid-reach. This will be heard as critical, she thought, a second too late. Sari's face clouded. Ava wished she could take it back.

"There's nothing wrong with the color. It's the way I like it."

"Mmm — that's why I asked first," Ava said lamely and moved closer to her sister. On a table next to Sari's chair was a fluted white glass candy dish with amber edging. She recognized it from the Mowbray family living room. It was circa 1920's dime-store, although maybe worth a bit more now, if discovered in a junk store. Sari had loaded the dish with gum trappings. Chewed Double Bubble and old paper wrappers. She hadn't even put the used gum inside the wrappers – the pieces were piled into a rubbery pink pyramid. Ava wondered when the last time was that anyone had cleaned in here. Or emptied the trash cans, all overflowing with empty chip bags.

Ava stood up, exasperated, turning so that her back faced the TV, trying to get her bearings for the unpleasant conversation about to start. Sari must have known it was coming. Maybe that's why she'd allowed so much disorder to surround her — to keep people off balance.

"Don't you ever eat any food that's good for you?" Ava asked.

Sari reached down along the side of the grimy upholstery and pulled up a cheese sandwich. "Sure. See?"

Ava didn't look because she'd spotted a cluster of Aunt Jemima figurines on the shelf behind Sari. "Good Lord. What in the world does Willi want with that Jemima stuff? It's degrading."

"They aren't hers. I got them at a thrift store. They're us, don't you know? It's who we were, which in that case means who we still are, or that's what my friend Spike says. It's called Black Americana when you go to flea markets, you know. It's starting to be worth a pretty penny, unlike everything else in this damn house, which is all broken. Like this lamp. Look at it."

"What's wrong with it? It's pretty."

"Try to turn it on."

Ava's hand had bumped against some kind of bottle collection and she had to snake her arm around to reach the switch. In, out, in, out, but nothing. "Do you have any spare bulbs?"

Sari jumped up and came around the back side of the table, reaching up under the shade and twisting the bulb with a flourish. "Da-da! See that? The bulb is fine. It's a broken switch."

Ava's patience was just about gone. "Well, change to another lamp, then, rather than make such a damn stink. The back porch should be jammed with lamps. Big John used to fix them up for extra money, didn't he?"

"Used to, is right. Until he got old and then he just *planned* to fix them. He got sick before he got around to any fixing. Now we got a porch full of broken lamps and toasters and god-knows-what-all. And it's not just the lamp. It's everything. I wear hand-me-down clothes; we sit on somebody else's furniture, and we walk over rugs that dogs and kids have peed or puked all over. Because white people can't get out the stink, the rug is good enough to pass on to a black person. What, they think our noses don't work? That we can't smell the stinking stains of their spoiled kids and filthy dogs, that their mistakes are our blessings – or is it they think that we're so used to living a trash life that we won't notice?"

"My God, stop that. You sound like Venus! She always saw the worst intentions in people. Any act of charity was some kind of insult. That's a mean-spirited and unchristian way to see people, Sari."

"Is it? Well, maybe these charity people are more mean-spirited than you like to think."

"Why else would they give you things except to help?"

Sari laughed, a harsh, ugly sound – worse than Venus's cruel snickering laugh. It was a sound so full of bitterness and hatred that Ava shivered from its impact, as if she'd been struck by a stone.

Sari wouldn't stop ranting. "You want reasons for their charity? They do it to cast out their own guilt. Rather than throw it away, they give it to a 'poor little darky family,' and then go to church and tell everybody how much charity there is in their heart."

Sari ran to her room and slammed the door shut, leaving Ava to figure out what in the world she had to give to this girl. She stood up, stunned and shaking, trying to think. She looked around at Willi's prized possessions. Books that had once been Celie's, magazines from the Jencks's. Calendars from years back, old paint-by-numbers, shepherded out by parents who thought their kids had forgotten. Willi had admired every one of them.

To an outsider, it might seem that Willi collected things nobody else wanted. But it wasn't like that. Here was the sofa she and Sari had played on at Celie's house, its far-right cushion chewed up by Hannah's beagle puppy and then taped shut with electrical tape. Bits of stuffing pressed against the tape and it was clear that a break-out wasn't far off. If the sofa cushion hadn't been beyond repair, would the Mowbray's have given it to Willi?

Ava closed her eyes and thought back to conversations she'd overheard from them. The talk of good-hearted people who shared what they had, as much as any people in the black community. Most likely, they'd had a windfall crop one summer and decided to replace the sofa, sending this one to the Red Cross ... until Willi stopped them. It was Willi who was unable to surrender anything with even a hint of life left in it. Having vacuumed and shampooed this couch a hundred times, she would have thought of it as hers and rescued it, eagerly, lovingly.

Sari didn't know this about Willi, not that she would have cared. Nothing Ava could say would make her care, because her power over Sari was gone. The promises she'd made to Sari now sounded hollow to her too. There was just one force strong enough to draw her away from Willi's nest, and that was Venus.

Over my dead body, she thought, grinding her teeth. She took a deep breath and thought – how could she get her sister out of here? She would have to choose her words with care. She had to do more than make promises of what might happen. She needed to make them come true right now, or else she'd be as bad as Venus. Sari was craftier and more self-protective now, enough to keep her on guard with everybody except Venus. 'Everybody' including Ava, now. There was a time when she trusted me too, Ava thought.

She could tell Sari, "I've never lied to the people I love." Isaac, Gabe, Celie. And you, Sari. Ava's version of the golden rule. With so few things to be proud of, this was one vow she'd never broken, thanks to Venus, who had encircled her daughters with her lies, big ones and little ones. Every time she opened her mouth to speak, she was testing out her words to see if she liked them. If she did, they became her truth, at least for that minute.

Long before her children had come along, Venus had traded truth for self-interest. Ava had escaped the habits of deception because of Minnie and Isaac, because of Celie's generous, open-hearted family. Gabe's gentle counsel. They had kept her safe from Venus's corruption, almost safe enough to live a fruitful life after life's most fundamental contract had been broken – the one where your mother loves and cares for you.

Sari opened the door and came out, her footsteps quiet, her face now composed. She had changed into a neat cotton sundress and sandals. Wearing no make-up, she looked fresher than she had in two years. She actually looked her own age.

Ava said, "I'm sorry for whatever I said that upset you, Sari. You've been telling me you're OK here, but it's clear to me that you aren't. Why didn't you tell me to come get you?"

"What do you care?" Sari answered. Her face contorted to reflect the contempt of her words, but there were tears in Sari's voice, and in her eyes. Ava found this oddly comforting. She was glad the girl's heart was still alive in there somewhere.

"I can see why you think that, but it's not true. I love you. I want to take care of you and now I'm old enough to do it. How about you come to the city with me?"

"You saying Mahm'll come see me if I live with you?"

Time to stretch the truth. "Well she'd not going to come while you're living here. She hates Willie."

"Is she even speaking to you?"

"I talked to her a week ago." At least this last statement was true. She didn't feel any obligation to add that the last words between them had been angry ones.

Sari grew fretful again and began spewing a list of complaints about life with Willi. Ava settled in and listened to it all, taking great care to keep her face sympathetic. She could sense that Sari was ready to give in. Wherever her Mahm was most likely to go next, that's where Sari wanted to be.

Willi had kept Sari at *status quo* here, a child half broken, half-grown, and she'd made no effort to try and heal her. In Willi's life, when people valued something you loved, it had a way of disappearing. She had collected Sari, kept her the way she was, and would probably fight to keep her. Her insistence that Sari didn't want to leave was partly true, but you don't get to collect people. It was Ava's job to pry her sister loose from the makeshift umbilical cord Willi had attached to her.

For now, she said, "I'll make you some soup."

She poked around the kitchen, thinking how you can find the stuff to make soup in just about anybody's house. When she came back with steaming bowls of noodles in broth, Sari had turned off the TV and was singing, but it was a song that made Ava's skin crawl.

Here's old Dan, he comes to town;
He swings the ladies round and round.
He swings one east, he swings one west.
He swings with the one he loves the best.

"*Tucker was a hardened sinner,*" was what came next, but Ava knew she couldn't stand another note. It was a particularly lewd version of "Old Dan Tucker."

"Where did you ever learn that god-awful song?"

"Hmmm?"

"That's an old minstrel tune that makes fun of black people in a very nasty way."

"Does it? Never thought what the words mean. Ifn' it upset yo', ah won' sing it no' mo'."

Infuriated with Sari for the degrading jargon, it was all she could do not to slap her. Where was all this venom coming from in a girl her age? For the first time she heard, really heard, what Celie had been warning her about. And why Willi was so vague about how Sari was doing. What in God's name had she done by leaving this girl behind with a bitter old woman? And what had Isaac been thinking, putting her here in the first place? All she could hope now was that it wasn't too late.

Sari sat with that mocking smile spreading across her whole face; the look said that she had antagonized Ava deliberately. That she had expected — maybe even wanted — a slap. And that was the moment when Ava let her hand fly up, mind of its own, and hit across Sari's left cheek, hard enough to sting but not leave a mark. It pained her that she'd chosen to control her sister through the kind of violence she'd hated when it had come from Mahm. Ever since Gabe accused her of punishing Celie in the way Venus punished people, she'd thought she had better control of her anger. She would need to control it every minute she spent with Sari. But she didn't regret the slap. Right now, Sari needed firmness more than kindness. Ava turned her back on her sister, knowing that if there were tears, they would be tears of frustration, without a shred of regret. That change would take time.

****

After Ava left, Sari sat on the porch, which she called the veranda, half as a joke but also because she'd always wished for one. Mornings on the veranda, the sun splashed its cheerful light on every surface. At night, the porch was a haven, so dark she could sit there and even Willi wouldn't know where she was. Sometimes, like tonight, she'd light a small campfire to remind herself of better days when Mahm and Ava were still around and when Ava was a comfort.

She was a burden to Mahm, to Ava, and to Willi. She was so *damned* tired of waiting. Always waiting ... for Ava to visit, for Venus to come, for a friend to pick her up and take her into town, for *something* in her life to change. But no, they all gave her a little taste of everything, just enough to know what she was missing, before leaving her to rot in her narrow room at Willi's. Even Ava's affection was empty. Why should anybody be surprised she'd found a sense of purpose on her own? A place to go where she wasn't a burden.

The campfire went from a low simmer to a bed of ashes, light and fluffy, like the delicate petals of the Mimosa tree in Celie's yard when they were growing up. Like with those tree petals, every wisp of air would pick up a handful of ashes and send them drifting up into the dark sky. She felt safe, meaning unseen, unrecognized. She hopped down and wove through the trees that lined the main road and made her way to the downtown. There was still business to be transacted tonight.

She was disappointed. The man she was looking for wasn't at the bar after all.

"He's in the woodshed out back," said one of his henchmen. Sari had just ordered an iced tea, the bartender frowning at her while she had fumbled in her purse for the exact change. She'd put the change in an ashtray on the bar top, taken a sip of her iced tea, and headed out the back door. Her glass had turned frosty in the heat, and with the lemon slice floating on top, it made her think of Venus when she was still with them, making them tea and fanning both girls when they'd become over-heated; all the while, saying, "I shouldn't be coddling y'all like this. I ought to let you just sweat, so's you won't end up soft. Your Pap would still be in your life if he hadn't gone soft." Every comfort had a price with Mahm.

She snapped out of her reverie when she spotted a man's hand waving her to come into the rat-infested storage shed that was used to store the restaurant's garbage on week-ends. It was all she could do to bring herself to walk into that godforsaken place. He was in there, alright, seated at a tiny desk with his back to her, his eyes focused on papers that he was sifting more than reading. It was all an act, for her benefit, she thought. He liked extremes. Rich man, polished to the nines, sitting in a rotting cabin. Sitting erect and aware that he was strikingly handsome, against hideous, sour-smelling surroundings. The henchman she hated most was the one who had waved, an ageless man called Pox, because of his deeply pitted face. His function seemed to be to keep people away from Calypso. He was holding up his misshapen hand, his forefinger raised, *wait a minute.*

Calypso finally acknowledged her, ambling over like he wasn't sure if he could make the trip from one side of the tiny room to the other. He put his arm around her and walked her outside to a pair of steel chairs, and they sat. They talked for almost an hour, the whole time with his oddly spicy fragrance permeating the air around her.

He had a mannerism that intrigued her – she dreamed constantly of him doing it – he would hold the soft tip of his finger against her lip while she was talking. She could feel that touch at night sometimes.

He was asking her to do something and of course she would, no matter what it was. She had to ask him a second time, what exactly, he wanted her to do, not as a challenge but to understand, and still his answer was vague. He seemed to know she was starving for details of his operations and withheld them because of that. She assumed he was very good at tantalizing people who were starving –withholding things they wanted inside a loop, just out of reach.

Just when he thought he had her to the point of feeling crazy, she sat back in the chair and said, "Never mind, doesn't matter. If I get there and can't make sense of it; I'll just leave. Find somebody who wants to jam a while. Maybe Cicero will be in town."

Calypso crossed his arms and let his chin drop to his chest. His beard covered the American Eagle gold coin that he wore on a chain and never removed. His eyes gazed at her above the rim of his glasses.

"Bitch. You don't want to be hanging with Cicero."

"I don't want to be hanging with you, either, yet here I am."

He reared back, laughed heartily, and then leaned forward again, the metal taps on his chair hitting the pavement with a clatter.

"Alright, Baby-girl. Got no more time to play tonight. Got a shipment coming in I need to spread around. Cops all over the place, so I need somebody I trust to keep it safe. You dig?"

"I have a perfect place. My sister works at the church and has a key. No one will think of searching in there, right?"

"He laughed again, and instead of touching her lips, he took her face into both hands and gave her a sweet, lingering kiss. She knew it meant absolutely nothing, that Calypso was like her. He liked a lot of people but loved no one. We're a perfect match, she thought. He's a lazy man, but he likes mayhem and needs people around him like me, who are good at making it.

He gave her one more part to play. If the fistfight wasn't sufficient to draw everyone to them, she was to toss a 'cocktail' into a parking lot until they finished the job. It's not just the drugs this time, she thought. Someone was going to be robbed.

She'd done tasks like this before, and once she'd even been caught. Gabe and Celie had come to get her released. In the car ride home, Celie asked why she did it.

"Did what?"

Gabe snapped, "We're not as stupid as you think, Sari, and the police aren't either. You're on their list now. The only reason you're not in jail is that no one caught you doing anything except making a ruckus. Was that it? You were supposed to create confusion to cover your partner's tracks?"

"I guess," she'd answered, sounding as vague as she could.

"Is this someone you're in love with, then?" Celie asked.

She spit out a derisive laugh. "Hardly! He's an asshole." She had expected to be scolded, but Gabe had instead found an open wound in Sari, something that finally hurt.

"She's Venus's child, Celie. That's the answer. Venus was the mother of chaos and Sari likes to be around chaos. Right, Sari? Makes you feel like you're home."

Chapter Twenty-Two

Strength does not come from physical capacity. It comes from an indomitable will.

—Mahatma Gandhi (in Attenborough)

After leaving Sari, Ava went to Isaac's cottage for the night, hoping she might get some sleep if comforted by the sounds of crickets and Isaac's gentle snore. But her head was too full of Sari — the girl's misery, her provocativeness, that sly laugh. She couldn't go back to Baltimore with Sari this way.

How could she tell Sari about her own secret, how the reason she hadn't kept her promise had been about protecting, not abandoning her? *Sari,* she would say, *sometimes it takes all my energy to stay on a forward track. When I look in the mirror, I see a girl tied together with string. I want to do some good in the world before the string comes undone.*

And it *would* unravel. She'd known it ever since the day at the migrant camp when Venus had told her she and Sari were doomed. No matter how she had tried to erase those words from her heart, she'd never been able to.

The curse had come because Venus overheard Ava scolding Sari for stealing clothes and jewelry from one of the farmer's wives. Ava was twelve then and Sari only eight or nine, a sweet child who just wanted to please. Venus had come up on them from behind, shoving Ava hard to push her away from Sari, screaming at Ava instead of Sari.

"Who you think you are? Why you thinking the likes of you could ever scold Sari? How you think you're so special? You ain't. Sari might be cursed, but guess what? You been cursed too. Your evil just a bit slower in coming, but make no mistake, girl. You born of bad blood. Even if you hadn't been, I done sold what's left of our souls to the devil. It's what got us up North and into good money. You listen good, Ava, cause there won't be no dodging the devil when he comes for you."

At first. she'd been sure she could overcome this harsh prediction. She had studied, and prayed, and sought advice from Isaac. Then the preacher. And yet no matter how much she practiced discipline in her life, the dark passion began to take shape. She was unable to bring herself to call it a curse, because this word made a person feel helpless, whereas a passion could be controlled.

She'd been fourteen when Venus's prediction hunted her down and consumed her. The preacher had asked her to stop by the church "for ministry" one afternoon when his wife and children were in town holding a prayer service. She had welcomed the chance for counsel.

He sat close to her, his eyes looking kind and soulful. He whispered softly, his lips near her ear, "I see you restless during prayer, Ava. Ain't good in a young girl. Maybe if you confess what's worrying you, I can help you cast out the trouble."

She'd been so relieved, confessing everything to him that day – about Venus, about Sari's attraction to the criminal elements, and finally about her own physical yearnings. "Mahm caught me looking at myself in the mirror and told me I better beware, what with me having a woman's body already. She said, 'When you fill out young like this, it means only one thing. God knows you gonna be a whore. God showing how you might as well be ready for it.'"

With these last words out of her mouth and tears threatening, she felt the preacher's hand on her thigh, sliding upward, rubbing her crotch, his other hand encircling her breast. She hadn't been able to say a word because his mouth was suddenly on hers, his tongue probing her teeth, her lips, until she found herself on the floor, under his weight, with her vagina throbbing from his horrible pushing and shoving – and then it wasn't horrible any more. It was this feeling, not the attack itself, that had undone her. She'd gone back to see him three times. Each time, she found herself aching with want for all the hours between their encounters.

Venus, of course, knew something wasn't right and followed her the third and last time. Ava was just leaving the barn, putting her skirt to rights, when Venus grabbed her by the arm and pulled her off the path.

"Well, well, well. If that don't beat all. You think you best off being God's whore, right, girl? Maybe you thinking it'll get you to heaven? Well, it won't. You'll see that damn preacher in hell, right there next to you," She walked away, hacking with laughter, barely able to walk a straight path she was so laughing so hard.

That was the night Ava left home to live at the church in Cambridge. The minister there, Reverend Benson, was an old man and she'd figured he probably didn't even know where his penis was anymore. She kept herself safe and free from following her temptations for two years, until she joined the Black Caucus. Then her life had seemed to explode, on the road for weeks courting danger, then hanging in the city with people who thought of sex as they would about scratching an itch. She'd settled into equilibrium, a pattern of work followed by escape, the boundaries intact between them, even if it felt more like resignation. She'd reasoned that if you're destined to be a whore all your life, you might as well spend part of your time with people who did good some of the time.

Of course, she couldn't bring Sari with her after that. How could she? Talking about it would give it life, might even jeopardize her own victory over Venus. Sooner or later, she would have corrupted Sari. She remembered how it had been with all Venus's "guests." The best thing she could do for her sister was leave her with better, more moral people. The best she could do for herself was pick out men who had a bit of character. Somehow that made her feel less soiled. That was of course, before she'd met Ethan.

****

The night Ava met Ethan Johnson, he'd been bar-hopping. It was his one night in town, free from work and worry. Often, he'd spend his time in bars where he might or might not find a girl he fancied. Whether he did or not didn't matter. He went for the release only alcohol could give him. Ethan lived in Cambridge with his mother, so he always went up the road a bit to Salisbury, where they let the races mix company in public places.

He was at a mostly white bar in a bad part of town, the *Keep Away Tavern*. They kept whiskey scarce, especially when people of color ordered. "Only got beer tonight," the bartender lied.

"No problem." Might be only beer, Ethan thought, but it works if you guzzle it fast and follow with one after the other.

Six days a week, he didn't drink at all. When the seventh day came, he aimed for rip-roaring drunk as fast as he could get there, rocketing himself past that point where you feel in love with every woman in the place. Past the point where your brain feels easy and your tongue's set loose, when the women can get you to talk by listening closely to every word. For years he'd been told he was handsome, but it wasn't looks he cared about. What mattered more was a sense of fun and a bit of a challenge.

This didn't mean he wasn't keenly aware of beauty in women, like the girl sitting next to him, a real looker and seasoned enough to be interesting. Her clothes hung just right, hugging her curves in some places, skimming over others. He liked that. The way she was looking at him told him she'd seen men drink the way he did and was waiting for him to get his head where he wanted it. He liked that too.

When he turned to her, she re-crossed her legs as if to get comfortable, flashing thigh and probably a lot more if he'd been looking in that direction. But his eyes were locked on her face. It was a face carved from stone and then painted with the colors of the ocean – bottomless greens and deep navy blue and shades of cavernous purple. He guessed that her ancestors had somehow kept their women out of the hands of white men. Much as he hated to blame his own women-folk for what men did to them, his own Ma – he found the woman's dark skin intoxicating.

She said her name was Ava and she talked without really looking at him. She wanted to know about his life, what he liked, who else he might know here, but he wasn't going to tell her about himself. Damned if he'd let a sexy little scrap of a girl cajole him to the bottom of a hole he'd spent most his life staying out of. Instead, he turned the tables, asking her one question after another, simple questions at first that meant nothing, so she would think they were making small talk.

She kept prattling and fiddling with her drink, and he saw this was going nowhere. He pulled in a deep breath, put his hand over hers, and spoke her name, drawing out the syllables as if they were the notes of a beloved song, crooning, "Av - a."

When he finally had her eyes, he asked, "So who loves you, Ava?" He'd intended for her feel a bit awkward, so she'd know she couldn't push him around. However, it was clear she'd learned not to be blind-sided by men. Having grown up with a crowd of bawdy boys, she told him, she was immune to his spiky teasing, no matter how he disguised it. Maybe she'd be a good challenge, just enough to keep his interest high without putting him on the defensive. A fun night for both and both gone by morning.

****

The one thing Ava hadn't anticipated was this guy's tenderness. His hand on her back was protective as they rose to dance. It wasn't the same man who a minute ago had used barbed compliments, as if to seduce and insult her at the same time. Still, like with all smooth-talking men, she didn't let herself feel anything good towards him. A snake can only be a snake, she thought, as he held her close, swaying to the music, caressing her bare forearm.

They sat down. He listed half a dozen reasons why she needed him to walk her home. Most of his arguments had to do with the danger of girls alone at night. She was tempted to upend him with a judo throw and then offer to walk *him* home, 'just to make sure you stay safe.' She settled for, "No thanks. Don't need a man to find the way home."

She wasn't sure what she wanted next. She needed a minute to think. She turned away, pulled her purse closer and reached inside it to grab a lipstick. When his eyes left her, she felt it, a chill on the top of her spine. Turning around, she saw only the back of him as he edged closer to the girl on his other side. Ava touched the back of his shoulder lightly, not like a possession, she was certain. To her disappointment, rather than trying to re-engage, he moved away, closing in on his new find. A white girl, all dressed in slinky black and trying to be oh-so-cool. Ethan was leaning into the girl, trying to impress her, unconcealed in his wish to dominate her. Ava wasn't going to stay to find out if it worked with this girl, or the next one. She was furious that she'd let him unsettle her, but when you lose a skirmish, you exit.

Once outside the bar, she felt the wind whip open her jacket. The filmy nylon of her dress made her feel colder than if she'd worn nothing. She walked briskly – she liked the icy wind because it made her senses sharp. She kept an ear out for unwelcome footsteps. Brave thoughts and judo skills notwithstanding, there was no sense asking for trouble.

The footsteps, when they came, were more annoying than frightening. She was positive they belonged to Ethan. His whisper shot out across the darkness, beckoning her to follow him. "I thought you'd never get here, Ava."

He slid into an alcove just ahead and she tried to picture how he could have gotten in front of her like that, without her sensing it. She tried to see his face and read his mood, but it was too dark. He was a shapeless indentation inside the alcove shadows, his body absorbing the energy from street lights rather than reflecting it. She was surprised when the door behind him opened inward and he backed himself through it, as if he knew where he was. He must be from around here. She followed him.

They were in a small room, oppressively dark, with no light except the pale remnants from the streetlights. She was close enough to him feel his warmth but still couldn't make out his facial expressions. She searched for other clues to remind herself of what she knew about him.

For the first time, she recognized how strong his scent was, now prominent without the smoke-wall of bar smells to block it. His aroma curled around him in an upward arc, reminding her of the perception she'd had of him as a snake. She moved closer to the smell, needing to understand it. Sweat mixed with soap, minty aftershave and something else … not sweet, not musky, very intimate. She couldn't place it except she knew he wasn't trying to smell like anything. It was something more basic.

"Who are you besides nobody's true love?" he was whispering, his lips on her cheek, sliding toward her neck. She was mesmerized by the touch of his lips, until his words brought her back to center. She was not going back to bar-side teasing. Out on the street, it's time to talk straight; and besides, she'd never felt like this with a man and she wanted more of that feeling.

He must have sensed the change in her reaction. His voice had lost its jaunty tone as he said, "The thing is, you're so beautiful. You don't need to hang out in bars. So why do you?"

"To find men like you, of course. Dangerous men who won't bore me."

"But I'm not dangerous," he said, his mouth against her ear again, his breath comfortably warm. She was filled with the scent of him, and it was all she could do to stay alert to his words. "Most men aren't dangerous, Ava. It's women who make their own selves weak, before any man ever thinks of it."

"Who cares?" she answered. "Weak is weak." He's either stupid about what bad men can do, she thought, or he's one of them. Approaching him had been a bad idea – gorgeous but not worth the risk. At best, with so many tiresome questions about her life, there had to be a way to get him to stop probing. But not this man, she suspected. This man would ask his own executioner about the denier of the rope as it was being tightened around his neck.

The room seemed to be swirling and she felt her body sway. His hand slid down her arm, just a touch at first. Maybe to hold her steady or maybe more. Then he began pressing harder, and harder, causing discomfort just shy of pain. She felt her own pulse through his fingers, then his pulse, then only the squeezing.

No matter what his intention had been before, he seemed to want her to react to his strength. Again, she thought of the snake in him. She took a deep breath, thinking to cool her brain, but instead it helped her recognize the elusive part of his scent.

Hormones, of course – but they weren't about sex, which is why she'd been confused. This man was driven more by adrenaline than testosterone. She had stood next to men when they were fighting for their lives, sometimes to the death. Ethan was afraid of something. His own shame, maybe, given he had worked so hard to make her feel shameful about her life. Maybe this was why he drank hard. To make sure he had no feelings about anyone else ... maybe no feelings at all.

Wait! That was supposed to be *her*! She was supposed to be the one who never got involved, and yet here she was, her nerve endings firing like cannons, her skin flushed with waves of warmth, the warmth turning to excitement. Soon, she'd be unable to walk away at all....

"Let go of me, Ethan. *Now.* Go back to that pasty-faced white girl you were talking to." She growled the words the way her judo-master had taught her. If he would let himself notice, he might feel her muscles tensing under his grip, readying themselves for a fight. A minute passed, with neither of them shifting anything.

When he finally let her go, it was a complete surrender. He backed himself into the darkness, wordless. When she left, it felt like an escape. She settled into the sound of her high heels clicking against the pavement, letting them jolt her back to common sense. As she turned the corner for home, she realized she'd been in more danger than if he had been some ill-intentioned madman trying to rape her. Ethan had wanted much, much, more of her than that.

Chapter Twenty-Three

For days after meeting Ethan, Ava had never felt more uncomfortable in her own body. Her feelings about him had intensified so quickly that it made her dizzy. Everything about the relationship was outside the bounds of her carefully established rules for directing the 'dark passion.' Intense sex was fine, but when handsome men who were practiced at sensuality set her body on fire, she was supposed to get up and out as quick as she could. Avoid the *Keep Away Tavern*. She'd done it before. Say *no thanks* to another drink. Leave the lights off so that faces could be blanked out and forgotten. You weren't supposed to memorize the curve of a bottom lip, the angle of a chin. Or notice a small scar and try to guess how old he'd been when – you weren't supposed to wonder about his past or imagine him as a little boy.

Her feelings had become a mystery to her so fast that it was impossible to know what to do with them. They had taken charge, forcing her to find out where Ethan worked, then looking up his teaching schedule. She'd sit in her parked car trying to catch a glimpse of him talking to his students, at which time her emotions and reason would both collapse under the weight of physical desire.

Maybe she was going crazy, after all. Venus's face was behind her in every mirror, sneering derisively, saying *what did you expect? All whores get trapped by the devil, sooner or later.*

Enough! Of Venus in the mirror and Ethan in her dreams, and of feelings taking over her life. She promised herself she would never see Ethan again.

But of course, she always did.

Today she would end it. It was Thanksgiving, a time for holidays and families, but she'd scheduled a road trip that would take her away almost until Christmas. That would give her the time and distance to get her sanity back.

The alarm and the phone rang at the same time.

The trip to New York had been postponed because of storm warnings and she fell headlong into her blue mood again. She would have to find something to do on the holiday to keep from thinking about Ethan. She called Sari, but the phone just rang out. God knows where Sari was staying.

She went outside to check on the storm and found the kind of murky Eastern Shore sky that colors everything on the ground a drab gray. Storm clouds were everywhere, threatening to dump out precipitation – could be sleet, snow, hail or rain. No matter what you wore against it, it would be wrong.

She almost didn't answer the phone when it rang again, given she was supposed to have been on a bus headed to Atlanta this morning, not here by herself daydreaming. *It could be Ethan.* With Sari refusing to see her since their confrontation, she would be tempted to see more of him.

But it wasn't Ethan after all. It was Celie.

"Oh good, you're there." Celie was breathless, even for Celie. "I ran back from work to try and catch you. Just in case you might have changed your mind about heading out before Thanksgiving. It's supposed to snow or something — hold on so I can breathe. Ok. I wanted to invite you to the farm for dinner. Unless you're spending the day with Ethan? How is Ethan, by the way?"

"No, I'm alone, and my trip got cancelled. I can come to the farm, if you want me." She would duck the question about Ethan.

"Want you? Are you joking? You being there will make it perfect. Gabe and Isaac are coming, and Hannah's home. Sari is welcome if, well … anyway, I'll pick you up after work."

"OK."

"You all right, Ava? You sound funny."

"How could I sound funny when I can't get a word in edgewise? I'll be ready."

Ava may have evaded talking about Ethan, but her skin was flushing, as it always did whenever she conjured up his physical presence. As she gathered her things, she couldn't help but think about her choices lately. She was still here in Cambridge because she'd cancelled two trips, including one to Atlanta where Medgar Evers was holding a multi-state meeting, not even giving herself an excuse. Her thinking seemed to have given way to raw emotion. When she was with Ethan, she was mesmerized with joy and desire. Away from him, her life was a misery.

She had never even imagined feeling like this. She had seen herself as living a life without romantic love, and not just because of her tortured family life. She knew what a successful marriage looked like and how people were supposed to treat each other. Minnie and Isaac. Celie's parents. Even Willi and Big John. All couples who were flawed, but their unions endured past their weaknesses and mistakes. As far as she could tell, the partners would have chosen to do it all over again.

If somebody had asked her how those marriages succeeded, she would have generated a snappy comeback, like, *Magic? Dumb luck, I guess. Or, because every dark cloud has a silver lining?* Beneath her cynicism, she told herself, was practicality. She'd spent years learning to deny her own passion, or else channel it through quick encounters with men who didn't matter. She was not destined to be part of a bonded couple. It wouldn't be the first time she'd run away from an attractive man, but it was going to be the hardest.

If she hadn't been at loose ends because of the cancelled trip, and because Ethan was with his own mom, and because she couldn't find Sari to arrange a sullen dinner at Willi's house, her life might have gone on the way it had been headed before that Thanksgiving dinner....

It was a lovely dinner. Isaac was in good spirits and looked healthy. Celie and Gabe were both acting like they had in the old days before they'd got so stupid about each other. The Mowbray house was dazzling with holiday cheer — the girls had brought in dozens of flowers – mums, asters, dahlias. Hannah, with her flair for arrangements, had added a handful of tall, ruby-red celosia to the centerpiece, although it had to be relocated to the sideboard when they realized that nobody could see over it.

The family had gone all out. Gabe was looking dapper in a white shirt and tie, and he'd even gotten a fancy vest onto Isaac. Celie was dancing around the table as she helped Mom lay out the spread. In her bright yellow dress, she looked like a butterfly. Hannah had turned into a beauty, nearly skinny now, although her love of desserts hadn't diminished. The meal began with jokes and happy reminiscing. The Felix the Cat clock was still in place and still kept time, although his tail had stopped counting the minutes and the moving eyes were permanently crossed.

Ava was enthralled by the warmth and the food. The table was overloaded, as expected, with turkey and trimmings — stuffing, green beans, two kind of potatoes, Parker House roles, sauerkraut, lima beans and –

"What's this?" Celie interrupted Ava's reverie, holding up a bowl of what looked like cherry jam.

"It's cranberry sauce," said Mom. "I found the recipe in *Good Housekeeping.*"

"You're kidding! What happened to the real kind?" Hannah asked. Daddy looked up from the turkey carcass he was denuding. "She has the real kind somewhere, right Mom?"

Mom blushed, yanked off her apron, and stormed into the kitchen. Nobody at the table said a word. Mom came back with a plate. On it was a can-shaped blob of gelatin, quivering hard to keep up with Mom's pace. Mom slapped the plate down on the table and the canned cranberry sauce lost its battle and slid off to the side. Mom tucked a curl under her headband, took her seat, and used her butter knife to slide the wriggly sauce back in place.

She said, "There, people. I just thought we could try something a little different for a change."

"Sure," Daddy said. "Absolutely. Something new. But I knew you had the real one, somewhere." They all began laughing until it seemed like they might never stop.

Later, when Mom and Dad had gone to take Isaac home, Celie said, "This place hasn't changed a bit, but it feels strange coming back to the farm now. Does it for you Ava? Gabe?"

No," said Gabe and Ava together. Gabe added, "It feels like home, more than any I've had. Except maybe Isaac's new cottage. There's no place I'd rather be than there. Sometimes I would swear he's really my father, or maybe I just wish he was."

"It's wonderful to be here," Ava said. "But to be honest, I feel like I've never had a home, not here and not anywhere. I think I'm a rolling stone. Maybe more like Venus than I want to admit."

The best part of any holiday, no matter what the weather, was when the "kids" would light a campfire, laying out blankets, even pillows, and settling in for stories about the past, or what was happening in their lives. A time to catch up with each other and a time for sharing secrets. Maybe because of that, or because she felt empty without Ethan, when Celie asked her what was worrying her, with those dazzling blue eyes looking right through her, she'd decided to answer. She had felt a wall slip out of place that made her want to relinquish a years-old secret. Before she even spoke, relief flowed through her, unshackling her thoughts and releasing her words as freely as if she was telling a children's folk tale.

About how Venus had cursed her future, how the preacher had violated her trust. How her mother had caught her and repeated the curse. She was able to put into words that it was her own behavior that was responsible for making that curse come true ... her giving in to the preacher and going back to him again and again, until Venus caught her.

While she'd been telling the story, she had let her eyes follow the flames as they were spiraling into the air, almost a little hypnotized by them. As she finished her last sentence, it occurred to her that no one else had made a sound since she'd begun the story. After another few seconds of dead silence, she looked up and encountered three pairs of horrified eyes.

"Hey, you guys, I'm not a complete ass. I can fight the curse most of the time."

"You're not a *what*? Jesus, Ava. Why would *you* be an ass?" Gabe asked.

"You poor, poor angel. There isn't any curse!" Celie was crying. "I can't believe even Venus could be that cruel. Don't you see? It wasn't you who was evil, it was her. She was jealous because you're beautiful and smart ... and because...."

Celie was prattling, always a sign of her misery. She's taking this much too hard, Ava thought. But it was Gabe who shocked her. He sprinted across the fire and grabbed Ava by the shoulders, first giving her a shake and then pulling her into a bear hug. He took a breath and then set her back in place, his face tight and angry. "Celie's right, she's worse than evil. That bitch of a monster mother of yours took a young girl's normal sexuality and twisted it into something ugly. You got raped by that minister –"

"Raped? For God's sake Gabe, didn't you hear the story? I went *back* to see him. I *liked* it. It's not called rape if you–"

"Let me finish. It's always called rape if you're a child. A child got raped by her minister and rather than help you and keep you safe from that damn pedophile, your mother cursed you. Then left you to make sense of the abuse on your own. No wonder you got such a warped view of sex." His voice was hoarse with fury. "Damn it all, Ava. You should have come to Isaac, or to me, when it happened. Why didn't you?"

His words bit into her like bullets. Ava sobbed instead of breathing, tried again and caught a gasp of air. "I didn't want you to look at me the way Venus did, the way that preacher did. I wanted you to keep believing in me."

"I always believed in you, Ava," said Gabe as he grabbed her up in another bear hug.

"Me too," Celie sobbed, as she joined in the hug, and then Hannah was hugging too.

Ava's tears subsided as she realized these people would love her no matter what she'd done. More than that, they saw a goodness in her she thought she'd lost forever. Something shifted in her, as if a devil had been cast out.

Gabe was pacing now. She'd never seen him so aggravated. "What they did to you was criminal. Bad enough that a man of God took advantage of a young girl who'd come to him for help. And that they blamed you. That wasn't even their worst sin. They made you doubt your own goodness. If that preacher hadn't died already, I might just have to go back and kill him."

Chapter Twenty-Four

In the mid-1950's, a thirty-foot, double-poled power grid had erupted throughout the farm landscapes of Dorchester County. Field by field, the corn stalks and soybeans gave way to wooden poles and glass transformers. (Author's observation)

On most farms, the power lines seemed to erupt right in the center of fields — often creating a still life of electrons and soybeans. The first lines began at the newly renovated power plant in Vienna. Within months, they were cutting through the fields just south of Williamsburg, carving out a center strip through the town proper in Federalsburg, skirting around the periphery of the Preston Trucking Company, and snaking along the edges of Easton. Participation was non-negotiable.

Each of the affected farmers were paid $6.12 per acre per month for three years for lost crop production under the Farm Bill and another $2000.00 per annum for two years, thanks to eminent domain. Even though the farmers each lost official ownership of a 20-foot swath of ground around the lines, they continued to plant crops right up to the poles, close as they could get. Everybody on all sides congratulated themselves for negotiating such a good deal.

Nobody knew exactly when groups of teen-agers began their rambles along the power lines. By the mid-1960's, the kids seemed to have formed an ongoing alliance that didn't stand for anything specific other than resenting the elements of life that pushed them toward adulthood.

In Cambridge, it wasn't clear who might set particular nights as party nights, and yet they always started at about the same time, and always in the same place, the graveyard next to the Faith Baptist church on Race Street. This cemetery displayed no iron gates, no carved angels, no ornate monuments. Simple headstones marked most graves, and, in some cases, not even that; just four-by-eight inch markers that might have a family name.

It couldn't be less like the 'Garden of Good and Evil,' but it was a cemetery with its share of eerie shadows. It was a fine starting point for the activity called 'going toxic.' Someone would bring a carton of cigarettes, someone else a few six packs of Pabst Blue Ribbon, and someone else would bring a couple of transistor radios with speakers so loud they could permanently blow out an eardrum if a listener got too close.

The walkers would follow the railroad tracks out from town until they got to the biggest intersection of the county power lines, about three miles south of Cambridge and two miles west of Trappe. Once there, they'd sit, singing, smoking and drinking, absorbing whatever electrons traveled out from the transformers. They'd take turns telling stories of great heroism, or more often, astonishing cowardice. It was here that the teenagers, mostly male and all of them white, learned about each other's differences. They learned even more about their similarities. They were all afraid of the same things, dying young in a fast-moving car – or if you could get a bit older, being blown up at war in a darkly forbidding country like Korea, or more recently, Viet Nam.

Cambridge — July 23, 1967

Tonight, Shrimpy Jones was the one who brought the radios, an Arvin 8 and his mom's leather-covered Western Auto Trutone. He set them forty feet apart from each other, tuned them both to WCAO, and blasted the volume.

Ray Petersen was singing, *But as they pulled him from the twisted wreck, with his dying breath they heard him say…*

"Turn it up," said Stacey, Earl's girlfriend. "I love that song!"

"Ugh," said Shrimpy, but he did it.

Tell Laura I love her, Tell Laura I need her, Tell Laura not to cry.

Six male voices warbled, *My love for her will never die,* right along with ol' Ray. The guys fell over laughing and the two girls began tossing pebbles at them.

"Good drag racer's theme song," said Jimbo Reid.

"Nah, too damn stupid," said Shrimpy. "If I got to die I'd rather be fighting."

Eddie said, "I'm ready for a fight. Tonight this famous homeboy is standing there in front of the Elks Lodge and he yells, *If Cambridge don't come round, we gonna' burn it down.*

"I don't believe it. They ain't got the nerve to say that," Shrimpy had said. "But if one of 'em did, I'd take care of him." He had drawn up his arms in the shape of a shotgun.

"He did say it, I tell you. It was one of those dudes was here back in 1963 – you know James Brown or something."

"Not James Brown you idiot. Rapper Brown."

"H. Rap Brown, you ignoramus," said Ernie Mac, the brain in the group.

"Anyway, he's yelling, *Whitey ain't your friend. You got to kill him, not love him to death.* You can read it in the paper tomorrow.'" Eddie must have felt everyone's eyes staring as if they didn't believe him. "I'm serious! It's true!"

"We can hear if it's true right now," Paige Janus said. "Earl, turn down one of those radios and dial the other one to the news."

"Why we getting so damn serious?" Ernie Mac grumbled.

"It's just for a minute – it won't kill you. Here, have another beer."

The radio crackled but it was a good, strong connection. The infamous words rung out across the Janus's corn fields, above the heads of the new-age crop called sorghum. They drifted out as far as the new irrigation system at Stillwater Farms. When the speech ended, and the ads started, Eddie said, "Well Shrimpy, you believe me now?"

"Yeah."

"So, what you got to say?"

"I say alright, I accept," he said as he stood up, scooped up a good size stone, and skimmed it out across the irrigation ditch. "We'll start with the fire, just like the man asked for. See where it goes from there."

Shrimpy had been shivering as he spoke, as his two strongest emotions, rage and exhilaration, began to grab hold. He had set fires before and there was nothing like it. Later that night, back in town, with the song echoing annoyingly in some part of his brain, he found himself agreeing to join a newly formed vigilante group with a plan to fight against H. Rap Brown and these Black Power people coming here. He'd found an enemy with a face he could identify, with motives he understood.

Cambridge — July 24, 1967 — 2:00 p.m.

Tate's Emporium, serving the town's black folks as a bar, restaurant, night club and pool hall, had become as much a community center as a business. Edward Tate ran a combination soup kitchen and mini-mart in the back of his restaurant, selling groceries at cost, or else giving then away, to people who ran short of funds at the end of the week. In the hours before his life's work burned to the ground, he did everything he could think of to prevent disaster in Ward Two, not just for his sake but for everyone's.

It had been a very long day and he'd kept himself worried sick nearly every minute of it. He spent the morning at the mayor's office offering reassurances of his cooperation with the town council. The afternoon was spent strategizing with Sister Jean, head of the women's choir, and with Reverend Doctor Hiram Benson, the Pastor of his church. They huddled together in the Reverend's office to brainstorm last-minute ideas to repel the outsiders that were here to stir up the local folks.

Reverend Benson could often see things that others couldn't. He was a seemingly ageless man, with gray-streaked hair and a quiet demeanor. People assumed he'd seen a bit of everything that humans can do to harm each other. Parishioners talked to him and he listened, nodding and smiling, never reproaching. Any advice he gave was without rancor, with the result that some people underestimated him, believing him to be far too merciful to use what he knew against them. Since childhood, he had used this aura of saintliness to gather information and then use it to benefit his community.

This afternoon, he turned in the swivel chair from behind his desk, facing it to form a circle with his visitors. Straightening his collar and crossing his legs neatly at the ankles, he took a small ceremonial sip from the cup of herb tea Jean had just handed him, and then he waited, like Jean, for Edward to begin.

"Has everyone read the report on this Hubert Brown – the new SNCC chairman – coming to tonight's rally? I don't have to say – you know from last time — I believe in us defending ourselves. This man is fearful. He preaches outright violence."

Jean said, "But I thought he was a friend of Gloria Richardson? I thought she invited him. I don't think she'd come down on the side of violence. Maybe being in New York, she can't see how things are here anymore. Whatever he wants, his people got signs posted everywhere. Could be hundreds of people, whole families, gonna be out there tonight." Jean mopped her forehead and her neck where her collar lay. More sweat replaced it, soaking through the bodice of her best church dress, a French crepe that looked almost like silk. "You know what it reminds me of?"

The Reverend had to cut her off, since she was about to retell the story of how her Raymond had been arrested and held in jail for three days back in 1963. Not that he ever minded listening to her story – that was his job – but not today. Edward saw and was grateful.

"Did you get to the CNAC meeting? What did they say the message will be?" he asked.

"It was same old."

"Same old what? What did they *actually* say?"

"Tell you the truth I didn't understand half of it. I don't think anybody did, but all the young girls was excited and they started chanting, *we will overcome*, you know, stuff like that. Too much like back in '63, you ask me. Some of 'em too young to remember it led to fires last time."

"It was all young folks in '63," said the Reverend. "This time it's going to be different. And Mr. Carmichael might have changed the message even before he left the SNCC and Mr. Brown took over. That whole group fell out with Dr. King's message, from what I hear. What they're different on, is using violence at rallies. And on the streets."

Edward said, "All I know is, half this town can't wait to shake Mr. Brown's hand."

Jean said, forcefully for her, "I remember him from '63. He didn't make any speeches, but I couldn't stand the man. Arrogant and mouthy. Pushed us all around. What's his first name again, because I ain't gonna call him 'Mister' anything."

Edward opened his mouth to answer but his stomach was pinching him bad, his ulcer not taking well to this discussion. He had a feeling it was going to go right on downhill. He swallowed the acid wash in his throat, so he could speak. "Harry or Henry, I think."

"No, it's Hubert, but they call him H. Rap Brown. His friends call him Rap."

"What-all he wants to call his-self, I call him Big Trouble." Jean put her foot on the library step for balance, then shifted her huge purse to her other shoulder, knocking it against the wide brim of her straw hat and setting it askew. It made her look ridiculously crooked, like she was standing sideways on a hill.

"In his speeches, he tells folks not to settle for second-class citizenship. That they have to make noise, have to fight – have to do whatever it takes."

"We'll have to stop this somehow," Edward said. "All our work for the new housing and things — the white people would vote it right out of here again if there was a riot. And can't you see the National Guard back here every day again?"

"What I can't get over is him telling folks to go against the church. To kill people. Why, that ain't even Christian!" Jean said, looking toward the Reverend. "Right, Reverend? Used to be you knew what young folks was thinking. You knew who influenced them because you knew every kid in town, every grown-up too, matter a fact."

Jean must have glimpsed herself in the fireplace mirror, being as she was shifting her hat. It still wasn't straight. On a different day, Edward would have smiled. She added, "Ever since that Bridge opened, all the kids talk about is getting across it to the city."

"The bridge isn't the problem," the Reverend said quietly.

"So, what is the problem, then?" Jean asked huffily. Jean hated to be upstaged.

How Edward longed for a solution that would calm people in time to prevent violence. He saw that his friend was deep in thought. The Reverend had pulled his hands back, deep into the cuffs of his cloak, the way he always did when he felt his ideas weren't big enough to face the problem at hand. Edward had once joked that the preacher was feeling around for a rabbit to pull out. Right now he regretted this joke at the Reverend's expense. Their joint helplessness was anything but funny.

Reverend Benson took one hand from inside his sleeve and removed his glasses, looking straight-on at Jean. He had wonderful warm eyes and he had learned to use them to comfort folks when nothing else would ease their troubles. He used them now to catch Jean's stare and will her back into her seat. She complied.

He said, "The problem comes to us from the other direction. All those riled-up 'students'. To me they look mighty big for kids. Coming over here across the bridge, squawking and yelling ... but they don't want anything fixed. What they want is trouble."

"Just like in '63," Jean nodded wisely.

"No. Worse," Edward said, massaging the pain in his stomach lightly.

None of them had wanted to admit the fires could start again. Edward asked, "you think there'll be buses full again? It was a couple hundred kids last time marching down the street. Most days, I didn't know more than 25 or 30 of them. Rest were strangers."

"I expect buses will come," The Reverend said, and pulled out a news article. "Let me read you this, what Mr. H. Rap Brown said in the last town he was in. He called all the white folks honkies. He said, 'Don't try to love whitey to death, shoot him to death,' and then, 'it's time to burn down your town.'"

Edward knew they'd each felt the same chill.

"Mighty lucky nobody got killed. God was looking out for us –" Jean began.

"Please shut up, Jean," Edward interrupted. "If God had been looking out so good for us, wouldn't have been no burnings and shootings at all."

It wasn't like Edward to be rude to his friends, especially to a lady, but his stomach had reminded him that he had the most to lose of all of them.

Jean said something again, too low to hear, probably not wanting her head bit off. Reverend Benson asked her gently, "What's that, Sister? Speak right up. Edward apologizes for his temper."

"Forgive me," Edward said. "I'm not myself. Think I'd best go home."

"All I said was when they come to our town, they got no respect for our way of life. Because they're strangers."

Edward pulled himself together for a speech, which would no doubt do him in for the afternoon. "Strangers? No problem. When strangers come through here going to the beach, no problem. When they all coming to St. Michaels for whatnots, OK. Eat supper at a fancy place, buy their what-nots, go home. But these agitators come here to put us in the newspaper. Our own folks start talking crazy. After a while, they talk themselves into not being satisfied with our ways. They see things on T.V., things that black people in the city can get, and they start wishing for things they never had before. And they all like to see their name in the paper."

"Wanting things they can't have has always been something I got to deal with," the Reverend commented.

Edward said, "Or even just to have the life they used to have before the packing plant closed up. When we all came up, getting along with white people was easier. Just go about your work, mind your own business. But now ... no jobs to get."

The Reverend said, "I heard Airpax is opening up lots of new jobs for folks."

"Uh-uh. Zero jobs," Jean said. She had moved across the room, apparently to get another look at herself in the little mirror. She straightened her collar and puffed up her chest, as if to make herself look more persuasive now that she had something real to report.

"Zero ... what do you mean?" The Reverend looked baffled.

"Only whites can work there. Lem Daniels showed us the paper-work yesterday. It says you got to have security clearance to work in the big plant. Talked to the Ward Two councilman and found out that so far, every colored citizen has got an automatic fail when they tried for it. Go look for yourself. Not a person of color anywhere in that place except the yard and the trash room."

"I – I didn't know that." The Reverend's face was tight with misery as he considered this latest bad news. After a minute, he got up, gave his collar a tug where it dissected his Adam's apple, and folded his hands neatly in front of him. "Well, we sure got to figure out where our folks can get work. I'm just saying it won't come from them marching around with paper signs, yelling and screaming and making threats to white people. All that'll get them is jail. Or worse."

"Jail or jobs is the way they see it," Jean pronounced, sitting straight and proper, now that she'd been successful at changing the tone of the room. Edward considered, for a minute, that she may have just been trying to gain attention – but she wouldn't have gone this far out on a limb if it wasn't true.

The Reverend said, "If you're right, Jean, what scares me to death is that when it all settles down, people here are only going to lose. Maybe lose a little, maybe lose a lot."

Edward added, "And I got a business I spent a lifetime building. I won't be able to go on if it's burned down." He slipped deep into his own chair. He saw things the rest of the church council didn't see. People who used to pay their bills on time, with some left over to come eat a meal with their families, these people didn't come to his place anymore.

"Let's not get ourselves overboard," said the Reverend. "People all love your place. They respect you. Why would they let anybody burn it?"

"When Mr. H. Rap Brown shows up and gets the crowds going, no one or nothing we have in the Second Ward can stop them. Ain't one blessed thing to do except sit and wait 'til it's done and hope nobody gets shot."

"If fires did happen – God protect us — we'd all build it back. We'd at least get us back to normal. We're a community. We can find a way to fix it. Right, Edward?"

"Right."

****

Edward had agreed but he didn't mean it. He'd come here today hoping Reverend Benson had nuggets of wisdom, but as a minister, he was so averse to change that he'd look for safe solutions. And as a holy man, he fought against most modern ways, like Elvis and rock and roll, and other things Edward knew were harmless bits of youthful self-expression. The Reverend didn't like to make waves of any kind in the white community. Believing every battle would end up favoring white people, he didn't battle.

Edward was old now. He could no sooner start it all over than make himself young again. His wife was after him to sell up and retire, but she had no idea he was in so much debt after so much unemployment in town. The preacher wanted peace, no matter what, but Edward had to protect the life he knew and the way he lived it.

Then try to keep his conscience from eating out his stomach.

"Clouds gathering from the South," Jean observed as Edward reached the pavement. Everyone looked skyward.

"Could rain," Edward said.

"You wish," said the Reverend.

As Edward walked back along Pine, he realized that evening was already here. Window lights were beginning to appear, and the pungent smell of sweet potato pie was in the air. All the way back from the church, he kept his eye out for violent agitators, but saw only well-dressed teens from Mace's Lane. He tried to relax. Children were laughing, yelling, pushing each other, then slipping into their houses one by one, no doubt called in for supper.

Tate's Emporium was getting ready for the changing of patrons, the emptying out of family men on their way home to dinner. Left behind would be older men who had no home to go to, who would stay until the young folks drifted in. It was still too early for the younger crowd, and for once Edward was glad of it. He wanted to sit for a few minutes with old men, peaceful men, even if they were a bit gloomy.

How many times in the last few weeks had he said that word – peaceful? As if by planting it in every conversation, it might take root and change something. It hadn't, and he was still in his office, eating milk stew with crackers, when the first fire siren sounded. He stuck his head out the window. "What is it this time?"

"It's just the Pine Street school again," called his neighbor. "Probably them white business men what been tryin' to buy the space for a parking lot."

Edward suspected other culprits. He scratched his head, wondering what it was that black men could possibly gain from burning down a black elementary school. He'd rather believe it was the work of one of those bused-in trouble-makers, not someone from their own community, stirred by the speeches. He was starting to feel like a puppet, rather than an actor, in this tragedy. An actor had choices; a puppet could only dance to the tune being played.

Well, the best thing to do was go home to Lena, get a good night's sleep, and see if anyone needed help in the morning. With him home, at least his wife would go to sleep happy.

Chapter Twenty-Five

Ava realized she had lost her head. She was supposed to be getting ready for the rally, and all she could think of was Ethan. It wasn't just that her logic had been swamped by Ethan's physicality. She'd expected that, just as she expected the strength of their attraction to fade in a few weeks. It always did.

Instead, she'd begun seeing things in him that increased his desirability. How loving he was about his mother, how his eyes fairly sparkled when he talked about his father, who before he passed, had been an inspirational teacher ... and the way his hair picked up deep blue highlights in the sun. To add to her confusion, they always ended up arguing, not about politics but about his refusal to discuss them. She wanted to recruit him, of course, and had taken it personally when he flat-out refused to listen to her platform.

"I know the philosophy Ava," he'd say and change the subject.

She'd expected resistance, of course. All outsiders were mired in faulty thinking at first, reciting trite phrases and tired logic. She was ready for that — you'd show them where their thinking had become stuck in a groove. You'd used data to discredit any erroneous 'facts' that clouded their thinking, since what they thought of as data was so often emotion, or even superstition. That's just the way people are ... entrenched. The recruiter just stays super-cool, until slowly, the target begins to see the light. This method of recruiting always got some level of buy-in, especially in the hands of a smart, persuasive recruiter like Ava.

But it hadn't worked with Ethan. Not even a little. The last time they'd been together, she had been explaining something and he'd cut her off sharply. "Drop it, Ava. It's fine for you but it's just not going to be my way."

"Don't you want the way that's best for the people?"

"Don't ask such a dumb question. I have a way to get where I'm going. My way doesn't rely on public bullying." He'd said this without a trace of arrogance.

"You got a way to go anywhere you want, any time you want? To get treated as an equal by white society?"

"I didn't say that. White people don't have that kind of way either. Nobody does. But I get where I need, and I get as fair a deal as any black man can. Fairer than most white people, sometimes."

She'd nearly jumped down his throat, vaguely aware that she wasn't being cool at all. In fact, she was very noisily and visibly mad. *"Aha!* There's your flaw. You're twisting words. *Fair* doesn't mean *equal*. You can't go in a white restaurant any more than I can."

"Assuming I want to, that is? All people discriminate, Ava. It's human nature. Every culture has a power hierarchy and a struggling underclass. I think some of your leaders have lost their focus. They've got you all chasing a bogus cause, and it's going to ruin the SNCC."

"What do you mean bogus? You think equality is bogus?"

"It's not equality that's bogus, no. Equality is merely impossible. It's your means of getting there that's bogus."

"What's the matter with you – you're saying you're just fine with the status quo?"

"Of course I'm not. But there's something wrong with the way SNCC is trying to get there. The organization has changed from the old days. Half of y'all are too idealistic and the other half are just angry. In fact, the group has got so it can't agree on much of anything, except to keep itself alive."

"How fucking self-righteous you sound. People are angry because of rotten housing, poor schools, crap jobs ... or no jobs."

"Of course they are, and they should be. In fact, most people we know have been handed a skimpy serving of the great society and most of us are plenty mad about it. I am too. And I'll even agree that those with the biggest portions are usually white. So your new leadership, H. Rap Brown and his friends, claim that all their troubles come from that greedy white guy. He tells you to go out and take what he has, and if you can't get it, burn it down. What intelligent person thinks that would fix things?"

"You're wrong! Everybody would rather see things shift peacefully, of course. Rap would too."

Contempt washed over Ethan's face, and for a second or two, he wasn't recognizable. She shuddered, hoping the fury he felt was for H. Rap Brown, not her. Ava said, "Your ideas are too vague. Even worse, you don't have a plan. You'd just go along with nothing changing. We've all done that too long."

Ethan leaned forward and laid a hand on her arm. "Your plan, as you call it, and your methods ... all they do is piss off white people and a lot of black people too. My ideas don't play well over a megaphone, it's true. But H. Rap Brown is a rabble-rouser, Ava, not a revolutionary. I don't know how somebody as smart as you can fall for his shit."

Ava bolted upright, leapt from her chair, and began pacing, right there in the public café, feeling some complicated mix of fury and disappointment. She had never allowed a discussion with a recruit to get this heated, especially not in public, but she couldn't find a way to stop herself. She said, "You've been beaten down by your own plantation mentality." It was the harshest thing she could think of. She had felt her voice rising, and people staring, and still she went on.

"What you're saying is still the thinking of slaves ... being afraid to piss white people off. But I didn't come up like that. My mother grew up in Jamaica, a child of privilege, raised by a loving family. She came to America with everything. Beauty, brains, and money to get by. She was seduced by the glitz of Miami, Florida, and by a charismatic jazzman in a Miami nightclub. She renamed herself Venus. Her life was all self-indulgence – no, make that *decadence*. But her sister, my Aunt Minnie, raised in the same family, gave her share money to Venus and married a very good, very poor sharecropper. Minnie and Isaac were happy. Venus never was, but it was her own greed that did that. I never once tried to blame discrimination in America for making Venus the way she is. Believe me, I can always tell who the enemy is."

She sat back down, her confidence bolstered. She'd been articulate, and she'd tamed her emotions.

Ethan turned his head slightly sideways, as if genuinely curious. "So why in the world, then, did you become a soldier in this particular army? Why you angry at *society* if your *mother* is the one who robbed you of life's fortunes?"

She looked away, determined not to be unnerved his sarcasm and instead, to find a connection. "Truthfully? When we came north, I was tired of Venus's craziness. Maybe I got too impressed with 'normal' families. Not just white ones, any normal family. I met Donna Richardson in college, before 'black power' became a marketing term. I saw how the status quo gets stamped into young kids. The people in SNCC made me to want to teach our kids to demand a square deal out of life. And to push on the system until it shifts to make room for them. I can't really explain how special people like the Richardsons are.

"You don't have to. I admire Donna and her family. I even used to agree with some of SNCC's ideas, but not all of them were realistic, even back at the beginning. Donna used to say, "basic civil rights aren't on the table for negotiation." I would have said back to her if I could, that if you can't compromise, you end up with nothing. Better to gain some freedoms now and then ask for more right after."

"Ethan, you're still not thinking this through. Don't you believe that every black kid has a right to the same things as every white kid?"

Ethan had pulled her the rest of the way up from her seat and swept her outside, cooing, for God's sake, like a lover. He whispered, "That's not a real question, is it, love? Just come with me for a minute … look at what white kids have, before you begin comparing."

He faced her toward the part of town where filthy white children were in the middle of the street, playing hopscotch with broken glass. With a jolt, the memories of Celie's internship family and the discarded baby overwhelmed her, and she let out a sharp, involuntary sob. Ethan must have heard the anguish in her voice, but he kept going. "The ordinary white kids around here don't have a fragment of what privileged white kids have. Most the white kids here grow up just as cheated. The cheating is different based on race, but the problem isn't caused by race."

Ava understood this at every possible level, probably better than he did. Most of the white kids she'd grown up with were nearly as poor as she was. Then she had listened to Stokely Carmichael and Medger Evers and something had caught fire in her soul. She'd wanted action. She had sacrificed so much, leaving her sister behind and living as a traveler for the SNCC, in the homes of white liberals, black militants, or peace-loving clergy, depending on what town it was. No matter what their differences, they all shared something important, a belief that if they kept pushing, things would change.

These people had been her friends. She had loved the camaraderie. It seemed impossible she could have been mistaken – not then and not now. She shook her head to clear away her confusion.

But Ethan was on a roll. "I believe that violence begets more violence. Men of peace, like Dr. King, have made the first real progress in fifty years. Have you read his essays and speeches? Or the works of Mahatma Gandhi? No, and you won't, will you? You won't settle for anything less than equality, NOW! Even if you were to get it, it wouldn't last. There are always different people coming up, trying to get more than their share."

"You're the one who's cynical. There doesn't *have* to be an elite, you know. If we improve education for our children –"

"Education? Where elitism is even worse, you mean? Only thing different is the currency they use."

"Did you say … currency?"

"Sure. They count IQ points instead of dollars. You try for good test scores on a loaded intelligence test. You learn how to pass this test by going to a white school."

He'd thought out his position too carefully and he knew so much more than she did about this. She'd been trained to fight against emotional arguments, not educated ones. For once, her logic had failed her. And so she gave up.

And then, just like that, Ethan had done an about-face, agreeing to come to Cambridge for the rally, "just to take a look." She had told herself he'd taken a step forward for whatever his reasons. She'd even bragged that night to her mentor at the Black Caucus about recruiting Ethan, without letting on that it was deep physical attraction, not ideology, that was their main connection. The thing was, he was coming to the rally. Soon, he'd be here.

Morgan State College — Baltimore — 4 p.m.

There were still five hours to go until the first explosion would send burning debris high into the air above Race and Pine. Gabe rented a car, a Carmen Ghia, so he could get to Cambridge in time to hear the speeches. He had missed seeing H. Rap Brown four years ago, and he wasn't going to let the chance go by again.

"It's a good little car, sir, although you're the tallest human ever to have driven this one," the agent said in a bright voice. "I wish I had a bigger one for you."

Gabe squeezed behind the wheel, smiling benignly, by now used to people telling him how he did or didn't fit somewhere based on how he looked.

He got back to his dorm in time to catch Ike, his roommate. Ike said, "Hey man! I was just about to leave you a note. They're predicting serious thunderstorms. You might want to wait til they blow over."

"People who are afraid to drive in rain are afraid of everything."

Ike laughed. "Well that's me, then. Folks from Arizona don't see heavy rain much. I didn't even know what a road slick was until I got here. Guess there's a right and wrong way to drive through rain?"

"Right way and wrong way for every little thing."

"Just be careful, man."

Ike narrowed his eyes to get a look at his friend. Being nearsighted and too vain for glasses, he sometimes had to get close to Gabe's face to capture the true meaning of his words.

Such a really serious dude, he thought, and wondered, not for the first time, what could have hurt him so bad in his childhood.

He'd been right about the storm.

****

It was almost time to head out. Gabe straightened his desk, shuffling the pages of his term paper. A copy of "Plessy v. Ferguson" lay upended against the window frame and he absentmindedly slid it away from where strong sunshine could fade it. He had just turned on the radio for news when the phone rang. He almost hadn't answered it, expecting it would be Celie, asking to help.

He felt childish and reached for the phone, half hoping, half dreading it would be her. He would tell her no, of course. Again. Each time he said it, it should get easier, right?

"Are you planning to go to it?" the voice asked, but it wasn't Celie.

It took him a second to recognize it was Ava, because she was muffling her voice. She was always sure someone was listening on the line. He thought she was overly suspicious, but he played along. No names. He said, "If I say yes, will you drop it?"

"Not on your life! That's why I'm calling. You need to stay back."

"What? Last time I didn't go, and you were furious. I thought you *wanted* more college students." Was he giving away too much by saying the word *college*?

It felt as if the air, itself, was perspiring. The plastic of his phone receiver was sticky with humidity. He felt his skin heating up, creating more sweat – he would have to change his shirt. He grabbed a magazine and began fanning himself.

"I need to explain," she was saying. "It's not about what you *want* to do. I know you want to, that you still got the same shadows in you as me."

It was true, his soul was darker now. Also true that there was not much he wouldn't do for a cause he believed in. Except violence, of course, but Ava knew that. And he knew the rest of what she was going to say, that he was better used here than on the stump, but he let her finish.

"Remember the night when I told you I was leaving that awful white high school?"

"Of course I remember."

"I thought then that you were the bravest man I knew. I've seen a lot of brave men since then and I still haven't met one who could stand up to you. I may be on a different path than you, but that doesn't mean you aren't still my hero."

He didn't feel much like a hero today. He'd hurt Celie bad, and he couldn't even listen to Sari any more. He longed to talk to Isaac. Isaac had a magic way of making you check yourself when you were headed wrong. When you left him, you'd be different, but you'd still feel worthy.

Ava went on, "We're not worried about how many screaming activists or even pissed-off rednecks will be there, although we'll have plenty of both. Our worry is thoughtful men with a purpose thrown into the mix. This time the thugs will outnumber you honorable types at least 5 to 1. We can't afford to have you in jail or worse. We need the educational pieces you're writing."

"I can do both."

"Listen, for God's sake, can't you? Your being there won't make a single bit of difference. If you get hurt or arrested, then there *will* be a difference, not a good one. You'd lose your place at the college. You'd be permanently sidetracked."

"That's not so. I have my own friends here in the department. Besides, wouldn't your people negotiate for – " he stopped himself to listen to his own heart thumping. Maybe she was right. He was already a jazzed-up fool, here in his own dorm room.

Ava spoke. "If you were going to say we'd fix things for you, you're wrong. I know, I'm one of the people who does the fixing. I'm the one who tries to get folks who've been arrested in front of the right judges. You know how well *that* goes."

He remembered friends from 1963 who'd got long jail sentences, immutable, no matter how many funds they'd raised. Other people since then who went to jail, basically for getting caught walking in the wrong part of town. The Freedom Riders had been jailed for sitting next to a white person on a bus.

"We need you as a different kind of soldier," she was saying.

A soldier. Invictus. She knew him too well.

He moved to his little kitchenette and lit up the kettle to make a cup of coffee. Coffee always settled his nerves. He said, "You're not just being over-protective?"

She said, "Darlin', listen. Sit and have some dinner. Watch the news and keep notes on what's happening. *That's* your job. We all have different roles to play at different times, and there'll come a time when we need you out there. Believe me, we'll ask." She raised her voice to say, almost harshly, "For now, this isn't me, who loves you, asking you a favor. It's me, a fellow soldier, giving you an order. Stay home!"

The phone clicked off.

He made himself a second cup of coffee and gulped it down. He still hadn't made up his mind. He hadn't really agreed, and despite all she'd said, he couldn't shake the feeling that he should go. Besides, he would make up his own mind. His choice would be for his own reasons, not because of some officious committee's directive. He knew who he was. He knew what he wanted. Like Martin Luther King, he wanted to change the world without resorting to thuggery. *Good people of strong will could move mountains.*

Straightening his desk, he saw that his history book was still open where he'd been studying for the entrance exam to law school. When he'd bought that book, he'd said he was willing to die rather than break his vow of non-violence. He would use the law.

What worried him was that if he actually went to this rally, he'd see something that might force him to react physically. He had seen first-hand how quick things could get out of control. Even though no one had died in Cambridge's so-called nonviolent marches of 1963, it wasn't because there hadn't been vicious fist-fights and many shots fired. People had been hurt.

By now he'd come to believe that his community had been used and discarded back in 1963, not just by the white men who hated them, but also by black men with agendas that had nothing to do with improving the lives of people in the Second Ward — or even of African-Americans as a whole.

And it wasn't like it was Martin Luther King who was coming. It was H. Rap Brown, a man who loved the spotlight with people shouting his name. A cowardly man who would let himself be spirited in and out of a target town in the cover of darkness, once his message grabbed hold, as long as he got credited with the chaos he left behind.

Gabe didn't want to be trapped into action by shouting men who lacked conscience. If Ava was right, for all the people who meant well at the rally, there'd be more who didn't. Meanwhile, good people like their own Reverend Benson, a man not unlike Martin Luther King, had become voiceless because of people like H. Rap Brown. If Ava was right, this rally would bring only trouble to his people.

Chapter Twenty-Six

The boys from the railroad tracks didn't need to rent a car to get to Cambridge. They had decided on the beat-up white one — "Because white is right," they said, 'raring to go. Their anger demanded a target – if H. Rap Brown didn't show up they could find someone else. They piled into the car, along with two cases of beer and a deer-hunting rifle.

At the end of the road where Mainstreet met Route 303, lived Otis Brown. His was the last house at the edge of town. He made himself stay in bed, not wanting to be seen by anyone, even just looking out his window. He had his quilt draped over his ankles, hot as it was, because he needed to feel some sense of protection. Ever since he'd been four, he'd had to cover at least part of his body while sleeping, even if just his feet, like now.

As he lay listening to the sound of tires against tarmac, he shuddered. Best not to imagine what might happen when these boys stopped their whoopin' and hollerin' and started firing.

****

Ethan kept his promise, arriving in Cambridge on the Salisbury Bus. When he stepped down, he could already smell Old Bay Seasoning. Crabs were steaming beneath handfuls of rock salt and spice, plunged into huge pots alive and pulled out minutes later, bright red instead of the blue-gray color of the Chesapeake. He knew he wouldn't make it past the stalls without at least a softshell crab sandwich.

The vendor at the walk-in stall had almost refused the order from a black man. Almost – he must have been caught by surprise, maybe by Ethan's stature or the way he was dressed, a tall man in an expensive suit. A white man's suit.

How could Ethan have forgotten that every single aspect of life in this town is dictated by your color? He could have been arrested just for being on the sidewalk he chose, as he headed to Ava's church on Race and Pine. The zing of the Old Bay stung the corners of his mouth. He'd forgotten that, too, the heat of the seasoning; and amazingly, he'd forgotten the cardinal rule of crab cuisine – don't let the spice touch the skin around your mouth. His eyes burned too – he must have touched his face at some point. A tourist mistake.

He decided not to wash away the burn of the spice because it reminded him to stay sharp. He mustn't let the rules of color catch him off guard and dictate how his day went. No scuffles today; there was too much to do. Settle things with Ava, make sure she was safe, then go see his mother. Old life, new life. He still fervently wanted to take Ava with him to his mother's, but he would honor Ava's request. She was probably right in wanting to wait until he'd prepared Mama before bringing a woman home. He'd promised to hear the Brown speech for one reason. To make sure Ava stayed out of trouble.

****

When she had set out for the church today, Ava was in the middle of the mental battle that played out daily in her head. A battle she didn't have time for on a critical day like this. To add to her troubles, last night she'd run into Baltimore for a rally that had gone wrong and she'd been hurt. And the final worry: she hadn't been able to find Sari and she had run out of places to look.

Above her were signs of a storm brewing from the southwest. Not close enough to rush her walk, thank goodness, because she ached too much for hurrying. The bones and muscles in her body felt like she'd slept all night under a tractor-trailer. Her face bore the marks of what could happen at any minute in her work – some over-excited boys had knocked her down during last night's rally. The cut stung like crazy, although this was mostly due to the make-up she'd used to hide it. She didn't want some nosy person at church asking questions today. The last thing she wanted to talk about today, of all days, was a rally that had gone wrong.

Inside the church, a few high school students sat and chatted, more about the Orioles than about H. Rap Brown's coming speech. A pot of gummy-looking coffee sat on a burner in the kitchen. The box that held teabags was empty. There was almost always iced tea in the refrigerator, but Ava saw the empty pitcher in the sink and knew the kids must have finished it.

She went further into the depths of the church hall and found Emma, the church warden on duty. "Hey, Miss Emma. How about I walk and get us some tea bags and make you some iced tea?" Emma's hand reached automatically toward an iced tea glass that was empty. When it was full, it served as a beacon of hope in the midst of her afternoon duties. When there wasn't any tea, she had once told Ava, she felt almost lonely.

"Well, I was gonna leave that to the good fortunes of another day, Ava. Afraid the collection plate was a bit on the skimpy side last Sunday. The Reverend's been bringing his own teabags from home." She looked up at Ava, letting her glasses slide to half-mast on the bridge of her nose, leaning back to flex out a kink in her back.

Ava said, "I can spring for a pitcher or two. Maybe even a six-pack of Coke to keep the kids happy."

"Well that'd be a blessing. It seems awful to send you out the minute you get here, but I'm not gonna say no." A tendril of hair had somehow escaped from Emma's stylish French chignon and she shoved it back in with a frown.

"That's a beautiful style for you," Ava said, smiling. "It won't hold up, though, if a lady doesn't get enough sleep. How late were you here last night?"

"It's a Paris, France look, and I do like it most days." Emma patted around the edges of the chignon without finding more trouble and smiled back. "They were up all hours, Reverend and Mr. Tate and Sister Jean. So upset. I couldn't leave until they got things settled, but they didn't, and then they picked it right back up today."

"I don't know how they'd get by without you. How long you need to be here today? It's supposed to be your day off. I'm here to spell you, you know."

"I know, I know. Going home soon. I just gotta finish these last few letters."

"I can do that. When I get back with the drinks, I'll take over the typing. After the kids go, I'll push Reverend Benson out too, if he's still here. I can stay until it's all over tonight, then lock up and leave the key behind the step for tomorrow."

Emma looked longingly out the open window. "Not sure you'll get him out of here until the rally starts. And the typing is my work. You got plenty to handle with the kids."

Ava put a hand on Emma's shoulder. "It's OK. The Lord doesn't care who typed the letters. I can handle both. Let me do my share."

The Reverend emerged from his office at just that minute, fanning himself, having long ago given up his rotating fan to cool the kids.

He said, "Afternoon, Ava. What say we lock up early? Mr. Brown's people called. They won't get here until the minute the rally starts. I don't want folks barging in here, thinking we're hiding him or something. I'll come back this evening and wait here to meet him, just in case he stops by here."

Ava could see he was desperate to get out in the community and be with his people. Emma must have seen it too. She stood up, ready to collude with Ava, purse strap dangling in her hand.

"Well, Ava, I'll give you the key right now then. I know what a good typist you are, and I know you'll help me get our good preacher out of here and where he wants to be."

Ava took a short cut to the small grocery store around the corner from the church. It probably wasn't open today, but Mr. Tink, Edward Tate's brother-in-law, lived in the back and would let folks in if they knew to give three taps on the kitchen door. She gathered the tea, the soda, some sugar and half a dozen lemons.

"Don't like to charge the church you know, Little Ava, but prices gone up and...."

"No apologies for having to earn a living. Thanks for being so kind to let me in."

Mr. Tink was a nervous man and he always made her think of the squirrels back on the farm. Today, he looked even more worried than usual, and she wondered what rumors had been circulating about the rally.

When she got back, the office was empty, its walls dark, and her own sounds were making long echoes. She looked for signs of the teenagers, but they had taken their signs away and cleaned up neatly after themselves. She'd trained them well. She moved quickly to make a pitcher of tea for anyone stopping by this evening during the rally, and then finished Emma's letters.

Ethan would be coming soon. She'd tackle the rest of the paperwork after the rally. Better to check the neighborhood for activity, then come back and wait for Ethan.

She pushed the rusty key into the ancient lock, her fingers throbbing as she tried to get the bolt to turn over. She thought of the Reverend's bony, arthritic fingers, opening and closing the church several times a day. She would ask Gabe to sand and oil the lock. Or she could ask Ethan when he got here. If he did get here, that is.

After her uneventful "surveillance," she again struggled with the lock, but this time a hand slipped over hers to help. His touch on her hand sent a jolt up her fingers that fanned through her whole body. She thought, how will I get through this day?

With both his hands on her shoulders, Ethan turned her around to face him and brushed her forehead with a light kiss. Her face was dripping with sweat that made her feel self-conscious and ugly. Was this normal?

She had been dying to talk to Celie about her feelings, but even after their renewed friendship, she was afraid to trust her. She was afraid to trust anybody.

Ethan slid an arm around her waist and was guiding her toward the enclosed park behind the church. He moved like he knew where he was going, just as he had that night they first met. If he was from around here, why hadn't she noticed him before?

They reached a clearing hidden in the center of the park, protected from outside watchers, then sat and talked for what seemed like hours, just talk, about the Kennedy family, the Chesapeake Bay bridge, the crops, Airpax – anything except tonight's rally.

The air around them began to change – sounds of people milling around and talking out on the street. She said, "We should go now. The kids will be at church soon for us all to go to the rally."

Within seconds, she'd been pinned backward against a large maple tree, Ethan pushing against her so hard that all she could see was the leaf canopy above her. Her body caught fire under his hands and his mouth — her heart thudding, her only thoughts, how much she wanted this man.

He whispered, "How can I help you tonight?" as if he wasn't holding her tight against him, as if his being here in her town, at her church, offering to help, was the most ordinary thing in his world.

She cleared her throat. Cleared her brain. "Just keep the kids together. Answer any questions they have about Mr. Brown and the meaning of the rally. And Ethan, we want them to care, but not to get riled up. We want them to get home safe. If there's violence, get them out and away."

"I'm a diehard pacifist, remember? Just make sure *you're* not the one to rile them up."

She opened her mouth to argue back before she saw he was teasing. She had to get herself focused.

The loudspeaker nearby crackled as someone toyed with it, getting the system ready to receive the voice of the great H. Rap Brown.

"Testing, testing. One – two – three — can you hear back there?" Crackling again and a long burst of static.

Ethan let her go abruptly and turned toward the church, hands in his pockets, ready to go; but she remained against the tree, immobilized. Her legs were stone, her heart the only part of her that could move.

"You ready?" he asked.

Her thoughts staggered wildly ... "ready for love," "rough-and-ready" "battle ready," and finally she said, "born ready?"

"Me too," he said, laughing heartily. Just knowing she'd made him laugh made her heart beat so fast she was sure she'd die of it; then he was pulling her along behind him and she found that moving her feet helped bring her senses back to balance.

By the time they gathered the kids and herded them to the makeshift podium by the elementary school, the Reverend was introducing the main speaker to loud applause.

Ava had finally steadied herself enough to listen. But less than two minutes into the speech, her emotions shifted again. The passion she'd felt just moments before had been replaced by rage. This was not the speech she'd been told to expect. It was a hate-filled, self-aggrandizing testimony to how crazy one angry black man can get. "It's time for Cambridge to explode, ladies and gentlemen. Black folks built America. If America don't come around, we gone to burn it down, brother. We going to burn it down if we don't get our share of it."

She realized she was gripping Ethan's wrist. Relaxing her hold, she whispered, "we have to get our kids away from here. This *cannot* end well."

Amazingly, Ethan wasn't ready to go. She couldn't believe how their roles had reversed. Maybe a man could stomach this kind of tirade, urging brutality, but she'd had enough. She already didn't know what she was going to say to the teens ... or to their parents.

"I mean it, Ethan. Let's go."

They got the kids home, made them promise not to head right back to the rally, then went back themselves to wait for the worst. However, by the time the speaker headed off with his party right after ten o'clock, there had been hardly a stir anywhere. It was so quiet that the National Guard was sent home. Not sure whether she was relieved or disappointed, she let Ethan prattle on, about teenagers and their jive talk, all the way to Celie's apartment.

"I'll call you when I get Ma settled. Could be a couple of days," he said and then kissed her as though he might never see her again. When she went inside the apartment, she was an emotional wreck. She couldn't wait to watch the TV news and see what the world had made of what had happened tonight.

Celie's Apartment

All day, Celie had been rehearsing what she'd say to Ava to let her know she wasn't going to keep her head buried in the sand this time. This time, she lived right at the edge of the Second Ward. Most of her patients lived here, too. She was toying with the idea that she might walk along with the – what did they call themselves this time? There were so many different groups, and she wasn't sure which of them would be there, but there'd be a lot of white supporters at the rally. She wanted to be there with them. She had said this to Gabe when she called him, expecting he would at least tell her she was brave for trying.

Instead ... well, she was still smarting from the harshness of his rebuke. "For God's sake, no! Stay home, Celie. How many times do I have to remind you ... you're not black." He'd made it sound like an accusation.

Afterward, she called Ava in tears, looking for vindication. Although Ava had agreed with Gabe's decision, she'd been kind rather than harsh.

"No, Celie. Gabe's right. Not that way. Not shouting freedom songs at a rally. If you want to help, you have to work from who you are."

"I ... I don't understand."

"I don't have the time to go around on this right now, Celie. Think of it this way – we'll need nurses, too. People are likely to get hurt tonight. You can be there to make sure the hospital doesn't turn them away."

Of course. That's how she would help. Ava had made her feel useful rather than ashamed. For a moment, the kindness had healed her pain. Then, with Gabe's words still ringing, she was crying again, no matter how hard she tried not to. She fought back the ache until she finally wore herself out with it and slept.

She woke to the sound of angry shouts and what sounded like a pair of gunshots. The clock said 8:00 p.m. She was afraid to look outside, not thinking of her own safety but of what might be happening to her community. Dressing quickly, she slipped to the window, standing behind the curtain in case someone should look up.

There was no one. She stretched out to the window edges to look up and down both sides of the street, but nothing there gave her a clue as to the meaning of the shots. She had to find out what was happening. On TV, the real news had been delayed. All they were showing was the Second Ward hours before the rally had begun, and interviews of local dignitaries.

It's not news at all, she thought, disgusted, as they bantered their canned opinions, all of them biased toward the mayor and his buddies. To get the truth, she would have to call Gabe or Ava, and then she realized they were probably out there somewhere, maybe on the front lines already.

She was suddenly afraid for them both. Even with the calm that had settled on the streets and the insipid nature of the news coverage, she'd never felt so afraid in her life. The only thing to do was go to work early so she could be ready for – whatever. She was dressed and ready to go at 8:15 for her 9:00 shift but was slowed by a last minute phone call. She hated to take calls when she was on her way out the door to work. It always took so long to get her focus back. With the rally imminent, she made an exception. The one thing she was going to make sure of was that this time her beloved friends felt her support.

Her heart sank like a rock when she heard the voice, not because it was Gabe or Ava, but because it was Daddy wanting to know about the rally. The last thing she needed was to argue with her father right before work.

"Celie, I hope you're staying put tonight with the doors locked."

"Daddy, it's not like that here. It's just a couple of speeches. And besides, I'll be inside the hospital, not outside."

"Just promise me you won't go into any dangerous situations."

"Don't act like you, you mean? Like when you saved Taffy from the charging bull? Or threw yourself in front of the harvester to save a litter of kittens? Or that time when there was a fire in the Nickerson's barn and you ran in to get their horses?"

There was silence from his end.

"Daddy, I spend half my time here in an emergency room. Practically everything we see there involves a dangerous situation. I'll be fine."

"Of course you will. I just wanted you to know ... I was ... I'm thinking of you. See you next Sunday, then."

A few months ago he'd come to the hospital to take her to supper. She'd been slammed with a last-minute intake, a multicar accident. He'd ended up staying to wait and had watched her in triage for over an hour.

Once they were in the car, he burst out, "I never saw anything like that in my life! No matter who came in there, you knew just what was wrong. You knew exactly what to say to every single person. Celie, you made all those people feel safe."

It had been the most wonderful, incredible feeling – to have Daddy not only see what she did, but to be impressed by it. Seeing herself through his eyes had changed her self-concept more than anything she'd ever experienced. For the rest of her life she would see herself as he'd seen her that day. As Wonder Woman.

Chapter Twenty-Seven

That is a night I will never forget — flames were flying all over the place.... They begged them to give us a hose. When they finally got one, it was too late.

— Gilbert Cephas (in Gates)

Combustion

Young Henry Johnson had kept himself hunched in the alley where he could get a birds-eye view of all the speakers. He was supposed to have been one of the students marching down the center of town, over to the white side, but his mother made him promise not to. So instead, he'd picked a spot where he could watch everything without being spotted by somebody who'd tell Mama.

He'd heard all the speeches, including H. Rap Brown's. He had to admit he didn't understand a lot of what he heard. His head was spinning from too many unfamiliar sights and sounds.

He sidled over to the barber shop where the old men could now sit talking, what with the National Guard gone. He heard them say, "Agitators" and" radicals."

Who did they mean? Did they mean the kids from around here — or just those college kids, now on their bus and over the Chesapeake Bay, back to Annapolis or Baltimore, or Washington? He decided to edge up to the old men without being seen and memorize what they were saying.

And he would have, if the conversation hadn't taken the turn it did. The barber was saying, "Now, how the hell all that mess do anybody any good? The man is crazy." *He must mean Mr. Brown.*

"Nah. Not crazy. They're trying to change things – make our lives better."

"Better? That crazy man? Stand there and tell all-a us *burn it all down* and he don't mean just the school. The stores and people's houses, he means. You call that better? I been working double shifts at Tate's bar and saving for a house. I need that job."

"Does he think somebody going to come in here and build everything back?" asked the barber. A voice from across the street shouted, "Why you want them back, old man? You don't own your shop or even your house. And if anyone be thinking the company store would ever give you enough for a house, you'll find out soon. You'll never have it, none of y'all will.

Henry had imagined excitement - camaraderie – and what he'd seen was chaos. Too drained to make sense of it, he decided the only thing to do was go home and sleep.

Henry may have thought he sneaked back into his room unnoticed, but the clatter of his window shutting had been enough to wake his mother. She had just, at long last, dropped off to sleep. Until his noise jerked her awake. Realizing that the shouting had ended, and her son was now home safe, she relaxed. The neighborhood seemed to be at peace.

She was too restless to go back to sleep, though, so she reached for her robe, pulling it over one of her arms. She felt around the floor for her slippers – one foot, then the other. The robe was still only half on, when she heard her neighbor, Old Samuel, who had stuck his head in the kitchen window.

"Them folks from the city, finally gone," he called.

"What time is it, Samuel?"

"After midnight."

"Thought I heard shooting," she answered, coming into the kitchen.

"Most of 'em just shootin' off at the air. Still could end in trouble, though. Stray bullet got an edge on Mr. Brown. Doc say he gonna be all right, but...."

"I hope so." She sighed heavily, pulled her robe the rest of the way closed, and reached for her glasses. "C'mon in. Samuel. You got your electric back yet?"

"Almost."

"Almost how? What, you stick kindling in your stove and light a match?"

"No Miss Smarty. Almost, as in I got $31.75 cents. Just need a dollar more."

"Well then. Not enough electric to get your coffee pot plugged in tonight. I'll make you some, if you want."

"Don't mind."

She figured he must be aching for something hot. It may be July, but a man liked his hot food and drink at the end of the day. She pulled some store-bought muffins from a cupboard, sliced one in half and fed it into the toaster.

"Thanks. Smells real good."

She added a pat of butter and some cherry jam to his plate and sat down across from him, stirring a tea bag rather than coffee into her own cup. She'd already lost too much sleep – no sense making it so she'd do nothing but toss and turn.

Samuel was chewing his muffin slowly, savoring it. She asked, "The soldiers back, I guess?" She hated to ask. How many more weeks of martial law could they all take? Soldiers blocking off one street or another, sometimes staring at them with their empty eyes, other times walking back and forth in front of the church, seemingly unaware of the old folks that wanted to go to services but wouldn't pass in front of white soldiers.

"Haven't seen any, thanks be. Things'll get peaceful now, maybe."

"I pray it will. With city folks gone back and both my boys home safe, I feel better. Tomorrow, I'll stop by the Reverend's after-church meeting. Maybe he'll talk about what happened and say what we can do to ease folks' spirits for a while."

"I won't be at church. Even the Reverend's sermon is a worry. I'm too old for it."

"I hear that. Night, Sam. Lord bless your sleep."

As she was drifting off, she remembered something. Samuel had not agreed with her that things would get peaceful. Instead he'd stuck his hand inside the loose placket of his shirt where the buttons should have been, a gesture he used when he felt confused.

What had he really thought, and why didn't he say? She sure did hate loose ends like that.

An hour later, she woke to the smell of smoke and Henry pounding on her door. "Mama, something's burning!"

She ran to her window and stuck her head out. She had a good view up and down the street. Boys and men were running, carrying buckets. A young man she didn't recognize ran across her front yard, close enough for her to call down to him.

"Hello there!"

He sat the buckets down and she saw they were full up with water. She asked, "Young man, what you need that water for?"

He used the sleeve of a very dirty white shirt to wipe his forehead. He was looking back down the street and she almost missed his answer. "They finally burned up Pine Street school," he said, retrieving his buckets and hurrying off.

"So where's the fire department?" she yelled after him, but he was gone. She felt an urgent need to get a glimpse of both her sons – just make sure they hadn't gone off again. There they were, huddled by their bedroom window, watching everything. She made them promise to stay put for the rest of the night, then she sat in the kitchen, sipping cold tea from her cup and listening for the sound of fire trucks.

A bowl of beans that needed trimming lured her into activity. Nearly an hour had gone by before she realized there still hadn't been any sirens.

10:20 p.m.

The first fire bomb, when it exploded inside the Pine Street Elementary school, blasted a hole through the retaining wall between the first-grade classroom and the cafeteria and clear through the ceiling. Burning debris spewed out through the hole and landed on the rooftops of the Pawn Shop, the Emporium, and the home of Miss Simms, the piano teacher. The elementary school was on fire – again. As loathsome as this was, it wasn't all that frightening. Everybody knew more or less what to do until the fire trucks came.

The fire department had been called right away, and then again, twenty minutes later. By then, men in the neighborhood were hauling buckets of water just to wash down buildings and hold back the spread.

From his window on the third floor of the Emporium, Edward Tate could see the fire trucks over on the white side, sitting. He saw the young men working and went down to help.

The fire burned high, then higher, catching on to the dry wood of building after building. One by one, residents approached the stalled firemen, negotiating frantically for help.

More minutes passed and became hours.

By the time the first fire truck was released to fight the fire, all that was left of the school was a dark, empty hole in the pavement and a single concrete wall. Next to it lay the charred debris of another thirty-three business and twenty-two homes, including most of Tate's Emporium.

****

Dennis James Johnson, Jr. lived just outside town. Hearing news of the fire on the radio, he grabbed his brother, dragged him into their rusty old pick-up, and tried to drive all the way to town, where his grandpa and two of his cousins lived. Route 50 was deserted as far as the eye could see, so the teens sailed along the highway.

Three miles outside town they were stopped by a State Police barricade. Behind the police line, the sky above Cambridge was glowing bright red.

"Go on home, boys," one of the policemen directed, but they didn't, of course. They retreated half a mile, stopped near the turn-off to Blackwater Farms where Dennis had a job tending duck blinds, and parked the truck on the gravel shoulder. By climbing to the top of the cab, they could see the sky above Race and Pine. They sat there for a long time, just watching the shifting colors of red and orange in the clouds. Even though they didn't learn a thing sitting there, it somehow felt right.

****

Early the next morning, Marian Emery got through the National Guard line by telling them she had business at the school. They were asking for identification, as if that would tell them who should pass and who should be kept out. She had a sense they had no understanding of why they were there.

She wanted to shout, "Go home! It's too late!" But what good would that do? Instead she said, "I work there."

It wasn't really true. Her class had been moved over to the temporary building, now that the Pine Street school was all but closed. She had taught at Pine Street for so many years that she just had to go and see if the rumors were true. Feeling ill as she inched along Race and across to Pine, she could barely finish the last two hundred feet to the school. Building after building, in ruins. Finally, she saw the long-ailing and controversial school, which was indeed, burned to the ground except for a single wall. They'd never be able to resurrect it this time. It was gone, as was her church, the five and dime, the Tate complex and God knows how many more.

She had to get somewhere to call her mother. She knew there was a pay phone on the white side of Race Street, but on the colored side – nothing. She would try the music store, a business anomaly that would wait on both white and colored.

Mama's phone rang and rang, and Marian was crying by the time she heard her mother's voice. "Oh, Mama. People are just walking up and down the streets. Some crying, most folks just staring. The buildings are still smoking. Almost all the businesses are – most everything is just — gone."

"Oh Lord. All those people who lived and worked up and down them streets. All those poor, poor people."

Papa got on the phone and asked the question everyone seemed to be avoiding, "Who started the fire?"

"They don't know."

"Somebody knows," he declared and hung up the phone.

****

Halfway across the peninsula in Caroline County, a beat-up white jalopy sat stalled, its nose in the woods, its rear-end sunk in a deep tractor rut at the sparse end of a cornfield. The car's owner could leave it here for only so long. A couple weeks before harvest, somebody would come by to check the crop growth and it would have to be hauled away by then.

What a night. Shrimpy Jones wondered if it was as bad as that time in '63 when those protesters all stormed Dizzyland's diner. White and coloreds together, most of them strangers to this town, yelling how if they couldn't get in there they were gonna close it down. He'd asked Pa why did they want to go in there? Lousy food, and everybody in there hating their guts. Pa said it was because they just wanted to fight. Every colored boy Shrimpy knew was like that – pissed off.

Well, probably it's the way all men are, right? If somebody pushes you, you push back harder. Pa told all his boys, "Any of you ever try to hit me, I'll knock your block off." It was a logic he understood. Stay strong.

He didn't need his father's reasons to be pissed off; he had his own. Not stupid ones, like his friend Bubba, who just plain hated colored people. Shrimpy didn't hate anybody. He was pissed off by real facts. He knew for a fact that colored people had applied for just about every job at Airpax. Some said they'd been at the docks, trying for jobs there too. They couldn't allow that. He had friends who still hadn't found work and now his own job was on the line — the rumor being the war would end soon. If that happened, the Army contract would disappear overnight. The last time that happened, jobs were gone inside a week. It was a fact.

When busloads of troublemakers got to town last night, he and his friends had been ready. As Nightriders, they were supposed to drive through, throwing bottles out the windows and whooping it up. A few people like Bubba had guns, but they were supposed to shoot in the air, not at people. He wasn't sure what Bubba had shot at, exactly.

The third time out of town, somebody between Cambridge and Hurlock had called the State Police. Thinking he heard a siren in the distance, Shrimpy hit the gas. 100, 110, and that was it, the car couldn't do more. He'd had to pull off the road and hide it.

His friends had been wasted drunk and of no help in moving the car. In fact they could hardly move themselves. Because of his huge size, Bubba hadn't been easy to dislodge from the back seat and they all three had to support him until he found his feet. Half-carrying his fat carcass, they'd stumble a few inches at a time until he could stand on his own.

The near-miss of police, if that's what it was, had scared Shrimpy more than when they'd been in Cambridge getting shot at, picking up bullet holes in the skin of his car. Maybe he was just less drunk by the time they crossed the city line, or maybe just feeling the down side of what adrenaline could do.

It was time to retire this car for good, anyway. For weeks, he'd been wishing his father would let him drive his new Galaxie. His friends shared his feelings about his dying car.

"Hey, Shrimpy - you think this old jalopy can even make it to Cambridge and back?"

"Sure. It has a way of getting a second wind under pressure. And don't bad-mouth it just because it's old. We've had a lot of fun in this car."

"Especially back when Frank was around," Whiner said. "No matter what kind of trouble Frank ever got in, he always had an alibi ... or some back door he went through."

Bubba expelled his booming guffaw. "I'll say. Never was anybody who could talk his way out of a situation as good as him." Bubba made it sound great, but Shrimpy remembered that Bubba had wet his pants, panic-stricken, in more than one of those 'situations.'

Whiner said, "I always thought half the stuff they said Frank did was made up. He'd have to be in two places at the same time to have done all that."

"Yup – he's a legend for a reason," Shrimpy added. "Not too many guys around like him."

"Not even him around, anymore," Bubba added.

To Bubba, Frank hadn't been around for a long time. Shrimpy knew better. Frank was always around, if not in person then in spirit.

Maybe his ma was right. Maybe he was getting too old for this shit.

Chapter Twenty-Eight

Earth provides enough to satisfy every man's needs, but not every man's greed.

— Mahatma Gandhi (Attenborough)

Celie's Apartment

It was quiet now. Too quiet. Ava found it hard to believe that those long weeks of preparation could end in that disgraceful speech. She still wasn't sure if what she felt was disappointment or relief.

Celie's TV was on, of course. It was on 24 hours a day so that Celie never had to come into a room alone. Ava listened to the news about today's non-event until it became repetitive. It seemed that the town had settled in for the night. With Ethan at his mother's, and Celie still at work, and Sari, God-knows-where, she may as well settle in too.

But the trauma of Brown's ugly speeches wouldn't leave her. Even the air around him had been noxious, reeking of his intention to poison the crowd. It had been a battle cry for destruction of the life and spirit of the community she loved. What if his plan had succeeded? Since it hadn't, why was she still shaken? She kept seeing the faces of her teens from the church and imagining the worst. When she closed her eyes, the faces grew larger, displaying fear, their mouths urging her forward — *something's wrong.* Could it be because she hadn't found Sari?

The only way she could possibly reduce her anxiety, she decided, was to go back and look for her sister. She called Celie at work. "Just want you to know I may be at the church when you get home. I just want to make sure my teens are all safe and sound."

"Oh, Ava. Don't go back out tonight," Celie begged. "Who knows what could happen?"

"Don't be such a worrywart. The rally is over. Even the National Guard went home. Besides, if any bad guys are left hanging around, I can take care of myself."

"Ava, you *are* upset. What aren't you telling me?"

"I never could hide my feelings from you. I don't know why I try." Ava swallowed past the lump in her throat, took a breath and steeled herself to confess her angst over Sari. But before she could say a word, Celie dropped her own bombshell.

"It's Sari, isn't it? I've been wondering when you'd find out. I didn't want to tell you. No, I *did* want to tell you, but at the right time. You were so frantic yesterday that I —"

"For God's sake, Celie, just tell me! What about Sari? Where is she?"

"The last place you'd want her to be."

"I already know about her hanging around Tate's bar. Remember?"

"No, worse than that. I wish it was Tate's. She was behind that liquor store where guys come to sell drugs. Standing outside a big car with New York license plates. She had a huge bag in her hands and there was this guy ... uh ... he had some guns."

Not buying drugs to use, then, Ava thought. Buying drugs to sell. Or she was some kind of messenger for those creeps at the after-hours club behind Tate's.

"Thanks, Celie. I know it was hard to tell me. I appreciate it."

"I'm not done."

What could be worse? Prostitution? Murder?

"I waited until the men left. Sari started back to the center of town. When she got close to me, I called out to her to get her attention."

"That was pretty stupid. What if those drug dealers were watching to see if there were any witnesses?"

"I didn't think of that, but it wouldn't have stopped me. I couldn't leave Sari there to fend for herself. Not when there was somebody around who knew her and loved her, to at least try to ... to ... I don't know what I thought I could do. She came over right away, even hugged me hello and asked how things were. I said, 'Sari, are you doing something with drugs?' She looked down at the bag in her hands, and said, 'Drugs! Are you crazy? Why would you think that?'

"I told her I'd seen her talking to those men from New York. She said, 'Oh, that. A friend of Omar's, my boyfriend. It's his cigarette connection. This guy comes up from North Carolina every week. On his way through, he drops off tax-free tobacco for Omar and his friends.' Ava, I know she was lying, but she did it so well. I've got so I can't believe anything she says anymore. She just isn't … right. I can see something in her sometimes — I don't know the word — but whatever it is makes me afraid of her."

"The word you're looking for, is evil. God knows I've thought it often enough."

"Evil? I didn't mean that! Look, I was *not* trying to say that about Venus last Thanksgiving. I was trying to say Venus was selfish."

"Well, I've thought about it a lot more than you. I've always been scared to death that Sari would end up like Venus, with absolutely no sense at all of right or wrong. Everything Venus ever did was because it gained her something. She had no friends and if you were an enemy, she'd hurt you, with no remorse. No feelings even. What else could you call that except evil? It was a good word to use."

Celie was silent, but Ava could tell by her breathing she was in pain. She wished she had time to listen, but now more than ever she had to go and find Sari.

****

Ava was bone-tired from her own emotions and everything that had happened today. She almost turned back home when she got outside. The storm still threatened in the distance and the air was saturated with humidity, draining whatever energy she had left. The cut on her face was being pulled too tight by the bandage. She yanked it hard to release the adhesive all at once, like Isaac had taught her.

"One sure thing in life," he would say, "things always all around, tryin' to hurt you. Secret is, face square up to it and give it a swift kick."

As the church came into sight, she saw people in their houses, looking completely normal as they prepared to end the day. She felt refreshed – maybe just by being near people who cared about each other, no matter how different they were or how they lived their lives.

She heard footsteps behind her – the click of a woman's high heels. Not scary, and yet her instinct was to pick up her pace.

The high heels did the same. Every nerve in Ava's body urged her to look around. A glimpse over her shoulder just to see –

What stopped her? The awkwardness of exchanging a look with a stranger, or of acknowledging an acquaintance? Maybe because she was much too tired for even that amount of engagement — or was it something more instinctive, a visceral unrest, a warning? *To look back is to acknowledge weakness.*

She forced herself to keep her eyes forward, her mind on guard. A small voice in her head asked, *if you're scared, why the hell do you keep on walking?* She didn't have an answer to what it was in humans that made them put up a brave front and try to stop their knees from quivering, to keep a strong stride, instead of, for God's sake, just breaking into a run.

By the time she got to the church, her heart thudding, the familiar walls and sounds in the vestry calmed her. A single tiny candle cast its faint light in all the vestibule corners. The room felt peaceful. *A haven from the storms outside, from strong emotions, from whatever it is you're hiding from.*

The candle flickered, its wax pooling until, finally, it drowned the wick. Darkness fell where just a second ago there had been that single point of light. She flicked on the lamp above her desk, illuminating the stack of papers she'd left for tomorrow. An envelope that needed an address caught her attention and she threaded it into the typewriter.

Later, she would remember the clacking sound. She would remember going back into the alley and talking to someone, then moving to the side of the alley, and then the fist that came out of a doorway and hit her hard in her right eye, knocking her to the ground and turning the world black.

****

Cambridge Hospital

The hospital was buzzing with the news of fire outside, of explosions in the Second Ward. The staff all watched on the small TV in the break room.

Hannah called and told Celie, "Find a TV."

"We're watching it now."

"Turn to Channel eleven."

They were playing a tape of a white car, flashing on and off the screen, racing down Pine Street. Another channel showed the same car making a U-turn on Race Street, then tearing back down Pine and out to Rt. 50. A newscaster said that shots were fired from it when it made the second run. The third and final drive-through, the car had pulled behind the Pine Street school and sat there for maybe three minutes before leaving. Three minutes was such a short time, unless you have a firebomb to throw, when it can seem like forever.

"I saw it. It was Betty alright. I'd recognize her anywhere."

"Who could have possibly —"

"You really don't want to know."

The police weren't able to identify the car, Hannah told her, but of course either of them could have. They also knew it wasn't the first time the car had been involved in skullduggery. Celie could remember when she'd first driven it, and when her brother raced it between the fields, on the river road, and in the NDHS school parking lot.

She took a quick look out her window toward Race Street, half-way expecting to see Betty there.

She'd wanted to tell Hannah that it couldn't have been Frank, that he'd have to be a magician to hop a plane from Formosa and get here without being AWOL, then sneak, unrecognized, into a town where people could identify him, and then reverse the whole thing to get back. Because if it had been true, it would eradicate everything she stood for and all the good she'd done in this town. How was it possible it was him? And if it was, what she could do about it?

She telephoned her family and a few close friends, certain that someone she loved was in deep trouble. The only person she couldn't reach was Ava, who wasn't home yet and wasn't at the church either. On her next break, she would go to both places. Just to make sure.

In the meantime, she would rely on her routine to keep her emotions under control. She finished her rounds, calming things as the night tucked itself in, as much as you ever could in a hospital. The wee hours were always the quietest, but they were also the most dangerous. Spirits sank, brains slowed down a bit too much and were in danger of switching off in those who were too frail to fight.

Mr. Becker was wide awake. He asked if she could wash down his skin, please, so he could get sleepy. She began lathering his forearm and the crook of his elbow, automatically swishing the water gently and letting it run back into the basin in a thin stream.

"Something wrong?" he asked.

"Wrong? No, not at all." She realized that she'd been staring at a blank wall.

"You had such a funny look on your face and I was thinking maybe you noticed how my skin looks *odd*. I noticed it earlier and I wanted to have them page the doctor, but the evening nurse made me wait 'til you got here. See? ..."

"Your skin is just fine. In fact, I was just thinking what a nice healthy glow you have today, I was just about to tell you."

"Why is it so red then?"

"You've been scratching in quite a few places."

"I itch."

"As it happens, I have a new lotion in my pack today I wanted you to try. It's supposed to work miracles for dry skin."

"Well why didn't somebody tell me before ..."

He was prattling about all the people he knew who'd been neglected in the hospital, (which would certainly never be true for him). She was glad for the chatter. It might help her worry less about Ava and Frank.

If not Frank, who else? Cousin Bobby? He was some kind of survivalist now, and he had always been a natural-born hater, exactly the kind of person to burn down a Black school, or any school.

This kind of thinking was useless. She snapped her mind back and finished the last bed-check. Back at the desk, a light flashed with an incoming call, infrequent on this shift.

"Third floor," she said to the switchboard. "Oh, Hi Gabe – you still up?" Dumb question.

Her face froze as she listened to his message. "Did they agree to admit her? OK, I'll be right down as soon as I get someone to cover."

Ava was downstairs, and unconscious, Gabe had said. She buzzed the girl who shared her shift, a new girl – where the hell had she gone – was she napping?

"Ginnie! Listen, you've got to get down here and cover! My friend just got brought into the E.R. You better get me a replacement. I might not be back." She took off for the stairs without waiting for acknowledgement.

Chapter Twenty-Nine

Ava could hear someone moaning. An aching, heartbreaking sound. She wasn't quite awake, but she should get up and see who was hurting so much. She was stopped by a man's voice, asking her, "Did you see anything? Everything matters, even little things."

The man had been talking to her for a while. Her body was aching all over and the pain in her head was excruciating. Suppose the groaning had been hers and this man was asking her about it.

She tried to remember if she was still in Baltimore. She didn't remember getting hurt that badly. All she could think to answer was, "No." Maybe if she kept saying it, the man would go away.

"Can we get some light in here?" asked another male voice. "Ask her again, Seth. In a case like this, timing is everything."

A case like what?

"Just one more minute and that'll be it, gentlemen," a woman said. "Then you have to go. Her blood pressure skyrockets every time one of you asks her something." That was a nurse's voice. She was someplace medical.

There was some rustling and then a thin light pierced the hospital-room haze. "Can you see me, Ma'am?" the first male voice asked her.

"Yeth," she answered. Christ! Her tongue felt fat against the roof of her mouth and there was a taste of metal. Blood, like she'd bitten through her tongue.

"I'm Detective Clive with the State Police. Are you up to a few questions?"

"Mm-mm." That would have to do for *yes*. Squinting, she could see he was decked out in a dress uniform, a jacket with a high collar, edged in gold trim. Handsome.

She tried to ask what happened, but it came out "whaa?"

"Someone, using fists and some kind of club, landed at least a half dozen hard blows, mostly to your head and shoulders. Any idea who he was?"

"Uh-uh." Moving her mouth even that much had hurt.

"Both of you were in the alley next to your church. Was anybody else there who didn't belong?" continued Detective Clive.

She shook her head no, an agonizing mistake inside a miserable cervical collar. What had he meant, 'both of you?'

The second detective, still out of sight, said, "I'm Detective Macy from the Cambridge force and I'm helping with your case. We'd like to get this guy, ma'am. There were lights there along the alley. You sure you don't know who might have hit you? Maybe somebody you knew only casually?"

Were they going to keep asking the same question over and over? She closed her eyes, an involuntary wince, and this led to an intervention by a nurse. Not the same nurse, it seemed – oh my God, it was Celie! Relief washed over her.

Celie sounded angry. "Why are you still asking her the same question? She told you she didn't see anyone, didn't she? Maybe you should write it all down if you can't remember."

Plain-clothes started to answer. "We know what she said, Miss..."

"Mowbray."

"Yes ma'am. I'm afraid you can't be in here. This is a criminal case."

Celie said, "First of all, I work here. Second, this woman lives with me. You can write down *next-of-kin*."

Silence. Ava counted, ten seconds. Twenty seconds. It was all she could do to hold back the agonizing push of a smile as she imagined their thoughts, filling in the blanks. Yes, it's the Eastern Shore and yes, a white girl just said she lives with a black one.

Had she just thought that or had Celie actually said it?

"I see," said Plain-clothes. "There are ... um ... very personal things we need to ask while the incident is fresh. It was a very brutal beating and the motive ... well ... let's just say it looks ... personal."

"Wasn't it just a mugging?" Celie's voice was shaking. "You mean somebody might have been waiting for them?"

"We don't know *anything* yet, Seth," said the dressed-up detective. He moved next to his colleague, and Ava saw that Plain-clothes was a black man. He directed a scowl toward his colleague, whose look said, *don't give away so much.* Plainclothes turned his head toward Celie, who appeared to be ready to block any attempt they made to get closer. "Can we have just a few minutes in private with her –"

"Not on your life," Celie said in a voice that meant she was the one in charge, not him. "OK, guys, time for *you* to go. She's in pain and they just gave her sleeping meds on top of the morphine. She needs to sleep. Besides, what do you think you're going to get from her after a concussion? What she needs is rest. You can come back tomorrow."

"Couldn't have put it better, myself," chimed in a third nurse, sweeping into the room and snapping the green plastic draperies so they closed completely around her patient.

"Gentlemen?" she added. Meaning she was now the one in charge.

Ava could still see their shadows through the curtain. Plainclothes was backing up toward her, until the night nurse slid a hand under his elbow. "Everyone out."

Ava heard several sets of feet scrambling. The men were gone but she would bet that Celie hadn't budged. The night nurse's tone softened. "Come see her tomorrow morning, lovey. You need sleep too."

Celie slipped through the closed curtain.

"Anybody you want me to call? Ethan?" Celie had her hand against Ava's, her fingers caressing her wrist, and it made her feel better. The lights went down, draining the room even further of color if that was possible. Celie's coppery bangs and shining blue eyes were the only parts of the room that weren't dull gray.

Ava mouthed, *no,* and then Celie was gone too. The light was darker now but not by any means was it empty enough for sleep. The night nurse scuttled around for a few minutes and then said, "I'll be right outside, making notes. Push the button next to your right hand if you want anything."

What could she want? A minute ago, she had come close to signaling Celie that she wanted Ethan to come. Now that they'd had adjusted her medication, she didn't want anything except sleep. She had remembered something and was trying to push it away.

Fists, no, one fist. A lot of sounds, gravel in her mouth, swirling visions of lights, the ambulance ride, the emergency room. Thoughts of what she might miss if he'd actually killed her. She'd miss her

friends and family. And Ethan, of course. Sari, and maybe even …
no, not Venus.

A pretty short list for a person of her age, but at least it was people and not French fries or dancing or something else stupid. In the
ambulance, she'd had a quick vision of her friends mourning her and
now she let herself relish the thought, surprised as she was by the
truth of it. A lot of people would miss her. Not Venus, who would be
surprised to learn that there were people who loved her. Her rapa-
cious voice, always somewhere in Ava's awareness, always predicting
the worst, was saying, *if you die after me, you'll be all alone.*

Wrong, Venus. I have a man who loves me, and friends, good ones.
The police were about to encounter just one of those good friends, a
brick wall named Celie, who would reveal nothing about Ava, not
even how long she'd known her. A girl couldn't have a better, more
loyal friend than Celie. She was lucky.

Lucky? I'm lying here with a head-splitting concussion, I can't
move any part of my face without agony, and I call myself lucky?
Her eyes filled with tears, something that almost never happened.
She couldn't tell whether she was crying from physical pain or from
the emotions that had been pounding her to a pulp lately.

She was supposed to push a button whenever the pain got too
much. She'd almost asked, "Too much for what — to want to go
back to my own life?" If so, the pain had been too much for quite a
long time now, but no one had suggested that there might be a way
out. Was there an equivalent of a morphine drip to fix a messed up
love life, or a job that took her places where it wasn't even safe to
go home? Or how about one for protecting children from places no
child should be in, like watching Venus hunt through men's pockets
for coins to buy milk? Those years had convinced Ava never to have
kids of her own. She never wanted to see the look on her own face
that she'd seen on Venus's, and then on Sari's.

The air in the room had become so thick she couldn't breathe it.
A yawn pushed hard at her jaws, trying to open them. The pain shot
through as if she'd actually widened her mouth in a full yawn. She
pushed the drip again, and then once more, until the jagged edges of
the curtains quivered, faded into each other, and disappeared. With
daylight now streaming into the room and the hospital staff bustling
in all directions around her, she finally fell into the deep, dreamless
sleep she needed so badly. The gruesome night is finally done with

me, she thought, as she drifted down.

But it wasn't to be. At the bottom of her dream, she saw another face — not the attacker, but Sari. Sari had been in the alley with her when they were attacked. She had to remember if Sari had been attacked too. She tried to pull herself up through the narcotic haze that slowed her thinking, but it wouldn't let go. Each time she'd start to wake up, the memories tried to get through and couldn't. Each time, she tried to clear her brain — put things in order.

Sari's face in the window – in the alley.

Sari fallen down and Ava trying to rouse her – *we have to run.*

Then it came, her trying to rouse Sari. Right before the moment the paramedics looked at each other, shaking their heads so very slightly. More a look than a movement — that awful, terrible, ice-cold medical short cut, the *no* signal. *No, she won't make it. No, no pulse. No hope.*

****

Ava woke to the sound of a bell. Alarm clock? Phone? Was it time for work already? She would let it ring til it stopped. *Please*, she thought, *no more interviews today.*

Ring number Five. Six. Seven. From the corner of her eye, she saw Gabe. He picked up the receiver and laid it down, leaving it off the hook. She needed to stir herself and tell him to put it back in case it was Ethan. *Put it back, Gabe. What if it's Ethan, or Sari* — No. It couldn't be Sari. Never again would be Sari.

****

When the phone rang again, she was wide awake and sitting up, eating Jell-O. Gabe answered it and said, "Alright, then, but just three minutes." He mouthed one word, "Your mother."

"Hello, Venus."

"Who the hell? Ava? Where's Sari. Nobody will tell me."

Damn, damn, damn. Venus, calling from God knows where, didn't know about Sari yet. Ava would have to be the one to tell her. Eventually, after she found the strength to speak to Venus, she said, "Why do you need Sari?"

Someone stirred behind her and she realized that Celie was also in here, and getting closer to the phone, no doubt trying to eavesdrop, but she wouldn't interfere unless invited. Meantime, the phone was spewing out pure Venus – her swearing and muttering, without consistency or clarity. She sounded drunk.

Ava sat back, listening, trying her best not to look desperate as her eyes switched from Celie to Gabe and back again. Neither of them had said a word, yet the room had mushroomed with increased energy and rising heat. Her skin was already sticky with it, maybe a result of letting Venus into her thoughts. She tried to gather the strength she needed to push her back out again.

Needing help, she looked from one friend to the other. Celie was striding out her distress by moving fast, twisting, winding her way back and forth in the room, tapping her fingers inside her pockets, preparing to explode. She would be too agitated to talk for several more minutes, but if a window was stuck or a pillow fell to the floor, she'd be the first to get there.

Gabe was on the opposite side of the room. His intensity was always concealed unless you knew him. If you did, you would watch for a tiny twitch in his right eyelid or a smile that didn't belong. His mind was what stayed in motion, planning and ordering and then focusing narrowly on what would work. An onlooker would see nothing unless Gabe reached to strike, a fast-moving lightning bolt, invisible until it reached for ground.

For this situation, it was Gabe's focused energy she wanted. She held the receiver toward him. He took it from her hand and his voice came out sharp as a blade. "Venus, both your girls were hurt during the attack. Sari got the worst of it. It was a bad wound and she wasn't able to – and I'm afraid she passed. I'm so sorry."

Ava found herself wishing her mother might now be asking about her too and was instantly furious at herself for wanting it.

"No, Ava can't talk anymore," Gabe said into the phone. "When she recovers enough, she'll call you and tell you what happened. Until then, I'm going to have you blocked at the switchboard so that – you want what?"

Again, the longing to have her mother care enough to ask about her. How astonishing to harbor such a hope after all these years.

Gabe was saying, "Go where? I can't understand what you're asking. They're not going to let you *take* the body, if that's what you're asking."

Gabe turned his back and she knew he was trying to muffle his voice. Ava could still hear every word. "You can't ask Ava that. You know, Venus, she's hurt too. Anyway, she doesn't have more answers. Nobody does. You need to stop trying — what? Say that again? I see. No, we didn't know." Gabe shifted his position and stood taller. "I would say I'm sorry, but the truth is, I'm not. I'm sure you deserved it. Good bye, Venus."

He clicked the button on the phone base and told the operator at the reception desk to block Venus's calls.

Celie said, "She'll get through that switchboard somehow and drive Ava crazy. She could even try and come up here. We'll have to find something to keep her away."

"No, Celie, we won't. Venus won't be coming to see Ava anywhere. She's in prison."

Celie's mouth dropped open. "In prison! And you told her you weren't sorry? That she *deserved* it? Seriously?"

Gabe's smile was sardonic. "Afraid so. Sorry, Ava. I couldn't stop myself."

Ava's face was killing her from the grin pushing at the corners of her mouth. It wasn't because she was glad about Venus, it was because Gabe looked just the way he did when she'd first known him as a boy. And because it was a relief to have things taken care of. The only thing that would have been better would have been to have Ethan sitting next to her.

The next time Ava woke to a groan, she knew where it came from. Was this progress? A man's deep voice was beside her.

"So the Knee-High Man, he hated being so short and he asked Massa Horse how he had got so big. That ol' horse, he said how he eats ten buckets of corn every day and then he runs twenty miles. Well, Knee-High Man did exactly the same as Massa Horse. When he was done, danged if he wasn't even shorter than before he started out."

"Uncle Isaac! How long you been here?" Ava had always felt comforted by Isaac's songs and stories and had never stopped missing them. She wanted to stretch her hand to him but by now she'd figured out that any movements from her shoulders up would hurt like hell.

"Been here a while. Sit here and watch my Lil Girl sleep. You stirred a bit, like you did when you were a young'un back at the camp, and I did what I always did –"

"Woke me gently with a story. Is there a reason for this particular story today? Or maybe you could just tell me why you like that story so much."

"Why'd I tell you this one? Sometimes a story's just a story. Why do I like it? Well, you see, my Grandpappy saw how I was only a mite of a boy and not likely to grow too big. He wanted me to know that I could still grow up strong. This story told me that by knowing my place in this world, I'd be the strongest I could be."

"Are you trying to tell me something about me knowing my place? Well, maybe I just thought I did. You know about me and Sari getting hurt –"

"Now you just hold up. Not you *and* Sari. She's one girl, you another. Sad thing what Venus did to that baby. That's what got her hurt. If any of us could've stopped it, God knows we'd have done it. But you getting hurt, well, that's a different story altogether. Your whole life, you always tried to do right. Made us all proud. Maybe because Minnie and me were blessed to help raise you, both of us knew you'd find your place someday. Minnie said when she first met you, 'Now this little girl, we can save.'"

"You did save me."

"Now looks like I got to come back here and save you all over again."

"No. I'm going to save myself this time. It may not be exactly the way I thought – I may have trusted some of the wrong people – but I'm going to be all right. When I need help, I got my brother to call on."

Isaac grinned, rocking a bit in the hospital rocker. "Mighty glad. People got to keep touch with the folks that can tell then what's right – bring 'em back to center time to time. Like Minnie always did for me and Hattie does now. Gabe's good for you like that until you can get your own man. If you want one, mind you."

She wished she could tell him about Ethan, but the way it was now, she might never see Ethan again. Isaac began patting her hand gently, like he'd done when she'd had nightmares after Venus left. When she drifted off to sleep, he was humming the nursery tune, "Rabbit and Turtle."

Chapter Thirty

The best way to find yourself is to lose yourself in the service of others.

— Mahatma Gandhi (Attenborough)

Race and Pine Street, July 25, 1967

Edward Tate was reconstructing last night's events, again. The end of H. Rap Brown's speech, everyone applauding, including his brother William. An act of politeness not agreement, William would tell him later.

Brown had left to walk a local woman home when a buckshot pellet struck him on the side of the face. He was rushed from the scene, treated privately by Cambridge's black doctor, then quietly escorted back over the bridge. Meanwhile, at 10:05 p.m. a small fire had erupted near the school and was put out. There might have been other gunshots, maybe from white nightriders, but no one was killed and thank God, there were no riots. By midnight July 25, the National Guard and the state police had been sent home because Pine Street and the second ward were calm.

Edward remembered how last night's report said, "10:05" instead of "around ten." He appreciated that someone out there was trying to be accurate. He had been so relieved, back then. After making sure the bar, the tavern and the pool room were empty, and checking every lock, he'd called his wife, so she wouldn't worry herself sick. He had told her to make him a light supper because he might be able to eat for a change, then grabbed an armful of paper work from his office and got ready to go home.

He kept replaying this scene over and over. The scene where everything was still fine, and he had been on his way home to continue
his life.

****

When the fire trucks hadn't moved by one a.m. or so, Edward and
his brother William had roused Councilman Charles Cornish and had
him call the Police Chief. Charles had looked so frightened as he told
the Tate brothers the bad news. Chief Kinnamon was angry – no one
knew exactly why. What he said was that he refused to put his men
in jeopardy. Snipers were waiting to ambush the fire trucks; they'd
fired at his men, he said, although no one had seen that.

Edward knew most of what he said had been made up. During the
fire, journalists were there taking pictures and creating broadcasts for
the next day, even interviewing the Chief for his thoughts. The man
wounded had been a black man, hours earlier. The Chief's insistence
it wasn't safe was obviously something he'd thought up later to justify
what he'd done.

It was the state's attorney who had commandeered one fire truck
and gone into the area after the four-hour blaze. By then, the sky over
his Emporium was bright orange. The complex burned to the ground
right under Edward's eyes while the fire trucks sat silent on the white
side of Race Street, watching. All the years he'd spent compromising
had amounted to nothing. All the sacrifices his family had made to
keep good relations with these people — and in his hour of greatest
need, they had treated him as an enemy.

****

Lena Tate had taken the water bucket from her husband's hand as
the last of the flames engulfed the complex.

"There's nothing more to do," she'd told him. "There's no way
to save anything." They had moved to the white side of Race Street,
where they could still see the remnants of his buildings as the wind
whipped the ashes in a swirl up and down the street.

It looked like the sky was falling. A crash sounded from the area which had been the pool hall. Edward moved toward it, but Lena's hand stopped him. "You can't go back. It's not safe."

"I keep asking *why us*? Why did those people have to come here? What did *we* do that turned them against us?"

"They don't turn against any one town, Edward. Or any one man. Don't you know that by now? They don't think at all about people where they're going. They look for where it's news. Because of before, because of 1963, we're a good story."

She was right, he thought. It should have made him feel better, but her words had struck him like weapons. The news truck drove up. He left his brother William behind to talk for them both. After four years of pleading, bargaining, and compromising on behalf of his community, he had nothing left to say.

July 29

They'd finally let Edward walk through his charred buildings. Firemen were still tramping through there, along with men in suits holding clipboards and wearing safety masks — sifting ashes, testing charred wood with chemicals. He had a *déjà vu* moment when he recognized three of the faces behind the masks – firemen who'd been there the night of the fire. They looked disinterested, as they had that night. He was probably imagining that, but it felt better than believing they could have cared and yet stood idle. He'd rather believe they may have felt frustrated and helpless, as he had. However, they could not have understood the depth of his despair. No one could, not even Lena, who knew his heart inside and out.

August 1

The Tates had breakfast as usual that morning in their house just outside of the Second Ward. He had never wanted this house, but Lena had insisted they move there.

"You can't spend the rest of your life at the beck and call of every drunk that causes trouble at the bar. Or when the delivery truck doesn't show up in the morning. You can't be there for every neighbor who comes to get coffee because he's run out, or he forgot to buy it. Or didn't have the money to buy it, most likely, knowing you're always good for a handout."

He had fought her on the new house as long as he could. "It's too far from the business. The neighbors will think we've got uppity. We can't afford it."

"Can't afford it? You already had one heart attack. We can't afford not to."

At breakfast, she'd said, "Aren't you glad now, we got this to fall back on? So many of our friends back there have no place to go to at all. We still got a life, thank God. And because of it, you'll still be able to help others.... Edward, please look at me!"

She had her hand on his face, cupping his cheek with her long, slim fingers, a comfort touch she used often, and as usual, it worked.

He smiled at her, and then broke the crust off his toast so he could dip it into the egg yolk. The egg was done just right, the yolk still runny but not raw. While he finished eating, Lena cleaned up the bright kitchen, absentmindedly tucking a strand of white hair beneath her pins while she worked. She rarely did anything absentmindedly and he loved it when she did. It made her seem a bit fragile, as if she not only needed him but would never take his love for granted.

She began looking through the newspaper, making little marks and tears for her own reference. A white woman's baby born (the mayor's daughter), to send a card. More important than ever to stay in their good graces now. *Wonderbread* on sale at the new A & P. The phone numbers of the other churches nearby. They would need a new one.

She looked up at him, maybe sensing his stare. "You need to think what you want to do today. Anything except go back to that damn complex, kicking ashes around and trying to find your past. It's time now we think ahead."

He nodded.

"Promise you won't go there for a day or two."

"Got to go tomorrow to meet with the insurance."

"I'll go with you when you need to go. Promise me, Edward."

Again, he nodded, very slightly, maybe a promise, maybe not.

He went up to his office on the third floor. She had taken great care to create a warm, workable space for him. His grandfather's old desk – thank God that had been spared from the fire. Pictures of his children and their children, all smiling from inside their silver frames. A chair for his comfort – she knew him so well. Not a new chair, as some wives would have been tempted, but the one from the first office he'd ever had, bought cheap at an auction. A huge, stuffed thing with fabric that he called tapestry.

Sister Jean from the church had corrected him. "It's not called *tapestry*. It's what you'd call napped velvet. Tapestry is like a wall hanging, with scenes in it ... flowers and such, and people. The stuff of life."

Jean was wrong. His chair had seen plenty of the stuff of life. It's where he had always hired and fired his staff, where the machinations of his business took place, where he scolded his young'uns when they argued for the freedom to be greedy, or just for freedom. When they'd got older and had more sense, asking for *real* help, it was where he'd handed out cash or checks. A neighbor had nearly birthed out a baby in this chair. It was this chair where he'd learned of the creation of each of his grandchildren. At those times, when he'd been swamped with responsibilities, it's where he learned when they were born and how much they weighed and who they looked like.

The fabric of his chair had long ago been worn down to a crisscross of threads on the arms. Some wives would have tried to recover them, but Lena had instead made little towels to put over, so he wouldn't have to cut away his memories.

What better way to start his recovery than to sit here in his office, in his chair. Maybe jot down some ideas. Call up people who'd lost even more then him and see how they're doing. He had so much to still be thankful for. If he wanted to give a bit to help others, Lena would approve. Maybe a ten-dollar bill to help with the electric, a box of fresh tomatoes to a housebound neighbor –

But there were no housebound neighbors left on Pine Street, were there? That world had disappeared. Hard as he had fought against it, and no matter how he looked at it, he would have to start over.

He looked over at the little cat's eye clock his nephew had brought him from New York City. Or was it Ocean City? One of those places he'd never been. Now he'd have the time to go.

The clock said 6 p.m. He had lost a whole day. Nothing had been done, nothing planned, nothing decided. All of it put aside until tomorrow.

His dinner would be ready, downstairs, warming in the oven. Two plates, two cups, waiting on the table for him to be ready for his dinner. Lena, loyal and patient, in her chair reading and clipping, ready to listen to how he felt about losing a whole day. Ready to listen, or if he couldn't talk yet, to keep busy while he ate.

He just couldn't face food, not with his stomach so bad. He would sit here in his beloved chair, rubbing the thin spots on the arms with his thumbs. He found himself calling up images – face after face of friends and family. His mind filled with memories of his whole life, the way people do when they're drowning. It felt like he was both mourning and celebrating at the same moment, if you really came down to it. A life with few regrets. He picked up his gun. Gently and steadily, he squeezed the trigger.

Chapter Thirty-One

The time is always right to do what's right.

— Martin Luther King, Jr. (*Remaining Awake*)

On Ava's first day out of the hospital Gabe and Celie hadn't left her alone for even a minute. When they'd got to Celie's, the TV was blaring, as usual. Robert Kennedy was asking the Maryland Governor who would be held accountable for helping folks in Cambridge start over. Celie almost tripped over the couch in her rush to switch off the TV, which seemed odd, Ava thought, but she was too worn out to ask why.

Celie had improved the sparse second room to make a longer-term guest room for Ava. The room was now a bright and cheery extension of Celie.

"Wow. Did you do all this by yourself?" Ava asked.

"Gabe helped me move in the bed and the dresser. I did the frou-frou stuff myself. Just look!"

Celie stuck out a toe to straighten the fringe on a large throw rug, moved in from Celie's own room, with neat tracks of vacuum-cleaner wheels formed in the pile. Fresh flowers were on the nightstand, and pressed curtains cascaded down the window in place of the 'greige' blinds of just a few days ago. The same puffy silk as the windows in Celie's other rooms.

"I know you don't go for ruffles and stuff, but I thought a homey setting might cheer you up. We can take them down if they're too different from what you're used to."

If she only knew, Ava thought. The kinds of rooms she was used to, even her own apartment, were austere and business-like. "Celie,

281

it's beautiful," Ava said as she sat on the bed. "You shouldn't have done so much. No, I mean thanks, sweetheart, it looks really great. I'm impressed with the curtains."

"You're welcome. I *ironed* them! Every little ruffle and tuck. All those years Willi tried to teach me how to iron paid off. Well I guess you can see that." She stopped to catch her breath. "Gabe put them up, by himself, while I vacuumed. And guess what, I think Gabe can cook."

"Is that what smells so good?"

"Actually not. The Reverend's wife made us some kind of casserole and a chocolate pie. It's all vegetarian. We'll heat it up later. Now come get in bed and let me wait on you."

"No," Ava interrupted. "I want to eat in the kitchen. I'm tired of being in bed and I'm even more tired of being waited on. All I want is to get on with my normal life, and back to my job at the church."

Celie stopped fluffing pillows and turned to face her, but it was not because she was ready to give in. With her legs planted wide and her hands parked on her waist, she was about to make a stand. Ava braced herself in case she had to battle.

"It's good you feel that way," Celie began, deceptively low-keyed. "I'm glad you want to get moving again." She moved closer and squatted so that Ava could see her face.

Ava got her breath. "I mean it. I have the funeral to go to and then I have to connect with people. Even a couple of days away is too much. Were there any calls for me?"

"No, Ethan hasn't called yet. Do you want me to try and find him?"

"No, I don't. I'm better off without him."

She looked out above Celie's head as she said it, so she wouldn't have to deal with those probing eyes. She changed the subject. "What are they saying on the news?"

"Nothing. *They* haven't heard from Ethan either."

"Smart ass.

"I didn't set up this room just to give you a transition space," she said. "Nobody wanted to tell you about the rest of what happened but now it's time. It's about what else happened the night you were hurt. There was a bad fire."

"I know there was a fire."

"But you don't know how bad the fire was. The doctor told us to tell you the worst things slowly, until you get some of your memory back."

"That's why you turned off the TV! You can turn it back on, now. I want to know."

"It's that the whole neighborhood, practically, was burned down."

"Was anyone hurt? Anyone killed?"

"Not then. No one except –" Celie stopped.

She'd been going to say except Sari, of course. She'd been pacing as usual, her pony tail bouncing as she crisscrossed through the room. She now picked up a stack of folded newspapers which she handed to Ava, and then plopped herself in the little white rocker that had been in her room back on the farm. The way she looked, she could have still been twelve years old, except that under the fluff and good cheer was a girl who was clearly in charge of things. She said, "I'm going to sit here while you read them, so I can answer any questions."

Ten minutes was all Ava took. When she looked up at Celie's face, she saw tears in her eyes; then Celie handed Ava one more paper, the one with the story about Edward Tate. Seeing the tears, Ava wondered how long she'd been letting people like Celie do all of her feeling, so she didn't have to.

"This breaks my heart. How's his wife?"

"She's still in their house and their kids are with her. She's at loose ends where to go or what to do. She's only in her fifties, you know."

Ava could feel her mind drifting and she tried to bring it back. "My church is gone, too?"

"They want to rebuild it, but it's going to be quite a while even to clean up what's left. I'm afraid there's nothing at all salvageable for most of the businesses."

"Then the work we did — it was all for nothing. All those people we were trying to help. They had no money, no jobs ... but they had their neighborhood, whatever we thought of it. It was theirs. It was home and family to them, and now they'll all be shoved into some housing unit somewhere."

"No, they won't. The riot drew so much attention that there's already money to rebuild all the houses, even the ones that had no insurance. Despite all they've lost, our folks are determined to keep their community."

"Good. That's something." Ava wanted to stand up but couldn't. "Celie, is Gabe still here?"

"I'm here. Do you need me?" So he'd been listening from the kitchen.

"Just to ask something. How are you helping them – the community?"

"The way I always do. At Mace's Lane, I just started a basketball thing, a summer coaching camp. And tutoring. Those are going on. And they're asking me to sit on the Board of Education next school year."

He came into the room, wearing one of Celie's frilly aprons. Both women burst into laughter and he looked sheepish. "Cut me a break. I don't have another clean shirt with me."

He had a wooden spoon in his hand which he used as a pointer as he continued. "There's only one good thing to come from this disaster, Ava. You'll have to find a less hazardous way to fight your cause. You now have a steel pin holding your shoulder together. Doc says you can't afford to keep getting knocked around." He grinned. "Now if you'll excuse me a minute, the stone soup is almost ready," he added, using their family name for pot luck.

Ava said, "First, I need to say something. I know I was wrong about some of those people in the Caucus. I never believed in violence, you know."

"We know," they said in unison.

But they didn't know, she thought. In the beginning, most of her friends had believed in the philosophies of Mahatma Gandhi. Gabe did and a lot of Martin Luther King's followers. Others – like Stokely Carmichael – split off. These people took an oath to do whatever was asked of them, even violence. Gabe and Celie would never know how close she'd come to joining them.

"Here," Celie was saying as she pulled a lined sheet of paper from the pocket of her nurse's uniform, unfolding it to read. "I made a list of Gabe's NAACP contacts in Baltimore, in case you need them. Some jobs he knows there, and some that I do. Or I can help you find a place to stay here in Cambridge for a while." She hesitated, and Ava could see she was struggling to say the rest, "...that is, if you don't want to stay with me. Which of course you can as long as you want."

Ava grinned and blew her a kiss. She'd forgotten the uncomplicated, optimistic outlook that Celie applied to everything and everybody in her life. Celie wasn't any more streetwise now than she'd been the day they'd first met. Somehow, she'd survived the meanest, poorest neighborhoods in Baltimore by expecting the best from everybody. She wondered what Celie would think of Ava's life choices, the ones she would never talk about.

She said, "Thanks, darlin,' That's sweet. I won't need the list, but thanks. I'll stay with you until I can make some plans; thanks for that too."

"What is your plan?"

"I might start over completely, away from here, but first, I need to think a while." She said it matter-of-factly, meaning it to close down the subject.

"Can we talk about it?"

"No, Celie, we can't. You've both helped so much, and I'm very grateful. But when it comes to what happens next, I need to do it alone. Let's drop it, OK?"

Ava lacked the will to argue her position right now. She hoped even Celie wouldn't disregard such a direct request. Maybe she'd try to tell them more over the soup, about how somewhere during her recovery, she had decided to leave her official place in the movement. Her reasoning about it was vague, even in her own thinking. All she was certain of was that being with the Caucus had brought out her vulnerabilities in a way that could someday be fatal. No matter why it was true, she wanted to live more prudently for a while. She wasn't sure what kind of role that would be since it also had to be useful.

Celie had laid some mail on the bed and now Ava picked it up, pretending to read, but mostly to deter more questions. It made her dizzy to look at the words, but she didn't let on. She kept sorting things into piles. She realized that Celie was still standing there, stiff as a soldier.

"I haven't got rid of you, I see," Ava said. "I'm not going to discuss it now, my dear friend. First of all, I'm trussed up like a stuffed turkey. You might not be able to see them, but I'm still loaded with bruises. Everything hurts, even talking. Even thinking."

"The doctor told us it would be like aftershocks from an earthquake. He said you might have had a mild concussion even before ... that night. Ava, I just want to help you get better. I have to say this! You weren't your right self, Ava, long before this happened. One of your friends told us that you hadn't been eating or sleeping for weeks before you came home. Gabe and I have been scared for a long time that the whole political thing was killing you."

Celie began wiping her tears with a bath towel she'd been carrying. As badly as Ava wanted to hug Celie, she didn't dare do anything that encouraged more intimacy. She was already feeling choked to death by too much attention. She picked up a random magazine from the bed and began flipping pages full of skinny white models in confectionary dresses. The last thing Ava could ever care about. Then, she did an unthinkable thing — she turned her back on Celie, hoping this would convince her to leave. She felt very mean for doing it and for saying, over her shoulder, "Can't I just be alone? Until the soup is ready? I need to think."

After Celie left, her head spun and throbbed until she felt she would die of it. Wasn't it just yesterday when she had been picturing her life with Ethan in it? Dreaming of the best of both worlds, a life that was meaningful without constant threat? What Ethan had wanted from her, the night of the rally, was a commitment to settle down in some normal way, and she had sent him to see his mother without an answer.

She thought of a line from Gabe's favorite poem: *I thank whatever gods may be — for my unconquerable soul.* Her unconquerable soul? She had committed herself to a mission, and it had mattered more than anything, more than even Sari. She couldn't stop thinking that in some way her actions were responsible for killing Sari, and maybe even for letting the Second Ward burn to the ground.

This kind of guilt would get her nowhere. It was what Celie called "original sin," the notion that all people are born morally defective — not capable of achieving even basic decency, let alone a loftier destiny. Just think, something useful from the Catholics for a change. If she could just get past that crippling guilt, she could go after the real culprits. Somewhere during the second hour of the fire, while she was being mugged and Sari was murdered, the good people of this town had watched a whole community, one they had sworn to protect, burn to the ground. It hadn't been fear of snipers that had made those firemen sit and wait. When they'd finally come to assist, it wasn't out of compassion. It had been the fear that the fire might cross over to the white district.

The mayor had been heard shouting, "Let them burn their own

asses up. Save us a lot of trouble." And in that hateful atmosphere, someone had murdered her sister, and no one seemed inclined to find out who it was. Even people out there who were the healers couldn't get their momentum back. Reverend Benson had visited her daily at the hospital, but his plan for the next step was an offer to keep his chin out for more. He'd said ridiculous things like, "I don't think there's any one group to blame." And, "Everybody's emotions got out of hand."

How in the world could she go "live a normal life," when the best of their leaders here would let themselves think such a thing? Poverty, inequality, suffering – were problems that would get worse, not better.

Isaac had said something profound when he'd told her his parable about finding her true self. He'd said, "You can't see who you are until you try and make somebody else's life better." He'd dealt with social crises by raising up his people, one at a time, but the crisis now was so big that men of good conscience were outnumbered by thugs.

A sociologist might say that this moral crisis in the Tidewater area was long overdue. The people who had lived in Tidewater for generations, who had breathed the same air as their ancestors, and as each other, had obeyed cultural rules that had kept them safely outside the margins of each other's struggles. They'd been blind to each other.

Martin Luther King said, "History will ... record that the greatest tragedy of this period of social transition was not the strident clamor of the bad people, but the appalling silence of the good people."

Isaac had a similar saying, "The Lord saves the hottest fires in Hell for people who mind their own business."

Nobody knew exactly when the balance of power had tipped so far to the white side, but the truce was broken for this moment in time. The people all stood face to face now, ready for battle, here in the summer of 1967. It was up to people like Ava to keep the walls down and work inside that gap, to make sure the blindness never returned. And somewhere on the other side of the boundary, she would find Sari's killer.

Chapter Thirty-Two

Shallow understanding from people of good will is more frustrating than absolute misunderstanding from people of ill will.

— Martin Luther King, Jr. (*Letters*)

Sleep was Ava's way of handling every dilemma these days. She woke to see Celie dressed for work and watching the evening news, chin in hand, eyebrows scrunched downward.

News. She hadn't heard the news since she'd been here. "What are they saying? Do they know who started the fire yet?"

Celie muted the TV sound. "Oh, rumors are flying in all directions. Mostly, the same political mumbo-jumbo they printed in the *Daily Banner*. A more important question is how are you feeling?"

"Mmm."

"I see. So bad you can't say. I didn't really mean how are you, anyway. What I meant was are you up to talking about Sari?"

"No." Trust Celie to always push to the core of things. Of all Ava's wounds, Sari's loss was the only one that would never heal. She'd been too heartbroken to talk about it to anyone, even Celie. But Celie would never let up, would she? Maybe she'd muted the TV because she knew how hard it was for Ava to concentrate on anything with the slightest noise in the room. Well, of course she would know that. She's an E.R. nurse. I couldn't have a better, or more annoying, babysitter.

Celie said, "I'm not asking you to lay your heart open this very minute, but it isn't healthy for you to say absolutely nothing at all. When you lose someone so important, it's just about all you can think about. So, how about letting a few of those words out?"

"My thoughts are – disjointed. I've always been so methodical — I'm hating this disordered-thought thing." She felt tears starting up, another damn intrusion to her method.

"It'll get better. Try not to get frustrated. Keep taking naps so your brain can heal. Meantime, I'm not asking you for an orderly report. I'm asking about your feelings."

"My feelings. Odd as it sounds, not grief, but worry. It's not that I have some fantasy that Sari's still out there somewhere. Worry was my last feeling before the – accident. That she'd been so lost, for such a long time. I think I'd been expecting a catastrophe for months. If I was surprised by anything when I saw her in the church window, it was that she looked so good. Not drugged-out or insolent. I have this perfect image of Sari just standing there, smiling. After that ... well, nothing clear after that. Until the hospital room."

Celie said, "So sad. I wish I'd done more. I didn't know how bad things were – honest, or I'd have told you. To me, she just seemed ... God, I'm chattering again. I should have stopped with 'So sad.'"

Ava smiled, grateful her face was starting to cooperate more when she tried to move it. "No, don't ever stop chattering. It gives the rest of us time to gather our thoughts and sound real smart when we finally get a chance to talk."

Celie collapsed in giggles and Ava's sense of well-being edged upward. As she saw the tension leave Celie, she realized how much of her own feelings Celie and Gabe had always absorbed, and the level of distress she'd caused them. For what seemed the first time in her life, Ava was feeling the weight of the responsibility that goes with loving people.

Each time the codeine had kicked in, she'd been flooded with visions of all the people in her past who'd tried to protect and comfort her – Isaac and Minnie, Gabe and Celie, Reverend Benson. Even self-centered Willi had kept things from her for her own good. She wished that in her floating vision of all these people, she'd seen herself returning something to them. To her great shame, the only person she'd spent time ministering back to in some way was Sari.

"Can I get you anything before supper?" Celie had been sitting as close to Ava as she could squeeze and yet Ava could see Celie's mind was already headed off elsewhere.

"No, but you can answer a question for me."

"Sure."

"I wonder what it is that's weighing so heavy on *you*."

"Me? Oh, not any one thing. Can I get you something from the kitchen?" Celie was standing and smoothing her skirt.

"Oh, no you don't. Now look who's being evasive."

"I'm not! OK, I am." Celie sat back down. "It's just that I've been thinking about other friends who might have ... who could be in trouble."

"If you mean Gabe, the answer is he didn't go to the rally. Nothing will come down to him."

Celie's relief was visible. "Are you sure? How do you – "

"I'm sure. I talked to him on the phone before and after the rally. He didn't get to Cambridge until long after Brown and his people were gone. He was in the hospital with us from then on."

Not exactly a perfect alibi, Ava realized, but Celie would trust her.

She said "I'm glad. Not that I thought he had anything to do with the fire or anything, but I'm glad the investigation won't come to him. I mean, somebody official *must* be looking to find who did this."

"It's always possible, I guess. I'm the last one to know about the investigation. But I do have another question before you go, about Gabe. The two of you have been spending a lot of time together taking care of me. Do I need to remind you what you promised me?"

Celie was trying to look cagey and Ava felt her temper rise. Celie said, "I know what I promised you. How do you know it's the same thing I promised him?"

Teeth clenched against pain, Ava said, "This isn't a joke, Celie. I stood by and let Sari head for disaster. I'm not going to do it with you, or Gabe. Or more to the point, the you-and-Gabe part."

Celie had taken one of Ava's hands in both of hers and Ava had felt Celie shudder when she'd said their names as paired.

Celie whispered, "I wasn't joking. Really."

"It's a relationship that's no good for him."

"You don't have to lecture me about what's good for Gabe. Just because the two of you agree, doesn't mean the two of you are right. I happen to believe you're both wrong, but I can't prove it any more than you can."

"The proof is ... well, the way people act. Look what just happened here!"

"I have been looking, Ava. I'm right in the center of it, just like you. What I don't understand is why you want to keep people divided.

I've always loved you as an equal, ever since we were little girls. At one point, I loved your being black more than you did yourself. Are you saying that you didn't think of me as your dearest friend? That you didn't love me?"

"I still love you! And Gabe is crazy about you. You think I don't know how he's always felt? He would give up everything for you. But I don't want him to ruin his life, not even for you."

Ava steeled herself, ready to argue, but Celie pressed Ava's arm as lightly as possible to keep her there. "Wait, let me talk. Despite what I believe, I accept that Gabe believes he has to go in a different direction. I've already told him to go, and I'll stick to that. But I'll be back here waiting. I believe he'll come to me some day."

It was all Ava could do not to jump up in protest. She said, though her mouth was aching, "Don't tell yourself that, Celie! It kills me to think you'd waste more of your life on a fantasy that anybody can love *anybody*. You don't even know what you're asking of him, do you?"

"Don't get high-handed with me, Miss. I'm not as simple as you think. I may not have your elegant turn of phrase, but I can see what's going on in Gabe as well as you can."

"You're right. I'm sorry for treating you like you don't know our troubles. You do know. But you can't change what you are. *White.*"

Celie let go of Ava's arm. "You sound like Gabe. What the hell does that mean? You don't think I know that I'm white and that he's not? What difference does it make? I've fought that battle before, you know."

"I'm not talking about standing up to the clerk in Nick's Luncheonette now, Celie. When it comes to life choices, you and Gabe have different goals."

"Let's see, a good job – love, friendship. In the end, what do you and Gabe want that's so different?"

"Just those things. But we can't just walk out this door and get them. To start with, we can't even get an equal job."

"Well, neither can I. A man in my job gets paid more. If I decided to become a doctor, I couldn't get into medical school either."

"It's not the same."

"The hell it's not. "

"A black man in your job gets paid less than you. A black person can't even get into any of the schools you went to. People have to know their own color and how it changes everything. Remember when you told me to stop wishing away my own skin color?"

"Of course I do."

"Then later you gave me a black doll to play with – so I'd have a doll my own color?"

"That wasn't the reason I gave her to you. It was so we could *both* have dolls of both colors, and as I remember you still played with the white doll the most. So, analyze that."

Ava leaned her head back and laughed, then grimaced with the pain it brought her. "I guess I did, didn't I? But what that taught me was that *you* were different, you Celie, as one person. It didn't mean other white people would be."

"You're still missing the point. What I was trying to do was get you to love yourself, and be yourself, no matter what anyone else thought."

"For *you* it was about that. For me it's been about figuring out where the self-hatred comes from in the first place. Loving people is what motivates *you*, Celie. It's who *you* are. But it's not who I am."

"Meaning your life is about hating people? I don't believe it."

"No, of course not, it's about changing things. About hating the reasons I had to work for a living at the age of ten, picking your family's damn crops."

Celie looked stricken, but Ava needed her to feel this. "I can't rest until my people are able to get to the front of the food line, the employment line. The line where equality is a God-given right, not a gift handed out by those in charge. Until these rights are *never* questioned."

"Never – really? Greed doesn't belong only to white men, you know. My grandmother had this saying and I never knew what it meant. She'd say, *the poor will always be with us*. Where she lived, they were all white and Catholic, but there wasn't equality then either. What she meant was that some people in society will always end up with less. That people can't live with each other without dreaming up a system to hog power."

"You got a way to overcome that? Because if you don't, these are the people who'll be your neighbors if you and Gabe try to live together."

"Not all of them. Some people are mean-spirited, but a lot of them are kind and open."

"And most of both kinds of people are complacent. Only a few are warriors, fighting to stir everybody else out of complacency. To warriors, there can be no compromise. Gabe is a warrior and so am I. We may have to fight oppression as long as we live."

"Is that the way you see me, then? As an oppressor?"

"Of course not. I see you as – as a miracle. An exception. Like a lot of those white civil rights workers at the rallies. Some of them were truly committed to us. The flaw they have, the people like that, is that they're trying to be color-blind."

"Color blind? You can't believe I want that for Gabe?"

"I don't know," Ava sighed. She felt better this minute than she had in weeks, despite her rush of painful emotions. Some kind of healing energy had been released – an energy that had been missing and that Celie always could boost in her.

She wanted to stand but knew Celie wouldn't let her get that far, so she patted the couch for Celie to sit. She looked directly into the unrelenting blue eyes, always so clear and open to whatever was out there. Celie had never been able to look away from anything. Her way of escaping the narrowness of her religion had been to keep her eyes open, saying, "You can do anything in the world you want, as long as you watch yourself doing it. And clean up the mess."

Ava said, "You want a world with one big group hug. I want a world where I don't have to negotiate for the right to be in the group. But there's never going to be that big group hug –"

Celie had opened her mouth to argue. Ava squeezed her hand to stop her. "Just listen to every word I say Celie, for once, instead of thinking up what to say next."

Celie hadn't been convinced by Gabe how impossible things were; it was now up to Ava. She said, "There must be a struggle, don't you see? Between races, between old and young, men and women. The balance, if there is one, is in 'push me, pull you,' like Dr. Doolittle's brilliant fictional beast. When people began pushing themselves to rise up, those higher up have to push them back down. They have to. It's what life is. So I hope that people are never color blind. I want them to know I'm black. I want black kids to have self-esteem – to see their own color as the best color to be. Not just equal – but best."

"How gloomy. How depressingly cynical. I thought we – our generation — would do better than our parents. Can't there be intolerance of intolerance itself?"

"No, Celie. Nonviolence and violence have to exist side by side. At this point in history, I stand for one and you stand for the other. You see?"

"I see what you believe but I don't agree. The difference is – forgive me for saying this – the imbalance you see, isn't based on your race, or gender, or religion ... or anything else so *grandiose*, so ... so *organized*. It's much more personal than that. It's because your parents treated you so terribly. They ripped a hole in your heart that you've spent your whole life trying to fill. Sorry to be so blunt."

"You're exactly right. And that's exactly what happened to Gabe, too. Call it our shared birthright. And when you add our race on top of that, it makes us seek the same mission."

Celie said, "There is so much more to these riots than equality. They are not about *push me — pull you*. The riots are about people losing everything. You think you know why all hell broke loose here in Cambridge this week? I say you don't. What I see is sheer panic, making all our folks crazy. People act out of character when they're scared. I see it in my work every day. People don't want to be reminded how vulnerable they are, so they segregate and make fun of people who are poor or sick. They're saying, *This can't be me.* The reason these rallies of yours scare the hell out of white people is because their families are on the brink of economic failure. They're afraid of losing everything. Just like Jesse's family hanging on to that damn skipjack for dear life, even when it makes no sense. It's panic that makes people forget we're alike, and instead see only their differences."

"You were dirt poor and you didn't forget."

"That's because I met you and Isaac and Minnie and Gabe. All I could see, all I'll ever see, are your beautiful souls."

Ava felt tears in her eyes again. She was sick to death of crying. She laid her head down on Celie's hand and for once, had nothing to say.

"And now, go back to sleep," Celie said, pulling an afghan up to Ava's chin and tucking it in lightly before turning off the lamp. Ava had been sure Celie was about to tell her something else, but she let it go and fell into a deep sleep.

****

For the past few days, Celie had felt like a dancer. Gabe would put his hand down in one spot, she'd make sure hers went in the other direction. If he moved to the right, she would feint to the left. So close ... so Goddamn close all the time that she could smell his shampoo and almost feel the warmth of his skin.

Once, just once, his arm had bumped against her hip while they were moving Ava into her chair. They had quickly choreographed a new maneuver – a 'no-contact' twist of things, with no risk of touching.

For hours afterward, her hip had fairly burned with the imprint of their encounter. She had replayed the scene over and over, memorizing it, so that if nothing else ever happened between them, she would feel his arm against her hip for the rest of her days.

Chapter Thirty-Three

We must develop and maintain the capacity to forgive. He who is devoid of the power to forgive is devoid of the power to love. There is some good in the worst of us and some evil in the best of us.

— Martin Luther King, Jr. (*Letters*)

Sari was reaching her hand out, and all Ava wanted to do was to wake herself up.

Gabe's voice interrupted her struggle. "Sorry to wake you. I can't wait, though. Ethan is here to see you."

She would have bolted upward but Gabe was holding her shoulders to slow her down. He said, "Whoa! Take it slow. Those painkillers make you forget ... you can't move that fast yet."

Her answer began with a sob. "Thanks. Can you hand me that – uh — I'm sorry. I seem to cry with every sentence lately. I ... I've been making up excuses why Ethan hasn't been to see me and ... now I'm afraid to find out."

"I know. I also know that he must have had a good reason."

"Do you know the reason?"

"I don't. Even if I knew the guy that well, I wouldn't ask him. All I can tell you is that he's here now. So what do you need to get ready? I can help you pick out some clothes and come back in twenty minutes. Or if you'd rather, I'll stay and help you get dressed." He was grinning.

"That'll be the day! Just my robe. And maybe a comb ... and, oh yes, a mirror." Despite their lighthearted teasing, Ava was sitting on a reservoir of irritability and it was all she could do to control it.

As Gabe went to the kitchen, he said, "Yell if you need anything."
The thin shell holding back her temper collapsed.

"Why does everybody think I need help with every little thing?
It's very annoying. Damn it, I'm not as fragile as you think." She
took a breath. "And twenty minutes will be fine."

Gabe disappeared, clearly ignoring her grumpiness. By the time
she was dressed, she heard him laughing in the kitchen. She heard
Ethan's voice too and felt an emotional jolt that played out, of course,
in her bones and muscles.

He was saying, "So give her the chance to send me away, then. If
she wants me to go, I will."

She pictured laid-back Gabe, shrugging his shoulders noncommit-
tally, and she called out, "I'm here!" her voice weak and pathetic.
Louder, she said, "Tell him to stay." She hated sounding like a victim, but she had no choice. "Gabe, can you help me out there?"

It was Ethan who came to get her. He supported her by placing
her arm on top of his shoulder, with his arm beneath it, holding her
waist. Her legs were trembling, which she'd expected, but his being
so close made it much worse. He ended up carrying her out. He
situated her in the overstuffed living room chair that had become
her constant partner, dragged from one place to another, now in the
kitchen. Gabe had helped with the chair and now moved to leave.

"Stay, Gabe! Ethan can talk in front of my family."

"He can talk better without us," Gabe retorted and disappeared
into the living room.

"Something to drink?" Ava asked, feeling idiotic.

"The last time we were together," Ethan said, as if she hadn't said
a word, "was right before the fire. Do you remember what I said
when I was leaving to see my mother?"

"Sure. You said you'd be back when things were fixed up with
her. I said something to the effect of, 'Do what you need to, you
know where to find me.'"

"A lot has happened since then."

She held up the arm with the cast on it, and cocked her head,
trying for the utmost of visual sarcasm, and said, "That's the under-
statement of the century. You – well, you didn't call to see how I was.
When you still didn't, I assumed something happened at your Ma's …
or that maybe you just changed your mind."

"Why in the world would you think that? How could I know you were hurt, Ava? I wouldn't even know now, except that I read about your sister's murder in the newspaper yesterday when I came into town to get supplies. Supplies including parts for Ma's broken radio. She lives in a marsh; she has one radio and no TV. Didn't I tell you?"

"She has a phone, doesn't she?"

"Sure she does, but people have to *use* it for it to be any good. None of you called me. You didn't; your friends didn't. Why didn't you?"

It had never occurred to Ava to call him. In fact, when she caught Celie looking through her purse for Ethan's number, she practically bit off her head for going too far in her efforts to "help." She owed Celie an apology. She owed everybody in her whole damn life an apology. She owed Ethan a lot better explanation than that.

"I guess the truth is that I assumed you were blowing me off when you said that about coming back after you fixed things. I've used similar lines. It's what you say to colleagues you like when it's time to hit the road. I thought that's what you were doing."

"You're such a little fool. I'm not your parents. And besides, you obviously have at least some people in your life who've never treated you that way." He swept his arm toward where Gabe had exited. "When are you going to start trusting people, Ava? When are you going to let people love you the way you deserve to be loved?"

"I'm so, so sorry. I missed you so much – needed you so much — but in my life, needing somebody has always been a surefire means of driving them away."

"I don't believe you for a minute. I've met Gabe and Celie, and I met Isaac yesterday. All three of them clearly adore you, and I'm sure others do too. The wedge between you and your folks is one *you* keep there."

She was crying. Again. She hadn't cried so much in her whole life as she had this past week. Ethan scooped her up into his lap and sat, cradling her, rocking her like a child. He held her like that until she fell asleep, and this time when her nightmare about Sari came back, he was right there, holding her.

They sat undisturbed for an hour and then Celie came home. Ethan said, "Let's eat." They slid the huge chair in place at the round kitchen table, already too small for all of them to have any knee room. For some reason, they all seemed to want to be close enough to Ava to touch her.

They drank mugs of soup along with the warm rolls Celie had brought home. Afterward, Celie rinsed out the mugs and Gabe refilled them with coffee while Celie somehow wedged a plate of cookies between the mugs. The two of them had worked fluidly, without exchanging a word. Ava tried not to notice whether there was electricity between them. She was tired of playing the heavy.

Once they were all back in place, Ethan said, "Tell us more about the nightmare about Sari. We're going to try and help you remember what happened because we think that, until you do, you won't really heal."

"I'm not sure I can separate out what's real from what I might have dreamed."

Gabe said, "It doesn't matter. Just say whatever comes to mind. We'll sort it out later."

"The first part is always the same. It starts with what I do remember, about how when I got to the church, it was quiet everywhere. No crowds left, just a few old men by the barber shop and some boys sitting on the steps eavesdropping. It could have been any summer evening. Inside the church, all I could hear was the sound of my typewriter... until a noise in the churchyard scared me. I got up to look, thinking a student might have missed his ride, but what I saw was Sari's face in the window. It was Sari and not-Sari. I know that sounds crazy. And that isn't even the fuzzy part! It seemed so real. Sari smiling a smile with no joy at all, no kindness. It cut into me like a knife because Sari had never looked more like Venus. The old Venus I mean."

"What do you mean, the old Venus?" Gabe and Celie asked at the same time.

"The last time I saw Venus — about a month ago – she'd turned into an old woman. She was using make-up to try and cover the damage, but it just made it worse – like she had drawn on a clown's face. Her lips were so much thinner, but she'd drawn an outline beyond the edges of her mouth with dark red pencil. She'd filled it in with thick, blood-red lipstick. And her hair –" Ava's voice faltered, and she felt three sets of hands, squeezing her hands and patting her arm.

"Her hair was shocking. She had no eyebrows. She'd drawn little feather lines there with an India black pencil. Her hair was almost bald at the hairline, and she'd pulled back what there was into a top knot ... and she put a fake ponytail in the knot. She made it swing back and forth in that exaggerated sashay of hers. Maybe it was attractive once, but now it only called attention to the shape of her skull ... a skeleton's head with a wig attached."

Ava knew tears were spilling down her face. She reached for the tissue box, vaguely aware of three hands shooting out at the same moment to push the box toward her. Tissues wouldn't do much, though. Tears flowing, words flooding, down from her brain to her tongue.... She couldn't have stopped talking if she'd wanted to, and she didn't want to.

"Venus's eyes are dull now, and the make-up makes them uglier. Her irises and cornea are almost the exact same dull ash color, like she has no pupils. Those eyes that used to blaze like they could shoot sparks, are now—dead."

Celie whispered, maybe not even knowing she said anything, "Like when flames die out and leave behind gray charcoal."

Ava reached for Celie's hand and gulped some air to clear her voice. "My Irish poet. Yes. Whatever it was that happened to her took away both her fire and her beauty."

"I'm glad I didn't have to see it," Celie said. "She was always so beautiful. I loved that about her."

"Sari did too," Gabe added, seeming to sense that Ava needed some of their words to fill in because her own were failing. He said, "Sari always tried so hard to look just like her."

"Now you know what I mean about Sari looking like the old Venus. When Sari popped into the window of the church like that, I had to look real close to see if she was Venus or Sari. I wanted to see if her eyes had gone dead. They hadn't. I asked her to come inside the church. I knew she'd been at the rally and I had to ask her about it."

"You saw her at the rally?" Gabe asked.

"No, but she was there. She had a sign, "Black Power." That was the other strange thing, the sign. Sari is less political than anybody we know. For her to show up at a rally, big payment of some kind had to be involved. Remember when we all played that marriage fortune-telling game, that night we moved Sari to Willi's? Remember she said the only thing she ever wanted from life was to be rich?"

Gabe answered, "I never played a game that silly, but I do remember her saying she wanted to be rich, no matter what. But she was just a kid then. Kids say stuff. There were other forces in her life besides Venus, you know, maybe even stronger ones."

"You mean men? Sari just used men. She used just about everybody she knew, just like Venus, who was the only person that really mattered to her. She never stopped wishing for her to come back, but even that changed into something ... I don't know, dark and complicated."

"Explain," Gabe said.

"I can only try. I doubt anybody besides me knew how Venus tormented her. Making promises she didn't intend to keep or never remembered making. By the time Sari was fifteen, she'd stopped believing there'd ever be anything close to love coming from her mother. The more she wanted it the more Venus pushed her away. And it was mutual after a while. They couldn't stop baiting each other. That kind of thing has a name – some kind of triangle."

"It's called co-dependency," said Gabe. "I read about it in my psychology class."

"I thought that term was just with alcoholics," Celie said.

Ethan spoke for the first time. "It's a little more complicated than that. But Gabe is close."

This man knows something about every topic in the whole world, she thought. Frowning, she said, "Whatever it's called, I *hated* watching it. I made up my mind not to be part of it. I tried to prepare Sari for how it would happen every time Venus came. I tried to make Venus clear in Sari's mind, but nothing I ever said was enough."

Celie had been sitting with her lips pursed, her chin nestled in her open fist, what Ava called her Rodin's Thinker Pose. She uncurled the pose, nearly tumbling her mug over the edge of the table as she stood, then catching it in the nick of time. She began pacing in a circle around them. "Wait. Sari was more than just a victim, though. Right? There had to be something she could hold over Venus. Tit for tat."

"That's right!'" Gabe said. "Did she, Ava?"

"You bet. She had lots of small things and one big one, that Venus was terrified for people to know. Sari would mock her about it."

"Don't tell me – not that old rumor about Venus being a witch?" Gabe sounded skeptical.

"No. It's true she learned Voodoo, or something like it, where she grew up in Jamaica. She talked it up so much that some people thought she was fooling around — that it was one of her scams. But Venus believed in magic and in spirits. She thought she was under the power of dark forces."

"That's what Sari held over her head? Dark forces? It doesn't sound like it would scare the Venus I know," Gabe said, frowning.

"Except Venus was convinced she was under a specific curse. It's why she was so inclined to curse everybody else."

"What kind of curse?" Celie asked, slipping back into her seat so she could hold Ava's hand again.

"That she'd be locked away for being crazy, the way our Pa was. No one besides Isaac and Minnie knew how bad Pa really was. A man that crazy does terrible things to his family. When Sari wanted to hurt Venus, she could make Venus feel crazy – or she'd act crazy herself. I used to think that's mainly what drove Venus away."

"Makes my head spin to think about it," Gabe said. "But I get it. I hated to be around Sari when she was acting like that."

Celie added, "Me too. But not you, Ava. When you saw Sari in that window, you wanted to rescue her, right?"

Ava nodded yes, or thought she did. Celie continued talking, squeezing her hand too tight as she said, "It might be the hardest thing you have to accept. That you couldn't have saved Sari. That nobody could have. That's what I had to tell my sister Hannah about what happened to Jesse. She swore she'd wait to marry him and then together, they'd save his skipjack."

"Who was Jesse?"

Gabe said, "You know who, Ava. The family that took me in from the waterfront. Jesse's father had one of the last working skipjacks in the harbor there – on the whole Chesapeake. He got hurt bad, and Jesse was supposed to save the business – which means their skipjack — from oblivion. Jesse loved that boat more than he did Hannah – or anyone."

"If it was that valuable, couldn't he get a loan or something?" Ava asked, annoyed at Celie for this tangent.

"No. Skipjack fishing had been dying out since the oysters began disappearing a hundred years ago. Jesse's boat was already obsolete. In fact, it was because of skipjacks and their dredging that the oysters became endangered in the first place. How's that for irony?"

"Like everything else we all grew up loving," Celie said with a sigh. "Did you want to stay there and help Jesse with the business, Gabe? Become a waterman?"

"Nobody ever asked me. I guess the answer was yes, back then.

There weren't many choices open to me in those days. When Isaac came to get me, I knew I wanted my real family more, what there was of it. Besides, I didn't think Jesse had a chance to do what he wanted. He couldn't see it, because to him, it wasn't just a boat he'd be losing. It was generations of the skipjack way of life. Celie, is that what you mean about none of us being able to save Sari? That her problems were larger than her own life? Like a self-fulfilling prophecy?"

Celie smiled and nodded.

Ava felt foolish. A minute ago she had flashed a look at Celie that meant, "What a dumb thing to say." As she often did, Celie had been looking at the heart of things, and as usual, Ava had underestimated what she had to offer. Celie didn't see the broadness of the world the way Ava did, but her views were often a godsend, and Ava had counted on her wisdom without realizing it.

Ava had a flash of insight. She might even call it a revelation. She saw herself as having spent her life as much under Venus's spell as Sari had. Whereas Sari was trapped by her longing for Venus, Ava had been mired in resentment, spending all her emotional energy trying to make up to Sari for having a rotten mother. It had given her own life meaning. Only when Sari dragged Ava into mortal danger was she able to break the spell.

Right now, she felt more connected to the people in this room then to anyone or anything on earth, except for Isaac, who'd been both father and mother to her. She'd been walking around with a hole in her heart that didn't need to be there. It's what Ethan had been telling her. She didn't have to choose one or the other – love or purpose. She felt like she could see her life forward as happening in Three-D, because of whatever it was that had shoved the last piece in place, the place where Ethan fit.

Ethan's hand had never left hers since he'd tucked her into the big chair. Celie and Gabe had taken turns holding her other one, letting it go only when she had an itch or needed a sip of something. An hour ago she had resented this "babying," and now it settled over her like a warm blanket. Like Sari's quilt must have felt to her back at Willi's house.

It would be hard for Ava to overcome Sari's loss and even harder for her not to see it as her own failure. But right now, except for Isaac, the people she loved the most in the world were here in this room, offering to help. For a change, she could feel them all. Maybe it wouldn't last forever, but it was true for now. Maybe that's all you really needed in this world.

Postscript

Celie: 1978

Celie had always imagined running across the quilt at a flea market or tag sale somewhere. Things like that happened. You'd be sorting through boxes and trunks and bump into a vase or a candy dish from your childhood. Once she'd found a hammer, one of Daddy's old favorites. He was as pleased to see it as if she'd brought him a new tractor instead of an old tool with a cracked wood handle and a rusty head. She knew he'd have it oiled and sound in no time.

Then she found the quilt. She actually sat on it twice before she recognized it in a jumble of things to sort through on Willie's back porch. She wondered if Isaac had brought it here since he had funny ideas about what should go where. She would ask Ava next time she saw her, although it was doubtful Ava would even remember the quilt.

The house hadn't been lived in for almost a year — yet it smelled fresh and there was a living plant on the kitchen windowsill, as well as a recent copy of *Reader's Digest* on the kitchen table. Willi's living room was cleaner than she'd ever seen it. She recognized the sofa that had been a partner in Dad's routine for so many years – eat, quick nap on the couch, and back to work.

Strong feelings were lurking in every nook and corner of her life lately, and poking around among Willi's things was reminding her too much of her losses. It was no better the next day when she had to go into the attic in Mom and Dad's farmhouse. She'd always had a love-hate relationship with that attic. As kids, she and Hannah had been fascinated with the rows of trunks and boxes. They'd spent long afternoon hours in that attic, imagining themselves transported to everywhere they could dream up. She could still visualize the way the light had sifted through the rafters, creating long bands of alternating light and dark on everything, even their faces. They always got themselves back downstairs by nightfall, the door shut tight and locked. You couldn't have paid either of them to go up those attic stairs after dark.

This time when she'd gone up, the dangers had been more practical. She'd had to check each of the steps to make certain there weren't boards so thin and rotten they could collapse under her weight. When she yanked the cord attached to its single dusty bulb, the cord dissolved in her hand. She'd had to reach up to the metal socket end and pull the stub with her fingernails. The light that spread out over the attic contents was dim, barely carving out the shapes of chairs, trunks, picture frames.

When she opened the first trunk, she half expected a ghost to try and stop her, but of course there was nothing scary unless you counted the dust, a thick, grimy layer of it that had trapped flies, a spider, other small insects. She hoped the seal of the trunk had done its job and kept the critters from crawling through, and was pleased to find that the inside of the trunk was clean and sweet-smelling. The doll clothes she'd saved from childhood were intact. Nestled between them was a large cardboard shoebox. The minute she opened it, a trap door opened wide and she tumbled through it, all the way to the bottom of her most unsettling memories.

The box held one of their cootie-catchers, Redsy's first dog collar, Dale Kent's picture, some 4-H blue ribbons she'd won at the county fairs, and the last thing she'd ever put in, a family picture of the boys who died drag racing. So many boys she'd known in school who would never grow up. Thinking about their lives now, she felt more like a mother to them than a friend.

As she closed the trunk and got ready to leave, she could hear Barry Klein's voice singing, *"Teen Angel, Can you can you hear me,"* the words so real they seemed to be dropping from the ceiling. She sang along. It comforted her — this whistling in the dark, bravely. Why did people do this?

She locked the attic door, took a hot shower and sprinkled the sheets with body powder she'd found in a dresser drawer, Avon's Night Magic. The house was so silent she could hear a dull roar from inside her head and she had been unable to give in to sleep. She read all the way through the night and faced the next day with only two or three miserable hours of toss-and-turning.

The next night, she switched to a crossword puzzle, putting words in boxes that bound her thoughts, with a clear end in sight. She finished the puzzle and stared at the ceiling, spelling out words in cross-hatch, still unable to plunge her psyche into darkness.

When she finally slept, she'd woken up panting for breath, her mind crowded with dreams of herself drowning, and of friends alongside her, struggling for air.

She knew immediately where the nightmare had come from. It was a version of the dream that started right after Frank had drowned ten years ago. He'd just left the Air Force and had been planning a birthday diving trip to Cozumel. His instructor had cancelled the class's scuba lesson at the last minute due to rough waves, but Frank had refused to follow the class ashore. He'd stayed in the river alone, and had fallen, bumped his head, and drowned in only twelve inches of water. His friends had not come rushing in to save him. They said they thought he was lying there deliberately, trying to see something in the water.

Nothing ever went bad for Frank, right? Nobody's fault, they said.

When they'd laid Frank out at Frampton's Funeral Home, he'd been holding a Sunday Missal, maybe the same one from his confirmation. He'd never held that thing more than one or two minutes in his life. Even when he'd say prayers in responsive reading at Mass, he would stand behind Mom and look down over her shoulder, picking out the phrases he liked to say: *Dominus vobiscum, Gloria Patri*, never *mea culpa* or *kyrie eleison*.

What had made Mom put that stupid white leather book into her son's hands? How would Frank have felt, sliding into eternity clutching that badge of submission, thrust on him by his mother and her priest? Celie had been so startled at the sight of the white pebbled leather and the gilt edges, that it had been all she could do not to rip the book from his hands, a woodsman's hands, with skin rough from the tools he used, his knuckles scraped and bruised from where he had tried to push himself up by grasping at the rocks at the bottom of Cozumel's choppy river.

She could see there were others at the service who felt the same way she did about the prayer book — cousin Bobby who'd been with him at the river that day, Frank's friends from the State Police, and anyone who'd known him at the karate studio or gone drinking with him. In other words, anyone who knew him at all.

For the first year after the funeral, she had chronicled the evolution of Frank's body under the ground. At first, he was clean and dry in his casket, his Air Force uniform still pressed and tight around him, a cocoon against dampness and worms. That's the way she thought of it because of that song of Frank's – he had sung it a thousand times, insisting his sisters sing it with him. He had seemed to know a dozen stanzas but now she couldn't remember any more than the first one or two:

> *Did you ever think when a hearse goes by*
> *that you might be the next to die?*
> *They wrap you up in a big white sheet*
> *from your head down to your feet.*
> *They put you in a big black box*
> *and cover you up with dirt and rocks*
> *And all goes well for about a week*
> *and then your coffin begins to leak*
> *The worms crawl in, the worms crawl out*
> *the worms play pinochle on your snout....*

In her chronicles of Frank's existence after death, she made adjustments to his appearance as the seasons passed. The changes she imagined had to be possible, and must exclude stereotypes, like a body springing to life with hands clawing at the satin cover of the casket, the victim shouting, "Get me out – I'm still alive."

In her version, the Catholic Missal was the first casualty, falling from his hands as they relaxed out of *rigor mortis*. Next went the hairspray holding his hair into the narrow, unnaturally straight part – it let go of the Charlie Chaplin flaps, thus exposing the small cut on Frank's forehead that marked where the deadly rock had hit him.

By the end of winter, she envisioned the cut as dried up into a thick scar. She'd read that skin cells continue shedding after death, some even healing. She imagined him experiencing the weather outside his grave. During the first freeze of that first winter, he had silently wished for someone to get him a blanket. By spring, his body thawed again, and his skin began to shrivel and peel away. By summer, she could see his bones.

She visited Frank's grave in real time, of course, adjusting her picture of him each time to what his body looked like now. This was a macabre secret between Frank and her, and he would have loved it.

She would later tell all this to Hannah, another of the many secrets that only they knew. They were the only ones who knew, for example, what Frank had really been feeling in those moments he'd dashed past the diving class, ignoring the divemaster's warnings of danger. "Trying to show the river who's boss," said the friends who only thought they knew him, shaking their heads at how often Frank pursued the kind of fun that could kill you. *That crazy Frank. He isn't afraid of anything.*

Not so. He had gone into the river because he was trying to lessen the fear that had plagued him all his life. He hadn't changed since the day, all those years before, when he'd leaned over to comfort Hannah, on the way home from the picnic grounds where a little girl named Becky had drowned. Hannah had been crying about how scared Becky must have been. Frank had whispered, "Don't cry. I've been thinking how drowning must be a very peaceful way to go … like falling asleep. I bet that little girl wasn't even scared." This from a boy who set fires in schools, and who people suspected of being part of the fire setting in Cambridge in the 1960's. A monster? Or not so different from the rest of them? She didn't know. What she did know was that all those times he sang, and made his sisters sing, that stupid song, it had been his version of whistling in the dark.

Then she unto the parson said,
Shall I be this way when I am dead?
O yes! O yes! the parson said.
You will be so when you are dead.

Acknowledgements Regarding Facts and Fictions

Larry Pinkett was the first black student to enroll at North Dorchester High School in 1962. He graduated and went on to college, the military, and a very successful civilian career. There was an Ava who enrolled at the school when he did, and who, like my Ava, did not last out the first school semester. Nothing else connects the two Ava's.

Larry generously shared details and feelings about growing up on the Eastern Shore, but none of the characters in this novel are meant to depict him or his family, with the exception of his anecdote about his enrolling at a white school after studying *Plessy v. Ferguson,* and "Invictus," which Larry used as a prayer to help him cope with the bigotry he faced every day.

The descriptions of Race Street, Cambridge, Hurlock, Secretary, and East New Market are recollections of the way the author saw these places. The accidental drownings and farm accidents all occurred mostly as written, but the names and dates are fictitious. Isaac and Minnie are as real and complete as can be remembered. The same is true for Celie and her family except for her brother Frank. The other main characters — Ava and Gabe — are fictional creations.

Peter B. Levy is a scholar whose seminal work followed the "riots" of 1967; his work is a critical help in separating out politicized explanations from the facts of what transpired in the 1960s. He also provides the reader with a demographic backdrop of the economy,

313

and defines the conditions that existed at the time across the Eastern Shore of Maryland and similar rural areas. I have treated his factual accounts as if coming from a bible – no one I know has been more accurate in any written treatment of this period of time.

There is no St. Paul AME Church and no Reverend Benson. Tate's Bar does not exist, nor does Edward Tate, although similar events occurred at Greene's Emporium, which was completely destroyed in the 1967 fire.

Appendix: History Capsule and Works Consulted

Tidewater is a peninsula bordered by the Atlantic Ocean and the Chesapeake Bay. Its early twentieth century prosperity came from farming, trapping and fishing — resources that became depleted by the mid-1950's. Beneath the visible social fabric of church manners and charity, as jobs diminished, poverty and injustice became unbearable.

In 1960, one-third of the residents of Cambridge, Maryland, were Black. They all lived in the Second Ward, represented for six decades by one black man on the five-member City Council. Three black people on the police force were limited to patrolling the Second Ward and they couldn't arrest whites anywhere. Black doctors had no privileges at mainstream hospital. Black schools received half as much funding per student as white schools; and all restaurants, churches, and entertainment venues were segregated. The white community's lives and businesses stopped on Race Street. Across from it, Pine Street was the black community; there were residences and dozens of small businesses in the neighborhood. They called it Black Wall Street and Little New York. It was prominently featured in the *Green Book*, (A travel guide for African-Americans in the 1950s and 60s, it reported which hotels and restaurants would be safe and welcoming.)

The Cambridge Nonviolent Action Committee (CNAC) was founded in the summer of 1962 to support protests (e.g. sit-ins and freedom rides) by The Student Nonviolent Coordinating Committee (SNCC)

315

and other national groups trying to desegregate Cambridge. In January of 1963, SNCC organizers, with 100 students and other civil rights activists, marched downtown to whites-only establishments. Freedom Riders came through Cambridge on their way South.

In the spring of that year, Gloria Richardson became the leader of the CNAC and met with city officials to discuss Cambridge's many civil rights problems. When these demands went unheard, Richardson led a protest in early summer of 1963. Her group was arrested for "disorderly conduct." In her absence, two 15-year-old high school students led the protests and were arrested for praying outside a segregated facility, held without bail, and sentenced to indefinite incarceration in the state juvenile facility. Large marches were organized in downtown Cambridge afterward to protest this harsh sentencing. Some 250 African-Americans went on a "freedom walk" to the Dorchester County Court House and were met by a crowd of 700 whites, protected by white police. Martial Law was declared for 25 days. Three days after the National Guard left, black demonstrators entered the all-white Dizzyland restaurant and were harassed and beaten by white patrons. The two groups were eventually dispersed by the Maryland State Police, after exchanging gunfire. The CNAC organized another protest, but this time, armed local African-American men circled the demonstrators to protect them. Fights broke out and several businesses in the Second Ward were set on fire. Gunfire was exchanged, resulting in many casualties. The white Cambridge Mayor blamed the violence on "outside agitators." The Governor reinstated martial law and The National Guard remained in Ward Two for two years, the longest occupation of an American community since the Civil War.

After the closing of Phillips Packing Company, the main local employer, there was no other industry to replace it, and Cambridge's economy floundered. Airpax bought the Phillips property and began delivering defense contracts in the mid-1960s. This new system favored white people: unions and security clearances were obstacles that no black person could surmount. Many black people became homeless. By the summer of 1967, black unemployment had reached 70%. 1967 saw a return of Civil Rights Activist groups to Cambridge. The national SNCC sent activists to a July rally where H. Rap Brown had been invited to speak. Within hours of his speech bidding residents to "burn down the town," someone set fire to the Pine Street

Elementary School. Several businesses were fire-bombed; shots were fired by both blacks and whites, and Brown was wounded.

Some reports said that crowds of blacks assembled and dispersed throughout the evening along Pine Street, setting small fires in the road and putting them out. An armed group of whites was photographed speeding through the neighborhood firing shots at random, coming back minutes later for a second and then a third run, and they were greeted with return gunfire. A white policeman was shot near his home.

Four hours after Brown left town, an estimated 1,000 people watched as white firefighters refused to respond to the call. The fire chief said he feared their being shot at. The fire burned without intervention and destroyed two city blocks and 22 buildings in the all-black Second Ward, including the Bethel AMC Baptist Church and Hansel Greene's popular Greene's Emporium. Once the fire seemed about to leap to a white gas station at the edge of the white district, the fireman worked quickly to put out the few fires that were left. Publicity was at the national level; there was a long investigation, but no one was ever found or charged for the explosions. A warrant was issued for H. Rap Brown, but he was not found and arrested. Parts of the Second Ward were rebuilt, including the church, but after Hansel Greene's suicide, Greene's Emporium did not reopen.

Works Consulted

Arsenault, Raymond. *Freedom Riders and the Struggle for Racial Justice.* 1961, Oxford University Press, New York.

Attenborough, Richard. *The Words of Gandhi.* 2001, William F. Morrow, New York.

Carson, Clayborne. *In Struggle, SNCC and the Black Awakening of the 1960s.* 1981, Harvard University Press, Cambridge Mass

Dubois, Laurent. "Vodou and History." In *Comparative Studies in Society and History* 2001. Vol. 43.1, pp. 92-100.

DuBois, W.E.B. *The Souls of Black Folk.* 1994, Dover Publications, Mineola, New York.

Eshelman, Ralph E. & Carl Scheffel, Jr. "Maryland's Lower Choptank River Heritage Cultural Resource Inventory." April, 1999. Project for Maryland Historical Trust.

Gates, Deborah. "Fifty Years after the Cambridge Riots, Scarred Community Heals: An Interview with Gilbert Cephas." 2 Feb. 2017. *DelMarva News.*

Kidd, Sue Monk. *The Invention of Wings.* 2014, Penguin Books, New York.

King, Martin Luther, Jr. "Letters and Sermons Prepared while in Birmingham Jail, 1962-63." Martin Luther King, Jr. Research and Education Institute, Stanford University. King Papers Project.

King, Martin Luther, Jr. "Remaining Awake Through a Great Revolution: Commencement Address for Oberlin College." June 1965. Oberlin College Archives.

Leatherman, Stephen B. *et al.* "Vanishing Lands: Sea, Land and Society of the Chesapeake Bay." 1995. Eastern Shore Conservation Center Archives.

Levy, Peter B. *Civil War on Race Street.* 2003, University Press of Florida, Gainesville, Fl.

Levy, Peter B. *Let Freedom Ring, A Documentary History of The Civil Rights Movement.* 1992, Praeger Publishers, Westbury, Ct.

Maryland Advisory Committee to the United States Commission on Civil Rights. "Migratory Workers of Maryland's Eastern Shore." June, 1983. University of Maryland Archives.

Michener, J. *Chesapeake.* 1978, Random House New York.

Omi, Michael & Howard Winant. *Racial Formation in The United States From the 1960s to the 1990s.* 1994, Routledge, New York.

Owens, Clay. "The History of Secretary." Sept. 2008. *The Star Democrat.*

Redding, Saunders. *On Being Negro in America.* 1951, Bobbs Merrill, Indianapolis, Ind.

Reid, Joseph D. "Sharecropping in History and Theory." In *Agricultural History* April 1975. Vol. 49.2, p. 429.

Rothenberg-Gritz, Jennie. "New Racism Museum Reveals the Ugly Truth Behind Aunt Jemima." In *The Atlantic* 23 April, 2012.

Shaw, Stephanie J. *W.E.B. Dubois and The Souls of Black Folk.* 2013, University of North Carolina, Press, Chapel Hill, N.C.

U.S. Department of Agriculture. "Soil Survey Dorchester County Maryland." Series 1959, No. 26.

CPSIA information can be obtained
at www.ICGtesting.com
Printed in the USA
JSHW012157290120
3868JS00005B/58